A Brighter Tomorrow

Rowena Summers is the pseudonym of Jean Saunders. She was a British writer of romance novels since 1974, and wrote under her maiden name and her pseudonym, as well as the names Sally Blake and Rachel Moore. She was elected the seventeenth Chairman (1993–1995) of the Romantic Novelists' Association, and she was the Vice-Chairman of the Writers' Summer School of Swanwick. She was also a member of Romance Writers of America, Crime Writers' Association and West Country Writers' Association.

Also by Rowena Summers

A Safe Haven

The Cornish Clay Sagas

Rowena Summers

A Brighter Tomorrow

CANELO

First published in the USA in 2000 by Severn House Publishers Inc

This edition published in the United Kingdom in 2022 by

Canelo
Unit 9, 5th Floor
Cargo Works, 1–2 Hatfields
London, SE1 9PG
United Kingdom

A CIP catalogue record for this book is available from the British Library.

Print ISBN 978 1 80032 776 4
Ebook ISBN 978 1 78863 474 8

Look for more great books at www.canelo.co

Printed and bound in Great Britain by Clays Ltd, Elcograf S.p.A.

1

Chapter One

Celia Pengelly shivered as she stood on the chilly Cornish railway station, awaiting the arrival of the train from London. According to her sister, still determined to go on living in the capital despite the threat of being bombed at any time, the river Thames had frozen over for the first time in more than fifty years, and it was cold enough to freeze the proverbial brass monkeys.

Celia smiled faintly, recognising the kind of slangy terms Wenna had picked up. She was practically a Londoner by now, and far more worldly-wise than the family had ever expected her to be. But Celia conceded that it went with the job. Singing in a nightclub all these years, and being the star attraction, no less, was bound to have an effect on her.

It was only when she came home to Cornwall that she resumed her proper place in the family – her younger sister's place, Celia thought with a grin.

'Here it comes, Miss Pengelly,' she heard the voice of the billeting officer saying. 'Get ready for the onslaught.'

Celia hitched the carrying strap of her gas mask more firmly onto her shoulder. She had faced this day with mixed feelings. Her mother was insisting that it would be marvellous to have children in the house again, and that the empty rooms of New World cried out for them. But these children would be strangers, coming from a different environment, and they would be frightened and bewildered.

'Not nervous, are you, Pengelly?' the more strident of the billeting officers asked her. 'They're only children, and you must be sure to discipline them as instructed.'

'Yes, ma'am,' Celia muttered, resisting the wild desire to snap her heels together and give a Heil Hitler salute. It would be the most disastrous thing imaginable in the circumstances, when they were all here to welcome the latest wave of these little evacuees from London and take them into their Cornish hearts.

Though, to be honest, the names of the four they had been allocated didn't fill her with enthusiasm. She glanced again at her list, even though she knew them by heart. Tommy and Mary Lunn, aged eight and four; Daphne Hollis, aged seven; and Butch Butcher, aged eleven.

It was this last name that had Celia wary of the whole thing. He sounded a real thug – even though she was well aware that it was wrong to judge him and expect the worst before he had even arrived.

But the train was snorting and steaming into the station now, and there was no more time to speculate. Nor had there been any chance of refusing the children. They had been allocated with the names and that was that. In wartime everybody had to do their bit and the Pengellys were no exception. They had plenty of room to take four, and four was what they would get.

'I'm not complaining,' her mother had said cheerfully. 'It will be just darling to hear the sound of children's laughter in the house again.'

'I doubt that laughter's the first thing you're going to hear,' the billeting officer had warned her, her eyebrows raised as usual at Skye Pengelly's quaint American way of speaking. 'There may well be problems at first, but we all have to cope with them as best we can. The children will be far from home, and the younger ones will be tearful, while others will be resentful at what they see as their parents' betrayal in sending them away.'

And that was what Celia fully expected from the eleven-year-old Butch Butcher...

As the train squealed to a halt and the carriage doors flew open, it seemed as though a great mass of chattering humanity was descending on to the small Cornish platform at once. The billeting officers and local teachers took charge, trying to form the children into some kind of order, shouting out names from their lists and inspecting the labels hung around the necks of those who were too frightened to respond at all.

Celia's heart went out to them. Poor little devils, she thought. They were clearly petrified by these bossy people with the strange accents ordering them about, even though it was the only way to organise the huge undertaking.

Moments later, she found herself looking into the faces of a brother and sister, the tiny girl clutching the boy's hand as if terrified of losing him. They each carried a brown paper parcel tied with string, which presumably contained their entire wardrobe, as well as the gas masks slung around their shoulders. These two, then, were Tommy and Mary Lunn.

Celia knelt down to their level, and looked into Mary's scared brown eyes.

'Hello, sweetie,' she said, smiling encouragingly. 'My name's Celia and you're going to come and live with me and my family for a while.'

To Celia's horror, the girl immediately began wailing, and Tommy put his arms around her protectively.

'She don't want to come and live wiv you, missis. She wants to go home. She don't like the country. They say there's cows and fings and we don't like 'em.'

'We don't have cows and fings – things,' Celia repeated, parrot fashion. 'We have a nice big house near the sea—'

'We don't like the sea. We ain't never seen it and we don't want to,' Tommy Lunn said at once.

Celia recognised his determination not to like anything at all. She had expected trouble from Butch Butcher, not from these two. She had thought a small brother and sister would be tolerably happy to stay together, but she realised she had been wrong to anticipate anything.

As Mary continued snivelling, a dark patch crept down her spindly legs in their dark wool stockings. Celia turned with relief when the billeting officer called her.

'Here are your other two, Miss Pengelly. Someone will be calling on you in a week's time to check that all is well.'

And with that, the woman moved away, leaving Celia to face an engaging little girl with the name Daphne Hollis pinned to her chest, and an overweight boy with ginger hair and freckles, whom she knew instantly had to be Butch Butcher.

She found herself full of anger at the inefficiency of the billeting people. Didn't they ever have the gumption to match the children? What the dickens did these four have in common, except having been brought to safety away from the dangers that London held for them now?

'She's wet herself,' Tommy said, pointing at Mary's legs.

'Me sister used to do that all the time,' Daphne piped up. 'I'll see to 'er if you like, missis.'

'Will you?' Celia said faintly, before mentally shaking herself, and steering the four of them out of the heaving station towards her waiting car. So far Butch had said nothing, but to her surprise Daphne caught hold of Mary's other hand and began pulling the small girl towards her, while Tommy tugged her the other way.

'I want to go wiv *her*,' Mary suddenly screamed, kicking out viciously at Tommy's shins. Her little boots were old and scuffed, but the kick was hard enough to make her brother howl with rage and give her a slap around the head, which made her scream still more.

'Good Lord, stop this at once, will you?' Celia said, appalled. 'That's no way to behave. We all have to learn to get along together.'

'I hate her,' Tommy yelled, though minutes before he had been Mary's champion, 'and she's welcome to her.'

He pushed his sister towards the other girl, and before Celia knew what was happening, Butch had got hold of him by his collar. It was just as she had feared, she thought, her heart sinking. This one was a bully of the first order.

'You behave yourself, half-pint, and do what the lady tells yer, or I'll give you what for, see?'

Butch looked at Celia as Tommy subsided with a scowl. 'Ain't that right, missis?'

'Yes. Well yes, I guess so. And you can call me Celia,' she said, when nothing else came to mind.

This whole situation was getting very strange, she thought, and who was in charge here, anyway? But the minute she directed them all to her car and debated about where Mary was to sit, considering her wet knickers, she heard Tommy's awed voice.

'Cor, are we going to have a ride in that car?'

She resumed her composure at once.

'Yes, you are. Butch will sit in front with me, and you other three can sit in the back. There's an old newspaper in the back for Mary to sit on for the time being, until we get her tidied up.'

'So how old is your sister, Daphne?' she went on, just to keep them occupied while they all piled into the car.

'Oh, she ain't nothing no more.'

'What do you mean, nothing? A person can't be *nothing*,' Celia said, abandoning any thought of grammar for the moment.

'They can when they're dead,' Daphne said cheerfully.

Celia's heart jolted. The country had been at war for nearly five months now, and bombs had been falling, but she had never met anyone who had been personally affected by the German air raids. She felt emotionally drawn to this little girl with the perky face who looked as if she had already seen far too much in her seven years.

'What happened, Daphne?' she asked quietly, as she began to drive home. She knew it was a bad thing to question her with the other children in the car, but she had to know...

'She 'ad the diphtheria like me brothers. They was all sick and they all died one after the other, and me Ma said I was a bleedin' miracle, 'cos I never got it,' she said, as proud as if she had won a trophy.

'Oh!' Celia said, too stunned by the enormity of such a tragedy to censure her for her language. In fact, apart from the way the child was revealing it so matter-of-factly, she couldn't help hearing the ghost of another voice from long ago, using the same words, in the same East End accent.

The very first time she and her sister Wenna had met her mother's acquaintance from the war that was supposed to end all wars, Fanny Webb had both shocked

6

and charmed the Cornish children by her frequent use of the words "bleedin' 'ell".

'Blimey, is that the sea?' Butch said suddenly.

All the children craned their necks as Celia said that indeed it was.

'Don't it end nowhere?' Tommy said nervously.

'It goes from here all the way to America, where my mother was born,' Celia told him, glad to give them something else to think about other than the deaths of Daphne's sister and brothers from diphtheria. 'In fact, I lived in America myself for about a year until last spring.'

Daphne spoke up again. 'Me Ma says all Yanks are film stars. Did you meet any of 'em, missis?'

'No, of course not,' Celia said with a laugh. 'Film stars all live in a place called Hollywood, but I worked for a family in New Jersey, picking apples—'

'You don't pick apples,' Tommy said scornfully. 'You buy 'em down the market.'

Celia gave up. Clearly, they all had a lot to learn about one another, and life was never going to be the same again.

They had known that long before Mr Chamberlain's solemn announcement on the third of September last year, in the many months preceding the event, when everyone had been preparing not only for war, but for the heartaches and separations of friends and lovers.

She let the children chatter on for a moment or two, remembering Stefan, as she did every night when she gazed up the brightest star in the sky. It was *their* star, he had told her during their last idyllic time together, before she had to return to Cornwall and he to Germany. And as long as that star shone, his love for her would remain just as constant and everlasting, however long their two countries were at war.

It was a lovely and noble sentiment, but it did nothing to ease the anxiety she felt when there had been no further news of him since then. Correspondence had dwindled to nothing, and the needs of lovers were very far down the pecking order of what was important now and what was not.

'What are those things?' she heard Daphne ask now. 'Are they mountains? I ain't never seen snow like that before.'

Celia dragged her thoughts back to the present and followed the child's gaze away from the coast to where the soaring spoil heaps of china clay glinted on the skyline on the moors high above St Austell on that cold January day.

'I don't like them,' Mary whimpered, starting to cry.

It was clear that Mary and Tommy were not prepared to like anything at all, and she spoke in a cheerful voice.

'It's not snow, Daphne. It's the waste material from something called china clay, which is a substance that helps to make plates and cups and saucers as well as other things like newspaper print, and even medicines.'

From their faces, she realised that this was too complic-ated for them to take in, and she changed tactics.

'They're not real mountains, of course, and my mother always called them the sky-tips, because it seemed as if they would reach the sky. It made my mother very happy to call them that. Can you guess why?'

When they didn't answer, she went on talking, starting to feel very foolish. She wasn't a teacher, and she didn't quite know how to handle this motley crowd of children. If they were all the same age, it might have been easier. As it was, she knew she was talking down to most of them, except for the infant Mary.

Tommy was older than his years, and Daphne already knew it all, Celia suspected. But she went on doggedly.

'My mother's name is Skye, and she liked to think the china clay heaps were called sky-tips just for her.'

She heard Tommy hoot with derisive laughter.

'Skye ain't a proper name! I ain't never heard of nothing so daft, and I ain't going to call nobody *Skye*!'

'I should think not,' Celia said evenly. 'You'll call her Mrs Pengelly.'

Mary started to wail again. 'I can't say that. I want to go home. I want me Ma—'

'Well, perhaps you could call her Mrs Pen. How about that? Would that be easier? Why don't you all think about it?' she said desperately, and was never more thankful to see New World come into sight as the four of them debated and squabbled over whether or not this was an easy thing to do.

She only prayed that her mother would take to the four of them. Celia was becoming increasingly sure now that she could not.

Mary was only a baby, and maybe Daphne could be handled in time, but as for the boys... Tommy was obviously what they called a loose cannon, and she simply couldn't make up her mind about Butch at all. Either he was a thug waiting to burst out, or he was a big softie, hiding behind a nickname he'd simply been given because of his surname. She just didn't know, and she wasn't sure she wanted to find out.

She had committed herself to staying on at New World to help her mother with these evacuees for a time, but she was itching to do some war work, the same as her cousin Seb who had joined the army the minute he was called up, and her cousin Justin, giving up his medical training temporarily to go straight into an army medical unit for what he called practical experience.

She envied them both. And even Wenna, under her stage name of Penny Wood, was saying that she fully intended joining a concert party to entertain the troops if Fanny Rosenbloom, née Webb, decided to close the nightclub for the duration.

Personally, Celia didn't think Fanny would ever close the Flamingo Club, but in any case Wenna wouldn't be prepared to stay there for ever. Her young man had immediately joined up as a war correspondent, and was already at some unknown destination. Wenna declared she would feel closer to him by doing her bit, as they all called it now.

Wenna was the lucky one, Celia thought, with a burst of misery. There was no way in this world she could be close to Stefan except in spirit. She and her lover were on opposite sides of a conflict that had nothing to do with them…

'Is that your house, missis?' Daphne said in awe.

Celia said that it was, and gave up the idea of persuading them to call her by name for the present. Presumably it would come in time, and meanwhile it was a relief to get them all out of the car, where the smell of Mary's wet knickers was starting to become vinegary.

She gave herself a mental reminder to scrub the back seats the minute she got the chance, and immediately felt ashamed of her uncharitable thoughts as she saw the child's pinched white face.

'Come on, sweetheart, let's go inside and see your new room, shall we?'

She saw Daphne scratching herself, and felt an urge to do the same. To her horror she suddenly recalled the instructions they had all been given at the last billeting committee meeting.

'Many of the children come from the slums. They will have scabies or lice, and will need to be de-loused immediately with disinfectant. This must be diluted to prevent sores, of course, but remember that all the children will be regularly inspected on arrival at school, so attention to hygiene is vital if our own children are not to be infected.'

Such a distinction had seemed mean and degrading at the time, but that feeling changed for Celia now, and with rising hysteria she suspected that the little beasts in her car had already infected her too.

And she didn't distinguish in her mind which little beasts she was thinking about.

'Wait here, all of you,' she said sharply, and left the four of them standing forlornly outside the car.

As she did so, her mother came out of the house to usher them in out of the cold, and after Celia had spoken to her rapidly, Skye Pengelly took charge.

'Tell Liza to get the disinfectant baths ready for the children. The girls first, and then the boys. I have some suitable clothes for them to wear for now; all their own garments must be washed and boiled before they can be used again. Go to it, honey, while I see to them.'

'But Mom, they'll infect the whole house.'

'They're babies, Celia, and they're scared. *Go*, honey, and don't make them feel worse than they do already.'

She walked towards the children, seeing how they huddled together. Skye had already been through a war, and fleas and lice held no fears for her. There were worse things. Any infestation obviously had to be dealt with quickly, but the most important thing was to reassure these infants that they were safe here.

'Let me guess your names,' she began with a smile.

'You don't need to do that, missis,' Tommy said rudely, jabbing a finger at his name label as if she was stupid.

'Oh, of course I don't,' Skye said. 'How silly of me to forget. Well, then, do you know who I am?'

They didn't answer, clearly silenced by the size of the lovely old house and grounds, so different from the crowded slum streets of London where they had all been born.

'It's Mrs Pen-something,' Daphne said at last. 'The lady said we was to call you Mrs Pen.'

'Well done,' Skye said. 'So now that we all know one another, let's go inside the house and get you bathed, and than we'll have something nice and hot to eat, shall we?'

'I don't need no bath,' Tommy yelled at her. 'I 'ad one last week. I just want me tea.'

'Mary needs a bath,' Daphne said importantly. 'She's gawn and wet 'erself again, but I can see to 'er.'

Dear Lord, thought Skye, eyeing the smallest one properly for the first time. The child was practically dripping by now, and none of them smelled too sweet. A hot bath was definitely a priority, but from the look of Tommy Lunn's face he was going to run a mile if he didn't have something to eat first. She made up her mind.

'Right. We'll change Mary out of those wet things in the outhouse, then go into the kitchen for some cake and lemonade, and *then* a bath, and then some proper dinner. All right?'

There was no way she could take Mary into the kitchen. She knew that Cook would throw a fit at the smell. The outhouse would have to do, and Mary could be wrapped in a large towel to eat her food while the offending knickers and woollen stockings remained well out of sight and smell.

–

A very long while later, four scrubbed, de-loused and well-fed children examined the rooms where they were to sleep.

'I ain't never slept in a room by meself,' Daphne said uneasily, her bravado finally cracking as she surveyed Wenna's old bedroom. 'There was five of us in one bed at home, top to tail, me Ma called it. Can't I sleep wiv the others?'

'I ain't sleeping wiv *girls*,' Butch said at once.

'Then Butch can have this room, and the other three can have the old nursery,' Skye said, revising all her plans.

'Nurseries are for babies,' Tommy argued at once.

'Well, providing you don't behave like one, it won't matter, will it?' Skye said crisply, getting his measure far sooner that Celia had.

–

'You were wonderful, Mom,' Celia told her when they finally had some time to themselves. 'I must admit I panicked when I saw them, but you seemed to know just how to handle them.'

'That's because I've had three of my own, honey.'

And by now, if things hadn't gone so horribly wrong, there would have been another babe of my own in the nursery...

She pushed the thought aside as Celia went on, 'Were we ever this bad? So *aggressive* and so ready to argue about everything?'

Skye's blue eyes sparkled as she looked at her daughter.

'Oh, honey, I assure you that you were – and you in particular! I'll never forget the little scenes at Lily's wedding, when you and Wenna were bridesmaids. You hated everything and everyone, especially your cousin Sebby, who you always referred to as a prize pig.'

Celia laughed too. 'My God, Mom, do you have to remember everything! I hope you're not including those kind of personal incidents in the history you're writing about the family. I'd be mortified if you did.'

'Don't worry, darling. I'm keeping strictly to business matters and the background of the clayworks. Even so, a business doesn't exist without the people who worked so hard to make it a success. I still sometimes wonder if I'll ever write it, though,' she added.

'Why ever not?'

Skye shrugged. 'Things have a habit of happening to prevent my giving enough attention to it. Like a war, for instance. There are so many more important things to do than writing up the memoirs of a business that doesn't even belong in the family any more.'

'But isn't that just why you should? It's what Daddy thinks, and what David Kingsley is always urging you to do.'

'David's a newspaperman, and he's always wanted me to get back to work with him in some capacity or other. But in any case, I'll have my hands full with those four upstairs now.'

As if to underline her words, the sound of wailing was heard again, and she gave a sigh. As Celia made to get up, Skye put a hand on her arm.

'Leave it to me, honey. You'll only lose your temper, and that will get us nowhere.'

Celia knew it was true, but she watched her mother's still trim figure move towards the stairs with a small feeling of anxiety in her heart.

Actually, Skye could have refused to foster four children and taken only three, but she hadn't demurred at all, and Celia suspected she was doing it as a kind of substitute for losing her own late-stage baby last year. She had insisted on including a very young child, which many other families didn't want, so Celia concluded it could only be so.

—

Her stepfather found her staring into space when he came home that evening. By then she had carefully pulled the black-out curtains until she was sure that no chink of light could escape, before switching on the lamps in the drawing room.

Nick Pengelly peered around the door in mock fearfulness.

'Have they invaded us then? Is it safe to come in?'

Celia laughed. 'They're here all right, and Mom's upstairs with them, trying to pacify the smallest one.'

'And do I take it that all went well, apart from that?' he said cautiously.

She shrugged. 'I guess so. I still think Mom's taking on far too much. She shouldn't have to be bothered with other people's children at her age—'

'She's not ancient yet, darling, and she won't thank you for doubting her abilities.'

'I know. And I shouldn't begrudge the poor little devils a decent home. I did, though, when I began to itch,' she added with a shudder. 'They were practically alive with lice.'

'Good God. I hope you've sorted that out,' Nick said.

'We have. We're all bathed, and their clothes are either burned or boiled.'

It was some time later when Skye came downstairs to join them, glad to find her husband home from his legal chambers in Bodmin, and already pouring her a glass of wine.

'They're settled,' she said, in answer to his unspoken question. 'It was Mary who was the noisy one, of course, but once she was asleep I realised Daphne was weeping into her pillow and needed the most comforting.'

'What?' Celia said in amazement. 'I thought she was the toughest little nut of all.'

'Not deep down.' She turned to Nick, not yet ready to tell them just how much agonised outpouring Daphne Hollis had revealed to her. 'So now we have a houseful again, honey.'

He raised his own glass to her. 'And here's to all who sail in her,' he said euphemistically. 'Let's hope there aren't too many stormy waters ahead.'

Celia groaned. 'That's the feeblest thing I ever heard.'

'And that reminds me,' Nick went on, unperturbed, 'have you seen the newspaper today? Food rationing's going to be stepped up, and it will soon apply to meat as well as butter, bacon and sugar. I hope your little darlings have brought their ration books with them.'

'It's all taken care of, Nick,' Skye assured him. 'Cook's already ingeniously planning new dishes that will make the most of what we've got, and seeing it as her life's work.'

'I wonder if this might be a good time to mention *my* life's work — or at least, a little bit of it?' Celia said. 'I said I'd help out here for a time, and so I will. But Mom, while everyone else is doing war work, I can't sit around twiddling my thumbs. The children will be in school all day except Mary, and I'll willingly take them and fetch them. But in between those times, I'm thinking of applying to be a tram conductress in Truro now that most of the men have joined up.'

'Good God, Celia,' Nick said angrily, just as she had anticipated, 'you've been to a Swiss finishing school and become an expert linguist. We didn't send you there for you to become a tram conductress, for God's sake!'

'Then let me enlist properly if you're so snobbish about it. I daresay my qualifications will be useful in some capacity,' she snapped.

'No,' he said sharply. 'Your mother needs you here.'

'Does anyone mind if I speak for myself?' Skye said, just as angry as the two of them. 'I'm perfectly capable of looking after children, and Celia must do what she feels is right.'

'That's the trouble. I don't know *what* I feel is right,' her daughter muttered. 'I only know I feel useless.'

'You're anything but that!'

'But it's how I *feel*, Dad,' she said, rounding on him. 'And people are starting to look at me as if I'm one of the privileged few—'

'Well, so you are, Celia,' he said. 'Your mother's family provided this house and the legacy of the clayworks, to say nothing of the successful pottery she founded. And I've always been able to give you children the best education.'

She gave a heavy sigh. 'I might have known you wouldn't understand. It takes more than an up-country accent to make someone acceptable today. In fact, I'm beginning to think it's the very thing that sets you apart in a community like ours.'

Nick's eyes flashed. 'Well, don't start talking like your Uncle Theo, or like that friend of your mother's in London, that's all, or I might just disown you.'

He was teasing, and she knew it, but it was on the tip of her tongue to say that right here in his house he had four little Londoners who used far less than perfect diction, and probably knew more choice blasphemies than even Theo Tremayne did! But of course, he hadn't met the children yet, and that was a delight still to come, Celia thought mischievously.

She turned to her mother.

'So do I have your blessing to call at the tram company tomorrow and offer my services, Mom?'

'If it makes you happy, honey, then of course you do,' Skye said at once.

But they both knew it would take far more than that to make Celia happy. It would take an end to the war that had barely begun, and a resumption of the heady life she had only just started to glimpse with Stefan von Gruber.

–

They both took the children to enrol at their new school the following day, knowing what an ordeal it would be for them. There were plenty of other evacuees there too, but they all stood out like sore thumbs from the local children and each faction stuck together warily at the sight of the others. To the Cornish children, it was clearly as great an invasion of aliens as if the Germans themselves had landed.

'You'd think children would all get along, wouldn't you?' Celia said to her mother. 'Somehow you don't expect them to have the same reservations as adults have.'

'Why not? They're as individual as we are, and they all have their own personalities.'

'Some more than others,' Celia added darkly, remembering how the self-assured Daphne Hollis had begun to assert herself as a leader among her own, even before she had been introduced to her class teacher.

'Well, we have some time to forget them, so since we're in town, let's call on Lily for half an hour,' Skye suggested.

'Do you think Lily will approve of this one?' Celia asked, raising her eyebrows at the sulking Mary as they walked back to the car, having just managed to stop her wailing at having been left behind while all the others went to school. Celia was quite sure she hadn't wanted to go, anyway, but now the small girl was all alone with two strangers who she was perfectly prepared not to like, and was determined to show it in the most eloquent way she knew.

'Have you wet yourself again, Mary?' Celia asked her.

'Only a bit,' she sulked.

'Never mind, honey,' Skye said cheerfully. 'We'll soon have you nice and dry again.'

'Me Ma says it's only cricket's piss, anyway,' Mary said, then without warning her eyes filled with tears while the other two were still gasping at this stunning statement.

'When can I see me Ma, missis? I want me Ma,' she howled.

'Good grief, if the billeting committee hear all that noise they'll think we're beating her,' Skye said uneasily. 'Let's get to Lily's as fast as we can, Celia.'

'And I'll leave you there while I go to the tram company, if that's all right.'

The less she had to deal with the fractious Mary, the better, she decided, and in any case, her mother was so much more tolerant than she was. During the months Celia had lived in New Jersey on the fruit farm, she had been able to deal with the brash and noisy Stone siblings, but that was over a year ago, and she knew she had changed since then.

Just before war had been declared, she had been able to meet Stefan for one brief week in Gstaad, and their love had been as strong as ever despite having been so long apart. But there was no guarantee that they would ever meet again, and Celia was now more moody and impatient than she had ever been. The fact that she fully recognised it didn't help to conquer it.

An hour later she arrived back at her cousin Lily's riverside house and pottery shop in Truro, having signed on as a tram conductress for six days a week, with Thursday afternoons free. The pay was ludicrous, but it wasn't the pay she was after, just the need to be useful.

She entered the shop and paused in astonishment at the sound of laughter coming from the upper storey of the building where the family lived. The shop assistant told her they were all in Mrs Kingsley's living room, so Celia followed the sounds and went to find them.

'Am I in the right place?' she said, poking her head around the door.

'Celia, come in,' Lily said with obvious pleasure. Lily was always happy with her company, seeing in Celia an echo of her own strong-willed character in the days when she had been a strident suffragette and proud of it.

'Where's Mary?' Celia said at once. 'What have you done with her, Mom?'

She hardly needed to ask. Lily's twin boys were eight years old, and home from school on the pretext of having colds. From being such a stalwart in days past, Lily was far too indulgent a mother, Celia thought, but the boys were obviously making a pet of Mary, and she was revelling in it.

Peace at last, Celia thought, as she relayed the news of her new position within the tram company.

'Good for you,' Lily said. 'We all have to do something, and if I was twenty years younger I'd join up like a shot.'

'We did our bit in the last war,' Skye said quickly.

'But if they decided to conscript women as well as young men, there'd be no choice,' Celia said, far too casually.

'I'm sure it won't come to that, honey. The war won't last for ever.'

'I bet that's what you said last time, didn't you?'

In the small silence that followed, the three of them looked at one another, and then Robert and Frederick Kingsley came shrieking into the room, with Mary chasing them as fast as her little legs would go.

'Mind the ornaments,' Lily yelled too late as a pottery vase shook and teetered on a side table and then went crashing to the carpet. It didn't break, but it stopped the children running around and brought a hunted look to Mary's eyes.

'Me Ma would've beat me for doin' that,' she announced.

'Well, nobody gets beaten here,' Lily said firmly. 'Nothing's broken and you can carry on playing, but just do it more quietly.'

Mary studied her for a moment. 'I like you, missis,' she said, and as an aside she added, 'better'n anybody so far.'

'Well, that's telling us,' Skye breathed, trying not to laugh. 'Anyway, never mind them. I haven't seen anything of Oliver for several weeks, Lily. Remind him he's got a home of his own now and then, will you?'

'I do, constantly, but you know what he and David are like once they get their heads together in the evenings. Sometimes I wonder why they bother to come home from the newspaper office at all, and why they don't take their beds there and be done with it.'

'I know what you mean, but Nick would like to see his son occasionally,' Skye said mildly, trying not to mind that Olly obviously preferred the company of this easy-going family to his own.

'I'll tell him,' Lily promised.

For a moment she hesitated as if she would say more, and then decided it wouldn't do to worry Skye unduly.

Chapter Two

Betsy Tremayne wasn't one to fly off into a temper without good cause. She left that to her volatile husband, Theo. Between his bouts of gout and his natural bad humour, there was rarely a day when the house wasn't in some kind of an uproar. There were times when Betsy thought wistfully of the comparatively peaceful days when Sebby and Justin were small boys, with the innocent ability to smooth things over even better than she could herself. Not that such sentiments had applied in recent years, she conceded. Nothing pleased Theo these days. But this was the last straw.

'What's upsetting you, Betsy?' Skye asked cautiously when they met in a Truro tea room on a late February afternoon. 'It's not like you to get so ruffled.'

'Can't you guess?' Betsy snapped, clearly having bottled up her resentment for too long. 'He's gone too far this time. He just can't leave things alone, always poking his nose in where he's not wanted. And 'tis not as if 'tis any of his business no more. He should be taking things easy now, but he just can't stop his meddling and interfering—'

'Hold on a minute, Betsy,' Skye said, putting a hand on her arm as she noticed the other tea room clients glancing their way. 'I presume you're talking about Theo. What's he done that's so terrible?'

She tried not to let the glimmer of a smile escape her lips, since this was obviously a serious matter to the normally mild-mannered and forgiving Betsy.

Whatever Theo did, Betsy could normally be relied upon to settle things, even to the extent of clearing up the unholy mess when Theo had hurled a vase through his precious television set. Not that it mattered a hoot now, thought Skye, since all transmission had been suspended after the outbreak of war, and their own set, that Olly had clamoured for so much, had been relegated to the attic of New World for the duration.

A good thing too, Nick had said, never happy about the thing sitting there like a blind, square grey eye in the middle of the drawing room.

Skye stopped her thoughts from meandering as Betsy's mouth became more pursed than usual in her tirade about Theo.

'You might not be so understanding when you hear where he's gone, and the rumpus because of it,' she said darkly.

'Not to the clayworks?' Skye said, reacting at once. 'We both made a bargain with the new owners not to go near the place. Theo fully agreed that it was for the best—'

'Theo will agree with anything for the moment. I know that better than anyone. I've lived with his lies and deceits for years, Skye, and I've overlooked it – most of it, anyway. But this could bring trouble on all our heads.'

Skye felt her heart lurch. How could Theo possibly meddle to such an extent? Ever since Killigrew Clay had merged with Bourne and Yelland China Clay Holdings Ltd, to become the combined Bokilly Holdings, she had truly believed that like herself, Theo had refrained from all contact with the new way of things. It was no longer their business.

This obviously needed discussion and she spoke more urgently.

'Perhaps it would be better if we continue this conversation somewhere else before you tell me what he's done, Betsy. Is he at home today?'

'He is not,' she retorted. 'Nor any other day.'

'Then why don't we go to the house?'

Betsy nodded, and Skye quickly paid the bill to the waitress. Even though she was becoming more alarmed than she allowed Betsy to guess, there was also a *frisson* of something else stirring in her veins. Until the arrival of the evacuees, there had been harmony in her own house since she and Theo had finally sold all their shares in Killigrew Clay and she had relinquished her interest in the White Rivers Pottery. Everyone had told her it was time she stopped being a businesswoman and took a more leisurely interest in life.

But in the secret heart of her, she had to admit that it wasn't a harmony she would have chosen. It wasn't her way to sit back and let the world revolve around her. It made her feel old and useless, which was why she had responded so readily to having the little evacuees at New World. At not yet fifty, being old wasn't how she wanted to feel.

The miscarriage she had suffered a year ago had undoubtedly made her assess her life, but not in the way everyone seemed to think. She had *wanted* that child, with a possessiveness that hadn't dawned on her until it was too late. It was a virtual certainty, now, that she wouldn't conceive again. And that made her feel old too…

Her thoughts became concentrated on the reason she was returning to the imposing Killigrew House with Betsy. Her cousin Theo was sixty-three years old, and clearly not ready to hang up his boots yet. And neither was she.

But she also began asking herself severely just what she was thinking about. She had been the one to push him into selling, following her husband's legal advice that a merger was the best way to keep both companies afloat. It seemed the best option for Killigrew Clay to cut the strings completely, but now it seemed that Theo couldn't let go so easily.

Once they were sitting in Betsy's comfortable parlour, she asked her bluntly to explain just what was going on.

'He's up there every day,' Betsy exploded. 'I swear to you I think he's going senile, Skye, and the clayworkers ain't going to play up to his shenanigans for much longer. He's up there lording it over them as if he's still one o' the clay bosses – far worse than old Charles Killigrew ever was in his day, by all accounts.'

'But they all know Theo has no authority any more.'

'Oh ah, they know it, and so far they'm all tickled pink by the way he goes on, and some of 'em are pretending to kowtow to him, funning with him, and then having a high old time aping his manner over jars of ale in the kiddleywinks, from what one o' the older clayers told me. Theo can't see that they're mocking him, o' course, but it can't last for ever, and I know they'll turn on him soon. He shames me, Skye, and that's a fact.'

She paused for breath, and Skye sensed her humiliation. It was bad enough that the clayworkers had bitterly resented Theo Tremayne's caustic manner when he was in charge. They had no say then. But now, he didn't pay their wages and he amounted to nothing, and she could just imagine the way some of the younger ones enjoyed jeering and mocking him.

'He must know they're just baiting him,' she said uneasily. 'He's not stupid, Betsy.'

'I told you. I think he's going senile,' she repeated. 'He rants and rambles on as if he's still a clay boss, and although he drives me to distraction, sometimes I fear for him. It's just like your Uncle Albie all over again.'

'Please don't say that,' Skye said quickly.

'Why not? The lapses happened to old Luke Tremayne as well before he passed on, and I ain't so sure the one who went to Ireland years ago didn't suffer the same kind of affliction too, so why shouldn't it be in the family?'

'Because I don't want it to be. Because I'm one of the family too, and both my parents were Tremaynes, and first cousins at that. If anybody's directly in line for any kind of abnormality, it's me.'

Betsy recovered from her brooding fury over Theo's antics to realise that Skye's voice had become shriller and that she was deeply distressed.

'Oh my God, I didn't mean to upset 'ee, Skye,' she said, acutely embarrassed now. 'You know I wouldn't do that for the world, and anyway, there's none so bright as you, so you don't need to take no notice of my nonsense.'

'But it's not nonsense, is it? It's just something I never thought about before.'

'Well, you can stop thinking about it right now,' Betsy said firmly. ''Tis Theo who's the madman, and he's been one since he were knee-high to a grasshopper, so there's no cause to think 'tis something that's just caught on, is there?'

Skye knew that was true enough, but she also knew that something had to be done to stop Theo making a complete fool of himself over a business that no longer belonged to them. The family had been steeped in the fortunes of Killigrew Clay for almost a century, but when it was time to let go, you had to let it go completely. She thought he had understood that.

'I'll have to speak to him, won't I?' she said slowly, knowing Betsy didn't have a hope of making him understand.

'I reckon you're the only one who can.'

–

She had intended going straight home to relax for an hour or so. Mary Lunn would be having an afternoon sleep in the old nursery, and their maid Liza always gave the child her afternoon tea now. Celia had managed to arrange her tram shifts so that she could fetch the others from school, and there wasn't much for Skye to do except to be the nominal matriarch of the family.

She shuddered at the word. A matriarch was an elderly woman, such as her Granny Morwen had been in her final years, and Skye wasn't ready for that yet. She instinctively turned her car away from the main road back to New World, and headed inland up to the huge, sprawling gash in the moorland that was Clay One, the remaining pit of the old Killigrew clayworks.

Life went on up here much as it had done for years, with the exception of the fine new electrical machinery that had been installed to make production faster and more efficient. The old days, that everyone referred to with such nostalgia, had been a time of hardship and poverty for the hundreds of clayworkers who had worked out in the open in all weathers, but this area had been reduced to a skeleton of those former times, and she doubted that any of her forebears would recognise it now.

The soaring white hills of the sky-tips didn't change, though, she thought stoutly, and nor did the milky green clay pools that looked so serene and beautiful in the sunlight. No visitor to Cornwall could fail to be affected by the wild, futuristic, moonscape appearance of it all. The phrase surged into her mind at that moment, and she stored it away to use in her record of the family background.

'Come to help your cousin on his way, have 'ee, Mrs Pengelly?' she heard a voice jeer, as she gazed down unseeingly, trying to recapture the memory of this place alive with hundreds of clayworkers, instead of the comparative few who worked here now. Nostalgia wasn't only for the old...

She whirled around at the sound of the voice, and saw a group of clayers nearby, leaning on their long shovels, their thigh-high boots caked in wet clay, their clothes dusted grey-white with the substance. They were strangers to her, but they clearly knew who she was.

'Is he here?' she asked, knowing at once that they must mean Theo Tremayne, and sharing Betsy's shame.

'You'll 'ear him any minute now, missis,' another one sniggered. 'He's been at the scrumpy, and he ain't feelin' too clever. Pit Captain says he shouldn't drive 'is posh car and he should stay here and sleep it off, but now I reckon you can take 'im home.'

'Where is he?' Skye snapped.

But she could already hear him, screeching his head off in the bawdiest song that was currently doing the rounds of the clayworks. Her face burned at the coarse words that weren't yet slurred enough to be mistaken.

'We'll fetch 'im for 'ee, missis,' the men laughed, clearly enjoying the sight of the company lawyer's wife looking so mortified. And an ex-owner at that. It was one more black mark against Theo, she raged.

The men half-dragged him towards her car, and bundled him inside it. The stink of the rough cider was almost overpowering, and whatever else she had intended chastising him about today was forgotten in her need to get him home as quickly as possible, with all the car windows already flung open to rid it of the stench.

'What the bloody hell's going on?' he snarled, still befuddled, but finally realising he was on the move, and that his belly was starting to boil as the car lurched over the uneven moorland track towards Truro.

'I'm taking you home where you belong,' Skye snapped.

After a startled moment he slurred on insultingly, 'Well now, if it ain't my sweet, beautiful American cuz, whiter than snow and twice as bloody angelic.'

'Shut *up*, Theo—'

'My sweet and lovely girl, who never let her knickers drop for her cuz, no matter how much he wanted her to,' he moaned dramatically.

'For God's sake, will you shut *up*! The car windows are all open—'

The next second, she was more than thankful that they were, as Theo suddenly swung sideways towards the nearest one and spewed up the contents of his stomach onto the track. He disgusted her so much; how he could ever have thought she would fancy him in a million years was beyond her. She wondered how Betsy ever had.

Mercifully the urgent eruption of his stomach contents made him pass out completely, and he slid down on the back seat without another sound until she had returned him to Killigrew House.

She ran to the house, and Betsy came to the door with her lips tight, calling to the menservants to bring their master inside. The quaintness of the request didn't escape Skye, and she presumed it was the only way Betsy could preserve a little dignity at this disgraceful exhibition.

'I wasn't able to speak to him about the other matter,' she said briefly. 'He was too drunk, but I'll do it as soon as possible. And don't worry about his car, Betsy. I'll arrange for it to be brought back to the house.'

'You can let it stay there and fall to pieces for all I care. He won't walk all that way with his gout.'

'But you know how he dotes on that car—'

'Serves him right. No – leave it where it is, Skye. And if the clayers find it amusing to daub it with anything that takes their fancy, that'll serve him right too.'

Skye drove away, sobered by the rage in Betsy's voice, and knowing that Theo had gone too far this time. But so had Betsy, in leaving his car to the wolves… and then, as the varying smells of Theo's presence in her car almost made her vomit herself, she decided that if this was what Betsy wanted, it wasn't her place to argue.

–

'We can't leave the car there,' Nick said angrily, when she had related all that had happened. 'The clayworkers will never leave it alone. His bombastic interference is well known by now, and I know just how inflamed they are at his insults. I've no doubt it will result in slogans and scratches all over the car. No, two wrongs don't make a right, Skye. Common decency demands that we bring it back, much as I deplore having to do anything for him.'

'Oh Nick, can't you forget your lawyer's conscience for once, and speak as a family member?' she said irritably.

'Not on this occasion. A lawyer is what I am, and you know it.'

'I don't always have to like it,' she muttered. At times she found his logical arguments for and against the smallest thing too much to take.

'Anyway, I can't do anything about it this evening,' Nick went on. 'I'm snowed under with paperwork, and I certainly don't want you and Celia going up there after dark.'

'It wouldn't be the first time. My family knew the moors like the backs of their hands, and were never afraid of walking up there, night or day, let alone driving. In my grandmother's time, they never had cars anyway.'

'Yes well, we don't live in miserable clayworkers' cottages, or have to scratch clay for a living.'

His arrogance was too much. 'Sometimes, Nick, you can be so *insufferable*,' she said. She marched out of the room in time to meet Celia with the evacuees coming home from school, and had to switch her mind to listening to Daphne's moaning, and Tommy's yelling.

'Don't they ever stop?' she asked her daughter.

'You wanted them here, Mom,' Celia said cheerfully. 'But I gather they've had a bad day,' she added in an aside. 'Some of the older children have been telling them their houses are going to be bombed, and they'll have to stay here for ever.'

'And that's a fate worse than death, is it?'

'Of course it is, poor little devils! What's wrong?'

'Nothing that can't wait for the telling,' Skye said, shamefaced at her black mood, and forcing a smile on her face for the sake of the children.

-

It was Butch Butcher who reported the news much later that evening. He and Tommy had been squabbling in his bedroom over one of Wenna's old books, and in the end it had got ripped, and Tommy was yelling that there would be bleedin' hell to pay now, and that Mrs Pen would give his arse a good old tanning the way his Ma used to tan his.

Skye was on her way to find out what all the commotion was about, preparing to talk to Tommy in no uncertain manner about his language, when she saw Butch standing by the window, his head pushed inside the blackout curtain, so that only the rear of his large, ungainly body could be seen.

'Come away from there, Butch,' Skye snapped. 'You know the slightest bit of light shines for miles, and I don't want to have the Warden coming down on us.'

He pulled his head back from the curtain, his eyes large and full of fear.

'I reckon we might as well go 'ome, missis, if the Germans have started dropping bombs on us here.'

'What? Don't be ridiculous. Nobody's dropping bombs here, and you should know better than to frighten the younger ones, Butch. We're perfectly safe in Cornwall, and besides, there was no air raid warning, was there?'

'What's that, then?' he screeched, opening the curtains wider, uncaring now whether or not he showed a wide beam of light to a non-existent enemy.

Angry at his apparent scaremongering, Skye strode to the window to snatch the curtains across again, and then gasped. The ground rose towards the high spine of Cornwall from here, and by daylight or moonlight it was possible to see the moors and the ghostly white sky-tips. It had always charmed her, but not now. Right now, all that could be seen was a huge fire burning brightly on the skyline, and at the same moment the sound of fire-engine bells as vehicles screamed towards it.

'My God,' she whispered.

'I told you, missis,' Butch was still babbling. ''Tis them Jerries dropping bombs on us, and we'll all be killed.'

'Are we going to be bombed, Mrs Pen?' Daphne Hollis said, dancing up and down, her eyes full of glee. 'My uncle was nearly killed in France in the other war, and he's got a hole in his head and a wooden leg now,' she added importantly.

'Don't talk such rot, Daphne,' Skye said, regaining her senses quickly. 'We are not being bombed, and it's merely a fire that's got out of hand on the moors. The firemen will deal with it. I daresay it was some foolish people playing with matches, as you children are always warned not to do.'

But she knew exactly what it was, or thought she did. Just as, years ago, she had known exactly what it was when her pottery had burned to the ground, and who had been responsible. There was no similarity between those two events, except for the gut feeling that the irate clayers had got their revenge on the hated Theo Tremayne at last by setting fire to his expensive car.

By the time she and Celia had calmed all the children down and spent an hour assuring the snivelling Mary that they weren't all about to be burned in their beds, Nick had driven to the site, and come home to confirm what she suspected.

34

'It was Theo's car all right,' he said grimly. 'The bastards had poured petrol all over it, though God knows where they got it from. The car went up like a bomb and as it spread it set the moors alight. The authorities are questioning folk in the area, but they won't find out who did it. The clayers are like clams when it comes to betraying one of their own.'

Although dumbstruck by what he was saying, Skye kept her eyes averted, afraid that he would see that she applauded this trait, no matter what the circumstances. And she shouldn't be approving of anything that resulted in an act of vandalism.

'We can thank God the night is so overcast,' Nick went on savagely. 'The German bombers won't be able to operate tonight, otherwise they might well have turned their attention westwards with such a beacon to guide them.'

Skye realised the truth of his words. But if he hadn't stubbornly refused to collect Theo's car, this would never have happened at all. She couldn't forget that, either.

'Someone had better let Theo know,' she said, full of a resentment she couldn't explain.

'My reaction to that is to let him rot until he sobers up,' Nick retorted, still bursting with uncontrollable anger at the irresponsibility of the clayworkers, and utter contempt for his wife's cousin.

Skye looked at him coldly, wondering how such a tender and loving husband could sometimes revert into such a monster.

'I shall go and tell him myself,' she declared.

'Mom, you shouldn't go out this late at night,' Celia put in. Skye rounded on her at once.

'Why on earth not? What the hell is wrong with all of you? Do you think I'm a child, or too senile to drive into Truro after dark?' she whipped out, immediately wishing she hadn't said the dreaded word.

But it was too late now, and she was damn well *going* to let Theo know what had happened. She had to be the one.

She realised the evacuee children were studying her silently now. Butch stood uneasily, while the other two, Tommy and Daphne, seemed oddly drawn together for once, with Mary burying her head in Celia's shoulder.

'Will you be all right, missis?' Butch said at last. 'I could come wiv you, if you like.'

'That's very sweet of you, Butch,' she said, touched by his red-faced concern, 'but this is something I have to do myself. It's family, you see,' she added, shutting them and Nick out completely.

–

By the time she reached Killigrew House and approached the front door, she could hear the raucous sound of singing. Theo knew some ripe old songs, and she could only thank God that the house was well away from any others.

Betsy opened the door no more than a fraction, red-eyed and clearly alarmed to find Skye standing there. Late night callers traditionally meant bad news in a community that rarely left their homes after dark except by invitation, and Skye quickly reassured her.

'There's no family trouble, Betsy, but I have to speak to Theo,' she said abruptly.

Betsy gave a shuddering laugh. 'Whatever 'tis, you'll get no sense out of him, Skye. But you'd better come in and see the state he's in, if you can stand it. 'Tis good of you to bother, and more than he deserves.'

The house smelled of vomit and disinfectant, and Skye had a job not to retch. She could only guess what kind of life Betsy had always had with her cousin in the past, with his philanderings and his evil temper. She followed the screeching sounds as Betsy led her to the parlour.

Theo was still bellowing out songs, of a sort. He was sprawled out on a sofa, a spilled glass of cider on the floor beside him. His face was puce, his shirt buttons stretched to breaking point as his beer gut protruded disgustingly through them. He was a disgrace to humanity, let alone his family, thought Skye.

But she tried not to let Betsy see just how much she despised him, knowing that the wife must still have some feelings for her husband, and truly amazed at her loyalty to him through all the years.

'Shall I leave you to him?' Betsy said.

'I think you had better stay and hear what I have to say, Betsy. He's not going to be too pleased,' Skye said, with the understatement of all time.

At her voice, Theo glared at her with narrowed eyes.

'What's this, then? Come to gloat, have 'ee, cuz? Like seeing your poor old feller in a poorly state, do 'ee?'

'I've got something to tell you, Theo, about your car.'

It took a few seconds for him to comprehend. Then:

'The bastards had best leave it alone,' he roared. 'If they've scratched one bit o' paint on it, I'll whip the hides off 'em—'

Skye spoke brutally, without emotion. 'They poured petrol on it – which I'm sure is against the law, considering the regulations,' she couldn't resist adding, 'and then they set fire to it and set the moors ablaze.'

It was a revelation to watch his face, and see the varying, flickering emotions that passed over it. There was bellowing fury; blasphemies of the most profound invention; a kind of comic disbelief; a pathetic howling of tears; and then he became a shadow of the old, powerful Theo as he finally slid from the sofa into a shivering heap on the floor.

'My Lord, I could have been a bit more subtle,' Skye said uneasily to Betsy.

She shrugged. 'Don't see why you should, Skye. Theo were always blunt in the way he spoke to other folk, weren't he?'

'But his car was his pride and joy—'

'Oh ah. We all knew he thought more of it than he did of me,' Betsy said matter-of-factly. 'Look at him now, the dozy old fool. Such a fuss to make over a bit of burnt metal!'

Skye caught her breath at such a provocative statement as Betsy tipped the toe of her slipper beneath Theo's arm to make him move. He didn't react at all.

'He's passed out again,' Skye said with relief. 'Otherwise he'd have been roaring at you for saying such things about his car.'

She paused, realising that Betsy was staring down at Theo strangely now. She knelt down beside him and pushed the great bulk of him over so that he sprawled on his back, completely inert. His face was grey and sweating, and his breathing was so shallow as to be almost non-existent.

Betsy's face was almost as ashen as her husband's when she looked back at Skye. 'I think we should send for the doctor,' she said quickly.

The official cause of death was a massive heart attack, but however incongruous it seemed, Skye thought privately that he died of a broken heart at the loss of his precious car.

'It was the most spooky thing imaginable to see the way Betsy sat there, stroking his face so tenderly, and crooning to him as if he was a baby, while we waited for the doctor to arrive,' she told Nick later, still choked and shocked at the swiftness of it all.

'My poor darling, it must have been horrible for you both,' he said gently, for once not condemning anyone at all.

'And I was the one to trigger it,' she said, starting to weep in his arms. 'If I hadn't rushed in and told him about the car so brutally—'

'Hush, my love, you know very well it wasn't just that. He was a prime case for a heart attack. The doctor said it was a miracle it hadn't happened long ago.'

'I wanted to stay with Betsy, but she wouldn't have it. She wanted to be alone with him until Sebby and Justin could be contacted. After the miserable life he led her, and all those other women...'

Nick held her close. 'But now he belongs to her alone, doesn't he? None of them can touch him now. He's totally hers, perhaps for the first time in her life. That's why she'll want to guard this last time with him so fiercely.'

She leaned into him. 'It's a long time since I had the feeling that you could be so perceptive, so *Cornish*,' she whispered illogically, since that was exactly what he was.

'It was always there, sweetheart. We never lose it, but sometimes we have a hard time saying what we feel.'

It comforted her to hear him say it now. She and Theo had been at daggers drawn for years, but now he was gone, she felt his loss more deeply than she could explain. She supposed it was because it was another one of the old Tremaynes gone, another link in the family chain broken.

But she hoped Betsy wouldn't have to keep up this silent vigil with him for too long before her boys came home. It wasn't healthy to sit over the dead, even though Skye knew it happened in many parts of the world and was thought perfectly natural. The body – the framework – was still there, and so was the soul, depending on your beliefs, but it still seemed creepy to Skye to watch over it, and talk to it, as if it could still comprehend. But maybe Betsy needed to do this, in order to make her own peace with her husband.

Skye shuddered, wishing time could move on, and they didn't have to go through the inevitable days of mourning and weeping… and as the thought slid into her head, she felt a huge shock at her own feelings. She realised she didn't *want* to mourn Theo, even though she knew she must. He had been a thorn in her flesh for so long, but he had chosen the way he lived his life, and to hell with the rest of them. And he was probably lording it over St Peter right this minute – if, indeed, his soul had winged its way upwards and not down.

She took a deep breath at the thought, and forced herself not to be too gloomy. Seb and Justin would soon be home on leave, and Wenna was coming back for a few days too. They still had a funeral to get through. The little evacuees were scared enough at knowing there was a death in the family, and had already clamoured not to have to go to it…

'Of course you won't have to go,' Celia told them. 'It's for people in the family to pay their respects and say goodbye, and he wasn't your uncle, was he?'

'Our Ma brings home lots of uncles,' Tommy Lunn said importantly. 'Sometimes we only see 'em once, and sometimes they stay all night too!'

'Is that so?' Celia murmured, guessing at the kind of men these uncles were, and not thinking too much of Mrs Lunn.

She was tempted to offer to stay at home with the children instead of attending the funeral, but that wouldn't be right, and the family needed everyone's support. Where there used to be so many of them, their numbers were dwindling, and unconsciously she echoed her mother's thought. The old order was changing, to use a boring euphemism.

Besides, Seb would need her. She didn't know why she thought of him particularly, but she knew he would take his father's death very hard. The two men had been so antagonistic towards one another, and yet she knew that love was there all the time. Some people just had a hard time showing it.

And right at that moment, Celia vowed that if she ever had children she would lavish all the love and care in the world on them, and never stop telling them she loved them.

It was a corker of a funeral, as an exuberant Betsy never stopped telling anyone who would listen. Theo would have heartily approved of the numbers of folk who turned out, bosses and clayworkers as well as family, all swelling the congregation in the little church and filling the churchyard where he was laid to rest next to his father's grave.

Back at Killigrew House for the bun-fight, which Betsy determinedly called it in Theo's own style, she flitted around as if she was the hostess at a society wedding.

'Is she all right?' Celia asked Seb uneasily.

Tall and dark in his infantryman's uniform, and clearly suffering with tight-lipped grief, he nodded.

'She'll do,' he said. 'This is her house now, and this is her way of stepping into Father's shoes.'

'Don't you think that's odd, after the way they've been all these years?' Celia couldn't help asking. 'I'm sorry, Seb, I don't mean to be crass—'

'You couldn't be crass if you tried,' he said, with a small attempt to be jocular. 'No, Mother's being the way she might always have been, if Father hadn't squashed her spirit years ago. He couldn't do it with Justin and me, and now it's her turn to be herself.'

He said it without any malice, which surprised Celia, but she was encouraged to ask more.

'I wonder what she'll do now. This house is far too big for her now with you and Justin away for the duration.'

She glanced across to where Justin was chatting to Wenna, just as if this was an ordinary family gathering, and realised at once how far away from them all the two of them had grown. Justin, the budding doctor, and Wenna, the nightclub star...

'She's already decided,' Seb said abruptly. 'She's going to offer the house for use as a servicemen's convalescent home. It won't be a hospital, and they'll have to be walking wounded, but I reckon she'll be needing helpers on a non-nursing basis, so if you're looking for a job in the area attending to a lot of helpless men, now's your chance.'

'Good Lord!' said Celia, too stunned at the thought of Betsy having decided on her future so quickly to consider anything else.

Chapter Three

Oliver Pengelly brooded over the fact that he hadn't been born a couple of years earlier. His cousins Seb and Justin had joined up, and the sight of them in their uniforms at their father's funeral had fired his blood anew. And the offices of the *Informer* newspaper were already depleted by several of the young men going off to war.

The very phrase had a dramatic and romantic ring to it, thought Olly. Not that he was stupid enough to underestimate what war meant. When you were in the newspaper business, you could hardly not know. But if only he had been born earlier there would have been no fuss about his wanting to join up at the earliest opportunity. It would simply have been accepted as the patriotic thing to do. As it was…

He gazed out of the office window on a late afternoon in July and scowled as he saw his sister approaching from the far side of the street, presumably at the end of her own working day on the trams, and knew he was in for a telling-off about not visiting home more often.

But New World wasn't home to him any more. He constantly argued with his stepfather, and he was far happier staying with David and Lily in Truro, where the Kingsley infants were his adoring slaves. He certainly didn't care for the influx of up-country brats his mother

44

had taken in, either. He'd met them once, and once was enough.

Uncharitable was definitely becoming his middle name, he thought uneasily, but he couldn't help the way he felt, and he thought his mother was too damn soft-hearted for her own good.

He put that down to a peculiar kind of guilt, and he'd been rash enough to say as much to David Kingsley recently. And when he'd explained what he meant, big as he was, he'd got a cuffing around his ears for his trouble.

'Well, I reckon she sometimes still feels guilty for not being a proper Cornishwoman, and for being from "over there",' he'd said belligerently. 'And I know that years ago a distant American relative tried to make contact with her old grandmother and caused her to have a stroke. My mother still feels guilty on that account. Both Americans, see?' he added, knowing he wasn't making sense, his ego still smarting over his cuffing.

'You young oaf,' David snapped, never mincing his words when he felt it was needed. 'You don't know the half of it. The man was related to the Killigrews, and only distantly related to the Tremayne family. I hope you've got enough sense not to say such things in front of your mother, anyway. She has nothing to feel guilty about!'

Olly's frown got darker. 'Well, she's American, isn't she? And you know what Mother's like. If anyone censures them, she takes a share in the guilt. Look how she fretted over the abdication crisis, as if she and the Simpson woman were practically blood relations!'

David looked at him thoughtfully. The boy was getting too hard for his years, and maybe it had been a mistake to bring him into the business so soon. But he knew as well as anyone that when Oliver Pengelly wanted something badly enough, Oliver Pengelly got it.

They both turned in some relief as Celia swept in, bringing the warmth of the July day with her.

'Mom wants to see you, Olly,' she said flatly, once David had discreetly left them. 'What the hell are you playing at by staying away so long?'

'I thought she had enough kids around her now without bothering about me,' he said, defensive at once. 'I don't see Wenna rushing home every five minutes, anyway.'

'Don't be ridiculous. Wenna's three hundred miles away. She still telephones every week, though, and she came home for the funeral, didn't she?'

'Oh ah, and she and Justin were acting the townies all right, weren't they? Wenna was always a proper little angel, phoning home every five minutes, and you're playing Miss Goody Two Shoes with the vaccies now, I suppose—'

'The *vaccies*?' Celia snapped. 'What kind of rubbish talk is that, for God's sake?'

Olly glared. He was too old for this, and he didn't need an older sister telling him what to do. He had always felt the underdog with her, and he felt it acutely now.

'Look, I'm doing a good job here, and I'll get over to see the parents when I can, all right? There's a war on, in case you haven't noticed, and somebody needs to report it.'

He puffed up his own role in the office, and was incensed as he saw her hide a smile. She never had much time for him, he raged, forgetting that she had been instrumental in persuading Skye and Nick to let him take this job and move in with the Kingsleys in the first place.

Such things could always be conveniently forgotten as far as Olly was concerned. In journalist jargon, he considered it sorting out the wheat from the chaff.

One day, he told himself furiously when she had gone... one day they'll take me seriously. And soon.

–

At least the evacuees were settling in after the first hiccups, thought Celia, as she drove back to New World. The drive was slow due to the restrictions of the hooded car head-lights everyone was now forced to adopt, even though she knew the road so well.

But she also knew the cliff edge was perilously near to the road in places, and she had no wish to go plunging over the side to the rocks below. Her great-uncle Walter had deliberately walked straight into the sea from somewhere along this stretch of coastline, breaking his mother's heart, and she had no wish to do the same.

In any case, it would be very bad form to have to have two funerals in such a short space of time, she told herself with mock cynicism.

Her thoughts reverted to the evacuees. Though Mary's sobbing bouts at home continued, the other three hadn't found school too much of a problem. Tommy had come home with a bloodied nose on numerous occasions, but had triumphantly proclaimed that they should see the other twerps.

Admittedly, a couple of irate mothers had telephoned Skye from time to time to complain about her charges. But apart from that, the children had dutifully written their laborious letters home – and sometimes the parents had written back. And all was well, Celia thought with supreme optimism.

She discovered the irony of that thought as soon as she arrived home. The sound of shouting came from the drawing room, and she was immediately enveloped in the smell of cheap scent as she went into the room. It was just as if a younger version of Fanny Rosenbloom had been reincarnated and appeared in their midst, as brash and blowsy as ever.

The only difference was that Mary Lunn, sobbing louder than ever, was clinging desperately to the woman's skirts.

Skye turned to her daughter with relief.

'Honey, this is Tommy and Mary's mother—'

'Pleased, I'm sure,' the woman said, without bothering to turn around. 'So let's stop beating about the bush, missis. I've come for me kids and I ain't going back wivout 'em.'

Celia intervened with a gasp as she realised what this was all about. 'You can't do that. They're really settling down here, and Tommy's enjoying his new school.'

Mrs Lunn looked at her through heavily made-up eyes. She was a tart, Celia thought brutally.

'He ain't enjoying nuthing. The kids want to come home where they belong and I should never have sent 'em away. My gentleman and me can give 'em a good home now, and no do-gooders are stopping us, see?'

'Your gentleman? You do mean their father, I presume?'

'That ain't your concern. He'll be back in a minute and if you're thinking of getting the rozzers on to us, we'll say you was taking our kids against our will, see?'

'Somebody's obviously schooled you well in what to say,' Skye said, wishing desperately that Nick was here.

Why was he always involved with other folks' affairs whenever she needed him? she thought furiously.

'We don't need no schooling. We just need the kids back.'

'Why do you need them just now, Mrs Lunn?' Celia asked, knowing that letters from their mother had been sparse indeed. The woman flushed under the heavy make-up.

'We gets a new flat if we've got the kids wiv us.'

'That's the most terrible and selfish reason I've heard for taking the children away from here where they're safe,' Skye snapped. 'Don't you know the danger you'll be putting them in if they go back to London? It's a terrible time.'

'They're my kids and I'll say where they live,' she shouted. 'You've missed me, ain't you, duckie?'

Mary snivelled that she had, and the next minute Tommy appeared from the nursery with their paper parcels of clothes. The other two children trailed behind him. Butch, never too bright, was uncertain of what was going on, and Daphne was clearly in admiring awe of the flashy Mrs Lunn.

'We're going home,' Tommy announced to Celia. 'Me Ma needs us and so does Uncle Bert.'

'Yes, well never mind all that,' his mother said hastily. 'Have you got all Mary's things as well?'

But it was becoming clearer by the minute now why she wanted these children home. 'Uncle Bert' was obviously on the look-out for an easy place to lay his head, and if they presented a united family, the flat would be theirs.

'You can't do this,' Skye said.

'I'm doing it,' the woman said rudely, and at the toot of a motor horn, she bundled the children out of the house towards the waiting car where a large man in an astrakhan coat pushed them into the back seat and slammed the door shut.

It happened so quickly that the others were left reeling.

'I didn't even get the chance to give Mary a hug or to say goodbye,' Skye said, her throat closing up.

'She 'ad to go wiv her Ma, though, didn't she?' Daphne said sensibly. 'You only borrowed 'er, Mrs Pen.'

Skye felt choked at the child's artless words. Oh yes, they were all on loan, all these children the country folk brought into their homes, and whose allegiance to them clearly meant nothing compared to what they felt for their parents.

That was absolutely right too, but she couldn't help feeling bad about not putting up more of a fight to keep the Lunn children here. She had wanted to care for them and keep them safe, and she had failed abysmally.

'We'll have to inform the billeting officer about what's happened, Mom,' she heard Celia's crisp voice. 'I'll telephone her now, and we can let the school know in the morning.'

Skye looked at her vacantly. Her daughter was the practical one, the strong one, while she was beginning to feel as if she was falling apart, the way she had felt when she lost her baby. And there were still these other two to care for... As if to echo her thoughts, she felt the unlikely touch of Butch Butcher's hand clumsily squeezing her arm, his voice rough with embarrassment.

'You've still got us, missis, and I ain't going nowhere.'

Skye gave him a watery smile, hoping the kindly meant remark wasn't a prophetic one. Hoping that at the end of this dreadful war, Butch Butcher would have a home and family to go back to...

She shook off the surreal feeling as Daphne tossed her head and resumed her usual toughness.

'They was cissies, anyway, and that stupid Mary was always stinkin' the place out wiv 'er widdle. We're better off wivout 'em if you ask me,' she declared.

'And there speaks the voice of experience,' Celia murmured, praying that her mother would see the funny side of it and not get too depressed at what she obviously saw as her own failure.

Celia knew very well that she was still grieving over her own miscarriage, no matter how she tried to hide it. It was one of the reasons Celia herself was still reluctant to think of enlisting, although she would dearly love to do so.

But if the London families wanted to withdraw their children from their country hosts, there was nothing to stop them, and everyone knew it. It was one of the things the billeting officers had impressed on the temporary foster homes before they took the children in.

And the worst thing any of them could do was to get too fond of the children.

Well, she would definitely never get too fond of Daphne, Celia thought now, seeing the way the little madam was noisily declaring now that she had never liked Tommy, anyway, and that Mary was a widdlin' weed.

Butch had turned out to be a gentle giant and not a thug, but what surprised Celia most of all was why her mother tolerated Daphne so patiently. She obviously saw something in her that Celia didn't. She gave up analysing and went to report the departure of the Lunn children to the billeting officer.

'Do we want to take in any more?' she asked Skye, careful to hold her hand over the mouthpiece at the officer's request.

Skye shook her head. 'Not yet. We'll see how things go, honey,' she said quickly.

She wasn't being cowardly, Skye told herself, but she just couldn't bear to have children coming and going and tearing her heart apart every time they did so. She knew she had babied Mary too much, and she dreaded what kind of life the child was going to have with that spiv of a 'gentleman friend' of her mother's.

No, Skye thought determinedly, if they had to open up their home to anyone in the future, it wouldn't be to any more evacuees – and she wasn't sure she could do what Betsy was proposing to do, either. She couldn't think any farther ahead than that for the moment.

—

One Sunday morning a few weeks later Lily and David Kingsley turned up at the house, and sent their boys out to play in the garden with the willing Butch and the reluctant Daphne.

'This is a surprise,' Nick said with a smile, 'To what do we owe the pleasure?'

'What is it?' Skye said, always more perceptive than he was when something was wrong.

Dear heaven, don't let anything be wrong with Lily, she thought, seeing her pallor. Lily had always been her strength when she needed it, but she looked positively ill as she put her hand on David's arm as if to caution him.

'Skye darling, we've got something to tell you, and I promise you we knew nothing of it ourselves until we found the letter this morning. There's one for you too, and we've brought it straight away. Don't be too hard on him.'

Skye took the envelope mechanically, but she hardly needed to open it to know what it was going to say, or who it was from. Olly's large, scrawly handwriting was all over the envelope, addressing them as if he wrote to strangers.

'What's going on?' Nick said sharply.

'Can't you guess? He's enlisted,' Skye said, choked, scanning the words that jazzed in front of her at speed.

'He can't enlist!' Nick exploded. 'He's too young.'

David spoke harshly. 'They're all doing it, Nick, and the hell of it is they're getting away with it. I grant you some of them are brought back with their tails between their legs, but Olly's too canny for that. The army needs keen young men like him, and from the size of him and his self-assurance, nobody would guess he's not yet seventeen.'

'And who gave him such self-assurance?' Nick said, rounding on him. 'I always knew it was a mistake to let him work in your bloody office and to live with you. His place was here where he belongs—'

'Nick, please,' Skye said, appalled at this outburst. 'None of this is David's fault.'

'It's all right, Skye, I don't blame Nick,' David said soothingly. 'It's the boy's own doing, and it's happened now.'

'Well, I'll see to it that it bloody *un*-happens,' Nick shouted. 'And please don't patronise me, Kingsley. You can always soft-soap my wife, but it won't work with me.'

'Nick,' Skye said warningly.

With his paying clients, he was always the cool-headed lawyer, but once he lost his temper he never did things by halves. And she couldn't bear it if he became vicious and made some sarcastic remark about always having known that David was in love with Skye. Not in front of Lily…

It was Lily who spoke calmly then, unwittingly diffusing the situation by her logical thinking.

'What do you think you can do about it, Nick? He says in the letter he's going to enlist, but he doesn't say where. I doubt that he'll have done it locally. In any case, people would know his family connections here.'

Nick's eyes narrowed. 'You're quite right. He'll have gone elsewhere. Plymouth or Southampton or Bristol, maybe. I'll make some telephone calls tomorrow. He chose the right day to leave the letters, didn't he, knowing we'd be unlikely to get after him on a Sunday?' he added bitterly.

'He's a clever lad, your Olly,' Lily said.

'Too clever and too proud to want to be hauled back here like a criminal or a naughty child,' his mother said slowly.

Nick turned on her. 'So what's your bright suggestion? Leave him to get on with it, knowing he's breaking the law? That's a fine way for a lawyer's son to behave, isn't it?'

'But he's not your son, is he?' Skye heard herself say.

She clapped her hands to her mouth as she saw Nick's stricken face and heard Lily's gasp. 'Oh God, I'm sorry, honey! I didn't mean that the way it sounded.'

'Was there any other way? We all know I'm not the boy's natural father but I seem to remember I adopted all three of your children after we were married, and I think I've always done the right thing by them,' he said, stiff with anger.

'Of course you have,' Skye almost wailed, wondering how this conversation had descended so rapidly into hurtful accusation and pain. And it wasn't helping things at all. It wasn't bringing Olly back. A small chill like a premonition fluttered over her heart then, and she willed it away.

She put her hand on her husband's arm. 'Darling, please listen a minute. I think we have to let the army deal with it. They must have ways of checking up on these young men who think soldiering is all fun and games. I'm sure he'll be found out and sent back home without us humiliating him.' She swallowed, imagining Olly's wounded pride. 'If we do that, he'll never forgive us and we'll have lost him for ever.'

She wasn't at all sure it was the right way, or if they too were breaking the law in not informing the authorities. Nick should know about such things… but this was a military matter and had no bearing on the domestic cases a country lawyer undertook in his everyday life.

She had to accept that her own instinctive need to hold the family around her like a kind of security blanket was of far less importance than the troubles in a changing world. The country needed their young men and women more than mere mothers did. All the government posters and propaganda told them as much, so it had to be true…

'I'm sorry, but I can't let it rest without making some enquiries,' Nick said firmly. 'He's still a child and we're responsible for him, Skye. If you can't see that then we're obviously on different sides.'

In the brittle atmosphere that was quickly developing, the Kingsleys called their sons and wisely took their leave, sensing the erupting situation between the two.

Celia arrived home from an exhilarating walk along the sands to find her parents practically screaming at one another.

Discovering the reason for it filled her with anger and guilt, knowing how impatient she had been with her brother. But common sense told her she couldn't have pushed him into this. The idea for enlisting must have been simmering inside him for some time.

'What are you going to do about it?' she asked flatly.

'Find him and bring him home,' Nick retorted at once.

'Nick, we *can't*,' Skye repeated.

'Would you rather see him killed? War isn't a game, however much these gun-happy children think it is.'

The words seemed to hang in the air between them all. Whatever else Olly was, he was still a child – *her* child. Skye was wretched, torn between the wish for her son to find his own feet and not be overshadowed by his successful stepfather, and her natural desire to keep him safe.

'Mom's right,' she heard Celia say scratchily. 'You can't humiliate him by bringing him back. The authorities will surely check all his personal details, and if they don't, then you should take it as a sign and let him go.'

'And there speaks our so-called modern miss, apparently still ready to trust in signs and omens,' Nick said coldly. 'I still intend telephoning the three army recruiting offices I suspect he may have contacted. It's my duty as a lawyer and father,' he added, without the slightest hesitation.

Skye knew then how much she had wounded him by her earlier remark, when in fact he had been all that a good father could be to her children.

'And if he hasn't reported to one of them you'll leave it alone?' Celia persisted.

She hardly knew why she was doing so, except that she felt bound to support Olly in this, having frequently been beastly to him in the past. And secretly envying him so much for his daring.

'For the time being,' was all Nick would say.

–

But his telephone calls produced nothing at all. Eventually he even called his one-time business partner, now the owner of an antique shop in Bristol, in case Oliver should have found his way there as a kind of temporary refuge.

'Nick, by all that's holy,' he heard his ex-partner's wife say delightedly. 'It's so long since we've heard from you, we thought you must have died or something!'

'Thankfully no. But it's good to hear you're still bright and cheerful, Queenie. Is William available?'

'I'll call him. He'll be tickled pink to hear from you.'

Even over the telephone line, Nick could hear her high heels clicking away, and her shrill voice calling for her husband. And then William was on the line, as hearty as ever, but instantly attentive when he heard why Nick was calling.

'I haven't seen him, Nick, but if he comes here I'll be sure to let you know.'

'Don't warn him, though. He won't think kindly of us if he thinks we're about to haul him back, but I'm afraid the boy's as wild and passionate as the rest of his clan.'

'I thought that was what attracted you to them – or one of them, anyway,' William said, and then his voice sobered. 'But don't worry, I'll be discreet if he does turn up here.'

A few days after the hunt for Oliver James Pengelly had turned out to lead precisely nowhere, he was signing on the dotted line as Jimmy Oliver, at a military base in Wiltshire.

The first thing he'd had to do was get as far away from Cornwall as possible. And he wasn't going to waste his shrewd journalist's brain on rushing into what would be his family's obvious conclusion. They still considered him a boy, but Oliver always thought things through before he made a move.

They would naturally assume he wanted to be a soldier, since army talk was all that anyone ever discussed. His cousins Seb and Justin had enlisted in the army, and his own father and Nick had served in the last war. His mother and female cousins too, he remembered, as he carefully worked out his plan.

Joining the Navy was definitely not an option, he thought with a shudder. There had been drownings in his family and their connections in the past, and although it didn't follow that any ship he joined would be torpedoed, the very thought of being sucked under the waves into that infinite underwater hell was enough to chill his bones. He had the inheritance of his mother's vivid imagination to thank for that.

He had never felt any particular passion for flying until he had seen some of the small airplanes whizzing about the skies in practice manoeuvres as he took the train away from Cornwall. Through the train windows he had watched them soaring into the blue, the sun glinting like silver on their wings, and turning them into shimmering works of art.

In those moments he had felt a brief and poetic affinity with the flight of angels... and the heady certainty of what he wanted to do had become as inevitable as breathing.

But he had no intention of enlisting as Oliver Pengelly. Jimmy Oliver he now was, and he blessed his size and powerful physique, and the self-assurance that easily persuaded the recruitment officer that he had left his identity card at home, but it would be sent on as soon as possible. He felt a pang on his mother's account as he told the lies so glibly, but he was almost seventeen now. A few months more, and they couldn't touch him. He was simply anticipating the day.

The officer was jaded and anxious to get home to his wife and children at the end of the day, and Olly held his breath as his papers were finally stamped. He was now one of the lowest of the low in His Majesty's Royal Air Force.

The rank didn't matter. He was *in*, and that was enough to give him an adrenalin rush in his veins as he collected his kit and went to find his billet.

-

'It's just as if he's vanished from the face of the earth,' Skye told Lily some weeks later, with a feeling of sheer desolation. 'How could he do this to us?'

Lily looked at her thoughtfully, and decided it was time for shock tactics.

'Why don't you think about his needs for a minute, Skye, and not yours?'

'What? Well, thank you very much for that. I thought I'd have your support at least!'

'Darling, you have my support in anything you do, and you always have. But I think that as usual you've got blinkers on as far as Olly's concerned. Is Nick giving you a particularly hard time over it?'

'You could say that,' Skye muttered after a few resentful moments. 'He's taking it personally, thinking he's driven the boy away. But Olly left us a long time ago, and I don't mean to throw any blame on you or David for that. Olly was always frustrated by having a clever stepfather and three women in the house who either made a pet of him or laughed at him. Poor love. He really couldn't win either way.'

Lily was silent, letting her work things out for herself. Privately, she admired Olly for doing what he felt was right. With the heavy bombing of London now, they needed every young man they could find to beat the Germans.

But, like Skye, she still remembered the trenches of France from the first war, and she shivered, not wishing for Olly or anyone to go through that hell again. She felt guiltily thankful that her own boys were far too young to be involved.

Skye saw her shiver, and tried to pull herself together. She had always known in her heart that Olly would enlist at the first opportunity. He was just jumping the age queue, like so many other young men, and all she and all those other mothers could do was to pray for his safe return.

God, she was being noble now, she thought in disgust… but she had to be, or go under. She drew a deep breath and tried to move her thoughts to other things.

'There's nothing we can do about it except what Nick's already doing, so let's talk about something else,' she said with a huge effort. 'How is the shop doing?'

'Poorly, since you ask. Few people have the money to spare on fancy goods these days.' She hesitated. 'In fact, I wanted to talk to you about that, Skye. So many of these evacuees are miserably dressed. What would you say to my starting a second-hand clothes section? People could bring in their unwanted children's clothing, things they have outgrown, for instance, and we could offer them at a small price for the evacuees, or even do an exchange arrangement. David could advertise the scheme in the newspaper…'

Her quick burst of enthusiasm faltered when Skye didn't answer. She knew it was a bad time to be discussing such things when Skye was so worried about Oliver. But then she saw that she had at least caught her cousin's interest.

'What a sensible woman you are, Lily. The clothes would need to be clean and pressed before we accepted them for sale or exchange, of course, and David would need to stipulate all that in the advertisement.'

'Can I go ahead then? It's your premises, and I wouldn't do anything without your say-so.'

'More than that. You have my blessing.'

–

They heard from Olly just after his eighteenth birthday. He was now stationed "somewhere in Wiltshire", he wrote grandly; he was in the Royal Air Force, and learning to fly a kite. They were not to worry about him. And he begged his mother to forgive him for running off the way he had, but life was good – oh, and he had some new pals who were simply spiffing.

'He sounds like a real toff, don't he?' Butch Butcher said when Skye read out the words to the family and the evacuees that afternoon.

'He sounds grown-up,' Celia commented, with an unexpected rush of affection for her brother.

'It ain't grown-up to fly a kite. Anybody can do it,' Daphne put in rudely. 'I 'ad one once. Me Dad used to take me up on Clapham Common ev'ry Sunday morning when he come out of the Nag's Head. Course, he was sometimes too tiddly to fly it proper,' she added, with a giggle and a nostalgic tear in her knowing young eye.

'Yes, well this is a different sort of kite,' Celia told her briskly. 'It's how the airmen refer to their aeroplanes.'

'Well, I think that's daft,' Daphne said.

'She thinks everyfing's daft,' Butch said. 'But she's the daft one, ain't she?'

Any minute now, Skye could see, battle was about to be done. She told them instead to get washed for their tea, ignoring Daphne's grumblings that she hated margarine and she wanted proper shop-bought jam on her bread like they had at home, and not the homemade stuff.

'She's lucky enough to get any at all,' Skye retorted after the children went upstairs, protesting all the way.

Now that everything was becoming rationed they all had to tighten their belts – though she had to admit it didn't do female figures any harm. She frequently longed for a good strong cup of tea, but now that tea was rationed to two ounces per person per week, even that resembled 'cricket's piss' – according to Daphne's colourful vocabulary.

But at any rate, now that they knew what Olly was doing she felt a little better. Ironically so, she thought wryly, since he was putting himself in the front line of danger. But not knowing was always the worst, and even Nick was showing a definite and belated pride in Olly's daring. She lulled herself into a false sense of optimism.

–

The Blitz began in September, with the heaviest bombardment that London had ever witnessed. As it continued unabated, through Christmas and into another year, Skye constantly begged Wenna to come home where she would be safe, but Wenna stubbornly reiterated that the show must go on to keep up people's spirits.

Even so, the Flamingo Club had put up its shutters except for Saturday nights, and once the air raid sirens started wailing, few Londoners risked turning out of their homes for anything so fancy, even to hear Miss Penny Wood sing.

Like most of them, she and Fanny hurried to the nearest Underground station, where temporary sleeping quarters and coveted family corners were the order of the day now. It was the new community shelter, and although the sights and smells were sometimes indescrib-able, Wenna recognised the weird sense of belonging, of beating the Hun by the sheer defiance of not moving out of London. This was where they belonged; they were all together; and this was where they would stay. Even the King and Queen said the same thing.

But families, friends and lovers were being parted, and she hadn't seen Austin in months now, although he wrote as often as he could and she knew he was due for a few days' leave soon. She knew that her cousins Sebby and Justin were stationed "somewhere in France" now, and that her brother Olly had enlisted. She was enormously proud of him.

But there was something else that drew Wenna to these people she now virtually thought of as her own. When the dull sounds of bombing grew louder and more frightening and rocked the Underground stations, no matter how deep they were, there were always those who started a sing-song to keep up the peckers of the rest, and to try to drown out what old Hitler was doing. She admired them all so much.

Even Miss Penny Wood wasn't averse to joining in the choruses, and eventually found herself leading the nightly singing. Most of the people who fled to the Underground were ordinary folk and not theatre-goers at all, and had no idea who she was. But they quickly realised they had a nightingale in their midst, and adopted her just as readily as she had adopted them.

'Gawd, I've forgotten me glasses. I'll have to go back for 'em, duck,' Fanny Rosenbloom said as they rushed towards the Underground station one early spring night in 1941.

The ritual was routine now, and people took so much of their homes with them that it resembled a huge under-ground refugee camp. Many of the older women took their knitting, since making socks and scarves for soldiers was their contribution towards the war effort.

Fanny Rosenbloom always took her showbiz and women's magazines, but she had finally succumbed to the inevitable, admitting that she was as blind as a bat without glasses.

'You can't go back,' Wenna said at once. 'Just join in the singing tonight or try to have a sleep instead.'

'I ain't sleeping while old Hitler's up there doin' his worst. I'll just be a few minutes, gel.'

'Fanny, please don't—'

But there was no stopping her, and Wenna watched anxiously as she picked her way carefully over bodies preparing to settle down for another night of mole-like existence; young mothers trying to settle down their children; babies crying fretfully while the older men belched or farted or drank more bottles of ale than they should to try to forget why they were all here. She couldn't blame any of them.

'Come on then, gel, let's see your pearly whites! Give us a song from that pretty throat of yours,' someone yelled, and others took up the call at once.

Wenna obliged at once, and the dimly-lit Underground immediately came alive with the sound of singing, so that the heavy bombardment didn't seem so bad. They could drown it out, and they bleedin' well would. Fanny always said so…

-

Fanny looked up at the maze of searchlights picking out the German bombers as they zoomed towards the London landmarks – like angry bleedin' dragonflies buzzing about, she thought irritably. The city was ablaze with light from the burning buildings by now, anyway, and they hardly needed the bleedin' searchlights at all. Fanny blasphemed cheerfully with the most inventive curses she could find, tripping and staggering through the rubble of a recently demolished row of houses on her way back to the Flamingo Club.

The buggers weren't going to stop her getting back to her own place, so sod 'em all. She gave the two-finger salute skywards as she reached the club, and stumbled in through the darkness and up to her bedroom to fetch her glasses.

She was deafened and consumed by noise now, as buildings all around her rocked on their foundations and the street was lit up with a blinding flash of light so intense that it was almost unearthly. But Fanny hardly saw it. Within seconds there was nothing left of her to see anything.

Chapter Four

The singing grew determinedly louder and more raucous as the noise of the bombardment from above penetrated the crowded Underground station. To those who were incarcerated below, it seemed to go on for hours, and voices were strained to their utmost as if to ward off the knowledge of what everyone knew was the destruction of their homes and businesses.

But one of them knew it was too long since her bene-factor had gone. The sweetest voice of all had become silent, her vocal cords drying up with what her family would call a true Cornish premonition.

'Fanny,' Wenna whispered brokenly. 'Oh Fanny, no...'

Finally, she could remain there no longer. There was a frail hope that Fanny would have sheltered elsewhere, and she had to know. She clambered over the bodies of those who were either trying in vain to sleep, or ignoring Hitler's whole bloody onslaught, and tried to reach the exit.

'Where d'you think yer goin', gel?' one and then another shrieked. 'The All Clear ain't gawn yet.'

'Let me go,' she gasped, as they tried to pull her back. 'I have to find Fanny. I have to know what's happened.'

As if to aid her determination, moments later they heard the long-drawn-out sound of the All Clear siren, and the sound of cheering replaced the hoarse singing.

Wenna clambered out of the Underground, swaying and blinking in horror at the carnage that assaulted her eyes.

Searchlights still criss-crossed the night sky in the moonlight for any stray German bombers, but there was little need for any natural or artificial light. It was a scene out of hell. The flames of the burning buildings lit the sky with a terrible red glow, and the acrid stench of burning flesh filled the air. Rubble and splintered glass lay everywhere, and the dust was choking and blinding. From several collapsed buildings where a bomb had struck a direct hit, rank sewage was pumping out with a stomach-turning stink.

People milled about in complete disarray. Among the rescue workers were half-clad folk peering out of home-made shelters in various stages of relief or fear or total disorientation. Others who had stubbornly remained inside their houses staggered outside the dangerously crumbling buildings, deafened and bewildered. But they were the lucky ones. They were still alive.

Wardens shouted angrily at Wenna to get off the streets as ambulances and fire engines screamed through them, seeking a passageway. Where they tried impotently to put out the worst of the fires, the firemen's hoses were instantly seared and scorched in the intense heat. It seemed as if the whole of London was on fire, lit up like a hideous red inferno.

Not knowing what to do or how to help, Wenna feverishly tried to ignore what the rescue workers were doing, willing away the anguished cries of the injured and dying. She closed her mind to the sight of blood and scattered limbs, screaming inside as she trod on a soft piece of flesh that had once been someone's arm, and at the sight of a bloodied and mutilated baby tossed into a pile of rubble as if it was a rag doll.

Weeping and almost demented, she ignored everything in her rush to reach the Flamingo Club and Fanny. She struggled through the winding streets and alleyways, and finally gaped in numbed shock and disbelief at what had once been Fanny and Georgie Rosenbloom's pride and joy.

There was nothing left of the entire street. Nothing but a heap of smouldering bricks and mortar. And somewhere beneath it all was the woman who had loved her like a daughter.

Galvanised at last into action, the sensations of pain and horror rushed through Wenna so fast that they made her gasp. Her chest was so tight with holding in the pain all this time that she was near to fainting. But she knew she had to do something, however futile the task.

She crawled over the broken stones and glass, ignoring the jagged edges that cut into her flesh, and began to tear frantically at the debris with her bare hands. They quickly began to bleed as the shingle ripped her tender skin, but she hardly noticed. Sobbing hysterically, she worked unceasingly until other hands pulled her away, and a man's voice she didn't know was shouting roughly in her ear.

'There's nothing you can do 'ere, duck. They're all long gawn, and you need 'elp yerself, by the looks of yer.'

Wenna turned on the air raid warden angrily.

'I have to find her,' she croaked wildly. 'You don't understand. I live here,' she finished, choking, and not noticing the compassion in his voice.

'Not any more you don't, gel. Come on now, into the ambulance wiv yer and get those cuts cleaned up—'

'I don't need a bloody ambulance! I'm not hurt. Go and see to those who need you.'

Was the man completely stupid? Wenna glared at him as the cruising ambulance pulled up alongside them, and then saw the kindliness in his tired eyes. And instantly, she knew he had seen far more terrible sights than she had this night, and with a whimpering cry, she slid to the ground at his feet.

–

'My God,' Skye said, white-faced, two weeks later.

She looked up from the letter that had been delivered that morning, her throat working and almost unable to speak.

'What is it?' Celia said sharply. 'It's not Olly, is it?' *Dear God, don't let it be*, she prayed.

'This is from Wenna's agent. She's been in a London hospital for more than a week now after one of those dreadful air raids. She's in a state of shock and hasn't spoken since she arrived. Apparently one of the other patients recognised her as the singer in the Flamingo Club and the hospital almoner contacted her agent. He thought we should know.'

She swallowed as she stared down at the letter, knowing how inane were her last words. Of *course* they should know.

'Go on, Mom,' Celia said, going swiftly to her mother's side. 'She's not seriously hurt or – or anything?'

Skye's eyes were flooded with tears now. 'They found her scrabbling through the rubble at the Flamingo Club. Trying to find Fanny. She never did, though.' She drew a shuddering breath, seeing from Celia's horrified eyes that she didn't need to explain any more.

'I have to go to Wenna,' she went on distractedly. 'She'll need me, and she'll have to come home now.'

'Mom, you can't go to London! Dad will never let you!'

'He won't be able to stop me because I'll be gone before he gets home. You can hold the fort here, can't you, honey?'

Celia recognised the determination in her voice, but it was still her duty to try and stop her.

'You know I can. But I can't bear to think of you being in danger from these awful bombing raids—'

Skye was suddenly calm. 'I've been in danger before, darling. And now I'm going to pack a bag, as I don't know how long I'll need to stay. Explain to Daddy for me, won't you?'

'Well, at least telephone this agent person first, Mom,' Celia said in alarm. 'You can't just go off like that!'

Skye nodded. 'You're right, of course,' she said, thankful for her daughter's common sense. 'I'll do that right away. And then I'll get ready to leave.'

She asked the operator for the telephone number on the agent's headed notepaper with a trembling voice. She remembered Martin Russell from the last time she had gone to London to comfort Fanny after her beloved husband, Georgie, had killed himself, his mind tormented by the treatment his fellow Jews were receiving in Germany. God, this bloody, bloody war that ripped people and families apart...

The voice that answered was crisp and efficient, but it changed at once when she said who she was.

'My dear lady, I was so sorry to be the bearer of bad news about Penny.'

In her agitated state Skye had to force herself to remember he was using Wenna's stage name, and that this man would naturally refer to her as such in the different world they both shared.

'Thank you for contacting me,' she said huskily. 'But how is my daughter, truly? Are there any physical injuries?'

'No more than a considerable number of cuts and bruises that will heal,' he assured her carefully.

'And what about her voice?' Skye asked.

Her beautiful, beautiful voice...

'I saw her yesterday, and she can whisper now. They say the voice will return to normal now that it's started to come back,' Martin Russell said, still cautious. 'She had a terrible shock, discovering the Flamingo Club razed to the ground like that. Especially as Mrs Rosenbloom had returned to the place earlier. Penny left the Underground and went there to find her, but there was no hope for her, of course. No hope at all. I'm sorry. Very sorry.'

His voice became jerky, and even though the words were short, Skye remembered that he had known Fanny Rosenbloom a long time. Probably longer than she had known her herself.

'Will you please tell Wenna that I'm leaving for London today and I'll be there to see her as soon as possible? And Mr Russell – I shall be bringing her home to Cornwall with me.'

She hung up before he could argue about that. It was none of his business, and besides, where else would Wenna go? She had made her home with Fanny at the club for several years now, but this was where she belonged.

The peace and tranquillity of Cornwall would restore her spirits, the way it always did, and always had, for all of them. It was their own private sanctuary.

–

By the time she reached London and found a taxi to take her to the hospital it was evening and getting dusk, and for the first time Skye felt real fear in her heart as she saw the full devastation of the Blitz. She had never imagined it to be quite like this – so many buildings demolished, and whole streets looking as though an earthquake had struck them.

Dust lay over everything. A strong whiff of burning still lingered on the air, bitter, pungent, and unforgettable. Remnants of possessions could be glimpsed amongst the debris – a child's shoe, a toy, a torn jacket, the burnt pages of a book – bringing the whole scene into heartbreakingly human focus.

'You got somebody in the hospital, lady?' the taxi driver asked her chattily.

'My daughter,' Skye said, her eyes as dark as midnight with fear and anxiety.

'In the Forces, is she?'

'No, she's not,' Skye said, swallowing hard and trying to ignore the images of destruction all around her. 'She's a – a singer in a nightclub.'

And dear Lord, but how *useless* that sounded, when all around her now, she could see young men and women in uniform scurrying about their business as night drew on. She was proud of Wenna, but right now, it seemed the most ineffectual job in the world for a young woman to be doing in wartime.

Clearly the taxi driver didn't think so. 'That so?' he said admiringly. 'We need gels like her to keep up the lads' spirits. There's more ways of winnin' a war than sticking a gun up a Jerry's backside, if you'll pardon me French.'

Skye swallowed again, blessing his generous heart, and thinking that he would never know how much he had done to restore *her* morale at that moment. People like him, in the midst of it all, could put things in their proper perspective.

When they reached the hospital she gave him a bigger tip than she had intended, and went to find Wenna's ward. Before she entered it, she was faced with the dragon of a Ward Sister and had to explain who she wanted to see.

'Is she all right? How soon can she come home?' Skye said all at once. 'And what about her voice?'

'Her cuts are healing nicely, and she can speak fairly clearly now. The temporary loss of voice was due to shock and not from any physical injury,' the Sister said efficiently. 'As for going home, the sooner the better. I need all my beds for the wounded.'

She swished away, leaving Skye feeling like a fly that had been squashed against a wall. Hateful woman. And then she tempered the ungracious thought, remembering that other war when she too, and all of them, had hidden their emotions beneath a wall of stoicism.

She strode down the ward until she reached the bed where Wenna lay, her lovely dark hair lank against the starched white pillow, her blue eyes looking listlessly the other way.

'Wenna, darling,' her mother said in a choked voice.

She turned at once, her expression disbelieving, the tears spilling out of her eyes at once. And then she gave a huge cry as she reached out towards her mother, and was at once enveloped in her arms.

'Oh Mom, I don't know how you got here, but it's so good to see you. It's been so terrible. I couldn't speak, and I was so afraid – and Fanny – poor Fanny – oh, you don't know—' she sobbed almost incoherently.

'Darling, I do know,' Skye said gently, overwhelmed with pity for her girl. 'That nice Mr Russell wrote and told me everything. I know Fanny's dead, and I know you lost your precious voice for a time – but in case you haven't noticed, you've got it back now,' she added, with a tease in her own at the sudden tirade.

'I have, haven't I?' Wenna said, unable to stop the sobbing all the same. 'Just as if it mattered about my stupid voice. I'm never going to sing again now that Fanny's gone. I'll never have the heart for it.'

Skye held her tight and let her cry it out. It was a long time before the paroxysm ceased, and when it did, Skye wiped both their eyes and spoke sternly.

'Now you just listen to me, honey. Do you think Fanny would want you to say such things on account of her? Don't you think Fanny would be the first one to tell you to stop feeling bleedin' sorry for yourself and to get on with things? She's probably somewhere up there right now, looking down at you and urging you not to let the buggers get you down. Can't you hear her saying it?'

She felt Wenna sniffling against her, and knew that several other patients were grinning their way, surprised to hear a well-dressed lady with an American accent speaking in such broad terms. But it wasn't *herself* speaking, thought Skye. It was Fanny, telling her what to say and how to say it. And forcing Wenna to give a wan smile at the end of it.

'She really is up there, isn't she, Mom? Or could she be somewhere much warmer? She was always a bit of a wicked lady, but in such a lovely, human way.'

'I'm quite sure Fanny's up with the angels, honey,' Skye said with a catch in her throat. 'And once this war is over, she'll expect you to carry on doing what she groomed you for. You're not going to let her down, are you?'

After what seemed like an endless moment, Wenna shook her head slowly.

'I know you're right, but I'm not even thinking about any of that now. Fame and fortune seem such paltry things compared with just being alive, don't they?'

'You're absolutely right, darling, but you'll think differently about your career when you've had a good long rest. I've told Mr Russell you're coming home to Cornwall, and I won't take no for an answer. I'll find somewhere to stay for tonight, and we'll take the train home tomorrow.'

She knew Wenna was about to argue, but before any more words left her lips the sound of the air raid siren wailed out, and the drone of many aircraft could be heard almost instantly. The heavily blacked-out windows blocked the sight of them, but they couldn't obliterate the noise of the bombs and the retaliating anti-aircraft guns as the hospital shook on its foundations.

Skye, still holding Wenna's hands, suddenly realised that it wasn't only the hospital that was shaking. With every burst of ear-shattering sound, her daughter was reliving the night when Fanny Rosenbloom had been killed, and she shook from head to foot.

'Take me home, Mom,' she whispered. 'Just as soon as you can arrange it.'

—

Celia stood in the fragrant garden of New World, looking up at the stars and breathing in the accentuated night-time scent of roses. The children had gone to bed, and her father was busy in his study. She treasured this time alone, when her thoughts always winged towards Stefan.

She fixed her gaze on one particular star, and remembered how her lover had told her that as long as that star still shone, they would be together in spirit.

A sudden burst of resentment split the serenity of her thoughts. It had been such a sweet, wonderful sentiment at the time, but now…

'What use is being together in *spirit*?' she said passionately, knowing that no one was around to hear her. 'When I want you close, to feel you and touch you, and feel you touching and holding me—'

She bit her trembling lips, wondering if it was wrong to want him so much. Wondering if they would truly ever meet again, or if it was a futile longing that could never be fulfilled, and full of bitterness at the cruel irony of fate that placed them on different sides in this awful war.

'Send me a sign, Stefan,' she murmured inadequately to their star. 'Anything, to let me know you're still alive, and still want me as much as I want you.'

In the soft dark silence of the evening, she finally turned away with her shoulders drooping, and went back into the house. The telephone was ringing, and she guessed it would be her mother telling her what time to meet her and Wenna at the railway station.

'Is that you, Celia?' a man's voice said.

She stared at the instrument stupidly for a moment. The line was not good and the voice was crackly and broken up. She didn't recognise it immediately, but she knew very well that she hadn't somehow conjured up Stefan by wishful thinking.

'What's up? Don't you recognise your cuz-in-law?' the voice went on teasingly.

'Good Lord, *Ethan*,' Celia spluttered into the telephone as the Cornish accent finally registered. 'You're the last person I expected to hear. There's nothing wrong with Karina or Ryan, I hope.'

God help her, she thought guiltily, but she had to think hard to remember the names of her mother's cousin Karina and her baby son. They had gone to Ireland to live right after Ethan and Karina's marriage, to escape from the disgrace of everyone knowing there was a baby on the way. Too many terrible things had happened between then and now to make it of such great consequence, Celia reflected.

'There's nothing wrong,' Ethan insisted. 'But I'm glad you answered, Celia, because it's you I wanted to talk to. Not that I'd have minded a word with Nick, of course. How is my brother? Still sorting out everybody's problems, I daresay? And your mother – and Wenna. How's Wenna?'

Celia was suddenly choked, remembering how Ethan had always been Wenna's champion in the days when she had been a moonstruck child, and the gangly fourteen-year-old Ethan had stood up to their Tremayne boy cousins in her defence. How long ago it all seemed now since they were children… She shivered, and made herself answer his questions.

'Everyone's fine, though Wenna had a bad experience recently when her lady boss was killed in an air raid. Mom's gone to London now to bring her home, and I thought you were her, telling me when to meet them…'

Her voice dwindled away, not knowing what else to say. With the intervention of time and distance and circumstances, they had grown apart, the way people did, even families.

'Well, I've got some news that might be of interest to you, Celia,' Ethan went on. 'We've got a prisoner of war camp near here, and the German soldiers are sent out to work on the farms. We've got a few working for us. They're supervised, and some don't speak much English, but they're sociable enough and one of them mentioned a name that you might know.'

'Go on,' Celia mumbled.

'I believe he's a distant relative of your von Gruber fellow,' Ethan said casually, never guessing how her heart was leaping now, fit to burst in her chest.

'Stefan!' Celia breathed.

'That's the one. Wasn't he the owner of some big vine-yard and estate in Germany?'

'That's right—'

'Well, it seems that the house has been taken over by the Gestapo, and because your man refused to co-operate, he's been interned. The relative has no idea where he is now.'

Celia spoke quickly without giving herself time to think.

'Ethan, as soon as Mom and Wenna get back, I'm coming over to see this man. I have to talk to him.'

His voice was dubious. 'He won't be able to tell you anything more, Celia. It'll just be a wasted journey—'

'He's a link with Stefan, and the first one I've had in months. I have to talk to him,' she repeated. 'I'll let you know when I can leave here.'

'Well, all right,' he said. 'Karina will be pleased to see you, anyway,' he added as an afterthought.

She hung up the phone, her hands damp and trembling. But her first sense of elation that she was going to speak with a relative of Stefan's – someone who would have seen him since she had done – was fast fading.

Instead, the word Ethan had used was seeping into her mind. Stefan had been interned. Locked up in his own country for refusing to co-operate with the Gestapo. She had no idea what that might mean, but her heart was breaking at the thought of him being tortured, or worse. And his lovely home that she had only heard about, being used by those evil men, must have broken his heart as well.

As the sobs welled up in her throat, she turned around to find her father watching her.

'Did you hear any of that?' she blurted out.

'Enough,' he said, holding out his arms to her. She went straight into them, glad of their strength and comfort.

'I can't bear to think of Stefan being interned,' she sobbed, when she had finally told him everything. 'What will they do to him, do you think?'

'I don't know, darling,' Nick said. 'He probably hasn't done anything so terribly wrong, but presumably he has to be punished in some way. What I do know is that it's foolish to let your imagination give you nightmares. There's nothing you can do about it.'

'I wish I could go to Ireland now, this minute,' she said passionately. 'This German soldier is the only link I have with Stefan.'

'You can't go right now,' Nick said more firmly. 'There are people who need you here, Celia. Your mother and sister will be back soon, and Wenna has been through a traumatic experience. It's upset the evacuee children too, reminding them of what could be happening to their families. You have to be here to give them the stability they need, Celia.'

'I know all that,' she burst out in frustration. 'But what about *my* needs? Don't they count for anything?'

As if to mock her, they both heard a sudden noise from the landing above, and Celia's head jerked up as she heard Daphne's voice, tinged with an unusually fearful note instead of her usual brashness.

'You ain't leavin' us as well, are yer, miss? Bleedin' 'ell, we might as well 'ave stayed at home.'

Celia was choked, not knowing whether to laugh or cry or reprimand her at that moment. In the end she did none of it, and merely ran up the stairs and gathered the wriggling Daphne close and told her she wasn't going anywhere right now.

Her time would have to wait, even if it sometimes seemed as if she spent her whole life waiting for something that was as out of reach as her shimmering star.

–

Skye and Wenna returned home several days later, and it was obvious to anyone that Wenna was far from her usual self. The shock of Fanny's death had affected her deeply, and even though her voice had returned now, the scars of what she had heard and seen were imprinted too deeply in her heart to be dismissed easily or quickly.

She still grieved desperately for Fanny, especially at the thought that she couldn't even have a proper funeral, since there was nothing left of her to bury. That seemed the most horrible thing of all. A life was over, yet it was as unfinished as if it had never been. It was immeasurably sad, and Wenna had never felt so alone and insecure.

Knowing that her sister needed the security of having her family around her now, Celia still delayed going to Ireland, while briefly toying with the idea of suggesting that Wenna accompanied her. But Wenna had once dreamed of marriage to Ethan, so she didn't even dare mention it.

With the resilience of childhood and her usual macabre curiosity, Daphne Hollis quickly recovered from her temporary fear of losing all her Cornish contacts at once, and eagerly quizzed Wenna about the bombing.

'What was it like, miss? Did you see lots of blood and stuff?' she asked, her big eyes almost popping.

'Don't ask such horrid questions,' Wenna snapped. 'If you can't be sensible, then don't ask anything at all.'

'I only wanter know,' Daphne said resentfully. 'Me Ma always says if I wanter know something, I should go ahead and ask. So what was it like?'

'If you really want to know, you can read the newspaper, and perhaps it will improve your education as well.'

The last thing Wenna wanted to do was to relive it all over again for this little madam. She didn't have her mother's patience with Daphne – nor even Celia's, she thought in some annoyance. Her sister seemed, oddly, to be marking time about something, and as yet, Wenna had no idea what it was. The old sweet sharing of secrets had temporarily vanished like will-o'-the-wisp, she realised, and knew it was partly her fault for holding everyone at bay.

Each of them had secrets now, that neither was willing to share. Hers was the very real fear of death that had seemed so near on that night of carnage in the Blitz. What

Celia's secret was, she didn't know, and couldn't guess, since she was closer than an oyster these days.

She became aware that Daphne was still glaring at her.

'I bet me Ma's dead and gawn by now,' she said suddenly.

Wenna flinched, and stared angrily at the girl.

'That's a wicked thing to say, Daphne—'

'Why? Do you wanter get rid of me and send me back?'

'Of course not. Well, not while there's a war on, of course. When it's all over, you and Butch will want to go back where you belong, won't you?'

Daphne shrugged. 'Dunno. Me Ma never liked me much, 'cept to fetch and carry for all the little 'uns. Now they're all gone, she won't want me back so I might as well stay 'ere if Mrs Pen'll have me,' she said nonchalantly.

She stared Wenna out, and despite the arrogant too-old look in her young eyes, Wenna suddenly saw the pleading there. Good God, she thought. She actually means it. The little madam *wants* to stay here – unless her Mum wants her back, of course. Daphne was the type to keep all her options open.

'We're not so bad after all, then,' Wenna said casually.

Daphne suddenly grinned. 'I dunno about you yet. I'll show yer where me and Butch found some blackberry bushes if yer like, and I'll let yer know later.'

She switched her thoughts with her usual mercurial speed, and reached for Wenna's hand. Without thinking, Wenna's fingers curled around the girl's. It was a gesture of a kind.

–

Celia had confided in her cousin Lily about the phone call from Ireland. She had to tell someone, since she and her father had agreed not to worry Skye or Wenna with Ethan's information. Lily was as practical as ever, sorting out the As-New clothes in her now thriving second-hand clothes department of the White Rivers Pottery shop in Truro.

'If you feel you need to see this man, then you should go, though I can't see why you should want to. Ethan said he wouldn't be able to tell you anything more – and he's a German, after all.' She almost spat out the word.

'So is Stefan,' Celia reminded her.

'But that's different. He's part of an old, established family business, not a soldier—'

Celia responded smartly. 'I doubt that any prisoners of war were born soldiers, Lily. He's probably some nicely brought up young man who was conscripted into the army, the same as our boys were.'

Lily said nothing for a moment, then shook her head. 'Well, I'm sorry, but I simply can't think that way. War's a bloody awful thing, anyway. So what are you going to do?'

'I haven't really thought, but since Wenna's still so unsettled, it seems a bit mean to go rushing off to Ireland. Maybe the man could be persuaded to write me a letter with all the details and let Ethan send it on to me.'

'I'm not sure the authorities would approve of your getting correspondence from a German prisoner of war,' Lily said doubtfully.

'Who's to tell them?' Celia retorted.

–

But as spring merged into summer, another call to Ethan established that the prisoner had been moved on elsewhere, so her chance of finding out anything more had vanished. She cursed her lack of resolve.

Before she could decide if there was anything more she could do, she received two visitors. The women and children were having tea late one afternoon when the men called at the house in an official-looking car bearing a flag.

'Dear Lord, don't say it's bad news,' Skye breathed. 'We haven't heard from Olly in weeks…'

Wenna was still at home, still finding it hard to come to terms with Fanny's death, and seemingly unable to concern herself with anyone else's problems. She spoke crisply.

'We'd be getting a telegram if anything had happened to Olly. They wouldn't bother sending two stiff-necked officials to deliver the fate of one young airman to his family.'

'Don't be cruel, Wenna,' Skye said evenly.

'I'm not. I'm being realistic.'

'P'raps it's about me,' Daphne piped up. 'P'raps it's ter say me Ma's bought it. Or Butch's Dad.'

'And you're a nasty, bloodthirsty little brat,' Wenna snapped at her. 'I'm getting you out of the way until we find out what's going on.'

Daphne grinned. 'I like you when you go all red and shout at me. You remind me of me Ma,' she said, at which point Wenna grabbed her hand and yanked her out of the room, with Butch following closely behind.

Skye answered the knock on the door, and moments later she returned, with the two men following her.

'The visitors are for you, Celia. I'll leave you—'

'No, please don't do that, Mom – unless it's something private?' she queried the men.

Though for the life of her, she couldn't see what it could be. The men were portly and grey-haired, with an unmistakable military bearing, and she knew she had never seen them before.

'Your mother is at liberty to stay and listen to what we have to say, Miss Pengelly. In fact, you may prefer it,' one of them said solemnly.

Celia felt her mouth go dry. Had she done something terrible? If so, she couldn't think what it could be. Unless it was consorting with the enemy... The thought was so ludicrous it almost made her laugh out loud. Almost.

'You're very young,' one of the men observed.

'I'm twenty-two – nearly twenty-three, actually,' she said without thinking. 'Not that it's anyone's business—'

Skye took charge. 'Please, won't you both sit down, gentlemen, and I'll organise some tea.'

A maid appeared as soon as she had rung the bell, and then she turned to the visitors. 'Now I think you owe my daughter some explanation of why you're here.'

The first one cleared his throat. 'My name is Brigadier Ralph Soames, retired, madam, and this is Major Dennis Beasley. Through our sources, we understand that Miss Pengelly attended St Augustine's Academy for Young Ladies near Gstaad, Switzerland, before living and working in Germany as a translator for some time for a Herr Vogl.'

'That's correct,' Celia said sullenly, resenting the fact that these two seemed to know so much about her, and wondering who the hell these sources were who could give so much of her personal details to strangers. It made her feel disagreeably exposed. In the way of interrogators, the men waited for her to say more, and in her nervousness she spoke too fast.

'Herr Vogl was a friend and business colleague of my mother's family, as well as my employer.'

'Ah yes. Your family were once the owners of the china clay business previously known as Killigrew Clay, and also of the associated pottery known as White Rivers, and you did much of your business with the German firm of Vogl's, I understand,' Soames said, smiling gratuitously at Skye.

'Look here, would you mind telling me what this is all about?' Celia snapped, losing her patience. 'So you know all about us. Is it a crime for me to have worked for a German firm? I'm sure many people did so in the past.'

'Quite so, my dear young lady,' Beasley said smoothly. 'In fact, with your academic credentials, it's a definite advantage. You are obviously fluent in the language in a far greater capacity than the use of schoolgirl phrases.'

She didn't answer. She loathed the pair of them with their snide manners, and when the maid brought in the tea, she childishly hoped it would scald them.

'Won't you please come to the point, Brigadier?' her mother said, with pointed American good manners.

'We want to offer your daughter an official position, Mrs Pengelly,' Soames said, turning to her. 'We have a specialised tracking unit in Norwich, where we are able to monitor incoming calls detailing German military move-ments. As you might expect, much of this is in code, but with her expertise and knowledge of idiomatic German, we believe your daughter could be of great help to us in deciphering these codes.'

'I see. Then her expensive education wasn't entirely wasted after all,' Skye said dryly, in an attempt to diffuse the suddenly charged atmosphere between them all. 'And what if she refuses?'

The officials glanced at one another. 'Madam, it's no great secret that by the end of the year, if not sooner, it's highly likely that all young women will be conscripted, either into munitions work or into the Services. This skilled work we are offering is essential to the War Effort, and we would much prefer that Miss Pengelly makes her own choice.'

'Excuse me,' Celia snapped. 'But I *am* here. I can speak for myself, and I'll be the one to decide whether or not I would be willing to take up such an appointment.'

'And would you?' Beasley asked quickly.

'Of course,' she said, without a second's hesitation.

Chapter Five

'Why on earth did you say yes, if you don't want to do it?' Wenna demanded a couple of weeks later, when Celia was trying to cram yet another item into an already overloaded suitcase, and letting off steam in the only way she knew.

'I don't know,' Celia snapped. 'I suppose it's better than feeling I'm useless here. Dad definitely approves, of course. He always thought it was beneath me to be a tram conductress, even though it was quite fun.'

'So you're taking on this new job just for his benefit, are you?' Wenna persisted.

Celia glared at her. 'Since when did you become so picky over everything anyone else does?'

'Since Fanny died,' she whipped back. 'Since I don't know where I'm going any more. I haven't heard from Austin in months and I'm sure he's missing or dead too, and who would bother telling me, anyway? I'm not his family. I don't even know if he had one. And since my life has been turned upside down, I'm feeling like the useless one, not you!'

As she raged on in her frustration, Celia paused in her packing, wondering where her soft and gentle sister had gone, to be replaced by this beautiful, brittle shell of a girl. And she could only feel immense compassion. Wenna had seen sights that she had never seen except in newsprint pictures. Her instinct was to put her arms around her and hold her close, but Wenna never invited such familiarities these days. In many ways, their old roles were reversed, she thought.

'Wenna, I'm sorry,' she said. 'But you were never useless. You were always the star in the family, and you've become far too insular since you came home. You've hardly moved out of the house, and you need to see other people apart from us and the evacuees. Go and see Lily – or visit Aunt Betsy, if you can't face Lily's straight talking.'

After a moment Wenna spoke grudgingly. 'Oh, I know you're right. You always are, darn it,' she added with a twisted smile. 'And although I don't want to seem ungrateful for all Mom's done for me, I do begin to feel stifled here. I don't know where I'll go, but perhaps I'll get out my old bicycle for a start and see if I can still ride it.'

'That's my girl,' Celia said, and resumed her packing.

For good or ill, she had accepted this decoding post in Norwich, and there was no going back on it now, although it had taken several weeks of paperwork and further interviews to get things properly organised. But as the stiff-necks had intimated, if she didn't take the job, she might easily be seconded into it when conscription for young women came in soon, as it surely would.

Despite her collywobbles, she couldn't deny more than a *frisson* of excitement too. She had left home before – for heaven's sake, half her life had been spent away from home, if she thought about it – and she would be doing a job for the War Effort. She would always think of those two words beginning with capital letters now, the way those pompous oafs had said them – but what the heck! Working for the War Effort was something she had wanted to do anyway, wasn't it?

Wenna cycled slowly away from New World, wobbling at first, but quickly regaining confidence on the long-disused vehicle. The sun felt warm and sensual on her back, and gradually the healing, fragrant air began to do more for her peace of mind than anything else so far. The sea was a sparkling blue that afternoon, and the forgotten silence of the summer lanes was wonderful.

She had made her home in a hectic world surrounded by show-business people in London, albeit on a minor scale, but now she realised guiltily that she had begun to feel smothered here by all those who wanted to do the right thing by her virtually stepping on eggshells in order not to upset her.

And she had needed Celia's healthy sibling ranting to show her some direction. She paused to watch some sand-pipers race across the edge of the cove far below, and saw how the wash of the waves made their tiny tracks disappear as if they had never been. It was beautiful, charming, and in an instant of time it seemed to Wenna's heightened senses to symbolise birth and death and everything in between...

...and in her head, she seemed to hear the ghost of Fanny's voice from long ago, the first time she and Celia had ever met her, both standing open-mouthed at this flashy friend of their mother's, the echo of another war and another time that they didn't know. A woman wearing bright clothes and garish make-up, and with a wonderfully wicked way of talking.

'Bleedin' 'ell, this effing place is deader than a cemetery, gel. How d'yer ever stick it?'

For the first time since Fanny's death, Wenna real-ised she was laughing out loud. Not cruelly, but softly, indulgently, with tears streaming down her face, because although Fanny might be gone, her memory would never fade. She had been too vivid a personality for that.

After a long while of letting herself indulge in pure nostalgia instead of trying to blank it all out, Wenna dried her eyes and got back on her bicycle. She still didn't know where she was going, but in the distance ahead of her was Killigrew House, where Betsy Tremayne lived all alone now, since her sons had gone to war and her husband Theo had died. But they all had to go on, no matter what, thought Wenna. It was the nature of things…

She thought briefly of the young war correspondent who had stolen her heart, and whom she knew deep inside that she would never see again. If that was Cornish intuition, so be it, she thought, but as she cycled slowly and unthinkingly into the grounds of the imposing house, hardly seeing any of it, she had already mentally said goodbye to Austin.

'Hey, watch out, babe!' said a voice she didn't recognise. 'You need a licence for that contraption.'

She realised at once that she wasn't alone, and that the grounds of the house weren't as silent as she had expected. There were more than a dozen young men strolling about, or sitting in the sunshine, and they were all in uniform.

And then she remembered. She had been so wrapped up in her own life and the trauma of recent times, that until that moment she had completely forgotten how, after Uncle Theo died, her Aunt Betsy said she was going to turn this house into some kind of convalescent home for the walking wounded.

None of the family had taken her seriously. It was the kind of thing people said spontaneously, and did nothing about. But Betsy had obviously lived up to her word, and as Wenna skidded her bicycle to a halt on the gravel, she slid sideways and fell straight into the arms of a young man with laughter in his eyes wearing the blue uniform of the Royal Air Force.

'Now that's what I call really falling for someone,' he went on teasingly, while she glared at him and tried to recover her dignity.

'I'm sorry, and if you'll excuse me—' she began frigidly, and then she heard her aunt's delighted voice and saw her coming out of the house, her plump arms outstretched, her accent still as rich and welcoming as Cornish cream.

'Wenna, my lamb, 'tis so lovely to see you, despite your recent bad news, but you'm as blooming as ever, and if dear Group Captain Mack will put you down, I'll introduce 'ee.'

She extricated herself from the man's arms at once, feeling incredibly foolish as she was clasped in her aunt's embrace, while the officer held on to her bicycle.

In the brief moment she had seen him, his striking appearance was etched on her mind. He was tall and fair-haired, with a rugged, outdoor look, and a severe and jagged scar running the length of his right cheek that did nothing to diminish his good looks.

'It's good to see you, Aunt Betsy,' she almost gasped, recovering her breath once she was out of both embraces.

'And you too, my lamb. Now you'm just in time for tea, so you can tell me all your news properly. Sebby was sore put out to hear about it, as were all my other boys.'

Wenna looked at her blankly, aware that this Mack person was following with her bicycle. His attention irritated her. She had imagined a quiet visit with her aunt, and suddenly she was surrounded by uniforms and idle chatter.

'Your other boys?' she said.

Betsy swung her arm around to encompass them all. 'These are all my boys now. They come for a spell and then leave, but they'm all the better for having breathed Cornish air.'

She suddenly remembered something and stopped so suddenly that the bicycle wheel cannoned into her, and she scolded herself for her stupidity.

'Bless me, where are my manners today? Wenna, this here's Group Captain Harry Mack. He's from Canada, but his folks originated in Scotland, so he's more or less one of us,' she added magnanimously. 'And Harry, this is my lovely niece, Wenna. She's just recently suffered a bereavement, so you be sure to be nice to her.'

Wenna squirmed, wondering if the man must think her aunt a complete country bumpkin, but he plainly adored her.

'I've seen your portrait, so I feel as if I know you already,' he said.

'Oh, I don't think so,' she said stiffly, unable to stop herself. She recognised his accent now. It wasn't as strong as her mother's, and there were slight differences in pronunciation, but it was definitely transatlantic.

'You've seen the picture of Wenna's grandmother,' Betsy broke in. 'People are always making the same mistake. It's Primmy Tremayne's picture over the mantel in the parlour, Harry, but Tremayne women all have the same rare colouring.'

'Stop it, Aunt Betsy, you'll make me blush,' Wenna said, not wanting to invite any compliments from the Canadian. He was perfectly charming, but she wasn't looking for charm right now. She was still too busy wallowing in her own grief.

She glanced back at him, seeing that jagged scar, more vivid in the sunlight, and the knowledge of her own self-centredness hit her with the force of a sledgehammer.

Everyone here – all of Aunt Betsy's boys, as she called them – had been wounded in action, or they wouldn't be here at all. And here she was, ready and more than willing to snub them. She was ashamed of herself, and gave the Canadian a warmer smile than she had intended.

'My aunt exaggerates, Group Captain Mack,' she said.

'I think not,' he said quietly. 'And the name is Harry.'

He offered his hand in friendship and she reluctantly took it in her own.

'Well now,' Betsy said in the small silence. 'Like I said, it's time for tea. Perhaps you'd remind the others that it will be on the lawn in five minutes, Harry, and you never know, we may just persuade Wenna to—'

'Aunt Betsy, *no!*' she said sharply, knowing exactly what she was going to say.

She had no intention of singing – of *performing* – today. It wasn't why she had come. She hadn't sung a note since the night Fanny had died, and her last memory of performing was of leading the songsters in a London Underground station while Hitler's bombs rained over-head and destroyed part of her life.

'Persuade her to do what?' Harry Mack asked.

'Nothing. Nothing at all,' Wenna said. 'I'll join you all for some tea and then I have to get back.'

'Why do you? We've only just met.'

She looked at him, reading the unspoken meaning in the words. Knowing that he was attracted to her, and sensing his desire to hold on to her presence as long as possible. She knew that look, that feeling, that instant

95

rapport. But she didn't want it. Not from him. Not from anybody.

She looked around in relief as several other men in uniform approached – but if she thought there was safety in numbers, she knew her mistake at once.

'Oh, my good Gawd,' one of the soldiers exclaimed. 'It's *you*, ain't it, gel? I seen you at that fancy club in London one time when I was home on leave and took my lady friend to hear you. You're that Miss Penny Wood, ain't she, missis?'

His voice became animated, and Wenna had no choice but to admit that yes, she was Penny Wood, but that was only her stage name, and she was really Wenna Pengelly, and the niece of Mrs Betsy Tremayne. And she didn't sing any more…

'Well, I'll be buggered – oh Gawd, beggin' yer pardon again, ladies, but I never expected ter see such a vision down here – 'ceptin' yer good self, o' course, missis,' he added to Betsy. 'So that's why that picture in the parlour looked familiar! Fancy Miss Penny Wood being your niece!'

'Ain't you going to give us a song, then, Miss?' his companion asked sadly.

'I'm afraid not,' Wenna said at once. 'I've – I've had some trouble with my voice recently…'

God, but that sounded feeble, when they must all have gone through some ghastly experience to put them here. She could see the disappointment in both men's eyes. And others, too, were crowding around them now, seeing that somebody new was here, and sensing that she was somebody special.

'Couldn't you give us just one song?' Harry Mack said quietly. 'Unless it would put too much of a strain on your vocal chords, of course. None of us would want that.'

'Well – I'll think about it,' she found herself saying weakly. 'Maybe after I've had some tea.'

She didn't know why she had said it. She didn't want to sing. *Couldn't* sing. Not for anyone. She certainly didn't want to give an impromptu concert on a Cornish lawn.

And then she remembered again the last time, and the raucous voices of the people joining in the chorus with her. Many of them terrified. Many of them too afraid to leave the shelter of the Underground because of what they might or might not find left of their homes above ground. But all of them had been ready and willing to sing their hearts out to drown the sound of the bombing, and to keep up their own spirits and those of all around them...

Of course she would sing. In the face of what these casualties must have gone through, she had no option – not if she wanted to keep some semblance of self-respect.

But first of all Betsy and her afternoon helpers brought out the trays of tea and scones and jam and cream, and they all sat around companionably on the grass or garden chairs.

It was blissfully informal, and Wenna thought fleetingly how different it all was from the days when they were children, and her Uncle Theo was alive, roaring his way about the place, with no one daring to speak above whispers. Now that Betsy held court, it was a different world...

Then, just for a moment, the scene in front of her shifted, and she had the weirdest vision of the way it must have been many years earlier, when this gracious old house had belonged to Charles Killigrew and his son Ben, who had married her own great-grandmother, Morwen

Tremayne. Against all the odds, too, Wenna thought, for who would ever have thought a clay boss would marry a lowly bal maiden who scraped clay blocks up on the moors in all winds and weathers?

'What thoughts are going through your lovely head now, I wonder?' she heard Harry Mack say beside her.

She flashed him a nervous smile as the vision faded.

'None of your business,' she said as lightly as she could, 'and you wouldn't want to know, anyway.'

'I would have to challenge that remark, since I would like to know everything there is to know about you,' he said.

She felt her heart leap. 'Oh, I'm just a singer, that's all. There's nothing special about me.'

'If you're seeking compliments, you can have them, but I think you must already know that I think you're the most enchanting young lady who ever lived.'

'Group Captain Mack, *please*,' she said in embarrassment.

'I told you, the name's Harry to my friends. And I very much hope you're going to be one of them.'

'Really.' She ignored the provocative remark and sought for something else to say. 'My brother's in the airforce. He was somewhere in Wiltshire the last time we heard from him.'

'Oh? I'm based nearer the east coast and I've been on ops for the last few months, but maybe I've come across him. What's his name?'

'Oliver. Oliver Pengelly.'

'I don't recall anyone of that name. I'm sure I would have remembered if I had. It's quite a mouthful, isn't it?'

'Not if you're Cornish,' she retorted, ridiculously pleased that she had made a tiny score over him.

She saw her aunt advancing towards her with one of the soldiers, and she gave a silent groan. There was no help for it now – but she was sadly out of practice, and she had a moment of panic as she wondered if any notes would come out of her throat at all. Her aunt spoke determinedly.

'Joe will play his piano accordion for you, Wenna.'

It was a far cry from the elegant piano at the Flamingo Club, she thought, eyeing the battered old instrument, and then felt a stab of anguish. However elegant that piano had been, it had gone the way of everything else in the street, and was no more than rubble and dust now.

Joe wore a private soldier's uniform and had a black eye-patch over one eye. Wenna didn't want to guess what was beneath the patch. She gave him a watery smile.

'I'd be happy if you would accompany me, Joe,' she said. 'What will it be? Do any of you have a favourite?'

The group of recovering invalids opted for 'Roses in Picardy' and she knew she should have made the choice herself. The song was far too plaintive, too romantic and emotive, but since it was a unanimous choice, she allowed Joe to play a few bars first, before she exercised her husky voice for the first time in weeks.

And somehow, as incongruous as it had seemed to be to sing in her aunt's garden in front of a motley and admiring crowd that was as far removed from her usual audience as was possible, the feeling of coming home, in more ways than one, gradually began to seep into her heart and soul.

Her voice grew in sweetness and strength as more and more songs were requested, until she was bound to protest laughingly that she could sing no more.

During the final burst of applause and protests, she heard one of the soldiers speak in a choked voice.

'The whole world should be privileged to hear you sing, miss, not just we poor wrecks.'

She caught Harry Mack's glance then, and her heart gave an unexpectedly hot surge. Whatever this man was, he was no poor wreck, she found herself thinking, and she had to lower her eyes at the expression she saw in his.

'Well, I've done enough for one day,' she said huskily, 'but maybe I'll come back another time, if you'll have me.'

'Every day!' they begged. 'But give us just one more today, miss. One of the old songs.'

'What do you say, Group Captain?' Betsy called to him formally, clearly delighted with the success of her niece's visit. 'You haven't made a request yet.'

He replied at once, his eyes never leaving Wenna's face, and seeing the warm flush creep into her cheeks.

'Do you happen to know 'Loch Lomond', lassie?' he said, exaggerating the Scottish-Canadian accent. 'To remind me of my ain folk, you might say.'

'Of course,' she said, and refused to look his way until the very last lines of the old song, when she simply couldn't resist it. In any case, it would have been churlish not to look at him, since it was his own request.

'...for me and my true love will never meet again, on the bonny, bonny banks of Loch Lomond.'

She looked fully at him then, and saw the way his mouth curved into a smile, and how the creases at the sides of his dark eyes almost met the curling fair hair at his temples. She saw how the sun still highlighted the vicious scar on his cheek that was surely not very old, and she felt a wild and primitive urge to run her fingers tenderly down its length, as if they held some magical witch's potion to relieve its anger.

She was shocked and enraged at her own reaction, coming so soon after the tragedy of Fanny's death, and her virtual goodbye to Austin. Was she so shallow, after all?

'That was a wonderful rendition, and I thank you for it, ma'am,' she heard Harry say gravely.

Before she knew what he had in mind, he had lifted her hand to his lips and kissed the back of it.

As she went to pull away from him in laughing embarrassment, her hand turned over and his kiss landed in her palm before she involuntarily enclosed it with her fingers.

It was symbolic, tore through her mind. Such a gesture and outcome would inevitably be seen as symbolic by those of a fey Cornish disposition. Certainly by old Morwen Tremayne, her great-grandmother; and her grandmother Primmy; and even her own mother, despite her American upbringing.

But she, Wenna, had long since dismissed all that spooky clairvoyant stuff from her mind, being the modern girl that she was, living and working in the sophisticated atmosphere of a smoky London nightclub.

And where had it got her after all? All of it was gone, and here she was, right back here with her roots. Feeling flashes of psychic nonsense that she didn't want, but seemingly couldn't escape...

'Are you all right, my lamb? Perhaps we shouldn't have pushed 'ee to sing for so long after all, and 'tis mighty warm this afternoon,' she heard Betsy's anxious voice say.

She blinked, realising her eyes had been tightly closed for a moment. 'I'm quite well, Aunt Betsy, but I really should be getting home now. I didn't even tell my mother where I was going, and she'll be anxious.'

'And you'll come back tomorrow? I can't tell 'ee what a power of good you've done for my boys this afternoon, love.'

Her instinct was to say no at once. She didn't dare come back while he was here... she wouldn't even think his name right now...

She was adamant that she didn't want any complications in her life, no more loves who were taken away from her, no singing, nothing at all, except the chance to let her heart recover from its traumas... and then she saw his face.

'I'll be back tomorrow,' she said huskily.

–

'You're looking much better, honey,' her mother told her the minute she entered New World. 'Celia said you'd gone for a cycle ride, and I can see it did you good. She had to leave for the train before you got back, but she said to tell you goodbye, and that she'd be writing to us all as soon as she's settled in Norwich. So where did you go today?'

A million miles away... to the moon and back...

Wenna sat down on the sofa and gazed unseeingly out of the window. Her cheeks were still flushed, and not only from the exertion of the ride. She hardly registered Skye's question and instead she asked several of her own.

'Mom, do you think everyone has the capacity for falling in love more than once? And if so, is it being disloyal to the first person you loved to have the same kind of feelings?'

'Good heavens, I didn't expect to be faced with such a deep-meaning discussion on a sunny afternoon,' Skye began with a smile, and then saw that her daughter was being completely serious. 'What on earth brought all this on, darling?'

'But *do* you, Mom? Think you can love more than one person in your lifetime, I mean.'

'I'm hardly the person you should question about that, Wenna. I think you know the answer already.'

Wenna felt her face burn. She had spoken unthinkingly, and she should have known better. It was more Celia's style to rush straight in, but their personalities seemed to have got all mixed up recently. Unwittingly, she echoed her sister's own thoughts.

'Oh Lord, I'm sorry Mom! I know you loved my father, and I'm just as sure you love Daddy Nick. And Great-Granny Morwen had two husbands too, didn't she? I don't know how I could have been so thoughtless—'

'You don't have to apologise, sweetheart. Remember what that young terror Daphne said her mother told her. "If yer wanter know something, then yer have to ask, don'cha?"'

The cockney accent was so false coming from her mother's lips that Wenna found herself laughing.

'So why don't you tell me *why* you asked the question, darling?' Skye went on. 'Or is it too personal?'

Wenna looked down at the hands clasped tightly in her lap and without thinking she opened her palm, where Harry Mack had kissed her. Her mother had always been a sympathetic and loving listener, but as yet her feelings were too private to share with anyone.

They weren't even properly formed yet. They were no more than a glimmer of warmth in her cold heart. And she was still too full of anger – about Fanny, about Austin, about how a so-called caring God could sanction all the killing and the pain that a war involved – to truly welcome them.

'It was just a hypothetical question,' she fibbed. 'But I should have known the answer, shouldn't I?'

And how could she possibly ask her very proper mother if it was so fickle – so *wicked* – to realise that despite all her passion for Austin, she had felt those delicious stirrings again, just thinking about Group Captain Harry Mack…

Skye sensed far more than her daughter guessed, but she resisted the overwhelming temptation to ask her more, and instead repeated her own question.

'So where did you go today, or is it a secret?'

'I called on Aunt Betsy,' she said abruptly. 'I suppose everyone knew she'd turned Killigrew House into a kind of refuge for the walking wounded after all, but I'd forgotten all about it, and it was a big surprise to me. I didn't expect to see all those servicemen there.'

'It didn't upset you, did it?'

Wenna shook her head, her voice rueful now. 'Between them all and Aunt Betsy, I ended up giving a performance, if you can believe it, and one of the soldiers accompanied me on a battered old piano accordion that had seen better days. Fanny would have been proud of me!'

The name slipped out of her mouth before she stopped to think, and without warning she was sobbing, and being rocked in her mother's arms as if she was a child again. Which was exactly how she felt right then, needing comfort and understanding, and getting it all in full measure.

'I'm sorry,' she finally gasped. 'I thought I was coming to terms with it.'

'And so you are. Do you think Fanny wouldn't have wanted you to cry for her, Wenna, or to mention her name ever again? She knew your soft heart as well as any of us. And you're right. She *would* have been proud of you today… So when are you going back to Betsy's to do it all again?' she said calmly.

'Tomorrow,' said Wenna with a gulp.

–

Oliver Pengelly, alias Jimmy Oliver, knew he was in his rightful element at last. He had been born to fly, he thought jubilantly, and his sharp-eyed abilities had been quickly discovered.

He had only been allowed up on practice jaunts so far, having had to fulfil the required number of flying hours before he could officially go on ops. He hadn't encountered an enemy plane in his life, and he had seen the best of it without knowing what real combat was.

He knew all that, and although some of the tales his fellow erks told him were horrific, he still longed to be up there in the thick of it all, giving Jerry what for.

He was training to be a wireless operator, and his world was peppered with an even more exaggerated vocabulary now. His chums were all good eggs, they were whack-oh and spiffing types, and everything was pip-pip or wizard prangs.

And although he was still an erk – the lowest of the low – once he had done the regulation number of practice flying hours, he'd be getting a seventy-two hour leave before going on ops. He had toyed between going home and staying around to make further progress with the pretty little NAAFI girl who had given him the glad eye.

But Cornwall won. He couldn't wait for his family to see him in uniform. By now he was sure they would have forgiven him for running off the way he had.

His natural optimism bubbled to the surface every time he thought about it. It would be good to see the folks again, but even better to get back to the base. Long before Christmas he expected to become a fully-fledged member of an air crew.

It was early December before he got his leave. By then he had phoned home several times, and knew that his sister Celia was doing important war work – 'somewhere in Norfolk', of all places, he thought with a sardonic grin. So much for her penchant for travel. And Wenna had joined the ATS and was now attached to ENSA, entertaining the troops.

'Good God, if that isn't the giddy limit,' he grinned at one of his pals after his last phone call home. 'Wenna will be a star yet. My sisters always fall on their bloody feet.'

'So do you, Jimmy-riddle,' the erk jeered. 'Even if we ditched our kite in the sea, I reckon you'd bounce up from the briny smelling of roses.'

'More like old Neptune's barnacles, the old fart-arse,' sniggered another. 'So you're really going home this weekend, are you, Jimmy?' he said, ducking as Olly threw a book at him.

'I should,' he said reluctantly. 'I haven't seen the parents in months, but you two just remember to keep your hands and eyes off Rosie while I'm gone, d'you hear?'

'Well, we might keep our eyes off her, but we won't bargain for the hands, will we, Sparks?' the first one taunted, his words resulting in a fierce pillow-fight between the three of them in the billet.

Just like children, Olly thought, with the superiority of an eighteen-year-old, remembering the incident as the train took him westwards on that cold December morning. Just the way he and his sister had once been. Or himself and his cousins Seb and Justin. Great days. Great times.

And he was in a hell of a sloppy mood to be looking back, he told himself severely, when he had everything in the world to look forward to.

He caught the admiring look of a young woman in ATS uniform sitting opposite him in the train compartment, and gave up reminiscing and turned to more immediate matters.

By the time he left the train, he had her telephone number in his pocket and the promise of a meeting if ever their leaves coincided. He doubted he would see her again, but flirting had been fun while it lasted, and took up much of the tedious travelling time across the country. Was a seventy-two hour leave ever worth it, he found himself wondering, when half of it was taken up with getting there and getting back?

The minute he saw his parents on the station platform, he knew it was worth it. This was home, and even the *smell* of Cornwall was different to any other place on earth, he found himself thinking, much to his own surprise.

He felt a surge of affection welling up inside him such as he hadn't known in months. It was a very different kind of affection from the easy-come, easy-go kind he felt for his fellow erks and the NAAFI girls. It was a fundamental affection that filled his brain with the sense that as long as everything stayed the same here, then all was right with the world…

He brushed off the stupid feeling that threatened to make his eyes water in a most unmanly way, and blamed the dampness on his cheeks on the way his mother was hugging him so tightly, as if she would never let him go.

'I swear you've grown six inches, Olly,' Skye said, 'and you look so distinguished in your uniform!'

'Well, thank you, ma'am,' he said huskily, seconds before Nick too was hugging this stranger who was their son.

But what the heck? This was wartime, when everybody hugged everybody else on railway stations. Olly gave himself up to their embraces, glad above all to be home, in a way he had never expected to be after his reckless need to leave.

But once the joy of reunion was over, there was an undoubted awkwardness between them all. It was mostly on Nick's part, still unable to fully forgive Olly for running off to enlist, while Skye overcompensated for Nick and was gushingly sweet to him in a way that both of them found completely false. Finally, Olly couldn't take it any longer.

'For pity's sake, Mother, why don't you rant and rage at me like you used to?' he finally snapped. 'I can't stand much more of all this sugar and spice – in fact, a little more spice would be very welcome.'

'You're right,' she said solemnly. 'I should treat you more like Daphne does, shouldn't I?'

He started to laugh. Daphne Hollis was still a miniature thorn in Olly's side, an irritating burr who wanted to know everything about flying, and how it felt to have your plane blown up in the sky and if it hurt to get a bullet in your guts from a German machine-gun, and if he'd jumped out with a parachute yet…

'She's a half-pint pain in the arse, and I don't know how you can stand her,' he admitted without thinking, at which his mother rounded on him at once.

'You can just stop that smart talk while you're here, Oliver, and save it for your barrack-room friends. Lord knows Daphne and Butch know enough swear words already without your adding to them.'

'Bleedin' 'ell, it wasn't even a swear word worth the candle,' he muttered beneath his breath.

'*What* did you say?' Skye asked.

And then they were both laughing, both remembering Fanny Rosenbloom's choice phrases all too well, and each reminding the other that they were two grown-ups now, and that Olly could no longer be treated as a child. The RAF had seen to that, Skye realised with a small shock.

Olly was a man now, and all her children were in uniform. And that was shocking enough for any mother to take, when it seemed like only yesterday that they were babies.

'I'm sorry, honey. I guess I forgot who I was talking to,' she said more solemnly, but with a twinkle in her eyes to remind him that she was still his mother, no matter how old, or how large, he got. She decided to change the conversation.

'In case you get stifled here with Daphne and Butch hanging on to your every word, go visit Aunt Betsy—'

'Why should I want to do that? Seb's not home, is he?'

'No, but you might want to meet some of her lodgers. Before Wenna joined up she got slightly friendly with a Group Captain in the RAF. He said he didn't know you.'

'Well, he wouldn't. We don't know everybody else in the Services,' Olly said uneasily. 'But actually, it's time I came clean about that, Mother. I know I've only made the occasional telephone call home all these months, but I think it's time I gave you my name and number, so you can write to me.'

'Well, I should think I know your name by now,' Skye began with a laugh.

'No, you don't. Not my RAF name, anyway. It's James Oliver, Mom. I couldn't risk you tracing me and dragging me back home, and I discovered it was incredibly easy to rig some false papers. Sorry,' he added more jerkily. 'You didn't know you had a forger for a son, did you?'

She stared at him steadily, hearing his voice shake a little and seeing how the colour warmed his young face. And she knew that whatever he had done to get himself into the air force, he was still desperate for her approval.

She put her arms around him and gave him a quick hug before she let him go. Physically and metaphorically, she thought swiftly.

'None of it matters, darling, as long as I still have a son. Just come home safe and sound.'

Chapter Six

'So your lot have come in at last,' Nick said to Skye a week later, when the tumultuous news of the Japanese bombing of Pearl Harbor had screamed out of every wireless news bulletin and newspaper headline, and caused America and Great Britain to declare war on Japan.

'*My* lot?' she echoed, still grieving that Olly's leave had been so short, and still wondering about the right time to tell Nick of their son's ruse to evade detection, which she privately thought quite cute. She wasn't sure what Nick would think, with his lawyer's ethics. It hadn't seemed important enough at the time to spoil Olly's leave by finding out, but she knew she couldn't keep it to herself for ever.

Right now, it took a moment for her to realise what Nick was getting at. America had kept out of the war in Europe as long as possible – and rightly so, in her opinion. It hadn't been their war, but now it legitimately was.

But Skye had felt so integrated in Cornish ways for so many years now that it came as a shock to hear Nick speak so.

'You're not going to deny your own birthplace, are you?'

'No. But I'm not denying my roots, either, and they're most definitely here,' she said smartly. 'Anyway, since the girls here seem to think that every American comes straight out of Hollywood, it will keep them starry-eyed once they start sending troops over.'

'I hope you're not implying that our own boys can't do that. Tell that to Olly.'

'Actually, Nick, there's something I've been meaning to tell you about Olly,' she said carefully, hoping that his mind was so full of the terrible news of the bombing of Pearl Harbor and all its implications that Olly's small deception wouldn't seem so terrible after all.

'He did *what*?' he exploded. 'Of all the deceitful young pups. I've a good mind to call the War Office and get him hauled over the coals.'

'Don't be ridiculous, Nick,' Skye snapped. 'Can't you for once admire his initiative and let it go at that? What's the point, anyway? He's over eighteen now—'

'The point is, he enlisted under false pretences, and he's living a lie in continuing with this false identity. If you don't understand the wrongdoing in all that, Skye, then I begin to wonder if I know you at all.'

'After all these years of marriage?' she said, appalled to realise how very narrow-minded he was being in all this, and desperate to lighten the atmosphere between them.

'Sometimes I wonder if we ever really get to know another person properly,' he said savagely. 'In my profession, I see far too many people living by their wits and cunning. I simply never expected my son to be one of them.'

It was on the tip of her tongue to blurt out the words she had said once before that had cut him deeply. That Oliver wasn't Nick's son at all, except by adoption.

She managed to resist the damning retort with a huge effort, and she spoke more pleadingly, swallowing her own pride in an effort to save Olly's.

'Nick, can't you see what it would do to Olly if you betrayed him over this? Couldn't you see how proud he was of his uniform when he was home? Our boy's a man now, honey, and if you take that away from him, he'll never forgive you.' She paused. 'And neither will I.'

He didn't answer for a moment, and she could see he was struggling with the damnable conscience that made him such a good lawyer, and such a difficult father at times.

'I'll let it go for the present, while I think about it,' he said at last. 'But I want you to know it's for your sake as much as his. I can never sanction what he did, but I wouldn't want to see you shamed over this, Skye.'

'Thank you,' she said, with more humility in her voice than was her usual style. But what was the loss of a little personal pride, when Olly's future was at stake?

And underneath it all, she knew there was something else destined to keep her head held high. Unbelievably, there were still folk in the close-knit clayworking community who still thought of her as the American upstart, even though she had lived among them for more than half her life, and had shared in their war the first time around. All her children were involved in this one, and now her compatriots were in it too.

Anyway, she thought, with an immense surge of pride that was as backhanded as it was tragic – had Cornwall ever been bombed? Let anyone dare sneer at her after Pearl Harbor... especially the clayworkers with their closeted outlook that couldn't see a world beyond the glittering sky-tips and the barren moors.

She didn't know why she thought particularly about the clayworkers at that time. Killigrew Clay had been out of their personal control for a long time now, and she had no contact with the company of Bokilly Holdings that had amalgamated the clayworks of Killigrew Clay with that of Bourne and Yelland.

Nick was still the associated company lawyer, of course, and occasionally reported talks of threatened strikes and squabbles, and the precariousness of the business as a whole, but none of that was new. It was the way it had always been.

Skye rarely visited the White Rivers Pottery nowadays, and she was sometimes alarmed at how easily her interest in it had dissipated. Once it had been all important in her life, just as the clayworks had been to her family. She must visit it again sometime, she vowed. Nick's brother Adam and her nephew Seb had bought it out, so it was still very much in the family. Butch Butcher was always asking how pots were made too, and she might take him and Daphne up there sometime.

She hadn't lost *all* interest, she told herself somewhat guiltily, and she still worked sporadically on the history of Killigrew Clay, trying not to overdo her family's involvement in it. But she felt she owed it to past generations, as well as future ones, to keep the history alive, and she sometimes regretted that she had been impetuous enough to burn all her grandmother's diaries without reading them properly.

She gave a heavy sigh, knowing it had seemed so right and so noble at the time, and in her heart she still knew it had been right. Morwen Tremayne's thoughts and dreams had been private, the way everyone's were.

They were the only truly private things a person had – and Skye knew that those had been Morwen's sentiments too. It was a pity, though, to have lost all of that. Just like Fanny Rosenbloom, who had left nothing but memories – it was as if she had never been.

Skye shivered, telling herself such a thought was nonsense. Anyway, how could Morwen Tremayne's ghost ever be destroyed completely, while the descendants who were her true legacy lived on – and while the clay was still gouged out of the earth, and the sky-tips still soared like gleaming white mountains towards the sky? No matter how the world changed, some things would always remain constant, Skye told herself.

By the time Nick sought her out later her thoughts had returned to Olly. Everyone else had gone to bed long ago, but she was still restless, still full of too many perceptions she wished she could dispel. Nick wrapped his arms around her and kissed her cheek, and she leaned against him with a sigh.

'About Olly, my love,' he said gently. 'We'll let things remain as they are. What harm can it do, after all, and what difference will it make to the outcome of a war?'

'What difference indeed,' she murmured, lifting her face for his kiss and feeling a surge of relief at his words. 'I do love you, Nick.'

'And I love you, my beautiful witch, in case you thought there was ever any doubt.'

'I didn't,' she said huskily. 'So why don't we go to bed and sleep on it?'

'That wasn't quite what I had in mind,' he said, his voice full of a seductive note she couldn't mistake, and didn't want to, anyway.

–

The news that Sebastian Tremayne's particular war was over came as a great shock to most of his family, and a huge, guilty relief to his mother.

'I just can't help it, Skye,' Betsy wept over the phone. 'I know you shouldn't be glad to know your son's been wounded, but they say 'tis not putting him at death's door, and at least I'll have him home again and out of harm's way. What kind of a mother could be sorry about that?'

'Nobody could condemn you for thinking that way, Betsy. It's perfectly natural,' Skye soothed her. 'So what exactly do they say about Sebby?'

She realised they were both speaking about him as if he was a child and had to refer to others to discuss his war wounds, but she let the thought pass. What the heck did any of that matter, as long as Sebby wasn't mortally wounded?

'They say the leg will heal in time, but the bullets severed some vital nerves, and he'll always have an acute limp. He's shell-shocked as well, so they won't let him go back to his unit at all, and they're going to keep him in this French hospital for a spell yet. Justin says we'll all have to be patient with Sebby when he comes home, as he'll probably be feeling very bitter about coming back to civvy street. But he's done his bit for King and Country, so I daresay he'll be more than glad to be out of it. Why should he be bitter?'

'Because he's a soldier, that's why,' Skye told her. 'And you should listen to what Justin says, Betsy. I'm sure he's seen plenty of severely injured patients who find it hard to come to terms with it. Lily and I had similar experiences with our boys in French hospitals in the last war, and it's true what Justin says. You must see some of that resentment in those who stay with you at Killigrew House, don't you?'

'Oh ah. But they're not my Sebby, are they?' she said. 'He'll be glad to come home where he belongs, and I'll make sure my other boys give him the red carpet treatment.'

Skye replaced the phone slowly, and immediately rang her cousin Lily.

'You've got to talk to Betsy,' she said urgently. 'She's got Sebby taking a starring role as a hero, which he may well deserve, but she'll drive him crazy if she doesn't let him get it all out of his system in his own time. And the other fellows are going to hate his guts before he even gets home.'

'I'll do what I can, darling,' Lily promised. 'But Seb's made of pretty strong stuff, and from what I can gather he won't be home for a long while yet.'

–

Right then, Sebastian Tremayne was staring at the peeling paint on the ceiling of the French hospital ward, gritting his teeth as he counted the length of time in seconds between the bouts of screaming from the bed at the end of the ward. He knew the reason for it. The soldier had had both legs amputated that morning, and had come round from the anaesthetic to the horrific discovery.

There had been no time to warn him beforehand. He had been close to death when they brought him in, and was only now learning the extent of his injuries. Seb could hear the starched swish of the nurses' uniforms as they hurried towards the soldier, pulling the curtains swiftly around the bed while they tried to comfort him.

'They're trying to shut him up so the rest of us don't know what we're in for, mate,' the young man in the bed next to Seb wheezed. 'Have you got a ciggy by any chance?'

'No,' Sebby said. 'I don't have any use for them. And neither should you if that cough's anything to go by.'

The youth gave him a beatific smile, hawking and spitting into the tray balanced on his chest in the disgusting way that had continued all night long, and almost turned Sebby's gut.

'This cough, mate,' he wheezed again when he could draw breath, 'is the only thing telling me I'm still alive, so don't you go knocking my bloody beautiful cough. Once I croak you won't be bothered with it no more.'

'You're not going to croak,' Sebby snarled. 'You talk too bloody much for that.'

'So they tell me,' the boy said with a strange sort of gurgling chuckle. And now that Sebby gave a bit more attention to it, he realised the boy's voice had begun to sound different, as if it was coming from under water. As if his entire lungs were filling up with water, or fluid, or blood...

Sebby hadn't taken too much notice of him until now. Listening to him all night long since he'd been brought in was bad enough. Sebby was too busy bemoaning his own fate, and the pain in his leg that was excruciating, even though they all kept telling him cheerfully that he'd live, and not to worry, soldier, and there were far worse than him... bloody Job's comforters, the lot of them, he thought savagely.

The boy next to him was making an odd piercing noise in his throat now, and Sebby looked at him sharply, in time to see the sudden glazing in his eyes and the gush of frothing blood and mucus that filled his chest tray and overflowed on to his bedding, forming a thick and ever-spreading stain.

'Nurse—' Sebby heard himself croaking. 'Orderly – *somebody* – come quick, for God's sake—'

Nobody heard him. Nobody was near. They were all taken up with the screams of the boy who had lost his legs and badly needed sedating. And Seb could only fix his eyes in horror as the boy next to him died with a final explosive vomit.

Then his chest collapsed violently, and he seemed to dissolve into the bed. As he did so, the putrid trayful of blood and vomit slid to the floor of the ward with a clatter, the vile substance moving insidiously towards Sebby's own bed, and sliding beneath it. Near-demented, and in the throes of shameful hysteria now, Sebby watched the nightmare lava flow coming for him, from which he was never going to escape…

He didn't know how long it was before he felt the sharp stab of a needle in his arm. These bloody orderlies were as brutal with their injections as if they sank their fangs into their victims, he thought. But right then, he didn't care. Right then, he'd have welcomed a whole bloody armful of drugs if only they would have given it to him.

Anything but having to relive all the sights and sounds and smells – above all the *smells* – he had to endure day and night in this place out of hell.

–

When he came to full consciousness a long while later it was night. He struggled to remember where he was and what had been happening. The lights in the ward were dim now, and all was quiet. There was only the distant sound of gunfire to remind him that he was still somewhere in a safe zone in France and that there was a war going on. The patient in the bed next to him had been removed, and he presumed that the amputee was heavily sedated. His own pain was temporarily under control from the cocktail of drugs they had pumped into him.

As his senses revived, he realised that the ward smelled cleanly of disinfectant, and he became aware that he could feel a cool hand on his wrist. As his eyes focused properly, he saw what looked like a white halo above someone's head, and the sense of gladness that rushed through him overcame any feeling of panic. He was obviously dead. He was in some transitional no man's land before he was whisked skywards into some mythical heaven, and he was never going to feel any more pain. Nothing else mattered but that.

'Are you an angel?' he muttered, his voice slurring through lips that seemed far too large for his mouth.

He heard a soft laugh. 'I've been called many things, soldier, but never an angel,' the female voice told him. 'My name is Colette and I'm to be your helper when you come to stay with us, while the nurses get on with their real jobs.'

Seb's eyes opened more fully as he realised he was not dead after all, and that this angel with the soft French accent but excellent command of English was no angel after all. She was...

'Bloody hell's teeth, you're a nun,' he ground out. 'Oh God, I'm sorry, Sister—'

'Don't be,' she said quietly. 'I'm sure God won't object to a few blasphemies now and then. And I told you, my name is Colette. If we're to spend a lot of time together, I prefer that you use it. You are Sebast something – how do you say? I find it difficult to pronounce, I'm afraid.'

'I'm Seb Tremayne,' he managed to say after a moment when his lips wouldn't seem to work again, wondering if this was a ploy to make him say his name himself. As if she thought he was some kind of blubbering halfwit who had lost his senses as well as... his hand went down to the cradle over his leg.

'Is it still there?' he said hoarsely.

'Don't worry, Seb, everything is intact.'

She was smiling down at him, and she truly had the face and voice of an angel, he thought. She was beautiful and serene, the way these bloody nuns always were. Nobody had a right to be that treacly, he thought mutinously, especially when their bloody calling put them out of reach of any healthy, red-blooded male who came into contact with them.

Something in her gently teasing words made him want to shock her.

'Everything? You mean you've washed me? Every bit of me? Is that part of your duties – Sister?'

She gave a small sigh. 'Every bit of you, soldier. And nothing has shocked me, nor will it. So take that mocking look from your face and I'll give you a sip of water before you go back to sleep.'

Well, at least he could thank God or whoever had been watching over him that she hadn't said he needn't make a fuss over such a little thing. His brief attempt to think lecherous thoughts subsided slightly as a wrenching pain shot through his leg, and he saw her reach for the jug and pour a small amount of water into a cup. She was trim in her grey habit, though he could only make a guess at what was underneath it, and he was hardly in a fit state or mood to take much interest, but the day he couldn't appreciate a pretty girl was when he'd know he was *really* dead, thought Seb, and he wasn't dead yet.

He knew she was young, and she was the best thing to happen to him since he was picked up and brought here, well away from the front line. He took the cup from her hand and took a deep draught of cold water, wondering if he dare ask for more painkillers yet.

'Slowly,' she urged him, far too late.

The shock of drinking too fast on top of the sedative cocktail made him throw up at once, and he spewed all over her clean grey serge. She folded it into her as if it was of no consequence, took the cup from his shaking fingers and said she'd be back in a few moments when she had cleaned herself.

He watched her go, and felt a fierce and unreasonable rage that she could take things so calmly. He had just *spewed* all over her, for God's sake, and she was no more upset than if he had handed her a rose. If that was what nunning did to a perfectly healthy young woman, he thought aggressively, then they could stuff it.

His brief interest in her as the only decent-looking female he had seen in months was fading fast, and he turned his face into the harsh hospital pillow and returned to his anger and self-pity.

–

Daphne Hollis was anxious to meet the war hero in the family. She and Butch had discussed it at length.

'I ain't never met one before,' she said. 'Do you fink he'll have a wooden leg by the time he comes home?'

'Nah,' Butch said. 'They said he'll limp, that's all.'

'I bet he will have a wooden leg,' Daphne went on positively. 'I wonder if he takes it off at night and hangs it on the bedpost like me uncle does,' she added with a giggle.

'You're so stupid, Daphne,' Butch said rudely. 'Anyway, he's not coming home for ages yet, so you'll just have ter wait and see, won'cha?'

She glared at him. Daphne was sorely put out by the fact that her mother hadn't sent her much for Christmas, promising to come and see her in the new year if she could. And now it was nearly February, and she still hadn't had a visit, while Butch's father had turned up out of the blue and gone away just as quickly, out of his element and needing London's frenzied pace of life as much as Butch hated it.

All the talk everywhere now was of the Yanks who were being sent over here in droves, and of the increase in the rationing system. Practically nothing was going to be available, no sweets or biscuits or tinned fruit – they might as well starve to death, Daphne had announced dramatically, to Skye's amusement.

For a child of such tender years, Daphne knew what was what in the world, Skye told Nick. Butch went on blissfully in his own sweet, unacademic way, but now that he was gone thirteen and the war showed no signs of abating, they realised they might need to find some occupation for him.

The children had come a long way since their first traumatic arrivals in the community, and Skye had got far too fond of them, she sometimes thought uneasily. They were only on loan, as Daphne herself had said loftily when the little Lunn children had been whisked back to London by their mother and her gentleman friend, and never heard of again... and Skye didn't want to look any deeper into it than that. But then, Mrs Lunn wasn't the kind to keep in contact, and she prayed that they had all fared better than Fanny had.

Skye still thought about Fanny a great deal, especially now that they had a casualty in their own family. She couldn't really understand why Sebby had been kept in France all this time, but Betsy had been told that his shell-shock had seriously affected his mind. When his physical wounds had healed, they had taken him to a monastery where the nuns were caring for him, and someone called Sister Colette was his chief nurse.

'I bet he'll come back all churchified,' Daphne observed, clearly disappointed at hearing that her hero might not be as dashing as she expected. 'Nuns make yer that way, don't they, Mrs Pen? They sing all day and pray all night, and live on bread and water. Bleedin' daft, I call it.'

'Daphne, I've told you before about your language,' Skye said, trying hard to keep a straight face. 'And with all this rationing we might all be living on bread and water soon.'

'Mrs Pen, when are we going to the pottery like you promised?' Butch asked, as gloom descended on them.

'Today,' she said, turning to him with relief. 'We'll go today, and it will cheer us all up to have something to do.'

'Oh, do I have to go?' wailed Daphne. 'Cook was going to show me how to make oatcakes. I don't want ter see how ter make those bloomin' old pots.'

'Then you can stay behind with Cook,' Skye said, 'and Butch and I will cycle up to White Rivers. We can't spare the petrol to take the car for a joyride.'

'He won't mind that, Mrs Pen,' Daphne said slyly. 'He'll do anyfing as long as it's wiv you!'

Skye saw the painful blush creep up the boy's freckled cheeks, and to diffuse his embarrassment, she said airily that as she was acting as his mother, it was just as well, and that Daphne could learn a lesson or two from him.

–

They reached White Rivers after a considerable effort. The weather was usually mild in the far west of Cornwall, but even so, the wind had taken their breath away long before they reached the end of their ride, and they had been obliged to get off their bicycles and push them uphill for the last bit.

'There you are, Butch,' Skye said, leaning on her handlebars and throwing one arm out expressively. 'How does it feel to be on top of the world?'

He looked around him as she spoke, following her gaze over the sky-tips and the scoured countryside, where the remaining pits of Killigrew Clay were now part of Bokilly Holdings. He gazed down at the clay pool, as creamy smooth as palest green milk, and listened to the whisper of gorse and bracken over the moorside. And he knew he was home. Truly home, in a place that he never wanted to leave. And because he didn't have the words to say all that his heart felt, he said the only thing that came into his head.

'It feels weird – like I should stay here for ever, Mrs Pen,' he blurted out. 'Like I belong. And now you'll fink I'm as daft as Daphne.'

'No, I don't, Butch,' she said softly, more touched than she could say. 'Because I felt exactly the same way the very first time I saw this place. But we can't stand here all day like two ninnies. Let's go inside and see how to throw a pot.'

They freewheeled the last hundred yards to the dip in the ground where the pottery was built, and Skye felt a burst of pride at knowing that starting this business had been her idea. It had been her choice of name too, despite her cousin Theo's derision when she had first mooted it.

She had no regrets about selling out to Adam Pengelly and Seb in later years, though, since it kept the business so very much in the family. It had been a delicious piece of continuity that very much appealed to her romantic heart.

For the first time, she wondered how Sebby was going to cope with being a partner in a business when he came home again. He was once so skilled at his wheel, but who knew how those hands might tremble now? Or how his injured leg might affect his abilities? However, those were problems for later, and she pushed them out of her mind as she saw her brother-in-law coming outside to greet her.

'Skye, by all that's holy. I haven't seen you in ages. What are you doing here? Not bringing bad news, I hope?' he said anxiously.

She shook her head at once. It was a measure of the way they all felt these days, that any unexpected visit might herald bad news.

'Not at all. Butch and I felt like some fresh air, and he'd like to watch you throwing a pot or two if you've got the time to show him, Adam.'

'Plenty,' he said, his voice giving away more than he intended. But they all knew that a luxury product like White Rivers pottery was of far less importance in wartime than providing the medical manufacturers with the pure white clay that the clayworks could supply. He turned to Butch.

'So you're thinking of taking up potting, are you, boy?'

'I dunno about that,' Butch mumbled. 'I just wanted to see how it's done.'

'And then you'd like to try it,' Adam finished for him.

–

'It was like watching fate reveal itself,' Skye told Nick that evening when they had finished their evening meal. 'Butch is a natural. He reminded me of the way Seb took to it – the way Tremaynes have always regarded the clay, I suspect, loving it and moulding it as if it was a living thing that required all the care in the world.'

'Good God, darling, you're getting quite poetic over that sloppy stuff,' Nick said, laughing at her eloquence.

She laughed back. 'So I am. And where would we all be without that sloppy stuff, as you call it? If my parents hadn't gone to America and raised a family and been unable to resist passing on the old tales of Killigrew Clay, I'd never have been so fascinated that I had to come over here myself to see what it was all about. And we would never have met. Why shouldn't I be poetic about that sloppy stuff?'

He caught her in his arms, and at the fierceness of his embrace, she knew why she had fallen in love with him. And as he looked down into her luminous, beautiful blue Tremayne eyes, Nick knew why he'd been possessed by her beauty, even when he'd thought she was no more than an enchanting portrait painted by an old uncle incestuously in love with his sister. But the reality of the living, breathing woman had been so much more electrifying than a face on a painted canvas.

'God, but I love you, woman,' he said huskily. 'Can you possibly know how much?'

'Oh, I think I have a rough idea,' she said with a catch in her voice, because such sweet moments were so rare these days, when other people demanded so much of them all.

'Then I think I should waste no more time in showing you how much. Let's—'

The scared voice floated down from the top of the stairs.

'Mrs Pen, I've wet meself. Can yer come quick?'

Skye heard Nick curse. 'Christ Almighty, she's nine years old now. Can't she control herself yet?'

'She's only a child, Nick, and this only happens occasionally when something disturbs her. She heard how excited Butch was today, and how he was boasting that he'll stay here forever if his father will let him, and become a potter. I think it's unsettled Daphne.'

She put her hand on his arm. 'I'll see to her, and then we'll go up. I won't be long.'

But by the time she had consoled the humiliated Daphne, changed her bedding and nightclothes and made her sweet again, Nick was already in bed and fast asleep.

–

Wenna had firmly believed she would be travelling all over the world with the ENSA concert party. She had made herself believe that, in the weirdest way, this chance that was brought about by a war was going to fulfil all of Fanny's dreams for her.

They were her dreams too, of course. She would sing in front of an enormous audience of servicemen, and among them would be all kinds of people, including agents and managers, and entrepreneurs of every kind. Surely at least one of them would see and hear the potential in Miss

Penny Wood – although as an ATS private, she was known to her companions by her real name now and only used her stage name for performances.

She had been convinced that future stardom would be staring her in the face through this most unlikely of sources, perhaps on a North African makeshift stage, where even important military men might hear her; or in Egypt; or wherever the army chose to send their little concert party.

Instead of which, the reality was like a cold slap in the face. They were sent to military installations all over England and Scotland, and entertained the troops wherever there was a need for them. It wasn't exactly what Wenna had imagined, but their troupe kept being assured that these people badly needed cheering up, especially those who had been repatriated due to injuries and were waiting to be sent home.

Knowing what had happened to Sebby by now, she knew that he could well be like them, glad of a soft voice and a welcoming smile, and she swallowed her disappointment at not being sent somewhere more glamorous, and sang her heart out on every occasion.

By now she had received confirmation that Austin had indeed been killed in action, and she had wept her tears over him. Group Captain Mack had written to her several times and the letters had followed her around the country. She had answered them cautiously, knowing that the attraction between them was mutual, but still determined to hold back from becoming involved with anyone else.

'I don't understand you, Pengo,' her accompanist said, using her current nickname. 'The chap must be crazy over you, and you're virtually giving him the cold shoulder. It doesn't add up with the emotional way you sing those songs, kiddo.'

'My songs are for every serviceman, Rita, and not for individuals,' she retorted.

They were performing that evening to a group of newly-arrived American servicemen. Real GIs, Rita had told her excitedly, and there were rumours that they sometimes brought chocolates and nylon stockings with them for the girls who caught their fancy. It would be better than painting their legs with gravy browning and pencilling in a dodgy wavy line for a seam, Rita declared.

It didn't impress Wenna. She turned around from the cracked mirror in their so-called dressing room and faced her counterpart.

'You just watch that they don't want payment in kind for their nylons,' she warned. 'Soldiers are soldiers, wherever they come from, and you've been bitten once already.'

'I never took you for a prude,' Rita said, offended.

'I'm not. I just don't want any entanglements, that's all. But never mind all that. How do my lips look?'

She pursed them towards her friend. Cosmetics were in short supply now, and the NAAFI cook was being constantly persuaded to give cooked beetroot juice to the concert party girls for them to colour their lips in lieu of lipstick.

'Looks good,' Rita said approvingly. 'A bit of soot on your eyelashes and you'll be all set.'

'I'm not going to bother. It makes my eyes sting, and I don't really need it, do I?'

Rita sighed. 'You know you bloody don't. Who'd bother looking at your eyelashes when you've got those great baby blues, anyway?'

'Which Hollywood flick did you get that line out of?'
Wenna said, glad that their brief spat was over.

But she felt excited too as they faced those GIs in their
tailored uniforms that evening, and knew how her mother
would approve of her entertaining her own countrymen
as she heard their enthusiastic whistles and foot-stamping.

'They know how to let themselves go, don't they?'
Rita breathed in her ear a long while later when they had
all gone through their routines and the concert party had
returned to their base. 'One of them in the front row was
definitely giving you the glad eye, Pengo, even more than
the rest.'

'That was hardly the glad eye. He looked as if he should
still be in school.'

'Don't they all?' Rita said dryly.

'Actually,' Wenna said carefully, knowing the reaction
she was going to get, 'he sent me a note after the show—'

'*What?* What did it say? Did he ask you to meet him?
You lucky stiff. I hope you ask him if he's got a friend for
me.'

'Now hold on a minute, Rita,' Wenna said, laughing.
'Actually, I think it's someone my sister once knew when
she lived in New Jersey.'

'My God, you people get around, don't you?'

'I told you my mother and grandfather were American,
didn't I? It seems as though this young GI lives on the
farm where my sister once worked. Years ago the place
belonged to my grandparents, only it wasn't a farm in
those days. Well, anyway, this Greg Stone knew Celia had
a sister who sang a bit, and we're very much alike in looks,
so he took a chance and asked if I could possibly be called
Wenna.'

'And you are.'

'Of course I am. You know that. Anyway, I said I'd see him in the canteen tomorrow for a chat, if he was free.'

'As if he wouldn't be! He's sure to bring along some of the others to meet you as well, so can I come along?'

Wenna sighed. Rita was so transparent, but she could hardly say no. And since she had absolutely nothing in common with Greg Stone, except a house in New Jersey that once belonged to her grandparents, another girl might be a useful ally if the conversation flagged.

She tried to recall what Celia had ever said about him, and came up with absolutely nothing, except that he was one of the younger siblings of the Jarvis Stone who had developed such an almighty crush on Celia at one time. The crippled Jarvis wouldn't have been able to enlist in this war, but she guessed that his brother must be about Olly's age and just about old enough to do so.

She smiled ruefully, thinking that for folk who were normally content to spend their lives working on a New Jersey fruit farm, being shipped overseas because of a war must be the strangest way of meeting people.

Chapter Seven

'You must tell him that if he's ever at a loss as to where to spend a leave, he's to come and visit with us,' Skye said at once when Wenna related the incident to her over the telephone.

'His unit is being sent overseas pretty soon, Mom, though I don't know where, of course. But don't you think it was a coincidence that he should have been at the concert? He told me a lot about the farm in New Jersey, and the time when Celia was there. It was so odd, hearing him talk about the house where you were born, and finding out that he knows it so well, when I don't.'

'But how lovely that he made sure you knew who he was, darling,' Skye said quickly, needing to overcome an enormous bout of homesickness at that moment, such as she hadn't felt in years. 'I'll remember to tell Celia the next time I hear from her. I'm sure she'll be pleased.'

When the call ended, Skye put down the phone slowly. How odd it was, she thought, echoing Wenna's words, that the endless continuity in this family should stretch out beyond the bounds of land and sea, and even now, should pull the tenuous threads together.

The Stone family had nothing to do with herself, except that this young Greg Stone had been born in the same house as she had. He would know and love the house in the same way she and her brother Sinclair had done.

The house where her mother, Primmy, had always been at pains to instil the love of their Cornish roots in her children. The roots that had brought Skye here.

'Oh Mom,' she murmured, 'you would have loved all this. And so would Granny Morwen.'

Even odder was the resolve she now felt to get the history of Killigrew Clay in order. There was no one else with the skill or the urge to record it all, and if she didn't do it, the intimate knowledge would end with her. She got out her bicycle and rode into Truro the very next day and went into the offices of the *Informer* newspaper.

She paused in the outer office before announcing herself. The hum of activity was the same as ever, as was the smell of printer's ink, of newsprint, of bodily sweat, and the indefinable air of excitement that came with a big story.

These days, among the more homely and domestic stories, there were always national and international ones that seemed to be ever bigger, but nonetheless still had their poignant moments. And no matter how dramatic the story, David Kingsley was an expert in sorting out the wheat from the chaff, she thought.

He caught sight of her from behind his office window then, and waved to her to come inside.

'Good to see you, Skye. Tea? Coffee?' he said, as busy as ever, but newly apprised of the trend towards coffee as an occasional drink now that the Americans had infiltrated.

'Tea would be lovely, David. And so would access to the archives, if I may. I'm going to produce some of those booklets we once talked about if it kills me in the attempt. I've already made a start on the scheme, but now I want to see it finished.'

She bit her lip as she spoke, as the insignificance of one tin-pot china clay business compared with the worldly state of affairs suddenly occurred to her. To her great relief, David evidently thought otherwise.

'Well, it's about time. When this damn war is over, Skye, people will be looking for ordinary pursuits again, and I've always said that visitors will discover Cornwall and want to get away from the big cities. The evacuees will have helped all that. They'll go home and tell their folks about how wonderful the countryside is, and we'll have hordes of them coming in, you'll see.'

'My Lord, how prophetic you are!' she said with a laugh.

'Don't you think it will happen? I'll bet that some of these kids won't even want to go back where they came from.'

'Maybe. Butch keeps saying he wants to stay for ever, anyway,' she said, realising David could be right. It went with the territory, of course. Being a newspaperman meant keeping your ears to the ground to know what was going on now, and also what was likely to happen in the future.

'Show me what you've done so far,' he said, when tea was brought in for them. 'You've brought it with you, I take it?'

She produced the folder containing her rough outlines of the time when Hal Tremayne was Pit Captain of Number One pit at Killigrew Clay, and his wife Bess, together with all five of their children, worked for the clayworks. One of those children was Morwen, Skye's own grandmother, but apart from brief mentions of them all, she had done her best to keep the story centred on the history of the clayworks itself.

David scanned it all, and then slowly shook his head.

'You've lost nothing of your storytelling skills, Skye, but what you've overlooked is the personal touch. Because of your family name and your own involvement in the growth of the clayworks, readers will want to know far more about the people than you've detailed. They'll want to know why Morwen's brother Matt went to America and how he came to be the patriarch of a new family of Tremaynes, and how one of them – you, my love – eventually returned to Cornwall, and stayed.'

'But that's exactly what I was avoiding. I thought people would be more interested in the china clay itself, and an industry that is unique to Cornwall—'

He interrupted. 'You, above all people, should know that a flat account of the way a business evolved is one hundred per cent less interesting that one that has a romantic human story included in it. And what could be more romantic than the son of a clay boss marrying one of his own bal maidens and starting a dynasty? No, you should think again about this, Skye. I know your idea was to keep it as impersonal as possible, but you and I both know that a story about a woman falling for the wrong man, or any kind of scandal, will always touch readers' hearts. And you have an important artist in the family, for heaven's sake. You can't leave out a mention of Albert Tremayne.'

'He had nothing to do with Killigrew Clay, except to be Morwen's adopted son.'

'But think of the readership, Skye,' David urged. 'Albert's parents both died tragically young – Sam, Morwen's oldest brother, in an accident on the moors, and his mother from the measles. Then the generous-hearted Morwen and Ben Killigrew brought up the three orphaned children as their own – including the aforementioned Albert – until an indiscreet word from a precocious American child tore their world apart again. The child who was destined to be your father, Skye! Think how your old magazine readers would have loved reading that!'

As he unfolded the story like a romantic saga of old, her writer's mind knew only too well its appeal for readers.

'It's private,' she said weakly. 'It's family business – and how the blazes did you know so much about it, anyway?'

He gave a short laugh. 'I'm a newshound, that's how, and I made it my business to know. I could write the story myself – but it would never have your feminine insight, nor your perceptive and heart-tugging way of writing it, and I wouldn't presume to do so.'

He could see her indecision, and he was quick to take advantage of it.

'Don't decide at once. Spend an hour or so in the archives by all means, and take home any relevant copies. Then discuss it with Nick, and see what he thinks.'

'It has nothing to do with Nick,' she said quickly, just as he knew she would. 'Whatever I decide to do, it will be my decision and no one else's.'

Just like a true Tremayne woman, she couldn't help thinking, avoiding his knowing eyes. And by the time she left, armed with a pile of old newspapers to study, her plans for the booklets had taken an entirely different direction.

And although she was quite alone as she rode home through the wintry lanes to New World, she got the weird feeling that someone was hovering at her shoulder and silently approving. It was a comfortable feeling that made her smile.

'All right, Granny Morwen, you win,' she murmured to the air, watching her breath leave her mouth in a soft cloud before it was borne aloft on a small, sighing breeze.

–

'Cor, are yer going ter write a book, Mrs Pen?' Daphne Hollis said in astonishment, gazing at Skye as if she was a creature from outer space.

'Maybe more than one, but it won't be a thick book like you read in school, Daphne. It may turn out to be two or three small booklets. They'll be a history of my family and the clayworks on the moors.'

'That's not a proper book then,' Daphne said scornfully. 'Wiv hard covers and all that.'

'Probably not,' Skye said humbly, seeing how important this was to her. 'Not that I ever see you reading one. Your teacher tells me you're not very interested in books.'

'I am too! Me Ma gave me one once, borrered it from the penny libr'y and fergot ter take it back – so she said,' she added with a grin. 'It had too many big words in it though.'

Her face flushed as she spoke. At nine, Daphne didn't like to be beaten in anything. Perhaps the teacher at the Truro school had mistaken Daphne's bolshie attitude, Skye thought quickly. If something didn't come easily to Daphne, she simply stiffened her aggressive little shoulders and refused to bother with it any more.

'Perhaps I could help you with that, Daphne,' she said carefully. 'We could read something together, if you like, and I could check your spelling with you.'

'If you like,' Daphne said, shrugging.

'We'll start tonight, and you can go through some of these old newspapers with me. It will make a change from reading a boring old school book,' she said calmly.

Daphne's eyes sparkled. 'I reckon you shoulda been a school teacher, Mrs Pen.'

Or a diplomat, thought Skye.

But helping Daphne with her reading by way of the old newspaper accounts of the daily business of Killigrew Clay was going to be a twofold activity. The booklets wouldn't be written for children, but she considered that seeing everything that had happened in retrospect and through a child's eyes might help her to discard the mundane events and stick to the more emotive and important ones. Life – and war – hadn't sent Daphne Hollis here without a particular purpose after all.

–

British Intelligence, like God, worked in mysterious ways, Celia thought, ignoring any thought of blasphemy in the analogy. How, or why, they had chosen her for the job she was now engaged upon was beyond her, but you learned not to ask too many questions of your superiors. For one thing, you were unlikely to get any proper answers, anyway.

By the summer of 1942 she wore a khaki uniform with the honorary rank of lieutenant, though she knew she had done nothing to deserve it. She also wore a special badge on her shoulder, and had a privileged amount of petrol and a driver assigned to her if she needed to go anywhere in a staff car. They appreciated her qualities, she conceded, and she had more than proved herself with her knowledge of German patois that frequently clouded the coded messages that came across the wires regarding German military and airborne manoeuvres.

She had become friendly with her immediate boss, a more highly ranked individual called Bertram Moon who everyone called Captain Moonlight because he preferred the evening shift to any other. On one of their joint assignments, Celia dared to broach something she had been dying to ask for weeks. By now she felt she could trust him.

'Moonie,' she said, with her own pet name for him, 'you know I worked in Germany for a time, don't you?'

'Of course,' he said, his attention still on the mass of gibberish coming through his headphones. 'That's how you got this job in the first place, sweetie.'

'Then you realise I must have known a lot of Germans.'

'Naturally. And learned the language amazingly well, including some very juicy phrases you keep threatening to teach me,' he teased. Then he saw her face. 'Go on.'

'I fell in love, Moonie. It was, and is, a really serious, passionate, forever kind of love, not one of those one-night things.' She blushed, knowing she was laying all her cards on the table and that this kindly man could shop her in an instant if he so chose. And she would probably lose this plum job if he did.

'Go on,' he repeated. 'I'm listening, but if you want to stop now, you have the choice, Celia. This passionate love of your life was obviously a German.'

'*Is* a German, God willing,' she said desperately. 'And that's what I want you to find out if you can. If you will.'

She knew he had access to places and people that she didn't. Despite the importance of the work she did, she knew she was no more than a link in a chain, while Moonie had a vast number of contacts in Germany.

Spies was what they called them in all the action novels, men who risked everything to send back news of the enemy's movements, and who infiltrated the most secret places of an enemy's headquarters, feigning loyalty to both sides, until no one was quite sure to which side they truly belonged.

They were shadowy men, Celia always thought, always having to conceal their true identity and allegiance, but remarkably brave, for all that, with the proverbial nerves of steel. Why, even Captain Moonlight himself could be one of these double agents for all she knew, feeding back false information to British Intelligence, of no use whatsoever...

'Drink this, Celia,' she heard his voice say in her ear, and she blinked, realising that she was sitting ignominiously on the floor of the operations room, and that Captain Moonlight was pushing a glass of spirits to her lips. 'I don't know what the hell got into you just now but you looked as if you had seen a ghost. You passed out for a moment.'

'I'm sorry,' she whispered, fighting down the almost irresistible urge to fling some crude and idiomatic German phrase at him and see if he reacted in any way.

'So tell me about this man of yours,' he said gently.

'I can't,' she said. 'I mustn't.'

'You have to now. I presume he's working for them?'

'Well, shouldn't he be? He's on their side, after all. He's one of the enemy,' she said, angry and frustrated at having to say it at all. 'But as a matter of fact, no, he *isn't* working for them. If my information is correct, he objected strongly to the Gestapo using his home as a base, and he was interned for his trouble. That's *if* my information was correct, of course.'

And now that she had said it, it sounded so thin, and from so unlikely a source. She only had a prisoner of war's vague word on it, and her cousin Ethan might even have got the name all wrong. She was a damn fool ever to have believed it at all, and in her reckless way of allowing her imagination to take over, she had endowed this nice and kindly officer by her side with the added indignity of thinking him a spy.

If it hadn't been so ludicrous, the shame of it would have made her weep. She swallowed her huge sense of disappointment and impotence.

'Why don't you start from the beginning, Celia? And by the way, you and I are on the same side, so if I can do anything to help, I will.'

She knew by the steady look in his eyes then that he had read her only too well.

'We were lovers,' she muttered, and if she had thought this would shock him, she was wrong again. 'I loved him – *love* him – more than I ever thought I could love anyone. He was eventually going to sell his estate in Germany, and we had thoughts of moving to Switzerland to live. That was before the war came and spoiled all our plans.'

'As it did for so many others,' Moonie reminded her.

'Well yes, of course,' she said, embarrassed. 'There are many people worse off than me, I know that. My mother's friend had a Jewish husband, and he killed himself rather than face what was happening to his family and friends in Germany. And then she died in an air raid in the Blitz...'

'Anyway,' she went on painfully, 'my cousins have a farm in Ireland, and some prisoners of war were sent to work there. One of them said he was a relative of Stefan von Gruber, and that he had been interned for the reason I gave you.'

'Sort of like a conscientious objector, then?' Moonie said thoughtfully.

'He's no coward!' Celia exclaimed angrily. 'But neither could he – or anyone with any sensitivity – sanction the things the Gestapo were doing, even to their own people. You should know that as well as I do, Moonie.'

'Calm down, Lieutenant, and get it in perspective. If your von Gruber was resistant to the Gestapo moving in and taking over his house, he as good as signed his' – he caught her agonised look and revised his words – 'own sentence. Not that it was such a terrible crime, compared with others, but why wasn't he conscripted anyway?'

'He's forty-two years old,' she murmured.

'And you're twenty-three.'

She turned aside, her face burning. 'Age has nothing to do with it, but if you're not going to help me, then say so. I'm sorry I bothered you.'

He gave a lopsided grin. 'My God, you've got a temper on you, haven't you? Is it a family thing, or do all Cornish women have it?'

'Tremayne women do,' she whipped back, and then began to laugh as she wondered why the hell she had said it. She wasn't a Tremayne, except way, way back. Her mother had been Skye Tremayne before she married Philip Norwood, Celia's father, and later married Nick Pengelly. But who the hell was *she*, she thought, starting to feel the sense of panic again?

'It's time we took a break, and you can explain that odd remark over a cup of hot sweet tea,' Captain Moonlight said briskly. 'That's the correct remedy for shock, I believe.'

'I'm not in shock—'

'You will be when I tell you how many strings I'm going to pull to get information about your von Gruber,' he said.

Her smile was dazzling. 'Oh Moonie, I love you!'

'No you don't, more's the pity. Save it for your man.'

–

There had been a time when Killigrew Clay was one of the largest and most important clayworks in Cornwall. Its steady decline had been due partly to the constant fluctuations in the industry itself, and partly to the intrusion of two world wars. Now that it was part of the larger company known as Bokilly Holdings, and no longer a sole concern, Nick Pengelly was still legally concerned in its fortunes.

But after a lengthy and painful meeting in Bodmin with the present clay bosses and their own lawyer after the product analysis at the end of 1942, what he had to tell his wife was no more palatable to him now than if she and her rip-roaring cousin Theo Tremayne had been in complete control.

'You can't be serious, Nick,' Skye said, white-faced. 'Things can't really have got as bad as that?'

'I'm afraid they have, darling. Many of the younger men have joined up or been conscripted, of course, which helped to keep the company finances afloat, although Bourne and Yelland promised to keep their jobs open for them. A vain promise, as it happens. Production is very low, and the Roche pits are as good as played out of china clay. Orders have dwindled to practically nothing, and they're simply having to let men go.'

'But what about the newsprint and medical contracts? I know it's a horrible thought, but wasn't this war supposed to bring new business for china clay on account of all the medical supplies that would be needed? And do you suppose Theo knew any of this when we sold out – about the Roche pits being nearly played out, I mean?' she added angrily.

'I'm sure he didn't, love. Theo was always looking to the main chance, you know that. And there was nothing underhand from Bourne and Yelland at the time. The pits have simply become exhausted.'

'But we're not paupers, are we? We still have dividends coming in from the combined venture, don't we?'

'We do while the venture exists. Once it closes for good, that will be the end of it.'

Skye felt her eyes blur. For all this time – a hundred traumatic years – the clayworks had been part of her family. Even after selling out, which had seemed at the time to be the biggest betrayal of all, the pits had still been there. They could still walk the moors and see the row of old cottages where Hal and Bess Tremayne had raised their five children and worked for old Charles Killigrew in the industry's heyday.

They could still see the scars of the four pits that had once comprised the proud Killigrew Clay itself. Through her own ingenuity, White Rivers Pottery had risen like a phoenix from the ashes to continue and further that name and industry.

What would happen to it all now? It was unthinkable to imagine it idle and still, with only the sky-tips to remind the world of what had once been Cornwall's pride and joy.

'Darling, it's a dying industry,' Nick said gently, as he registered every emotion on her ashen face.

'How many times has that been said?' she cried, with a passion worthy of her grandmother. 'How can you say it now?'

'Because it's true. Bourne and Yelland are planning to close, and there's nothing we can do about it. They'll offer it for sale of course, and some other firm will snap it up at a pittance, hoping to make a go of it, but it won't last.'

'Then we could buy it back, Nick! I don't care if we're in production or not. We don't need huge profits right now. We just need to keep control of it until this war is ended and we get back our European markets. I know we could do it—'

'Skye, for God's sake, be realistic. How could we possibly buy them out?'

Even though she knew he was right, and that he would put every obstacle in her way, her thoughts went off at a tangent, seeking and hovering over a new solution. A solution that seemed so daring, so grand, so impossibly forward-looking, that she knew it must work.

'They won't get much for a dying concern, will they? A pittance, you said. The cottages go with the clayworks and a couple of them are empty so they can't be many clay-workers left now. If we guaranteed to let them continue doing what work they can, it would salvage a little of their pride as well. We still need clay to supply White Rivers,' she pointed out, 'and I prefer to use our own clay than to buy it in from outside sources.'

Nick couldn't see the sense in it, but he couldn't help but be stirred by her passion. These wild and crazy clay-folk, he thought, distancing himself from the whole lot of them – especially from the hot-headed Tremaynes.

'You're completely mad,' he said finally.

'You haven't let me finish,' Skye rushed on. 'It's something David said—'

'What the devil does he have to do with it?' he said, jealousy of his wife's long-time admirer showing through.

Skye ignored it. 'David reckons that in time Cornwall is going to become a mecca for visitors. Think about it, Nick. Once this war is over, people will want somewhere calm and peaceful to visit. They'll want the beauty of the countryside, and they'll have had enough of bomb-damaged cities and want somewhere to restore their spirits.'

'And you think the sight of an old clay-pit is going to do that?' he said sceptically.

'The evacuees have already discovered Cornwall and will want to bring their families here. That's partly why I'm writing the history of the clayworks and my family – to interest those visitors who have never seen such places before. And maybe if one of those old pits was turned into a vast area where visitors could go and see just the way it was all those years before, including the old cottages – well, don't you see the potential in it? Someone else may do it if we don't.'

When he didn't answer immediately, she plunged on as her imagination took hold.

'We could have my booklets for sale, and some of Uncle Albert's pictures to add more local and family interest. And if you don't think our finances will stretch to buying out Bourne and Yelland in the first place, you know I still have a collection of Uncle Albie's pictures upstairs. I'd willingly sell them to raise the money. So do you still think I'm completely mad?' she added.

It had been an inspiration to remember the legacy of Albie's pictures. Dozens of them were stacked in a locked room at New World, and those that had already been sold had always fetched a handsome price. With the proper advertising, and David's help in it all through the newspaper, it couldn't fail. Skye was sure of it.

It would *all* work. And the need to do it, to continue everything that had always been theirs, was as urgent and necessary to her as breathing.

'We'll think about it and discuss it privately later on,' Nick said, as cautious as ever, as Daphne and Butch came bursting in from school with tales of how their classes were going to rehearse Christmas carols to sing at the local hospitals and for the poor soldiers at Aunt Betsy's place.

Skye felt a glow in her heart, because nothing could have told Nick more plainly how integrated these children were now, and how they would want to come back to Cornwall after the war, and bring their folks, and how successful her new venture promised to be, given half a chance.

She felt more optimistic than she had in a long time, even though her own children had left the roost, and these two had sometimes been more troublesome than she had bargained for. She thought she knew now exactly why Morwen Tremayne had opened her heart to her brother's children when he and his wife and died.

Tremayne women had a huge capacity for loving, and there was always room for more, though she had never expected these two to be the catalyst to some new challenge that would stir her imagination and keep her business brain alive. She hugged them both, ignoring their squirming, and recklessly promising them something special for tea.

'Bread and scrape, more like,' Daphne observed, prosaic as ever, which made them all burst into hysterical laughter for no logical reason at all.

They decided to call a family council. It was only right that all members of the family should be aware of their proposals. Even in the middle of a war, domestic matters still had their place, though those who couldn't be present had to be informed by letter of what Skye Pengelly had in mind for the future.

By now Sebby had returned home to Killigrew House, and was proving as difficult as his brother Justin had predicted. He couldn't accept what had happened to him, and while his participation in the war was past, the battle within himself was far from over.

He had been driven to the pottery a few times, and had played around with the clay, but his fingers were out of touch with it, and he had flung it down in frustration when the once-skilled hands didn't do what his brain told them they should. Even Butch Butcher could do better, he thought bitterly, and was bragging to all and sundry that the minute he left school next year he was going to be apprenticed to Adam Pengelly.

It was more than likely now, since the day the billeting officer had arrived at New World to tell Butch his father had been killed in an air raid. After a wretched night of crying, Butch had emerged, red-eyed, to say that he wanted to stay here for ever now, if Mrs Pen didn't mind.

She had seen the fear in his eyes that he might be sent away, and she had taken him in her arms and said that of course he could stay. After all, where else would he go?

The legalities could wait until after the war, she told Nick determinedly.

The family council consisted of Skye and Nick, Betsy and Seb Tremayne, Adam Pengelly, and Lily and David Kingsley. David wasn't strictly family, but since he was going to have more than a hand in what Skye envisaged, she insisted that he must be included. Apart from that, she had already got her own children's written approval. Justin had written to say it was all right by him whatever they did, and in any case he'd never had his brother's intense interest in china clay.

'You all know why we're here,' Nick said, taking charge. 'I've given you all a plan of what Skye wants to do, and I'll leave it to her to explain further.'

'We'd like her to explain how she plans to raise the money,' Betsy said, glancing apologetically at Skye. 'I don't have no business brain, my lamb, but I know how tight things were when you and Theo decided to sell Killigrew Clay, so how come you can manage to buy it back now?'

Seb snorted. 'Her family has always managed to find money when it was needed. They never went short, sending their girls to their fancy Swiss school and sending Celia to America.'

'Neither did you, Seb,' his mother said, 'so mind your manners and let Skye speak for herself.'

He glared at them all, and Skye hoped he wasn't going to make things awkward. Then she saw how he grimaced with pain as he stretched out his leg, and she readily forgave him.

'You all know that when Uncle Albert died he left his studio and paintings to me,' she said evenly, trying to ignore the little lurch of her heart at mentioning his name.

'So does that mean Lily has to sell up to fund your little scheme?' Seb jeered next. 'You'd better watch out, Mother. It looks as if we might all have to move out of Killigrew House as well.'

'Shut *up*, Seb, and don't be ridiculous,' Skye snapped. 'Nobody has to go anywhere, and if you would kindly keep your stinging remarks to yourself for a minute, I'll tell you what I have in mind. I have a large collection of Albert Tremayne's paintings still in store. They belong to me, and I have the absolute right to do what I like with them. Is anybody about to dispute that?' she said, looking directly at Seb. He pursed his lips mutinously, and said nothing.

'Then what I propose is that I sell them and put the money towards buying out Bokilly Holdings, including the old cottages. Nick has already checked that I can get it all at an acceptable price. I am not going to bother you with the details, because this will be solely my business. I'm not asking anyone for any money, and nor do I want any partners.'

Her voice shook a little as she continued, because it suddenly seemed like such an enormous leap in the dark. And they could well think her a complete madwoman for even considering buying a virtually played-out clayworks.

'What I do want your approval on is this,' she went on. 'Once the clayworks are in my control, I propose renaming it Killigrew Clay. What do you think?'

Please approve, she begged silently. *Please say you feel as charmed by the idea of preserving our past as I do...*

Seb snapped, 'I'm sure you and your man have already got it all sewn up between you, so if that's all we've come here for, we might as well have stayed at home.'

'I think it's a simply marvellous idea, Skye,' Lily said. 'People are always interested in the old ways.'

'Yes, but all that will have to wait until the war is over. We're hardly likely to get hundreds of visitors right now. And meanwhile, I must stress to all of you that the idea of this scheme goes no further than these four walls. The important thing is to regain control of the clayworks.'

'But it's something that I'm sure the townspeople will approve of when they hear,' Lily went on. 'And it's good that the name of Killigrew Clay will live on after all.'

'You always had a clever brain on you, Skye,' Adam put in approvingly. 'Anything to breathe new life into an old industry has my approval, and once Sebby gets his old skills back, I know he'll see the sense in it.'

'You can speak for me as well now, can you?' his partner scowled at once. 'I might have lost some of my slickness, but I can still think for myself.'

'For God's sake, man,' David Kingsley said angrily. 'Can't you give this idea a chance?'

Seb's voice oozed sarcasm and innuendo then. 'Oh well, we all know why you'd think it so wonderful, don't we?'

Skye could see that Nick was more than ready to grab him by the throat and throw him out, and before it all got completely out of hand, she rapped on the table and called the meeting to order.

'Then if we're all agreed, I intend to arrange for an art expert to put a reasonable price on the paintings before offering them at a public sale. We shall need advertising to attract people from farther away than Truro and St Austell, but I'm sure David will see to all that.'

She went on before Seb could open his mouth again.

'So I can now tell you that I have made a nominal bid for Bokilly Holdings, subject to our approval here today, and Nick says it will be held as a true and faithful offer until the sale of the paintings goes through.'

'See?' Seb burst out. 'It's just as I said. It was all cut and dried before we even came here.'

'And it's just as my girls always used to say, Sebby Tremayne. You were a prize pig when you were a child, and you're an even bigger pig now – oink oink,' Skye flashed back at him, so fast and so unexpectedly, even to herself, that his eyes almost popped out of their sockets.

Then she saw his slow grin and heard his grudging hand-clap, and she was suddenly laughing back, and the atmosphere in the room palpably changed.

'Come on Sebby, let's get home while we'm all in a good mood for once,' Betsy said comfortably, and as they got to their feet, Adam called them back.

'Come up to the pottery again soon, Seb. I could do with you to show Butch a thing or two at weekends.'

Skye held her breath, wondering if this was going to light the tinderbox again. But to her surprise, Seb shrugged and said he'd think about it.

'Why not?' he added, with a spark of his old arrogance. 'If the master can't teach the pupil how to throw a pot, it's a poor do. I daresay I'm still good for something.'

Chapter Eight

The plans weren't the kind that could be settled quickly, and another Christmas had come and gone before negotiations with Bourne and Yelland could be properly concluded. To Skye's regret, none of her own brood had got Christmas leave, and the house would have seemed appallingly empty but for the noisy evacuees, who definitely filled a void, she thought guiltily.

But by now, thinking ahead to the way the clayworks might one day be given a different face for future generations to enjoy, Skye was filled with an energy she hadn't felt in years. No other company had shown the slightest interest in buying out Bokilly Holdings, since all were feeling the same pinch with the closing of foreign markets and the fall in prices for china clay.

In the end, the growth of the amalgamated company had been its downfall, since they were unable to provide enough work now for the numbers of clayworkers needed to keep them in production. And pittance though the sale price was – in terms of the vast turnover of the business in other years – to find the necessary funds, Skye knew she couldn't put off sorting through Albert's paintings any longer.

The room where they had been stored since they had been bequeathed to her and brought from his old Truro studio to New World had been locked and out of bounds for many reasons – not least because Skye knew that once she saw the many beautiful images of her mother, she would be reminded again of the creepy and possessive love Primmy's brother had felt for her.

Seeing the pictures would unleash the memory of the unfulfilled love that Skye had felt in her soul was slowly and incestuously being transmitted to herself, because of her uncanny likeness to Albert's sister.

It was an obsessive love that had saddened Skye even while it repelled her. Sometimes she even thought keenly that this much-admired family beauty and likeness was more of a curse than a blessing.

But if her visionary project was to go ahead, there was no help for it, she told herself briskly. She had arranged for an art expert to come to the house in early February, with the sale already being advertised for the end of March. Bourne and Yelland had agreed that they would dispose of the spring despatches of clay and then the transaction would go through.

And before any of that happened, the paintings needed to be aired and properly displayed for the art expert's assessment and costing.

'You can't put it off any longer, darling,' Nick told her, knowing her reluctance to even enter the room.

'I know. It's just that so much of my life is bound up in that room and those paintings.'

'It's not *your* life, Skye. Whatever life Albert and Primmy led, it was theirs. It belonged to them and not to you. You have to believe that and let it go. We've discussed this a million times, and I can't believe it's been festering inside you all these years.'

'I can't believe it either,' she murmured. 'I never expected to be still so affected after all this time.'

She shivered, wondering if you could ever really rid yourself of the past, or if aspects of it would always be there to haunt you when you least expected it.

'I know I'm being an idiot,' she went on slowly. 'So I'm going to go up to that room right now and unlock the door. And then I'm going to go inside and dispel those ghosts for ever. And I'll take a duster with me,' she added practically.

'Shall I come with you?'

'No thank you. When were you ever interested in dusting?'

She gave him a half smile and headed for the stairs before she lost her nerve completely. It was only a room, for God's sake.

Only a roomful of memories…

–

The stuffiness inside hit her the moment she entered the room. It smelled old and musty, almost choking her, and for a moment her heart balked, because it was so much like Uncle Albie's studio had been when they had finally had to clear it out after he died. It was almost as if he was still *here*…

She forced the windows open, their hinges stiff with disuse, and let in the cool February air. She leaned against the windowsill, pressing herself against it without realising that she did so, facing the sheet-covered groups of paintings that were stacked like shrouded ghosts around the room.

One step at a time, she told herself shakily. *Uncover them slowly, just one at a time*…

'What yer doin' up there, Mrs Pen?' she heard Daphne's raucous voice yelling up the stairs, making her jump, making her feel sick at the unexpected sound of another voice.

Skye tried to call back at her to stay downstairs, but the words didn't come out, and the next minute Daphne's footsteps were inside the room, followed by Butch's much heavier ones. The children stood, goggle-eyed and saying nothing for a moment.

'Bleedin' 'ell,' exclaimed Daphne, predictably. 'Did somebody die in 'ere?'

'Shut up,' said Butch, nudging her violently. 'Can't yer see Mrs Pen's upset about somefing?'

'No, I'm not,' Skye said, automatically reassuring them as she had done for so long. 'I just have to sort out these paintings. I told you about them.'

'You didn't tell us they was *'ere*,' Daphne complained. 'You said they was going ter be in some sale. Can we 'ave a look then?'

Before Skye could stop her, she had lifted one of the dust sheets and pulled it away from the stack of paintings. She stared at it, not saying anything for a moment, while Butch simply gaped.

'Christ-church,' he finally said, awestruck, and forgetting how he tried very hard not to swear in front of his idol. 'Is that you, Mrs Pen?'

'What do you think?' she asked in a cracked voice. 'Do you think it's me, Daphne?'

'Nah,' the girl said. 'It's somebody else who looks like you, but it ain't you.'

'Why not?' Skye said, surprised at her perception. She looked at her mother's image fully now.

Primrose Tremayne had been so beautiful, in an ethereal, yet utterly bohemian and free-spirited way that had captured more than one man's heart, as Skye well knew. They had always been compared as mirror images of one another, and Wenna in particular had inherited all the Tremayne looks too, so what was it that this streetwise child saw that wasn't evident to other people? The need to know overtook all other emotions.

'She's dead, and you're alive,' Daphne said positively, after a few moments of cocking her head on one side like an inquisitive little bird. 'This one ain't lived 'ere wiv us, has she? She looks diff'rent, like somebody from a long time ago, and – well, she just ain't you. She's that lady in the picture in the drawing room, ain't she?'

'She *looks* like you,' Butch said hastily. 'But you're prettier,' he added, with an enormous blush reddening his cheeks, at which Daphne hooted with laughter.

It was a sound that was out of place in here, thought Skye angrily. This room was a reverent place, a sacred place, dedicated to the memory of her mother and another lifetime.

And just as instantly, she knew how ludicrous she was being. It was just a room that needed airing, and which needed to be sorted out for the sale of her uncle's paintings. The memories would still be in her heart, and they didn't need this stuffy mausoleum of a room to keep them safe.

'Now you're both here, you can help me,' she said, after drawing a deep, steadying breath. 'We need to uncover the paintings carefully, so mind you don't scratch any of them. Then we need to arrange them so that the expert can see them all and say how much he thinks they're worth.'

'I bet it'll be a lot,' Daphne said sagely. 'Pounds and pounds, I'll bet.'

'Even more than a hundred,' Butch echoed, at which Daphne hooted again and told him he was dafter than usual if he thought a few old paintings could be worth so much.

–

Skye was staggered when the art expert told her how much he thought the paintings should fetch. Albert Tremayne's work had grown in value since he died, and the fact that much of his work portrayed the same woman only added to its appeal to collectors.

Primrose Tremayne's beauty had an air of mystery about it, and she had obviously meant a great deal to the artist. The art expert said as much to Skye, and then paused, as if hoping to hear more – but he waited in vain. Just how much Primmy had meant to Albert was a secret that she might guess at, but that no one else would ever know, Skye vowed.

'Don't underestimate the worth of these paintings, Mrs Pengelly,' he went on. 'In fact, a provincial town is hardly the best place to stage such an important sale.'

'You're probably right, Mr Hatch,' she replied, 'but I don't think that showing them in some London gallery is advisable in these hazardous days, do you?'

He gave a slight smile. 'I assure you that not all of London has shut down because Mr Hitler sends over his regular messengers of death,' he said delicately. 'And the city is quickly recovering from the darkest days of the Blitz.'

'All the same, the sale will take place in Truro,' she said quickly, not wanting to be reminded of that time, and finding herself beginning to loathe the oily man. 'Truro is where my uncle lived and worked, and if people wish to attend the sale, they must come here.'

'As you wish, dear lady,' he said with a small stiff bow. 'Then, when it is all arranged, if you will allow me to have the full details I will gladly distribute them to collectors outside the area who would be interested.'

'Thank you,' said Skye. 'I'll see that you're informed.'

She couldn't wait for him to leave, and she told Nick vehemently that she had no intention of advising him of the sale, and that she hoped the paintings would all stay in Cornwall where they belonged.

'That would be very short-sighted of you, darling,' he said, to her surprise. 'You want to sell the paintings, and he'll know where to find the keenest buyers. You can't afford to be sentimental over this, Skye.'

'I'm not—'

'So you would prefer all the best families in the area to buy one of your mother's portraits as a collector's item, and risk seeing them every time we're invited out to tea?'

'You're exaggerating, aren't you? When do we get invited out to tea by all the best families?'

But she knew she was going to cave in. What he said made sense. She had her own paintings of her mother, and they were her own choice, and very different from the stack of them they had discovered long ago in the late Albert Tremayne's studio.

She had shut those paintings out of her life for so long, and until that moment she had never fully realised that the reason for it was because she couldn't bear to see the variety of expressions Albert had drawn out of his sister.

Whether or not Primmy had truly known he was in love with her, somehow Albert had dragged every ounce of sensuality out of her to put on to canvas. In his own twisted way, he had manipulated her for his own lecherous needs, and Skye knew she never wanted to see those paintings again.

But did she really want other people to see them too, and forever speculate about the artist and the sitter?

'Nick, tell me honestly. What do you see when you look at those portraits?'

She was desperate to know, and afraid to hear the answer.

'I see a lovely woman, of course.'

'And nothing more? No − I can't find the word I'm looking for. No concubine − or − or—?'

'Darling, all I see is a woman who was painted many times by the artist who happened to be her brother, and found himself a ready sitter. The fact that there are so many of them and that he's captured her in so many moods is the only thing that makes it intriguing.'

She had to believe it. *Had* to believe it, otherwise she would feel she was exposing her own mother to whispers and gossip. And it wasn't the first sale of Albert's work. They had gone through this before, and to her knowledge there had been no questions in people's minds. She was letting this whole thing get out of proportion, and it was time to stop.

She needed money, and her uncle's paintings gave her the means to find it. End of problem.

−

There was no doubt that the first few months of 1943 saw the start of new hope in everyone's mind that the war was being turned in the Allies' favour. The Germans had surrendered to the Red Army in Stalingrad; Berlin had been bombed in daylight for the first time, proving that the RAF could penetrate deep into the enemy's heartland; American troops were driving back Rommel's forces in Tunisia, and Prime Minister Churchill announced that the sound of church bells could be resumed around the country now that the fear of invasion was past.

In early April, Wenna Pengelly's friend and pianist sought her out in their ENSA practice room.

'Have you heard the latest, Pengo? We're detailed to perform at an American army base next weekend. The GIs need a bit of cheering up, being so far from home,' she said gleefully, 'and I reckon we're just the gals to do it.'

'You would think so,' Wenna said. 'And no, I hadn't heard. Where is this base?'

'Oh, I don't know. Somewhere in Wiltshire, I think—'

'Really? My brother used to be stationed in Wiltshire, but I don't know where he is now. I haven't heard from him in ages. I wonder if his unit will be invited as well?'

'They usually bring in all and sundry – including local girls, more's the pity. I know you're partial to these RAF bods, but they can't hold a candle to the Yanks. There's going to be a dance later on in the canteen,' she added.

'You be careful, Rita. You know what I mean.'

The other girl giggled, tossing back her fair hair.

'I know, but heck, there's a war on. We might all be dead tomorrow, so if you can't be good, be careful!'

Wenna had to smile. Whatever happened, nothing was going to get Rita down. She seized any opportunity for fun, and sometimes Wenna wished she could be more like her. If she was, she might not have snubbed Group Captain Harry Mack quite so obviously. She hadn't heard from him in a long while either, but then she hadn't even answered his last letter, simply because it had got over-familiar and frightened her off.

After what had happened to Fanny and then Austin, and knowing how difficult a time her cousin Seb was having getting used to civvy street again, she had no intention of getting involved with anyone.

There was a war on, but that didn't mean you had to seize every moment with reckless abandon. It was what many girls did, and a lot of trouble it got some of them into. One of their own section had been ignominiously dismissed through having got into trouble with a sailor.

She sighed with irritation at her own thoughts, knowing how pompous they were. What right did she have to think herself above everybody else, when she knew she would be no different from the next girl if the right man came along?

That was the trouble. She had a soft heart, and she knew she could easily fall in love again, if she wasn't careful. She had fallen for Austin, giving him her heart, and more – and she could just as easily have fallen for Harry Mack...

'Are you decidin' whether or not you're going to let your hair down at the dance, Pengo?' she heard Rita say slyly.

Wenna laughed. 'There's not much of it left to let down now, is there?' she said, deliberately misinterpreting, and patting the sleek new cut she had chosen to go beneath her service cap, with the dark fringe almost meeting her finely-arched eyebrows. It changed her appearance, and on anyone else it might have been almost mannish. On Wenna Pengelly, alias Miss Penny Wood, songstress, it was piquant and stunning.

'Anyway, I thought you'd hooked one of these Yanks, as you called it,' Wenna said with a grin, 'so you shouldn't be looking for another one so soon.'

'Why not?' Rita said lazily. 'There's safety in numbers. And you can stop nursemaiding me. He showed me this little instruction booklet they've all been given. It's a scream.'

'As long as that's all he showed you,' Wenna said.

'Do you want to hear some of these bally instructions or not?' Rita said, ignoring her.

'Oh, go on then.'

Rita recited them so clearly, it was obvious that she and her Yank had studied them and found them hilarious.

'It says that the GIs can make many boners in British eyes – that's *mistakes* to you, Pengo – and that it isn't a good idea to say "bloody" in mixed company,' she gave a snort of laughter, 'and that if you say "I look like a bum" the British will think you're looking at your own backside.'

'Rita, you're making this up!' Wenna exclaimed.

'I am not, I swear! A couple of the other instructions creased me up too. "If you're invited to eat with a family, don't eat too much or you may eat all their weekly rations—"'

'Well, that makes sense.'

'We're also supposed to be more orderly at football and cricket matches. The GIs are told that the men will be generous and shout out "good try" even if they louse things up. Oh, and they must never criticise the King or Queen, or tell us that the Americans won the last war, or mention war debts—' She was laughing so hard now, she couldn't go on.

'Would any of them really bother about such things?' Wenna said in amazement, remembering the happy-go-lucky audiences at several previous concerts when the GIs had just wanted to talk about home, or show pictures of their girl friends, or find out if the British girls wanted any chocolate or nylons or anything else that was in short supply here.

'Dunno. The ones we've met so far have been extra polite, and I like being called "ma'am", don't you?'

'Well, it's better than some other things I could mention. Anyway, hadn't we better go through some of our numbers for the next show?' Wenna said pointedly.

–

By now, London had reasserted itself following the end of the Blitz, the dwindling of enemy air raids over the capital to little more than reconnaissance raids, and the advent of the flood of glamorous American servicemen into Britain.

Seeing the breezy GIs with their smooth, tailored uniforms and money to spend, and joining in the growing sense that victory might not be so far off now, others surged back to the once beleaguered city to join in the almost reckless enjoyment, eager to laugh at anything and thumb their noses at old Hitler. The warning phrase "the calm before the storm" was pushed aside in the new air of confidence that all would be over soon.

"Make do and mend" might be the stern instruction from the government, and utility garments might be the order of the day now, with home-sewn undergarments made out of scraps of parachute silk, but there was a longing for freedom and life after darkness that wouldn't be denied. *Gone with the Wind* had been showing at the Ritz Cinema for four years, and attracted far more people than Pathe News. Life went on.

'Why don't we go down to London one Sunday?' Rita asked Wenna, when the concert and dance at the US base was over, and they had jitterbugged the night away and were still too keyed-up to sleep. Rita's Yank and his friends had related all that went on in the city and filled her with restlessness.

She turned her head towards Wenna when she didn't answer. 'Well, what do you say? We could get to London and back easily enough. You used to live there, didn't you?'

'Yes,' Wenna said tersely. 'And I don't want to go back.'

'Why not? There aren't any air raids now.'

They had both flopped down on their bunks in the billet after the vigorous evening, not even having undressed yet. Now Rita leaned up on one elbow, kicking off her shoes to ease her throbbing feet.

'Did something bad happen while you were there?' she persisted. 'You never talk about it.'

'I don't want to talk about it now, either.'

'Why don't you? You don't have anything to hide, do you? Not you of all people!'

'Of course not,' Wenna snapped, all her nerves on edge now. 'You're so shallow, Rita. All you think about is enjoying yourself. You never think what terrible experiences other people might have gone through.'

'Hey, I'm in this war as well, you know,' Rita said resentfully. 'Go on, then. What terrible experiences have you gone through, with your posh family house in Cornwall and your Swiss finishing school and your lawyer Dad!'

Her inverted snobbery made it all sound like less than nothing, thought Wenna furiously. Instead of which, it had all made her what she was – and proud of it.

'If you must know, for months I spent every night in a London Underground, sheltering from the air raids, and trying to help keep up everyone's morale by leading the singing,' she snapped. 'I'm no Vera Lynn, but it seemed to help. Anyway, one night after the All Clear I left the Underground to go and search for the woman who was my boss and my friend, and there was nothing left of her or the nightclub or the street where we lived. There was just rubble and dust and the stench of burning flesh everywhere. Is that terrible enough for you?'

'*Christ*, Pengo, why didn't you tell me any of this before?' Rita said in a hushed voice.

'Because it was none of your business. Because it hurts like hell to talk about it or even think about it, even now. And that's why I don't want to go to London ever again.'

'Well, that's just why you *should* go,' Rita said. 'You'll never get over it properly unless you do. What kind of woman was this friend, then?'

'I told you, I don't want to talk about it.'

Rita said nothing, and when the silence became too oppressive to bear, and the images of Fanny were all too vivid in her head, Wenna gave a small sigh.

'She was flamboyant and brash and swore like a trooper, but she was the kindest, most big-hearted woman I ever knew. I loved her, and she loved me like her daughter, and I was bereft when she died, because it wasn't her time. I never had the chance to say goodbye and there was nothing left of her to bury. Her whole life – everything – all blown to pieces, unfinished,' she said bitterly. 'Now do you understand?'

'I daresay the street's still there,' Rita said. 'So let's get some flowers and say a few words over the place. I don't believe in all that church stuff, but if it'll make you think she's resting in peace, then let's do it.'

'What good will that do?' Wenna said.

'What harm will it do?'

Wenna didn't speak for a long while and for once Rita had the gumption to let her mull it all over.

'I suppose my mother would approve,' she said finally. 'Fanny was her friend long before she was mine.'

'That settles it then,' said Rita. 'We'll make our pilgrimage to Fanny's place on Sunday, and then we'll go and whoop it up in Leicester Square. That's where everyone hangs out nowadays,' she said knowledgeably.

–

Wenna knew it had been the right thing to do, no matter how hard it had seemed at the time, when she received Skye's emotional reply to the letter telling her about it. She scanned her mother's words quickly.

> It was a wonderful gesture, darling, and in a strange way it will have helped you to revisit the place you and Fanny both loved. I'm sure it put some sad ghosts to rest. Your friend Rita is a very wise young woman.

It wasn't quite how Wenna would have described her, remembering how the glamorous Yanks in the Square had plied them with drinks and chocolates before they returned to their billet. Rita had got quite squiffy, and in daylight too. But it had also been a headier day than she had thought, and Rita and her mother had been quite right. In a very sad and loving way, it *had* laid a ghost to see the now flattened street where she had once known such happiness. She had placed her flowers there as reverently as if they truly marked Fanny's grave.

She blinked back the tears and carried on reading the newsier part of her mother's letter.

'You would have been surprised at the numbers of people who turned up for the sale of Uncle Albert's paintings, and the prices they fetched! I'm sure he would have been amazed to know he was so well thought of, all these years later. You might even see one of them turning up in some London art gallery, since I've no idea who some of the buyers were.'

Wenna doubted that she would, since she wasn't in the least interested in touring art galleries. But she was pleased for her mother, and with the news that the purchase of the one-time Bokilly Holdings had gone ahead. It had been officially renamed Killigrew Clay, even though production was virtually confined to supplying the pottery now, and any post-war plans for the clayworks were to be kept strictly private for the time being.

'I heard from Celia yesterday,' Skye continued in her letter. 'She doesn't sound too well, and had a dreadful bout of flu recently, but she refused to come home to recuperate. She takes her job so seriously – to her credit, of course.'

Wenna studied those last words. The innocent comments made her feel less than adequate. Her sister was engaged on important work for British Intelligence; her brother was now a wireless operator in Bomber Command; her cousin Seb had been honourably discharged after being wounded in action; and Justin was a field doctor "somewhere in France". She was just a singer in an ATS concert party who couldn't ever compete with the popularity of Gracie Fields or Vera Lynn or George Formby.

For all the glamour of her one-time blossoming career, it seemed to be going nowhere very fast now, and sometimes she envied Celia very much for having such purpose in her life.

—

Wenna wouldn't have been so envious if she could have seen her sister that evening. Celia had fallen in love with Norwich, much to her surprise. It wasn't a large enough town to be pompous, nor small enough to be full of busybodies. In many ways it reminded her of Truro, and it was that very similarity that sometimes made her heart ache for the security of times past and the uncertainty of the future.

But she loved her job. It was intriguing, exciting, and sometimes hugely frustrating when the supposedly important coded messages turned out to be nonsense. At other times, when her expertise helped to thwart some enemy attack by providing their own lads with some prior information, it was more rewarding than anything she could have imagined.

There were also times when she wondered just where it was all leading. The war reports these days led them to believe that victory was just around the corner. Hitler was being defeated. The Japanese weren't getting things all their own way, and the Allied troops had become a mighty force with the Americans behind them now.

One day, all this would be over, and as the song said, "there'll be love and laughter and peace ever after".

But not for me, she sometimes thought, in her gloomier moods. *Not for Stefan and me…*

She shuddered in the cool of the evening air, and pulled her jacket more firmly around her shoulders. The city was as dark as always, the black-outs in every building firmly in place now, the few cars that were in the streets with their headlamps shrouded and dimmed. Overhead the sky was overcast, with only a few breaks in the clouds to show that stars still shone in the heavens. *Their* star was still there, Celia thought fervently. Even when it was temporarily hidden from view by clouds and rain, it still remained, as constant as their love. Nothing could kill a star...

Her shoulders drooped as she leaned on the railings of a narrow bridge, looking down into a stream where her own reflection was no more than a shadow. Wondering, not for the first time, if she was holding on to a dream that was over. Because for all Captain Moonlight's endeavours to find out more about Stefan's whereabouts nothing had come to light.

It was as if he had simply disappeared, as so many others had done. Celia tried very hard not to let her imagination tell her what that might mean in these evil days of reprisals and death for such slender crimes.

She didn't dare think about the future any more either. They had once envisaged such a bright tomorrow, but in her heart she had already begun to wonder if it would ever happen.

Even if they both survived this war, what did the future hold for them? Could Stefan return to his home, or even want to, knowing it had been violated by a regime he despised? Could she go back to Germany to work among people who would have been so recently her enemies? And how could Stefan go to Cornwall to be with her, when *he* would still be regarded as the enemy in many quarters? Old hates weren't dispelled in a day or a year.

She shuddered, wondering how he would view her part in decoding his country's wartime activities.

Long before this war began, their dream had been to start a new life in Switzerland, in the place where they first met, near the beautiful Alpine village of Gstaad. It was still her dream, but how fragile it seemed now, without the touch of his hand, or the whisper of her name on his lips, or any communication at all to tell her if he was alive or dead…

'I thought it was your delightful shape I could see,' she heard a voice say, and her reflection in the stream was joined by another, more solid one. She swallowed the lump in her throat, knowing who it was without turning around.

'Do you think I'm a completely hopeless case, Moonie?' she said sadly. 'I know you've already pulled far more strings than you should on my account, and if you can't trace him, I begin to wonder if anybody can.'

'Now just you stop talking that way, Lieutenant,' he said briskly. 'I haven't exhausted all avenues yet, and even if I had, you needn't think the worst. Never give up hope is my motto, and since you look as if a bit of cheering up is in order, and the wind's getting up, I suggest we repair to the local hostelry and drown our sorrows in whatever watery grog they call beer these days. Sometimes I swear it comes straight out of the North Sea instead of from our fine Kentish hops.'

Celia began to laugh. 'Oh Moonie, you do me good.'

'All part of the service, ma'am,' he said, in a pseudo-American voice.

He held out his arm and she tucked her hand in it. He was her superior, but he looked after her like a Dutch uncle, she thought affectionately, and with no ulterior motive. He was right about the wind getting up, she thought. It was time to move on before she got thoroughly chilled. She glanced up at the sky where the clouds were scudding faster now, and her heart stopped for a moment as she saw her bright star shining steadily through the gap before they covered it once more.

–

With rationing extending to every commodity now, the local hostelries had a shortage of beverages. Spirits were limited to two drinks per customer, but there was always plenty of beer available to satisfy the many servicemen and women from the nearby camps.

They had to provide something, Moonie observed, if they were to keep open at all, and it was best not to ask where they got their supplies for customers who were specially favoured. The black market could supply anything these days, and it seemed that everyone knew someone who could get something…

Celia made do with a glass of the wishy-washy drink that passed for beer. She didn't particularly like the taste at the best of times, and this weak variety suited her palate well enough. Moonie bemoaned the fact that the only decent brandy around these days was for emergency purposes only, and she asked him smartly if he'd like her to faint again so he could get them both a swig or two.

'I think I'll survive without that,' he grinned at her. 'But I'm glad to see you've recovered your spirits anyway, no pun intended!'

'None registered,' she grinned back.

Someone had begun to thump out a tune on the pub's battered piano, and a group of squaddies had crowded around it and begun belting out the words of "This is the army, Mr Jones".

Moonie nodded his head slightly towards a noisy group of RAF personnel who were hogging a far corner of the public house. The services tended to stay in their own groups unless a fight broke out between them, which wasn't unheard of.

'Friend of yours?' he asked. 'He keeps looking your way. The RAF bloke over there, I mean.'

Celia's heart leapt with excitement. Olly! It had to be Olly... Her pleasure faded when she looked across the smoke-filled room into a ruggedly handsome face she had never seen in her life before. It certainly wasn't her brother; this man was an officer, hob-nobbing with a couple of fellow officers and some lower ranks.

'I've never seen him before,' she said, abruptly.

'Well, he seems to think he knows you,' Moonie said. 'He's coming over.'

Celia was aware of the man weaving his way through the crowded groups, and deliberately turned away. She wasn't an unaccompanied female, and she wasn't looking for company apart from the safety of Moonie's. But she sensed that the officer was standing nearby, and then she heard his voice.

'Pardon me for intruding, but you are Miss Pengelly, aren't you? No one else could look so much like Wenna unless she was her sister.'

Hearing Wenna's name unexpectedly made Celia's head jerk around so fast she felt her neck crick.

'You know her?' she asked stupidly.

'May I join you?' the officer said after a brief nod, taking charge so effortlessly it was like poetry in motion, she thought, as he dragged a stool from nowhere and perched on it, his tall frame fitting it awkwardly. Now that Celia looked at him properly, she could see the scar running down his cheek, and registered his accent. He might wear a RAF uniform, and from his wings she could see that he was a pilot, but she knew by his accent that he wasn't British.

'Please forgive this intrusion, but won't you put me out of my misery?' he went on with a smile that would charm the sparrows from the sky. 'I spent some time recuperating at a house in Truro, and a young lady called Wenna Pengelly came and sang to we poor wounded mortals. You look so much like her I thought for a moment you must be her, until I remembered hearing that she had a sister.'

'Wenna sang at Aunt Betsy's?' Celia echoed before she could stop herself, beginning to feel like a parrot.

Harry Mack smiled in relief and spoke with a hint of triumph in his voice. 'Thank God it is you. I began to think I was going crazy and seeing double. Look here, may I get you and your companion something more interesting to drink? I might be able to persuade the landlord to rustle up a bottle of red wine. He owes me a favour or two.'

Celia gaped. Red wine was for Continentals, she thought irrationally, and nobody persuaded this landlord to do anything, as far as she knew, but moments later the officer came back to the table with a bottle and three glasses.

'I'm impressed,' she said. 'But you may have a riot on your hands if you're so privileged.'

Why should he be, she thought resentfully, just because he wore a Group Captain's uniform and had what she had now deduced was a slick Canadian accent? She felt her hackles rising, whatever the hell they were, at the thought that he might think her an easy pick-up just because she was here in a pub with a man old enough to be her father.

'It's all right,' he said. 'They know me here, and Wally's henchmen will keep us from being lynched. I know this is an imposition, Miss Pengelly, but can you tell me what's happened to Wenna? I've tried desperately to keep in touch but she doesn't answer any of my letters. Do you have an address for her, by any chance?'

He was slick all right. But slick with a desperation in his eyes that she recognised all too well, because it echoed the way she so longed for news of Stefan. Just to know that he was alive and still thought of her and wanted her.

It stuck out a mile that this man was in love with Wenna, and that was the only reason he had sought her out. When she didn't answer immediately, he went on rapidly.

'I'm sorry. I can see that I've embarrassed you. But we're leaving here in a few days. Obviously I can't say where we're going, so if you would please just let Wenna know that Harry Mack was asking after her, I'd be very obliged.'

He stood up to go, and she nodded at once.

'I'll be sure to do that, Group Captain—'

Her voice was drowned then as the raucous singing in the bar grew louder, and he smiled down at her.

'Thanks. And please finish the wine with my compliments.'

He saluted them both, then walked swiftly away to rejoin his companions. Celia turned to Moonie with wide eyes.

'Well, what do you make of all that? It seems my sister made a conquest whether she wanted to or not!'

Chapter Nine

By the middle of May the whole country was in a state of intense excitement as news of the Dambuster raids in Germany became the main topic in every newspaper and every wireless broadcast. Led by the fearless Wing Commander Guy Gibson, the bombers of 617 Squadron had breached the huge defences with their new bouncing bombs that had skimmed the surface of the water and then exploded at the foot of two major German dams.

Walls of water had burst through, flooding the valleys of the Ruhr and Eder rivers, destroying a vital power station, causing massive damage to coalworks, ironworks and railways, crashing through the industrial city of Dortmund, and causing thousands of people to flee their homes.

'They were the lucky ones,' Nick said grimly to his wife. 'The poor devils who thought they were safe in their air raid shelters stood no chance at all. I know they're our enemies, but most of them were probably ordinary people like us, going about their daily business. That's the hellish side of war. We're all puppets in the hands of overlords.'

As she was normally the one to show such compassion, Skye was touched by his words. But she had other things on her mind as she read the later reports in the newspapers.

'How quickly they gloss over the fact that eight Lancaster bombers were lost in the raid,' she said. 'They treat us like children, keeping the grim details from us. The young men in those planes won't be coming home—'

He broke in. 'Stop it. I know where your thoughts are going, but we don't even know if Olly was flying Lancasters.'

'We don't know that he wasn't, either,' she retorted. 'We don't know anything, do we? He never writes, and we might as well be on the moon for all the real information we get.'

'Would you rather be in London?'

Skye flinched. 'I would not,' she said.

The news that Wenna and her friend had gone to London and revisited what had once been the Flamingo Club had touched her at the time. Now, she could only think what danger they might have been in. The German bombardment of the capital might have stopped and moved to other vulnerable cities, but occasionally there were horrific tales of undetonated bombs in burnt-out buildings suddenly exploding and causing untold injuries and deaths to unsuspecting victims.

There was a tale of one such bomb being found beneath a family's doorstep in Notting Hill, and the whole family being sent away. It had been made safe by a controlled explosion, but they had been left with no home to return to. Better that than losing their lives, everyone had said at the time, but it still made the family evacuees and the rest of them aware that danger still lurked in such a silent and obscene way.

Skye also couldn't rid herself of the thought that Olly might be flying in one of these powerful Lancaster bombers. The last time he was home he had sounded so grown-up, so brash in an oddly endearing way, and it had been easy to see he believed himself invincible. She prayed that he was, and that God would forgive her for asking him to protect her own.

In June came the sad news that one of Britain's most beloved actors was 'missing believed killed'.

'He wasn't even involved in the war,' she almost wept when the news about Leslie Howard came through among all the regular reports of war casualties. 'It says he had been giving lectures in Spain to promote British films there and he was in a civil airliner shot down in the Bay of Biscay. It's so tragic. What had he ever done to the Germans?'

'What have any of us done?' Nick said shortly. 'We don't take account of the civilian population when we bomb their cities, either, do we? War's a cruel game, darling, and in the end, it's the little people who are hurt the most.'

'Only a philistine would call a famous actor a little person,' she retorted angrily.

'They still eat and sleep the same as the rest of us. And break wind too, I shouldn't wonder,' he added, trying to lighten the tension between them.

'You're as much of a pig as Seb sometimes, aren't you?' she snapped, knowing he would have put it far less delicately.

'Not at all. Just realistic. And if you're going to spend your days mourning every person who is killed in this war, you're going to depress us all. We all have to get on with living, Skye.'

She knew that. She just couldn't rid herself of the nagging fear that Olly was up there somewhere, flying those abominable machines that looked so fragile and beautiful in flight, but could bring such death and destruction to innocent people, and to the men who flew them.

Whether the words were 'missing in action' or 'missing, believed killed', they had a terrible finality about them, and were being delivered via yellow telegrams with agonising regularity these days. Sometimes to a family whose sons were fighting the war at sea against the dreaded enemy U-boats; or engaged in the war in the air; or still fighting on the ground in Sicily or Tunisia or the western desert…

Nowhere was safe any more, and the thing most women dreaded was to see a telegram boy leaving his bicycle outside their house and coming towards their front door. When a loved one was declared missing, everyone automatically assumed the worst, and mourned him in their hearts.

–

Daphne Hollis went missing after school one sunny June afternoon. By now, she and Butch had mastered the bicycles that had been Christmas gifts from their generous Cornish hosts, and rode to and from their Truro school each day.

Butch didn't always wait for Daphne. For one thing, it was getting to be beneath his dignity to hang about for a bumptious nine-year-old girl whose school friends always giggled and huddled together when they caught sight of him. For another, he liked being alone. He liked riding through the lanes and catching sight of the sea, and he liked the smell of the wild flowers, and he liked to think of himself as a proper Cornish lad now, and to pretend that he was here to stay.

On that June afternoon, he dawdled on the way home, knowing Daphne would catch up sometime. The lure of his favourite cove beneath the cliffs was too strong to resist. The whiff of the salt air and the glitter of the sunlight on the waves made it a magical place, though Butch was far too inarticulate to ever put such thoughts into words.

When the tide went out and the sun baked the sand dry, it was firm enough to ride on and catch the spray as the waves crashed on the rocks nearby. It was a sport Butch loved, and the tingling touch of the sea water on his face invigorated him. That day he spent longer in the cove than he should, collecting shells and a few fossils. When he finally cycled back to New World, he was aware of the prickly heat on his skin, but decided it had been worth it.

'Where's Daphne?' Skye said, the moment she saw him come into the house, long past tea time.

He blinked, having been ready to show her his shells and fossils, and share her own pleasure in such simple things, and was momentarily thrown off balance by the anxious look on her face.

'I dunno. She's here, I s'pose,' he stammered. 'I ain't seen her.'

'Hasn't she been with you, Butch? Didn't you wait for her after school?'

The reddened colour on his normally freckled face deepened still more as he heard the accusation in her voice.

'She don't want me to,' he said, his adolescent voice cracking more than usual. 'She's always off wiv her mates, and she says I'm spoilin' their fun if I'm hanging around.'

'What kind of fun?' Skye said sharply.

'I ain't saying,' he said sullenly.

'Oh yes, you are!' Skye said, suddenly alarmed. Daphne might think herself worldly-wise and a cut above her country cousins, but she was still only nine years old –

almost ten, Skye reminded herself – and a large girl for her age at that. And Skye was still responsible for her. She resisted the urge to shake Butch and spoke more calmly.

'I think you had better tell me all you know about the fun Daphne and her friends get up to, Butch.'

In his own slow way, he was troubled by Daphne's wildness, but he didn't want to betray her. But in the end he knew he had to do it.

'They go down to the river where the soldiers sit outside the pubs in the sun, 'cos they give 'em sweets and fings. And once,' he gulped, 'I caught her smoking a Woodbine—'

'*What?* And you said nothing about it?'

'I told 'er she'd better stop it before she got in trouble,' he howled. 'But you know what she's like. She finks she knows better'n everybody else. It weren't my fault!'

'I know it wasn't, Butch,' Skye said, trying to keep her fury under control. 'But you say these little girls hang around the pubs where the soldiers sit in the sun. How long has this been going on?'

The town was more overcrowded than ever before, what with the dozens of evacuees and the servicemen who were billeted in every corner of the country now. Skye felt a new fear crawling inside her. A fear that only adults could know, but of circumstances in which children were the victims. Dear Lord, had she been so involved in her own affairs that she had become lax in taking care of Daphne, and allowed this to happen?

'Stay right here, Butch. I'm going to make some telephone calls and then you and I are going back to Truro.'

The first call was to the school, to be told by the caretaker that everybody had gone home long ago and there were no bicycles left in the stands.

Next she called the newspaper office, and asked for David Kingsley's personal number. She quickly related what Butch had told her, and he responded at once, saying he'd go down to the riverside pubs and take a look around.

None of them would be open at this time of day, of course, but the old wooden benches outside had become a mecca for the servicemen stationed down here, as many of the older local girls had soon discovered. But Daphne wasn't old enough to take care of herself in the way those girls were, and while Skye despised herself for thinking the worst of them, she knew there could always be a bad apple in the best of crops.

'The girl will probably saunter in at any minute as large as life,' David assured her. 'Try not to worry, Skye, and report back to the office the minute you know she's safe.'

But she couldn't wait for that, and as soon as she had hung up, she called Nick's chambers in Bodmin to tell him what was happening. Then she and Butch set out for Truro again. He constantly apologised, until she snapped at him to shut up and just concentrate on cycling there as fast as they could.

She hoped against hope that they would see Daphne coming towards them, her head in the clouds as usual, but there was no sign of her, and the sun was getting lower in the sky now, sending a sheen of red and gold across the calm sea.

'What d'you fink's happened to her, Mrs Pen?' Butch finally said cautiously.

'I dare say she's playing with her friends and they just forgot the time,' she said, mentally crossing her fingers.

She didn't dare to think what the evacuee billeting officers would say if Daphne was missing for any length of time, or had been harmed in any way. Those stiff-necked townswomen had frightened the life out of the children when they first arrived, and the thought of them interrogating Daphne was something Skye didn't care to imagine.

It would depend on Daphne's mood, of course. Daphne, scared and snivelling, would be easier to handle, even though she'd be a sitting target for a billeting officer's wrath. But Daphne, defiant and belligerent, and peppering every sentence with inventive cuss words, would be something else – and a bad reflection on the household she had been living in for the last three years.

Skye caught her roving thoughts up short, realising that this was no time to be thinking of her own part in all this. What did any of that matter, compared with the safety of a child?

When they reached the town they rode straight to the riverside pubs. David met them there.

'Nobody's seen her, though a group of soldiers offered to start a search party for her if we needed one. I told them it wasn't necessary. No need to alarm people yet. I called home to see if she'd gone there, as she likes playing with our boys, but Lily hasn't seen her either.'

'What about her friends, Butch? Do you know who they are and where they live?' he asked the boy.

Butch, always nervous of David's direct manner, looked hunted. He couldn't think and couldn't help.

After a fruitless hour of searching, and asking anyone in the area if they had seen Daphne, Nick arrived from Bodmin and said shortly that if she didn't turn up soon, they must inform the police. He anticipated Skye's protest and spoke sharply.

'They're the professionals, Skye, and it's been more than four hours now since she left the school – and she's our responsibility,' he added, echoing her own feelings.

'But it might be nothing at all, and now everyone will know. Her teachers, the billeting officers—'

'Do you want her found or not?' he demanded.

'Of course I do!' She turned to Butch again. 'Was there anywhere else she liked to go, Butch? Somewhere you haven't thought about yet?'

'Well, sometimes she said she was going to do what your girl does. She had a terrible screechy voice, but she kept saying the men at Aunt Betsy's liked her carol singing at Christmas. P'raps she's gone back to London to be a singer.'

Skye threw up her hands. 'Oh, that's the last thing I want to hear, that she's tried to get back to London—'

'Hold on a minute,' Nick said. 'She'll know the way to Betsy's, and I bet that's where she is. She'll be there preening herself, singing to a captive audience. And knowing what a devious little liar she is, she'll have told Betsy it was all right with us to stay as long as she likes.'

'I don't care how many lies she's told, as long as she's safe,' Skye declared feverishly. 'Let's go there right away.'

'You two go with Nick,' David said, 'and leave your bicycles here. I'll get someone to bring them back tomorrow.'

'Bless you, David.' Skye got into Nick's car with shaking legs, and Butch breathing down her neck in the seat behind her.

For one crazy moment she had the strangest feeling of *déjà vu*, from when her own little girls and the precocious Sebby and Justin Tremayne had been breathing down her neck in a car on the way home from a fitting for wedding outfits for Vera's wedding to Adam Pengelly, all those years ago…

She brushed the feeling aside at once. This was a far more desperate occasion, and she urged Nick to drive at more than his usual careful speed towards Killigrew House.

The minute Betsy came to the door, astonishment on her face at seeing the deputation, Skye's intuition told her they were out of luck.

'Well, this is a surprise, my lambs,' Betsy began. 'But if you're wanting that pretty little minx of yours, you've missed her by a long while.'

'She's been here then? Daphne, I mean? How long ago? When did she leave?' Skye said in a rush, sick with disappointment.

'Oh ah, she were here all right, along with a few of her school friends – all making eyes at my boys, the little madams,' she chuckled. 'Most of t'others went a long while back, but your girl and a little friend stayed for tea, saying you knew all about it. You *did* know, didn't 'ee, Skye? I didn't do anything out of turn in letting her stay, did I?' she added, finally aware of the tension in the other three.

'I didn't know, but it wasn't your fault, Betsy. I know how plausible she can be. She hasn't come home from school, and we've been out looking for her for hours—'

'Oh well, she'll be back home by now, sure to be,' Betsy said complacently. 'You'll have missed her, that's all.'

'Can we telephone New World?' Nick said, taking over. 'We need to be sure before we do anything else.'

And if she wasn't there, the next thing they would have to do was to inform the police, Skye thought, feeling sick.

-

'Are you sure this is the place?' the smaller of the two girls said uneasily. She and her clever friend seemed to have toiled over the moors for hours and were now crouched in a hollow near the very peak, gazing towards the hovel with the curl of smoke rising into the still air.

Daphne snorted. "Course I'm sure. There's a witch living there, and she'll cast a spell for yer, quick as lightning."

'What sort of a spell do you want then?'

Daphne glared at her. Tilly was soft and a bit stupid, but she usually did what Daphne said. They all did. Daphne was the leader of the gang, though the others had gone home long ago, and only Tilly Green had agreed to come with her to try to find the old witchwoman the locals spoke about.

Tilly's mother thought she was spending the evening at her Granny's, and her Granny would just assume that Tilly had gone home instead, she had told Daphne triumphantly.

Daphne wasn't scared of witches, but Tilly's jitters were starting to affect her, and she began to wonder if this had been such a good idea. But Tilly was still waiting for an answer, and she said the first thing that came into her head.

'I'd ask her for a spell to send me back to London.'

'Don't you like it here then?'

Daphne looked at her in exasperation, needing to think about why she'd said it. 'Mrs Pen's all right, but I'd rather be back 'ome. I miss the pie and mash shops and the jellied eels me Ma used ter buy on a Saturday night—'

'Ugh!' Tilly squealed. 'It sounds *horrible*.'

Daphne grinned as Tilly's pasty face paled still more... or was that because they were surrounded by a bit of a mist, now she came to think about it? She sat up cautiously and felt a shock as she saw that they seemed to be sitting in a sea of fog now, where minutes before it had been a bare expanse of moors.

'Jesus Christ!' she said out loud.

'Daphne Hollis, you know you shouldn't take the Lord's name in vain,' Tilly said at once.

'I didn't say the Lord's name. I said Jesus Christ,' Daphne snapped. 'And p'raps he'll tell us how the bleedin' 'ell we're going ter find our way back.'

Tilly gave a terrified cry when she saw what Daphne had seen. Without warning she wet her knickers, and the shame and discomfort of it set her wailing even louder.

'Shut up and let me fink,' Daphne snapped.

'We're going to die,' Tilly wailed. 'Nobody knows where we are, and I want my Mum—'

'I want mine too, but fat chance I've got of seein' 'er,' Daphne muttered, with a small catch in her throat. 'I reckon there's only one fing to do. We'd better see if the witch can help us.'

Tilly screamed, and Daphne clamped a hand over her mouth, so that only her scared, tear-filled eyes showed above it.

'It's either that or die of starvation and cold,' Daphne said dramatically. 'I dare say there are wild dogs roaming about up here as well, ready to come and tear us apart and eat our flesh – and when they've done wiv us there'll be nothing left but bones,' she added, warming to her tale. 'I bet they're surrounding us right now—'

They suddenly heard a thin, cackling voice close by, causing them to cling together in terror.

'You tell a fine tale, my pretty maid, one that even old Helza couldn't improve on.'

For a moment or two they couldn't see her properly for one of the pockets of mist that frequently slid across the moors at the end of one hot summer's day and heralded a similar one tomorrow. And then, as ever, it moved away just as miraculously, and they could see the old crone leaning on her stick not two yards away, wizened and hunched, and puffing away on an evil-looking clay pipe.

'We know who you are,' Daphne said as bravely as she could, considering that her voice was so croaked.

'We don't need no introductions then,' Helza cackled. 'I know who you be too. You'm the girl staying with the clay and pottery folk, and this one's a local, I dare say.'

'She must be a real witch,' Tilly whispered, trembling.

Daphne recovered herself quickly. 'Don't be daft. She can tell from the way we talk where we're from. Are you going to cast us a spell then?' she demanded of Helza.

'Just ask her to get us home,' Tilly said in a fright, the chill of her own urine and cold wet knickers making her shiver still more.

'The devil helps they that help themselves,' the old crone wheezed. 'You don't need no spells now the mist's lifted. Get on with you and leave old Helza in peace.'

She turned and hobbled away, seeming to melt towards her hovel. Tilly scrambled to her feet.

'Let's go before she comes back. As long as we keep going downwards we're bound to get off the moors, aren't we?' she said, her voice ending on a squeak.

Seeing her fear, Daphne was filled with guilt now that the adventure seemed to be over. Tilly might be a stupid little cuss at times, but she had been her friend from the day Daphne arrived. She put her arm around the smaller child.

'I'll look after yer, Tilly, even if it gets dark.'

She bit her lip. It wasn't dark yet, but the sun had gone down and after the heat of the day the air was chilled. And those damn wispy bits of mist still kept coming and going.

With one accord they turned and ran, heads down, their chests tight and heaving, then screaming in unison when the ancient standing stone with the hole through its middle that they called the Larnie Stone suddenly seemed to loom up in front of them. They had almost barged straight into it.

'Bleedin' stupid place this is,' Daphne snarled between her gasping breaths. 'Who'd wanter stick a bleedin' great rock on top of the moors where people could fall over it?'

'I wish you wouldn't keep saying that awful word,' Tilly almost sobbed. 'If my Mum heard you, she'd stop me playing with you, Daphne.'

She was clinging on to Daphne with vice-like fingers now, pulling at her cardigan sleeve as she tried to keep up with Daphne's scrabbling feet. She knew she couldn't do it. Her legs were too short, and her chest was hurting too much, and she couldn't see where she was going because her eyes were smarting, and the insides of her legs were being rubbed raw by her navy knickers now...

With a sudden almighty shriek of pain, she lost her footing in a rut in the ground, flying past Daphne, but somehow still managing to hold on to her cardigan, so that the two of them went hurtling forward and crashed to the ground together, completely winded.

It took a few minutes for Daphne to untangle herself from Tilly's arms and legs that seemed to be stuck out at all angles. Worse than a bleedin' octopus, she thought sourly, having no real idea what an octopus looked like.

She peered down into Tilly's white face and then sat back, feeling a momentary grudging admiration at the way the girl could act like she was dead just to give her a scare.

'Come on, you ain't hurt that bad,' she said roughly, and aware of an almighty headache the size of St Paul's, 'I ain't carrying yer, that's for sure.'

Then she saw the slow trickle of blood on the girl's forehead, and her heart skipped a couple of beats. She spoke fearfully, her throat threatening to close up completely.

'Tilly, stop pretendin', fer Gawd's sake. Come on, open yer eyes, there's a love. We've got ter get off these moors before it gets dark.'

Tilly still didn't move, and Daphne smothered a sob. But she could see now that she wasn't dead. There was a pulse throbbing away in her throat, though she wouldn't open her eyes.

Daphne panicked, not knowing what to do. Instinct told her she shouldn't try to move the girl. She could screech for the old witchwoman to come and help them, but she didn't know how far they had run, and she doubted that the old crone would hear her anyway.

The pottery was somewhere around here, she thought next, but even if she could get to it, it would be shut now that it was getting dusk. However, there were cottages at the top of the moors above the old clayworks, she remembered, and perhaps she could reach one of them and get help.

She started to scramble to her feet, and a searing pain like red-hot needles shot through her ankle. She had been so busy worrying about Tilly and her next move, she had hardly thought about herself. Her agonised scream was strangled in her throat as she looked down at the ankle that was rapidly swelling and turning several shades of blue and purple, and she found herself blubbing hysterically.

In a wild panic, she began to shout as loudly as she could, but her voice was quickly carried away until her throat ached and dried up with trying, and still nobody came. There was only the soughing of the evening breeze through the bracken to break the silence.

'There's nothing for it, Tilly,' she said hoarsely to her unconscious friend. 'We've just got to sit it out and hope somebody will miss us and come looking for us.'

Her words ended on a sob, because how could anybody even guess where they were? They were going to be in a God-awful heap of trouble when they were found, too. And the night ahead of them would be very long and cold.

But she knew this was all her fault, and she tried not to notice the stinging pain in her ankle as she covered Tilly with her own body as gently as she could to try to keep her warm until somebody came. Somebody would, she thought, with a faint echo of her usual cockiness. Somebody *must*.

–

'They've got to be somewhere,' Skye said frantically to the police sergeant who had come to the house and was now in charge of the investigation. 'Children can't just vanish.'

His constable was taking such an interminable time in writing down all the details that she could have hit him. Didn't they sense the urgency of the situation?

'Mrs Pengelly, I assure you they'll be found,' the sergeant said complacently. 'We've contacted the school to find out the other child's surname, and contacted her parents. They'll be here any time.'

Nick spoke angrily. 'You've asked them to come here? What good will that do, man?'

'People like to be together in a crisis that affects them all,' he said pompously.

Skye groaned. The last thing she wanted was the arrival of two hysterical parents who would be blaming Daphne for taking their little girl away – and that blame would obviously be transferred to the Pengellys. But she smothered the thought, knowing it was uncharitable, and that Tilly's parents would be as frantic with worry as they were.

They arrived a little while later in a police vehicle, a red-eyed mother and a rough-hewn father, unused to the company that lived in a spacious house near the sea and who were posher folk than themselves. As if any of that mattered, Skye thought, and tried to smile reassuringly.

'Please sit down, both of you,' she said swiftly, as they stood awkwardly together. 'Would you like some tea?'

God, how *inane* that sounded, and of course they didn't want any tea, or any kind of comfort from herself and Nick. They just wanted their child home, safe and sound.

The sergeant cleared his throat and addressed Nick.

'We'll start a search party, Mr Pengelly, and some of the soldiers have offered to help, so we're accepting their offer. My men are combing the shore first, to see if they've fallen down the cliff' – he ignored the cry from the suffering Mrs Green – 'and then we'll spread out and cover a wider area on the moors.'

'They wouldn't have gone up there,' Skye said. 'Daphne knows the dangers of the old mine shafts and how the mist can come down quickly and people can lose their footing—'

Dear God, why was she putting such ideas in these simple folks' minds? she thought, as Mrs Green's cries became louder. Her husband seemed to have no idea what to do about it other than to pat her back as if she was a family pet.

'You'll realise it may be a difficult task, since we'll have to keep our searchlights to a minimum,' the sergeant went on carefully. 'The regulations still apply—'

'You think some stray German bomber is going to pick tonight to swoop down on a couple of frightened children, do you?' Skye said angrily. 'Where's your humanity, man?'

'We all have to abide by the rules, madam,' he said stiffly. 'We won't rest until we find these children, though things would naturally be easier in daylight.'

She hated him. She was tempted to say they would have a repeat performance if it suited him better, and let the girls go missing in the morning instead of at night, which would make his job far easier. But she knew how ludicrous that would sound, and it wouldn't help. Nick's steadying hand on her arm told her so.

The sound of the doorbell ringing made them all jump, and the constable went to answer it without giving anyone else a chance. He came back into the room a few minutes later.

'They've found two bicycles at the foot of the moors, Sergeant. There's no sign of the girls, but it looks as if they dumped them there, and went walking.'

Butch had been sitting quietly, afraid to speak up after being questioned earlier, and still feeling guilty for not waiting for Daphne. But he couldn't keep quiet any longer.

'Daphne sometimes talked about that witchwoman who lives on top of the moors,' he said reluctantly. 'She liked to scare the younger ones with spooky stories.'

'The young devil!' Tilly Green's father suddenly spoke up, aggressive and guttural, his fists clenching. 'She needs sending back where she belongs and locking up, and if I get my 'ands on 'er—'

'Now then, Mr Green, there'll be none of that talk,' the sergeant said sharply. 'The important thing is to find these children as quickly as possible, and now that this young scallywag has given us a lead, we've got somewhere to start.'

'I don't know if that's where they've gone,' Butch said, near to crying. 'I only said she talked about it sometimes.'

'It's all right, Butch,' Skye soothed him. 'It's good that you remembered it, isn't it, Sergeant?'

He gave a curt nod, unable to resist complying with that unflinching stare from the woman's blue eyes. He wasn't a ladies' man, but he could guess that people would do anything to please her, even this young evacuee lad.

'Would you like to stay while we wait for news?' Skye asked the Green parents, praying they would say no, and not wanting to see their accusing faces any longer than she had to. She didn't waste her energy on feeling shame at the thought either. They had each other, and all her anxiety was for the children.

'We'll get off and do our own searching, thank 'ee, missis,' Mrs Green sniffed. 'If we don't find 'er, I dare say we'll be told when they know what's 'appened to our Tilly.'

'But you have no idea where to look.'

They didn't answer, and Skye gave up protesting as they left, together and yet so alone in their separate miseries. She looked at Nick.

'We're going with you,' she told the sergeant.

'It's best if you stay here, Mrs Pengelly—'

'Sergeant, I've never been rude to a police officer in my life before, but if you try to stop me walking these moors tonight I shall demonstrate the extent of my vocabulary.'

'I'm coming too,' Butch said, standing close to her and Nick and presenting a united front.

'Of course you are, Butch,' Skye said, knowing how important this was to him.

–

The night was overcast by now, and the sky-tips loomed up ahead of them like ghostly sentinels. There were huge numbers of people about now, as word had spread through the towns, and police, soldiers and local folk all joined in the search.

'It's ridiculous,' Skye said to Nick, as the shouting for the girls echoed up and down the moors. 'Even if they called back, we'd never hear them with all this din going on. Can't they see how stupid it is?'

'We should have let the police do their job, Skye. We're only adding to the confusion.'

'But we're involved. We couldn't sit at home twiddling our thumbs when Daphne might be – might be—' She was choked suddenly, as the realisation of just what could have happened to Daphne struck her forcibly.

These moors had long been mined for china clay, but they were also criss-crossed with old mine shafts from the days when tin was king. Theo Tremayne's own natural grandfather, Sam Tremayne, had died when Ben Killigrew's rail tracks had collapsed taking clayworkers on an outing to the sea.

The thoughts flitted in and out of her head like a dire presentiment of what could be happening. Her grandmother's best friend, Celia Penry, had drowned in a clay pool belonging to Killigrew Clay. Accidents had happened over the years on these moors, and some things that weren't accidents…

Already they seemed to have been searching for hours with the dim lights of the torches like useless glow-worms in the dark. The old moorswoman had been questioned and said she had seen the children, but it was hours ago. Skye could still hear her indignant screeching and cursing as the police insisted on searching her hovel, before reeling out of it, having found nothing but the stink of her and her animals.

Then at last the piercing sound of a whistle stopped her heartbeat for a long moment. It was the signal that something or someone had been found…

'Dear God, let them be safe,' she whispered aloud, and with Nick's and Butch's hands holding tightly to hers, she struggled to reach the area where the sound was coming from, somewhere beyond the old Larnie Stone.

Chapter Ten

It was inevitable that Daphne would see herself as a heroine. She had saved Tilly's life, she told Butch dramatically, by keeping her warm until they were rescued.

They had both been taken to hospital, where Tilly was treated for cuts, bruises and concussion, and Daphne had her sprained ankle strapped up. The nurses petted them, and visitors brought them sweets from their rations. They remained there for two days for observation, and were then allowed home. But if Daphne thought she was going to get off lightly just because everyone was relieved that no real harm had come to her and Tilly, she was very much mistaken.

'Do you know just how wicked and stupid you were, by going off like that?' Skye railed at her. 'Anything could have happened to you on the moors at night, and I've had nightmares just thinking about it. You were a very foolish girl, Daphne, and you'll be lucky if you're allowed back to school at all after the summer holidays.'

'*Good*,' Daphne screamed at her, still wrapped up in her own little euphoric cloud, and not wanting to hear anything different. 'I don't want to go back to that bleedin' stupid tin-pot little school anyway.'

'*Daphne*, I've told you before about using such language,' Skye said, incensed. 'I won't have it in my house.'

'Well, we can soon change that an' all, can't we?' Daphne bawled back. 'I don't wanna be in your house, neither. You're not my mother, and I hate you!'

Skye felt as if she had been slapped in the face. Lord knew she had done her best with this girl, and it had got her precisely nowhere. She turned away from the sofa where Daphne was sitting in state with her feet up to rest the swollen ankle, and fought the urge to retaliate at this little tyrant. And then she heard the sound of sobbing, and Daphne's voice, thin and weak and aching with remorse.

'I didn't mean it, Mrs Pen. I don't hate you, honest.'

Skye turned back to her at once, kneeling on the carpet beside her and gathering the stiff little body in her arms. So what if she was being a sucker and Daphne was using her the way she always used people? The evacuees were as much war victims as any wounded soldier. Daphne was in her care, and she had to see this through, no matter what.

'It's all right, honey. We all say things we don't mean in the heat of the moment, and I dare say your ankle's giving you hell, isn't it?' she said, giving her a let-out to save her pride, and knowing it.

Daphne nodded. 'You shouldn't use such words, Mrs Pen,' she said with a ghost of a smile, and Skye laughed as they hugged one another, both perfectly aware that Daphne was careful to wince dramatically for maximum effect.

–

'It's true what she said, though,' she said to Nick later. 'I'm not her mother, and I should remember it. One of these days, her mother will want her back, and I'll miss her.'

'Like you'd miss a thorn in your foot, you mean,' Nick commented, never able to be as forgiving as Skye.

'That too,' she grinned. 'She can be impossible, but she's still vulnerable, and she's got a birthday in August, Nick. She'll be in double figures, as our children used to say. We should give her a small party, don't you think?'

'If you like,' Nick said. 'As long as I don't have to be there. But who are you going to ask, anyway? Do you imagine the Greens will allow their ewe-lamb to come after Daphne nearly killed her?'

'Stop exaggerating, and yes, of course we should ask Tilly, and a few more of her school friends. It will be a nice gesture, and by the time they go back to school after the holidays, hopefully all this will be forgotten.'

In her heart, she knew it was a vain hope. Daphne would be bragging about the incident for ever more, and had begged for a copy of the *Informer* newspaper for herself after David Kingsley had felt obliged to put the whole story in print, much against Skye's wishes.

'It has to be done,' he'd said. 'Everyone's got wind of what happened, Skye, and it's better that they get a tempered version in print than garbled stories spread from mouth to mouth. Before you know it, they'll have Daphne tarred with the same brush as old Helza, and there are still superstitious folk prepared to believe in witches and the like. You don't want any scaremongering to result in the kid being hounded out of New World, with you in the thick of it.'

'I suppose you're right,' she said with a shudder. 'Go ahead then, but don't make her out to be too much of a heroine. She's preening herself enough as it is.'

–

'My mother's going gaga,' Wenna declared to Rita, incredulous at the news. 'This appalling child has turned the whole town upside down and managed to get her name into the newspaper as if she's a little angel instead of a villain, and now Mom's going to give her a birthday party.'

'Not jealous, are you, Pengo?' Rita said, too excited over the fact that at long last they were going overseas to entertain the troops, to bother too much over one wayward child in a remote Cornish town she'd never heard of before.

'Jealous! Of Daphne Hollis?'

'Well, she seems to have conned your mother all right. What did it say in that newspaper cutting? "Daphne is very contrite about her misdemeanour. Mr and Mrs Pengelly have forgiven her for her irresponsible behaviour, and trust that others will do the same."'

'My mother's a very forgiving person,' Wenna defended her. 'She stuck up for my brother when he enlisted under age and refused to let my stepfather bring him back home.'

'That's the first time you've referred to him as your stepfather,' Rita noted. 'In fact, you hardly mention him at all. Don't you get on?'

'Of course we do. He's a darling, and I said it without thinking. We're one big happy family,' she added glibly.

'Cripes, do such things exist? Don't answer that. Where do you think they'll be sending us, anyway?'

'Somewhere warm, I hope,' Wenna said, stretching like a sleek cat. 'Somewhere where the sun shines all day—'

'And the Yanks are ready to play all night,' Rita added with a grin. 'That'll be enough to raise our temperatures. But with our luck, it'll be the back of beyond.'

She eyed her friend thoughtfully. 'So are you going to tell me who your other letter was from? The one you read mighty quickly and then tucked away.'

'No,' Wenna said flatly.

'It wasn't from your Canadian then?'

'He's not *my* Canadian.'

'It was from him though, wasn't it?'

Wenna sighed impatiently. Rita could be as tenacious as a limpet when she wanted to know something.

'All right, so it was. He wrote to my aunt's house, and she passed it on to my mother, and it finally got to me.'

'And?' persisted Rita.

'And nothing. It was a letter to a friend, that's all. I doubt that we'll meet again, anyway.'

'That's not what Vera says, is it?'

Wenna looked blank for a moment. The only Vera she knew was one of her mother's cousins, and she had died years ago… and then she heard Rita humming tunelessly, and realised she was referring to the song that Vera Lynn had made her own.

'You're letting all this sentimental romance stuff go to your head, Rita.'

'And you're not? Are you telling me you don't put your heart and soul into those slushy songs you sing? Especially when you go all gooey-eyed over "I haven't said thanks for that lovely weekend"…'

'That's different. That's work,' Wenna said crisply.

'So when you come off stage with tears in your eyes and your throat working overtime – that's work too, is it?'

'I'm fed up with this conversation, and you're getting far too nosey,' Wenna said.

But she couldn't stop thinking about it all the same. She couldn't stop thinking about Harry Mack either, nor the sweet things he had said in his letter. She hadn't wanted to read them, nor to remember his voice, nor the look in his eyes when she had sung the words of the traditional Scottish song he had requested at Aunt Betsy's house.

But somehow, no matter how hard she tried to put such emotions out of her personal range and limit them only to her stage performance, it was gradually becoming impossible to do so. The shock of losing Fanny and Austin, and everything that had happened since – including getting used to the sight of the badly wounded and shell-shocked servicemen who were brought by nurses to hear their concerts – had made her close her mind to becoming involved with anyone else for the duration.

She gave a wry smile as the phrase entered her head. It was one of the phrases they all used so thoughtlessly now. But the duration of what? This terrible war? Her lifetime? Who knew how long that might be? How did any of them know? She shuddered, knowing how fragile life could be these days.

And the sweet, polite, handsome Harry Mack was in the thick of it, maybe flying regular sorties over Berlin by now, and longing for a letter from a girl he knew, just to have a breath of home. So what sort of a monster was she to refuse?

–

'Yer going to give me a birfday party?' Daphne echoed suspiciously when she heard. 'Me Ma would still be givin' me a cuff round the ears of a night, for what I done.'

'I told you, it's history now, Daphne,' Skye said. 'You have to try to forget it and just be as pleasant as you can at school and not cause any more trouble.'

'Why do I have to keep goin' there?' she said, as sullen as ever. 'Nobody plays wiv me now—'

'Yes they do,' Butch broke in. 'Don't tell such lies, Daphne. You should see 'er, Mrs Pen. She's still telling everybody how she saved Tilly Green's life, and as Tilly can't remember much of it, she believes it an' all. They all hang around Daphne when she tells her tales.'

'They ain't tales, anyway,' Daphne scowled. 'It was all in the paper for everybody to see. And I don't remember *you* saving anybody's life, donkey-drawers!'

'All right, that's enough,' Skye said, seeing another battle about to begin. 'The fact is, Daphne is going to have a birthday party. Auntie Lily's two boys will come, and you can choose which of your school friends to invite, honey.'

'I bet their mums won't let 'em come,' Butch sniggered.

She turned on him. 'Butch, please go into the garden and pull up a lettuce for tea, while Daphne and I talk.'

'I hate lettuce,' she said at once. 'It's yukky stuff, and it's fer rabbits, not yoomans.'

'Well, you'll either eat a lettuce sandwich for tea or go without,' Skye said grimly. 'I don't exactly like seeing my lovely flower garden turned into a vegetable patch, either, but we all have to dig for victory these days, and grow what we can. So are you going to tell me which of your friends you want to invite to your party, or shall we forget it?'

'As long as you don't give 'em lettuce, then,' Daphne said, scowling.

'We'll try to do better than that,' Skye promised.

–

'There's something on her mind,' she reported to Nick that evening. 'I thought she'd be pleased about the party, but she just droops about the place and scowls at everyone.'

'She always did,' Nick replied.

'But not like this. I wonder if the ordeal on the moors upset her more than we realised. Tilly was concussed, but Daphne probably stayed awake half the night until we found her, imagining all kinds of horrible things. She must have *some* sensitivity, Nick.'

'I doubt it. But if anybody can find out what's bothering her, it's you. You're the one she trusts the most.'

'Do you think it's because Butch is leaving school now and going to work at the pottery?'

'Why should she care about that?' he said, too busy with his own work problems to worry overmuch about Daphne Hollis, who, he thought, could very well take care of herself.

'I don't know. Maybe she feels we're favouring him. His father's dead, and I know he wants to stay with us when the war ends, now that he's got nobody else. I don't know if it's possible, but I wouldn't object. He's a cute boy.'

Nick laughed. 'You're too soft with them, Skye. I can't imagine anyone else calling Butch cute.'

'Well, so he is. You have to see beyond that large, awkward exterior to the good-natured person inside.'

He slid an arm around her shoulders and kissed her. 'And you would, wouldn't you? He's not the only one who's cute and good-natured around here.'

She kissed him back and then went back to her theme. 'So what do you think is troubling Daphne?'

'Lord knows, and he's not telling,' he said carelessly.

'O' course,' Daphne said in a superior tone to the admiring crowd of little girls sitting in a circle around her in the school playground, 'I don't really want a bleedin' party at all, but Mrs Pen wants me ter have one, so yer all invited, if yer wanna come.'

'My mum might not let me,' Tilly said uneasily.

'There'll' be more grub fer the rest of us then, won't there?' Daphne shot at her. 'Yer mums will have to bring yer all anyway, and Mrs Pen's written out the invitations.'

Since Daphne had never had anything so grand happening to her in her life before, she handed them round as solemnly as if they were made of gold. Despite her airy voice, she desperately wanted every one of them to come and see the posh place where plain old Daphne Hollis lived now.

It was a bit different to the two-up, two-downer in the East End where she'd been born, crammed in with her Ma and Dad and all her brothers and sisters, though as far as the tiny house went, things had got easier when one after another of the younger ones had died of diphtheria. At least then the six of them hadn't had to sleep head to foot in one room in three narrow beds, all sweaty little bodies and smelly feet and sniffling noses. Daphne swallowed an unexpected lump in her throat, remembering those contrary little devils, bawling and screeching the night away when her Ma and Dad were down the pub, until he'd gone off and was never heard of again. She didn't really miss any of them. Well, not often.

What she did miss more and more, though she wasn't going to tell a living soul, was her Ma. Only Daphne herself knew how bruised and bewildered she was that her

Ma never wrote to her now, except to send her a miserable little note from time to time, saying she hoped Daphne was being a good girl for the lady who was looking after her, while Daphne dutifully wrote a letter home once a month.

She had already written an extra one, telling her Ma about the birthday party. Her stiff-necked pride wouldn't let her beg her Ma to come to Cornwall for it, and anyway, she knew her Ma was far too busy working in her munitions factory to bother coming all this way for an afternoon. Or far too busy making eyes at the Yanks... but Daphne didn't want to think about that.

By the time her birthday arrived, a small group of Truro mothers and foster mothers had brought their daughters to New World, most of them curious to see this grand house, and confident that Mrs Pengelly wouldn't let things get too riotous with the unruly Daphne and her evacuee friends.

'Mrs Pen's made me a cake,' Daphne announced, the minute anyone arrived. 'You can all 'ave a piece, as long as there's enough left to keep a piece fer me Ma.'

'It'll go rotten by then,' Butch sniggered, annoyed at having been made to attend the party, when he'd far rather be up on the moors or messing about with the clay at the pottery.

'Shut up, fat-arse,' Daphne hissed, at which several Truro Mamas glanced at one another, wondering how the elegant Mrs Pengelly was going to handle this.

'We're going to play some games before tea,' Skye announced, refusing to rise to Daphne's bait. For days now, the child had been verging on the edge of fury, ready to fly at anyone who came within earshot, and Skye prayed that the day would pass without incident.

One of her little friends had been unable to come at the last minute. Their family had received one of the dreaded yellow telegrams, and the mother had telephoned, choked with tears, to say that their soldier son was missing in action, and that little Lena was too upset to come to a party.

'She's a cry-baby, but she'll soon be bragging about 'er bruvver being a hero, 'specially if 'e's dead,' Daphne had snorted, at which point Skye had felt ready to throttle her.

'We're going to play Hunt the Thimble now,' she went on determinedly after they had played several exhaustive games of Pass the Parcel, all of them squabbling and fighting to regain the package. 'As it's Daphne's birthday, she can have the first chance to hide it while we all go out into the garden for exactly five minutes.'

As they all trooped out, her cousin Lily spoke under cover of the excited children. 'How on earth do you put up with her, Skye? I always said you were a saint.'

'I'm anything but that,' she retorted, aware of her earlier murderous thoughts towards the little madam. 'I just try to be tolerant, that's all, and to remember that she's not in her own home.'

'She's been here for three years now. From all you've told me about her miserable home life, I imagine she gets far more care here than she did in London.'

'But I'm not her mother, and that's what counts,' Skye said, unwittingly echoing Daphne's own thoughts.

The screams from the children told them it was time to go indoors, and that the thimble had been hidden. It wasn't difficult to find. It was more difficult to find Daphne.

'Where the dickens is she?' Skye fumed. 'Tea's ready, and the star of the show is nowhere to be found.'

'We're having a new game,' Butch yelled. 'It's called Hunt stupid Daphne—'

'Butch, it is *not* a game,' Skye snapped, but she was talking to the air. The children scattered, racing about the place like lunatics, while their mothers stayed outside in the warm afternoon.

After another ten minutes of fruitless searching, and the threat of tears from some of the smaller children as it all began to get out of hand, she decided that tea was the best option. If Daphne wanted to be absent at her own birthday party, it was up to her.

They wouldn't cut the precious cake without her, though, having decorated it with some candles carefully stored from previous occasions which were practically burned away to nothing now. But blowing out the candles was for Daphne, and no one else.

Once the guests were all sitting down to the amazing sugar-free concoctions Cook had managed to create to please the small appetites, Skye slipped away from the dining room to make a last search for Daphne. It was ridiculous. She had wanted this party so much, and now it seemed that the ungrateful little tyke had just turned her back on it.

Skye thought she had searched everywhere by the time she heard the sound of muffled crying from the room that had held Albert Tremayne's paintings. It was no longer locked, but now that the paintings had gone, it remained empty and unused.

Skye turned the handle and saw the small huddled figure sitting by the window. Her Sunday best dress that she had put on especially for the day was crumpled and creased by now.

'Daphne, what are you doing here?' she said softly. 'Don't you want to blow out the candles on your cake? Everyone's waiting for you—'

'Everyone ain't here. *She* couldn't be bovvered to come, could she? I *hate* her now, and I 'ope she never comes.'

'Who are you talking about?' Skye said in bewilderment.

She knelt down beside the girl, but resisted the urge to take her in her arms. The small body was too stiff and unwelcoming, the hurt in her eyes too intense. Skye knew at once that she wasn't the one who was wanted.

'Me Ma, o' course,' she lashed out. 'I wrote and told 'er about it, and even if I hadn't, she shoulda known it was me birfday, shouldn't she? But she couldn't even be bovvered to send me a letter or nuffin'. She don't want me no more, so I shan't want 'er no more.'

'Oh, Daphne, of course your mother wants you,' Skye said. 'But you know it's not always easy in wartime to do the things we want. She may not even have got your letter—'

'In case she's dead, you mean?' Daphne said viciously.

'No, I don't. Letters can go astray these days, and there's probably one in the post for you right now. I'm sure she would have wanted to be here if she could, because being ten years old is an important milestone. It's almost being grown-up, so dry your eyes and come downstairs and let's show them all what a young lady you're becoming.'

Her response was a series of sniffles, then she finally shrugged and stood up, brushing down her crumpled skirt.

'Might as well, I s'pose,' she said grudgingly.

'And we'll be sure to keep that piece of cake for your mother, won't we?' Skye went on, wanting her to agree.

'If yer like. She won't come, though.'

Skye knew that. It hadn't occurred to her to write to Mrs Hollis to suggest it. The distance between London and Cornwall was too great, and it was obvious that the family was a poor one. Some of the evacuees had visits from relatives, but in the end it usually unsettled them and caused more tears when they had to leave them behind again. In her opinion, such visits were best never made. But the children wouldn't see it that way.

'By the way, Mrs Pen,' she heard Daphne say in a small voice as they left the room. 'I fergot something.'

'What's that?'

'I fergot ter say thanks fer me lovely party,' Daphne said in a rush, at which Skye had to turn away and walk ahead of her down the stairs, her eyes smarting.

–

At the beginning of September the woman in the short, home-made swagger coat fashioned from an old grey blanket toiled the last half-mile to New World, and paused to catch her breath.

The train from Paddington was crowded with servicemen, but the crush was no problem to someone who had lived cheek by jowl with neighbours in a sweaty London Underground shelter all through the Blitz. Someone who enjoyed a saucy joke or two and had a store of her own to tell, despite some of the disapproving looks she got. It all helped to make the long journey pass quicker, and once out of the train station, she had caught the bus out of Truro as far as it went.

Now she took in the sight of the lovely old stone house set near the cliffs. The endless, unfamiliar expanse of sea was enough to make her light-headed too, and she let out her usual expletive as if to assure herself that it was real.

'Bleedin' 'ell, duck, you never let on that it was as grand as this, did yer!'

At the sound of the voice, but not the actual words, Skye looked up from her garden, where the flowerbeds had long been taken over by vegetables now, and leaned on her hoe.

'Are you lost? I'm afraid we're a bit isolated here.'

The woman grimaced, shifting her chewing-gum from one side of her mouth to the other. 'Well, I ain't too sure this is the place I'm lookin' for after all, 'spite of what the bus conductor said.'

Skye felt her heart begin to pound. The woman didn't look like Daphne, except for the sharply pointed and determined chin. But there was something in the voice, and the quick way of speaking, so different from the Cornish drawl, that she knew by now could only belong to one place.

'Are you from London?'

''Ow d'yer guess?' the woman said, her voice faintly mocking. 'I've come looking fer me kid, see, and I know she's livin' around 'ere somewhere—'

The next moment something like a small whirlwind flew past Skye and into the woman's arms, and what had been two separate figures suddenly became one huge blur of grey swagger and clinging arms as the coat enveloped them both.

–

'I swear that it was symbolic, the way that coat just folded them both inside it,' Skye told Nick, when Daphne and her mother had gone off together for a walk down by the sea. 'It was as if nothing could separate them again. It was almost – well, beautiful.'

'And you're having a hard job not to get emotional about it, aren't you, darling?' he said. 'Don't get carried away by the moment or the woman's sudden appearance. She hasn't bothered much before, so what do you think she wants?'

'She wants Daphne, of course.'

Now that she had said the words, Skye knew it had been inevitable. From the moment she had seen the handsome woman in the shabby grey coat, and the glorious happiness Daphne couldn't hide as they hugged one another, she had known why Mrs Hollis was here. What she didn't know was what she was going to do about it.

Anticipating her thoughts, Nick spoke firmly.

'You can't keep her, Skye. If her mother wants to take her back, there's not a thing you can do about it. You know that. You've always known it. It happened with the other two children, didn't it? None of them belong to us.'

'But what kind of a life will she have in London?' Skye said passionately. 'They say the danger is past for now, but who knows what Hitler's got up his sleeve for the future? The war's not over yet, and I thought at least we'd have them here for the duration – and don't you dare suggest we take on any more, because I just can't bear all this coming and going.'

'For heaven's sake, Skye, get a grip on yourself. Daphne's been away from home for three and a half years, and her mother will have been missing her. Don't you think she deserves some consideration?'

Privately, Skye thought that if Mrs Hollis had been missing Daphne all this time then her almost total lack of communication was a strange way of showing it. If Daphne had been *her* child, evacuated to a different part of the country to live with strangers, she would have moved heaven and earth to keep in touch... but Daphne wasn't her child.

'I know you're right, Nick, so let's wait and see what they have to say when they get back from their walk.'

'Maybe this is just a visit, anyway,' Butch offered, having learned all about it by the time the Hollis pair returned to the house in time for a late afternoon tea.

The minute Skye saw Daphne's shining eyes, she knew it wasn't just a visit. Daphne had a huge capacity for grasping any opportunity, and as the words tumbled out of her eager lips, they all discovered that a great opportunity was coming the Hollises' way.

'Me Ma's come to take me 'ome, Mrs Pen, and now that she's heard that me Dad's passed on – Gawd bless 'im,' she added with false piety, 'she's going to marry 'er Yank, and we're all gonna live in America after the war! What d'yer fink of *that* then, Butch Butcher!'

Butch gaped at her, unable to say anything at all, and struck dumb by the fact that Daphne was hugging and kissing this stranger and behaving more like a normal person than he'd ever seen her. But going to live in America was something he just couldn't comprehend.

'Is this true, Mrs Hollis?' Skye said, aware that it wasn't her place to question or criticise or doubt, but feeling a mixture of all of those things at Daphne's outburst.

'Oh, it's quite true, Missis. Me and my feller have decided to tie the knot as soon as possible now – and we'll be shippin' out the minute the war's over,' she added grandly. 'I'll be one o' them GI brides, and me and Daphne will be nicely set up wiv my Gary.'

'Well, that's – wonderful,' Skye said. 'So when will you be wanting Daphne to join you? You're not thinking of taking her back to London yet, are you?'

'Course I am. That's what I've come 'ere for. If yer've got room to put me up fer the night, we'll be going back to the smoke tomorrer.'

Daphne squealed with joy. 'Course we can put yer up, Ma. This is a *yooge* house, and yer can sleep wiv me, just like we used to. She can, can't she, Mrs Pen?'

'Of course,' Skye said mechanically, feeling as if these two were taking over the entire household by the force of their personalities and determination.

Her brain seemed reluctant to function properly. But weren't there formalities to go through? Anyone relinquishing an evacuee had to go through procedures. There was the billeting committee to be informed, and the school... evacuees didn't just disappear on a whim whenever their parents summoned them back home...

Even as she thought it Skye knew that was exactly what did happen. It had happened to the little Lunn children, and now it was happening to Daphne.

But it mustn't happen to Butch, thought Skye, seeing his apprehensive face. Butch had no one in the world but themselves now, and no authority on earth was going to drag him away from the place he loved as much as any of her family.

She made a silent vow to that effect while they were all listening to the excited babblings of the Hollis mother and child, and she decided to ask Nick to find out about putting an adoption order in motion as soon as possible.

It was a thought to keep her sane during the hours in which the speed of Daphne's proposed new station in life took precedence over everything else. By the time they had all had breakfast the next morning, Skye was heartily sick of hearing about Edna Hollis's Yank, who was winning the war singlehandedly, by all accounts, and of Daphne's predictable boasting that she'd soon be meeting all the movie stars.

But all the same, when she and Nick drove them to Truro railway station, she felt a heart-tugging such as she had never expected when Daphne suddenly threw her arms around her neck, and whispered in her ear in a strangled voice.

'I do love yer, Mrs Pen. It's just that me Ma needs me back, see? We're gonna be a real fam'ly again.'

'I love you too, Daphne,' Skye said, choked. 'You just remember to write to me, and I promise to write back.'

'I will. And when I get to 'ollywood, I'll write and tell yer all about it.'

Then the train was ready to crawl away, and they waved them off until they could see no more for the smoke and steam, and the sparks that stung the eyes and tightened the throat.

'Come on, love,' Nick said roughly, understanding more than she knew. 'We'll waste a bit more of our precious petrol and make a visit to the pottery and the clayworks. Let's take a look at our new acquisition. And don't forget, when all else fails, we've still got each other.'

'And Butch,' she reminded him huskily.

'And Butch,' he agreed with a grin.

–

By the end of the year Skye had recovered from the shock of having Daphne wrenched from her control so abruptly, but she still missed her badly. Another Christmas was only weeks away, and Daphne had assuredly made the most of the previous ones with her raucous behaviour. She had livened up the house, and it was emptier without her. Butch was never the liveliest of companions, fond though Skye was of him.

She found herself aching for Christmases past, and there were times when she wondered fearfully if it was a sign of age that made her wallow in nostalgia far more than was good for her. At other times she told herself severely not to be so stupid, and that it was simply because she was giving more and more time now to her history of the clayworks and her family involvement with it.

How could she help being nostalgic? She was forced to remember all those times past, whether they belonged personally to her or to all those who had gone before. But it was a task of love as well as duty, and now that the house was empty all day long, she threw herself into researching and writing the Killigrew Clay booklets.

Two weeks before Christmas came some news that filled her with very mixed feelings. There was guilt, because no one should rejoice in someone else's misfortune. But there was also an overwhelming elation and thankfulness, because Celia was coming home.

'I know I shouldn't be this happy,' she said to Nick, almost shaking with the delirium of it. 'I know this Captain Moon's letter advises us to treat her with extreme care, because it was such an unexpected illness, but she'll recover here, you'll see. Cornwall has always been our place of refuge and strength. It's our personal heaven, and I don't care if it's blasphemous to say so. In fact, I'd go as far as to say that what the Lord has recently taken away – meaning Daphne – he's giving us back in full measure, by sending Celia back to us. It was obviously meant to be.'

She was almost dizzy with joy and the sense of destiny, and when Nick's face came back into her focus, she became aware that he was less than pleased at her outburst.

'Stop it, Skye,' he snapped. 'You're getting this all out of proportion, and I won't have all this nonsense. Celia's coming home to recuperate, but once she's better she'll be eager to go back to her job. And she won't thank you for implying that her enforced homecoming was fate compensating us for sending Daphne Hollis home!'

'Well, I think you're wrong. This time, Mr Smarty Pants know-all lawyer, I know I'm right.'

Chapter Eleven

Celia didn't feel ill. She didn't feel anything but relief that the decision had been made for her. She hadn't even been aware that anything was amiss until the night she and Moonie had been working late and she had suddenly burst into tears of rage and frustration as all the letters and figures on the code she was working on seemed to dazzle in front of her eyes in a crazy ant-like war dance. And when she had begun screaming and trying to fight them off, it became obvious to Captain Moon that something was seriously wrong.

She didn't remember anything after that until she had woken up in a hospital bed and told she had been sedated for two days, and that she was suffering from severe exhaustion that threatened her physical and mental state.

'You mean I've had a nervous breakdown,' she had stated to the military doctor, staring him in the eyes and daring him to deny the stigma attached to the words.

'You're suffering from nervous exhaustion, Lieutenant Pengelly,' he prevaricated, making her sigh with impatience.

Why couldn't they call a spade a spade and be done with it? They were only words, for God's sake. It was her body and her brain was being sent into turmoil, and whatever label they put on it didn't alter her sense of panic and anxiety and disorientation.

But she could still argue with the best of them when it came to dismissing incompetents.

'How can I be suffering from nervous exhaustion?' she had said perversely. 'I'm not fighting in the trenches or dropping bombs on enemy territory. I'm doing a desk job, that's all.'

'But we both know it's a job that requires immense concentration and expertise,' he said, giving her all the status she deserved. 'My dear young lady, we all have our limitations, and when one has personal worries as well as everything else required of us these days, we can all reach the end of those limitations. That's when the mind as well as the body closes down and demands that we take a rest.'

God, he was good, Celia had thought. Patronisingly good, of course, but good nonetheless. How much he knew of her "personal worries" she didn't know, but if Moonie hadn't confided all her fears for Stefan, she had probably blabbed it all herself before being doped up to the eyeballs.

Now she was being sent home, and no doubt all the family was feeling sorry for her, and were ready to tiptoe around her the way they had done around Sebby for the first few days after his arrival. But contrary to what everyone might expect, she was guiltily glad to be out of a job she hadn't volunteered for in the first place – and she was never going back.

She sobered at the thought. She would have to do something else, of course. She was able-bodied, even if she'd been half out of her mind for a while, and she was still only twenty-four years old. Her country still needed her, she thought cynically.

But one thing she wasn't going to be was a nurse. She'd seen enough of that in the short while she'd been in the military hospital. She admired them all enormously, but she couldn't stomach some of the things they had to do. She couldn't go back to being a tram conductress either. Her father would hate that, and stuffed shirt though he might be in many respects, she wouldn't put him through that indignity again.

As the train took her homewards, away from the cities and through the green fields that could still look amazingly peaceful and so very pastoral, even in the midst of a war, she remembered how she and Wenna and Olly had relished visits to their Aunt Em's farm in Wadebridge all those years ago. It had been such fun in those far-off, halcyon days, following country pursuits; feeding the chickens, rounding up the cows for milking, and pulling up carrots and turnips to make Aunt Em's famous stews.

She remembered it all, the sights and sounds and smells, with a warmth of affection for her aunt that she had all but forgotten. And long before the train arrived in Truro, Celia knew what she intended to do with the remainder of her war.

–

'You're going to join the Women's Land Army?' Lily asked Celia after a few weeks, when she had settled into an uneasy routine of vainly trying to make everyone see that she wasn't about to fall apart, and was dutifully making the round of family visits. 'Good for you. What does your mother say about it?'

'I think she understands. I have to have some training first, but I shall ask to be posted in this area – on the grounds that I'm still a bit feeble-minded and need to be near home,' she added airily, to take the sting out of it.

'Dad's not too keen on the idea,' she added, 'but that's to be expected. I knew you'd be sensible about it, though, Lily.'

'Oh, that's me, darling. Always the sensible one, and leaving the glamour to somebody else!'

Celia looked at her sharply. 'What's that supposed to mean? You never used to bother about such nonsense.'

'About my looks, you mean? I don't bother now, but perhaps I should have thought about it a bit more.'

With one look at her downcast face, everything clicked into place in an instant. Celia drew in her breath.

'You're not going to tell me you think David's straying, are you? I can't believe that—'

'Why not? What makes him so different from other men? He always had a passion for your mother, but I knew all about that, and it meant nothing. It was never going to upset our applecart. Now, well, perhaps my plainness does mean something... God forgive me, but I never meant to unload such things on you, Celia, in your delicate state of health.'

'You're not plain – and I was never delicate, any more than you were. We're the tough Tremaynes, remember?'

Lily's mouth twisted. 'So they say, but neither of us were born Tremaynes, were we? We got diluted some-where along the way.'

Celia brushed aside her weak attempt at humour. 'The name doesn't matter. We believe in self-preservation. We're survivors. Look at Sebby – look at *me*! And I can't believe you're not going to fight for David. You *have* confronted him with whatever it is you suspect, haven't you?'

'Not yet.'

'Why the hell not?' Celia sucked in her breath, realising how belligerent she was becoming. 'Oh Lord, I'm sorry, Lily. I shouldn't speak to you like this. You're my elder, and I've got no right.'

'Never mind about calling me your elder,' Lily said, more sparkily. 'I'm not in my dotage yet, and you have every right to tell me what I should have been telling myself.'

'So why do you think there's something wrong?' Celia said carefully. 'Don't tell me if you don't want to, mind, but since you've got this far…'

'It's a relief to tell somebody. I'd tell your mother, but she was too full of you coming home to worry her. Oh, I don't know – perhaps I'm just seeing things that aren't there. He works late every night, or so he says, and when he comes home, he seems so distracted, and he's always too tired to—' she gave an embarrassed little laugh – 'well, I can't tell you *everything*, you being an unmarried girl, but you might guess what I mean.'

'Oh, Lily,' Celia said, ignoring her own blushes. 'Do you think Stefan and I never made love? Do you think I never long to have him in my arms again? I long for him and ache for him every single day. I miss him so much, and I don't know if I'll ever see him again—'

Without warning, the tears overflowed, and she was held tightly in Lily's arms. The comforter badly needed comforting, she thought ashamedly, although by now she wasn't sure who was supposed to be comforting who.

'Forget about me,' Lily said eventually. 'Have you thought about going to see Ethan, to make contact with that prisoner of war working on his farm who he thought might be Stefan's relative? I know I thought it was a bad idea at the time, but now I'm not so sure.'

Celia shook her head. 'I wrote to him about it, but the Germans have been moved to a different camp, and Ethan didn't know where. He couldn't tell me anything more, anyway, so that idea was a no-nstarter, like every other one.'

Their conversation dried up, as each brooded on her own troubles, and by the time Celia left she could see how Lily's shoulders were drooping again. On an impulse she went straight to David Kingsley's office and demanded to see him.

'Celia, my love, it's good to see you starting to look more like your old self,' he began with a smile. It quickly faded at her reply.

'I doubt that you'll think so when I tell you why I've come,' she snapped, never one to mince her words. 'What the hell are you playing at, David?'

—

It was odd, but championing someone else's cause put her own miseries in the background for a while, and even went a little way to putting it all in perspective. David had been so uncharacteristically abject when she told him in no uncertain terms that he was in danger of ruining a good woman's life that she could almost smile about it later.

The shock of realising that Lily had been aware of his shortcomings, and that now Celia knew all about them too, had blanched his good-looking face and made him stutter like a schoolboy caught stealing apples.

'My God, Celia, Lily has no grounds for suspecting me of philandering. It's pressure of work that keeps me here—'

'Oh, not that old thing! I've heard plenty of excuses, and that one doesn't wash any more.'

'Really? And what gives a young woman like you the right to censure me, or even question me?'

'*Love* gives me the right, David. Love and family loyalty. And if you don't know what I'm talking about, then you're denser than you look – and you look pretty dense right now, if I may say so.'

He gave a rueful grin. 'You always did have a knack for words, didn't you? You're in the wrong business, Celia. You should come and work for me.'

'No thanks. And don't change the subject. Are you honestly telling me Lily has nothing to worry about except being neglected?'

'Cross my heart and may God strike me down dead this minute if I'm lying to you.'

Celia relaxed as she saw his elaborate attempt to reassure her, but she couldn't dispute his sincerity.

'In my experience, God rarely does what you ask him to on the spur of the moment,' she said dryly. 'But I'll believe you, partly because I'm fond of you, and partly because I badly want to on Lily's account. Don't let her down, David.'

'I won't. I promise. And if I do seem secretive and distracted at times, it's in a professional context, not personal. My whole working life is concerned with finding out information from my various sources, and I'm constantly having to suppress anything of any importance in the interests of government security. You of all people must know there's something big in the wind, and it's enough to play on any newspaperman's nerves.'

Celia flinched. She knew all about living on her nerves by now, but she also knew what David was getting at. For months now, the planned invasion to liberate France had been an open secret. The only uncertainty was when. Every reporter would want to be the first to know.

She looked at him squarely. 'I can't tell you anything, and I wouldn't if I could. That part of my life is over.'

Without warning, she began to feel stifled. The varying smells of a newspaper office might be full of nostalgia to her mother, but to Celia they were nauseous, and reminded her too vividly of the small decoding office where she and Moonie had worked for so many long hours. She stood up abruptly.

'You won't forget everything I've said, will you, David? Lily needs you. But don't tell her I came here today.'

'It's our secret.'

'And I suggest you explain things to her more openly. Don't keep all your worries to yourself. She has a right to share them.'

She knew she shouldn't be talking to him like a Dutch uncle. He was fifty-six years old, and showing it. But she had never been slow in speaking her mind – and the next day, a telephone call from Lily told her she had been right to do so.

'I just want to say that everything's all right again. I challenged him, Celia, and now I know how wrong I was. Thanks for making me bring it all out into the open, darling.'

'I'm glad,' Celia said cautiously, knowing her mother was within earshot. 'I'll see you again soon, Lily.'

'What was that all about?' Skye asked, when she had replaced the receiver.

'Oh, Lily was a bit worried that Frederick had a temperature, but he seems to be all right now,' she invented. Wild horses wouldn't make her reveal that she had gone to David and told him what was what.

'I think I'll go up to the pottery and see how things are, Mom,' she said next. 'For some reason I can't seem to stay indoors for long.'

'Do you want company?'

'Not unless you're desperate to come. Do you mind?'

'Not at all. I'm planning to sort out the old Christmas decorations today, so I'll see you later, honey.'

Skye watched her daughter leave, her own eyes troubled. Celia was still suffering, no matter how bright a face she put on it. But although Skye ached to get back the old closeness they had once shared, she knew it wouldn't come yet. Celia needed time alone, and the last thing she needed was to be fussed over. It had never been her style.

–

Celia relished the vastness of the open moors and the weird sense of being alone in the world, or even on some other planet, as she contemplated the wildness of the scrubland and the soaring sky-tips ahead of her. *Their* sky-tips, she found herself thinking with an odd sense of possessiveness, now that her mother had managed to acquire the land back where it rightfully belonged. Killigrew Clay it had always been and would always be.

She found herself twisting the pearl and garnet ring on the third finger of her left hand that Stefan had given her. Businesslike, she had worn it on a chain around her neck all these months, but since her bout in hospital she had experienced the need to feel its cold unfamiliarity against her finger, as if to reassure her that he was still alive, still somewhere in the world. To remind her that some day they would be together and able to live the normal life of two people in love.

Her throat closed painfully, knowing that even when this war was over, in many eyes they would still be regarded as old enemies for some time. It had happened in her mother's war, and who was to say it would be any different in this one?

She gazed unseeingly ahead for some minutes, forcing herself to remember that she and Stefan had already made tentative plans. They would live in Switzerland, the beautiful country where they had first met, fallen in love, and been everything that a man and woman could be to one another. They would start their own hotel business and begin their own proverbial happy-ever-after, so beloved of story books…

A sob caught in her throat as the plaintive sound of a seagull far from the coast echoed the futility of such hopes and dreams. Why should they be the lucky ones, when so many others had lost sweethearts and lovers?

She was still some distance from the pottery when she saw the small, ungainly figure hobbling towards her. Old Helza frequently terrified walkers on the moors with her unexpected appearance, as if she metamorphosed out of nowhere whenever she chose. But she no longer terrified Celia. As she stood very still, it was as if she had been waiting for the old crone, and they both recognised the fact in an instant.

'So what is it you want of me, girlie?' Helza cackled, her wizened old head on one side as usual. 'Is it a potion perhaps, to settle the raging in that pretty head o' yourn?'

'My head is fine, and there's nothing I want from you,' Celia retorted. 'Unless you're able to see in your crystal ball – or whatever evil instrument of witchcraft you use – just where my fiancé is right now.'

Helza's button-like eyes flashed. 'Mebbe I can, and mebbe I won't. And what makes 'ee think all witchcraft be evil, Miss Snot-face? 'Tis the oldest religion in the world—'

Celia heard nothing beyond her first sentence. 'What do you mean, maybe you can?'

The cackling laugh rang out again. 'Got your attention now, eh? Well, I don't give no help to non-believers, so you'll just have to go on wond'ring about your man.'

'I *do* believe,' Celia said desperately. 'My great-grandmother Morwen Tremayne and her friend Celia – the one they named me after – *they* believed, and they consulted your sister or mother, or whoever she was.'

She began to feel the sweat trickle over her skin as the old crone stared at her. She was furious for letting herself be mesmerised by the witchwoman, but she couldn't seem to help herself. If Helza could truly give her some inkling about Stefan's whereabouts, she would go to any lengths to find out. In that instant, she knew she was just as vulnerable as that earlier Celia had been, nearly a century ago.

'Show me your palm,' Helza said abruptly.

Celia breathed a sigh of relief, even while she hated the fact of her own hand being grasped by Helza's claw-like one. But it was preferable to being invited into the hovel with all its weird potions and smells. With her panicky sense of being stifled anywhere indoors right now, Celia knew she couldn't have stood it for more than a moment.

The old woman studied the lines and contours on Celia's palm, tracing them with her cracked nail and making her squirm. She longed to snatch her hand away and end this farcical confrontation. But she couldn't. She was as transfixed as if their two hands were gummed together.

'I can't tell 'ee any more than 'ee already know,' Helza said at last, and the spell was broken as Celia furiously rubbed her palm against her skirt.

'Well, so much for your magical powers,' she snapped.

She was disorientated with disappointment. But had she really expected this madwoman to say she had seen a vision of Stefan in some castle stronghold deep in the German countryside, where he was being incarcerated from indulging in any suspected subversive activities…?

Her head spun wildly at the thought, and she realised that Helza was already hobbling away from her.

'Wait,' she called weakly.

Helza turned and called back, her thin voice carrying on the breeze. 'You don't need me to tell 'ee what your own senses know, missie. There's only one man in your life, and your heart line is strong and unbroken. Bide your time, and you'll be together again.'

She was gone, while Celia was still asking herself whether she had in fact seen a vision of the place where Stefan was. Or had it all been a hideous fantasy because she wanted so much to believe that, because of his status in the community and what she knew would have been his dignified refusal to co-operate with the Nazis, he had not been severely punished?

However feeble the hope, she told herself that she *had* to believe it or she would end up completely mad. The alternative was to think that it was her own Cornish feyness providing what she so longed to know.

She shivered, not sure she wanted to believe that either. But whatever the reason for the thought or the vision or whatever it had been, she walked on with an ever-quickening step.

Seb saw her coming. He was taking a break outside, and he greeted her with a scowl on his handsome face.

'Sorry, cuz, you've caught me at a bad moment. It's no joke to find out that a young whipper-snapper is better at doing your job that you are.'

Despite her own tormented feelings, Celia couldn't resist a small smile at the indignity in his voice.

'If you mean Butch, why shouldn't he be good at it? He's had enough tuition from experts, hasn't he? You and Adam should be proud that he's such a good apprentice.'

'And when did you become such a diplomat? You're wasted down here in the sticks, Celia.'

She didn't miss the sharpness of his reply. It matched the way she used to be, what seemed like a hundred years ago. Now, she simply didn't have the energy to be sharp – and even as she thought it, she knew it was a terrible way to feel for someone of her age. It was the way old women thought, and she mentally and physically straightened her back.

'This is where I belong – for now, anyway,' she amended. An image had flashed into her mind at that moment of where she dearly wanted to be, and it wasn't here.

It wasn't anywhere remotely near here. It was among the foothills of mountains where sweet-scented wild flowers grew in profusion, and where the air was as clear as wine…

'Hey, what's wrong?' Seb said at once, seeing how her face suddenly crumpled. 'This isn't like you at all. You've always been the strongest one among us.'

'Have I?' she said, her eyes stinging. 'Well, perhaps I don't want to be strong. Perhaps I just want somebody to lean on, the way people have always leaned on me—'

Without warning, she was in his arms and sobbing on his shoulder. He had always felt affection for her, and she knew that, but thankfully she recognised that there was nothing in the least sexual in the embrace. There was just sweet, much-needed comfort. Eventually she drew away from him.

'Thanks,' she said, her voice tight. 'We two old crocks should stick together, shouldn't we?'

'Old crocks?' he said, the old aggression back. 'Since when did a Tremayne ever become an old crock? My father resisted that until the end, and so will I – and so will you.'

'But I'm not a Tremayne, am I?' Celia said, ready to argue. 'There's not many left with the name now.'

'Tell that to the stars,' he retorted. 'Once it's in your blood, you never lose it. Nor the name of Killigrew, either. Your mother's plans are going to see to that, aren't they? She's a woman after old Morwen Tremayne's heart, and so are you. Don't let anybody ever tell you different.'

'My God, Seb, you're the one who's wasted here,' she said in honest amazement, never having heard him be quite so passionate about their heritage.

She didn't dare let herself get emotional about the fact that he had mentioned the stars. She had to keep the faith. She only had to look into the sky at night and see *their* star to know that the love she and Stefan shared was still bright, still strong and everlasting.

She swallowed. 'Hadn't you better get back to work? I've come up here to see how things are going, not to have a pep talk – but I thank you for it all the same, Sebby.'

She hugged his arm to take the sting out of her words. He was her cousin and her friend, and she needed him now.

'Come and see how young Butch is getting on, then,' he said roughly. 'He's our rising star now.'

–

Christmas 1943 was a frugal affair as far as normal fare went, but like people everywhere, the Pengellys and their family were determined to make the most of it. As always, Skye and Nick were determined to host the day for as many of the family as could turn up. Wenna was out of the country now, and 'somewhere in Europe', according to the sparse letters she was able to send.

But, amazingly and without warning, Olly arrived home on Christmas Eve, amid tears and laughter from his mother and sister, and a manly hug from his father.

'Did Wenna get leave?' he asked, once the first excitement of reunion had tempered a little.

'No,' Skye said, feeling the familiar tug at her heart. 'It would have been so marvellous if we could all have been together again.'

'Not only for us, Mother,' Olly said. 'I've brought somebody with me for the holidays. I hope it's all right.'

'Of course it is. You know that.'

'Have you got a lady friend at last, Olly?' teased Nick.

'It's not a lady – and he's more interested in Wenna than me, Dad. He's gone to see Aunt Betsy right now, but I said I'd go and fetch him later. It's Wenna's Canadian. We ran into one another a few weeks ago and discovered we both had a seventy-two hour pass, so I invited him here. I hope that's all right.'

'Wenna's Canadian?' Celia said quickly.

'Group Captain Harry Mack. She must have mentioned him to you. He was recuperating at Aunt Betsy's when she came down here some time ago, and he was besotted with her. They've been writing to one another for some time, I gather.'

Celia stared. Her parents seemed to know all about this affair, while she had allowed herself to become so insular that she hadn't even been aware that Wenna had had a beau after Austin had been killed in action.

She knew she *should* remember it, but sometimes her memory was so hazy that she could recall nothing from before the nervous breakdown. It was frightening, and something she didn't care to mention to anyone.

But she did recall that Wenna had said she was never going to lose her heart to anyone again after the trauma of Austin's and Fanny Rosenbloom's deaths. So it would be interesting to meet this Group Captain Harry Mack and see how far the association had gone.

Even as she thought it, she knew how much she had changed too. In the past she would have known a sibling rivalry for Wenna's new man, while now she only felt a protective need to look him over, to ensure that he wasn't taking advantage of Wenna's vulnerability. She had changed, as they all had. War did that, tearing people apart, changing lives, making some of them strong and some of them fall to pieces...

'Are you all right, Celia?' Olly said now. 'You can come with me to collect Harry, if you like. He asked me to call him Harry while we're on leave,' he added, 'even though his rank is much higher than mine.'

Celia smiled at his obvious pride in having become an associate of this man. Olly had grown so much in stature and maturity, she thought with a rush of affection. He was no longer her little brother. He was a man.

'Yes, I'd like to come with you. Mom knows I don't like being indoors for too long, and in the new year I'll be out in the fields all day long, I dare say.'

'Good God, when Mother told me you were going to be a Land Girl, I didn't believe it. You haven't changed your mind about mucking out the cows and dishing out pigswill then?'

Skye forestalled her with a laugh. 'When did you know your sister change her mind about anything she had set her heart on, Olly? She's a true—'

'If you're about to say I'm a true Tremayne, I'd rather you didn't,' Celia cut in swiftly. 'I've heard it so often, I sometimes begin to wonder just who I really am.'

'It's meant as a great compliment, darling,' her father told her. 'Anyone who ever knew old Morwen Tremayne – and your own grandmother – knows that.'

'I know it too,' Celia muttered. 'I just want to be myself, that's all. I'm nobody's reincarnation, and I don't want to be. I'm sorry if that offends anybody.'

'It doesn't, honey,' Skye said softly. 'Because I have so often thought the very same thing.'

-

'Mom's remark didn't help. It just makes me feel even more that we're all somehow one and the same person,' Celia said to Olly a while later, when they were bumping along the lanes towards Truro in their father's car to collect Harry Mack. 'It's spooky, isn't it?'

'Only if you let it be,' Olly said. 'This isn't like you, Celia. I know you were unwell some time ago—'

'I had a nervous breakdown, Olly,' she said brutally. 'I'm not afraid to say the words, and I wish other people wouldn't hedge around them either. Thank God for Lily and David, who don't patronise me by pretending it was something as simple as a summer cold.'

'All right, so you're over it now, and you don't want to hang on to it like a comfort blanket. That's good. Forget it, and live for the moment. It's all we've got, anyway.'

His accurate summary took her by surprise. 'You're such a philosopher all of a sudden, aren't you?'

'Takes one to know one,' he said with a grin. 'But you know I'm right. The past is behind us and tomorrow's still an unknown quantity. So we've just got to dig in our heels and make the most of today.'

She was touched by this new, mature Oliver. He was all of twenty years old now, but he had the wisdom of Solomon compared with the muddle in her own mind lately.

And yes, he was right. She couldn't reach Stefan now, except in her heart, and they could only live each day as it came, until they knew what the future might hold.

'I love you, Olly,' she said, the words leaving her lips before she could stop them.

Immediately, she gave a rough laugh to hide her embarrassment. 'Oh Lord, just forget I said that! What kind of a soppy, halfwit sister tells her strapping brother that she loves him, for God's sake?' He squeezed her hand for a second until he put his own back on the steering wheel again.

'The best, that's all. And you're no halfwit. For the record, I love you too, but if you don't want me to run this damn vehicle over a cliff, you'd better change the subject or you'll have us both blubbering. So has anybody heard from the ghastly Daphne child yet?'

'We had a home-made Christmas card,' Celia said, glad that he had so cleverly turned the conversation. 'She's full of importance now that she's going to live in America when her mother marries her GI.'

'God help America then. If they're not careful, it will be Daphne for President in a few years' time,' Olly said solemnly, at which they were both convulsed.

–

'We've met before,' Group Captain Harry Mack said, shaking Celia's hand. 'Don't you remember?'

The instant she saw him, she remembered the pub in Norwich, and the motley crowd of servicemen singing and laughing, and this handsome Canadian plying her and Moonie with the unexpected luxury of wine. And Harry Mack mistaking her, ever so briefly, for the girl he obviously adored, her sister Wenna.

'I do indeed,' she said. 'How nice to see you again.'

'I hear you've been ill. Are you better now?'

The easy manner with which he said it was as refreshing as a summer breeze to Celia. There was no guile about this man, and she responded instantly.

'Well enough to look forward to a change of occupation. I've just completed my training for the Women's Land Army.'

Harry whistled approvingly. 'Good for you. There's nothing like good country air for putting some healthy colour back into a person's cheeks. I should know.'

'Do you come from a country background then?'

'Canada's one huge backyard,' he said engagingly. 'I miss the wide open spaces at times, but I'm getting used to it here – and there are compensations, of course.'

'Though unfortunately she's not here for the holidays, old bean,' Olly put in, pushing his luck with the familiar RAF jargon, in Celia's opinion.

'But at least I can be with her family, and feel her presence in her home,' Harry said.

'Good Lord, my mother would say those words are worthy of a true Cornishman,' Celia said, caught by the simplicity of the statement.

'Well, thank you for the compliment, ma'am,' he said with genuine delight, but his teasing words told Celia it was a mark of how deeply he felt for Wenna. She only hoped her sister appreciated the fact.

Chapter Twelve

'My sister's working on a farm near Penzance,' Wenna reported to her friend, when the letter finally caught up with their ENSA unit in northern Italy.

'She must be mad,' Rita said baldly. 'All that muck and animal stink wouldn't be my cup of cocoa, I can tell you. You can keep the country as far as I'm concerned.'

'That's because you're a city girl.'

'*You* left it for the smoke, didn't you?'

'That's different. I had a career opportunity,' Wenna said. She realised how grand she sounded, and gave a half-smile. 'Oh well, all right, I suppose I did. It doesn't mean I don't love the country too, though.'

'What else does she say?' Rita asked lazily. She wasn't really interested, but anything was better than being confined to barracks now that their tour was over, and they were preparing to return to England.

'They had a lovely Christmas, and my brother had a friend staying at New World with him.'

'Not peculiar, is he?' Rita sniggered.

'No, he is not,' Wenna said crossly. 'As a matter of fact, it was Harry.'

'*Your* Harry?'

Wenna sighed. She had long since given up protesting to Rita that Group Captain Mack wasn't her Harry. Besides, by now, she was fairly certain that he was – or could be, if they ever got the chance to see one another again.

As yet, it was no more than a long-distance relationship, built mainly on correspondence, but the memory of his voice was strong in her head whenever she read his letters, and to Wenna, that had to mean something significant.

Already, she knew he was more than a friend, and, inevitably, the searing pain she had felt when Austin had been killed in action was fading from her mind, no matter how much she had tried to cling on to it.

'So?' Rita persisted. '*Was* it your Harry your brother took home to Cornwall for Christmas leave?'

'Yes, it was my Harry,' Wenna said softly. 'And I wish I'd been there as well to see everybody. My mother always makes a big thing of Christmas, and invites all the family. My stepfather's widowed brother is courting again too,' she added, 'so it looks as if we'll be having another wedding in the family sometime.'

That was another surprising bit of information from Celia, thought Wenna. Adam Pengelly had kept this very quiet – but then, he was a very quiet man, and rather a dull old stick in Wenna's opinion. His new lady friend was also widowed, and fifty-something like himself, according to Celia, and they were clearly looking for companionship rather than passion.

Wenna wondered fleetingly how fulfilled a marriage it would be… and without warning her thoughts turned to Harry Mack again, and the look in his eyes that had told her instantly that he desired her. Her heart began to beat considerably faster. The woman that Harry Mack married certainly wouldn't enter into a quiet, middle-aged marriage…

'Where's your brother stationed now, Pengo?' Rita was saying. 'Is he still in Wiltshire?'

Wenna had a job to drag her thoughts back from the erotic image of being held tightly in Harry Mack's arms and tasting his kisses on her lips, and was irritated with Rita for obliging her to let the image fade.

'I don't know. You'd hardly expect him to tell anybody, would you?' she snapped. 'He's with Bomber Command now, though, and Celia says he's dropped a few heavy hints that he might be involved in the invasion – if it ever happens. But now that he's come clean about getting into the air force under age, Olly's become a stickler for the rules. He's quite a character, my brother.'

She'd never truly thought about it before. But she realised she admired him tremendously for his tenacity in getting what he wanted. Olly always did, she thought.

Celia too, seemed more like her old self now, she thought thankfully. For a time, the nervous breakdown had been a worry for all of them. It was so unlike Celia, whom Wenna had always considered so much stronger than herself.

One of the other girls in the concert party popped her head around the barrack door as Rita went out.

'Pengelly, there was another letter for you. It must have been left on my bed by mistake, and I've only just got back from the ablutions. Sorry,' she said.

Wenna took it absently. Such things happened, and it was nothing to get het up about. And then her heart leapt as she recognised Harry's writing on the envelope, and in an instant she knew that whatever feelings she had for him, they were definitely far from platonic. She'd never really believed that old chestnut about absence making the heart grow fonder, but she was beginning to believe in it now. She opened the letter with shaking hands. It was two months since Christmas, but the letter had only just caught up with her.

"I couldn't believe we had missed one another," Harry Mack wrote. "It was so poignant, being there in your home, touching the things you used to touch, breathing in the atmosphere you knew so well, and imagining other times when you would have joined in singing the Christmas carols around the tree and raising your glass of hot punch for the toast to absent friends. You must know who I had in mind when your mother made that particular toast. I was so happy to be there, and yet so sad without you. It was like stumbling about in the dark and being unable to see the sun and be completely warmed again. You see what effect you have on me, my sweet girl? I dream of you, Wenna, and whenever I hear the words of a love song, I hear your voice in my head."

"Even when you're not beside me, I can still feel your presence, and I'm writing this letter slightly under the influence of too much English beer, otherwise I wouldn't be so free with my words. I shall post it without reading it again, or else I'm quite sure I'll never dare to tell you how much I love you and ache to see you again."

"Maybe someday when all this is over, I'll show you how vast and awe-inspiring the Canadian prairies are – but nothing could ever be as beautiful as you are to me."

Wenna pressed the letter to her mouth, her eyes stinging with tears. He was so sweet, so utterly and adorably open and sweet, and oh yes, she knew she was falling in love with him. She no longer fought against it. Every love song she sang, she sang for him. Every prayer she offered up was that he would come through this war safely. Every longing in her heart was that someday, someday...

She heard the door of the barrack room open and bang shut, and then came Rita's alarmed voice.

'Good God, Pengo, you look as if you've seen a ghost. Not bad news, is it?'

'No,' she said huskily. 'Not bad news at all.'

–

By the beginning of April, everyone knew that something big was in the wind. The invasion had to happen soon. By now thousands more American and Canadian troops had poured into Britain as General Eisenhower directed his final preparations for the long-awaited invasion and subsequent liberation of Europe from the Nazi stranglehold.

Every coastal area in Britain was banned to visitors as the dummy manoeuvres were conducted on and off shore, fooling the enemy as to where and when the actual assault would originate. Everything was being rehearsed, from airborne landings by parachute, to amphibious operations for landing guns and tanks and personnel. By the end of the month all foreign travel was banned, except for troop movements.

Oliver Pengelly was impatient for it all to begin, and, with the optimism of youth, he was euphoric with the feeling that he could conquer the world single-handed.

'Do you have a death wish or something, brainless?' one of his fellow erks commented. 'I'm not half so keen to fly over enemy territory as you seem to be. You should have been born a Yank with all that crazy enthusiasm.'

'Thanks, Tom,' Olly said with a laugh. 'I'll take that as a compliment. My mother's American, and she thanks you too.'

The other grimaced. 'Doesn't anything ever get you down, you bugger?' he said with wry good humour.

'Why should it? I'm doing the job I was meant to do, and once we've gone in to support the invasion forces, we'll be laughing. It'll all be over by Christmas.'

'And where have I heard that before?'

'Well, it can't go on for ever, can it?' Olly said reasonably. 'Though I intend to stick with this job permanently. Maybe I'll go into commercial flying or get some backing to start my own flying service—'

'Listen to the monied bastard!' Tom and his other cronies started jeering. 'None of that's for me, mate. The minute this is over, I'm back to my desk in the bank.'

'Good. I'll know where to come for a loan then, won't I?' Olly said crisply.

He hadn't really meant any of it seriously. He hadn't even thought about after the war. All he knew was that he wanted to keep on flying, to be as near to reaching the stars as it was possible for a man to be. And *that* little bit of poetic licence was something he wasn't going to share with these bastards, he thought cheerfully.

But it all had to end sometime, and when it did, there would be thousands like him, looking for something to do. Looking for something to replace the mixture of excitement and fear that was so intense that it was almost sexual. Something to replace the rush of adrenalin that came when their silver machine soared into the sky, with no more attachment to the earth they left behind; as free as birds and almost blinded by the welcoming sun.

Olly wasn't religious in the slightest, but he had to admit that when he was flying, he felt nearer to God – if there was a God – than at any other time in his life.

'Who's coming down to the NAAFI?' he said, before his thoughts began to get too serious. 'I'll stand anyone who beats me there to a pint, and the rest is on you buggers.'

He would miss the camaraderie too, he admitted to himself, as Tom slung his arm loosely around his shoulders and gave him a friendly punch in the solar plexus to wind him and slow him down before they all raced towards the canteen.

—

Skye missed Daphne Hollis more than she had expected to. She had been gone a long while now, but her presence had been so forceful that even now, Skye sometimes imagined she could hear her scathing remarks as she burst in from school, especially during her last few days.

'Bleedin' stupid lessons. Who cares about stupid old history, anyway?'

'You have to do your lessons, Daphne. It's important to know about what happened in the past—'

'Why is it? It don't matter to me. I'm prob'ly going to end up famous, anyway, like Wenna. I might even be a picture star, and I won't need to know about stupid old history when I'm making pots of dough, so there!'

Skye smiled, remembering, and wondered if Daphne's prophetically wild remarks had been due to the mystic influence of Cornwall. Whether they had or not, she was apparently going to live in America one day, and her young head would soon be filled with dreams of storming Hollywood.

Mentally, Skye wished her well, and admitted that if anyone could manipulate dreams to make them come true, it would probably be Daphne Hollis.

Her own dreams for the re-invented Killigrew Clay were going nowhere. Nor could they, Nick told her reasonably as they got ready for bed that evening. Not yet, anyway.

There was no sense in trying to build a flourishing new empire out of a dying industry, since there would be no tourists, curious to see how an old clayworks operated, for the foreseeable future. She knew she should be content that the pottery was still in business, with the clayworks still ticking over. It just didn't suit her productive and impatient mind to have to wait until Hitler was crushed before she could begin on her new venture, which was what it amounted to.

'You can still draw up some outline plans and sketches for the preliminary ideas, darling,' Nick told her. 'And the research for your booklets should give you a better idea of how the open-air museum should take shape.'

'Is that how you see it? An open-air museum?' she said, pausing in her undressing.

'Well, isn't it?'

'I suppose so. I hadn't thought of it in exactly those words, though. I like the sound of it, Nick. And you're right. There are things I can do, even if the reality of it all seems so very far away.'

He put his arms around her. 'My poor love. You always did want everything to happen at once, didn't you?'

Skye smiled ruefully. 'You think that at my age I should have learned more temperance, I suppose.'

His arms tightened around her. 'I do not. I don't want to change a single thing about you. Why do you think I fell in love with you in the first place if it wasn't for your quicksilver mind?'

She spoke teasingly. 'Oh, was that the reason? I thought it was more physical than mental.'

He laughed. 'Well, maybe so, at first. What red-blooded man could resist such a beautiful woman? It was only later than I discovered that you had brains as well as beauty.'

'I'm not sure whether or not that's a chauvinistic remark, honey,' Skye said, ready to bridle.

'No, it's not. It's simply the truth. The man who gets a wife who combines brains and beauty is twice blessed,' he said, more solemnly. 'I fear Adam has yet to discover the lack of brains in his new lady when they tie the knot.'

'Oh, of course he won't,' Skye said, defending her at once. 'Felicity is quiet and charming, as well as being an excellent homemaker and cook, so I'm sure they have everything they both want. No two marriages are ever the same, Nick, and in your profession you should know that only too well, so don't be so patronising!'

He laughed again at her indignant voice. 'I always love the way your eyes sparkle like sapphires when you become defensive about something. And as I didn't marry you simply because you were an excellent homemaker and cook, I've got my own ideas on what makes a good marriage.'

'Oh, really?' Skye said, perfectly aware that he was hardening against her, and teasing him a moment longer. 'Perhaps you'd better tell me what they are then.'

'I'd far rather show you,' Nick said meaningly.

As his hands went to her shoulders and slid the remaining article of clothing from them, she felt the familiar surge of desire at his touch, and sent up a silent prayer of thanks that this marriage was still so good, and so passionate, after all these years.

David Kingsley telephoned her in the middle of May.

'Betsy's in a hell of a state,' he said. 'Lily's gone over there now, but I thought you'd want to know.'

'What's happened?' she said at once. Betsy Tremayne was the calmest of women and almost *never* got into a state, so it must be something pretty bad, she thought fearfully.

'Justin's caught a packet,' David said baldly. 'He was patching up some of the wounded when he got caught up in the firing line somewhere in Italy. Betsy doesn't have the full details yet, except that he's already been sent home to a military hospital, but she's in a real panic. After all the comfort she's given to the boys recuperating at Killigrew House, it's a pretty rum do that her own two sons should have caught it, isn't it?'

He went on talking in his quickfire way, but Skye couldn't concentrate. All she heard was the word Italy, a place she hoped and prayed Wenna was well away from now. And all she could think was that both Betsy's two sons had been wounded, while her own was blessedly still safe – as far as she knew. As far as any of them knew...

'Are you still there, Skye? I thought you'd want to get over to Betsy's as well.'

'Of course I do,' she said, fighting down the brief panic that had taken all her breath away for a moment. 'I'll get there as soon as I can.'

She put down the phone with clammy hands. Just as you got a little bit complacent, thinking things were going the Allies' way at last... just as you thought your own family was somehow charmed and invincible, something happened to remind you that everybody was vulnerable...

'I'm going up to the pottery now, Mrs Pen,' she heard Butch Butcher's voice say. 'Are there any messages?'

She turned with a start. Butch had become so much a part of the family, so much her faithful shadow, that she sometimes forgot he was there. But she wondered now if Seb had gone up to White Rivers before Betsy got the telegram, and if he was unaware of what had happened to his brother.

'No messages, Butch. I have to telephone Sebby myself. You run along now,' she said, her voice thick.

'Are you all right?' he asked anxiously.

She nodded, unable to answer sensibly. Just wanting to be left alone, and to gather her thoughts for a moment before she picked up the phone again and asked the operator for the number of the White Rivers Pottery.

'He's not here,' Adam answered. 'I don't know what's happened to everybody today, but we don't have much business anyway—'

'Adam, Justin's been wounded. I don't know how bad it is, but if Sebby's still on his way to work it could be that he doesn't know yet. Break it to him gently when he gets there. I'm going to see Betsy, and I'll call you again later.'

She couldn't say any more. She needed to get out of the house and gulp some fresh air. Whatever happened to one member of the family affected all of them, and even though Justin had been the most self-sufficient of all the cousins, she knew that sometimes the most independent were the ones who fell the hardest. Like Betsy herself...

She was proved right the minute she entered Killigrew House and was enveloped in Betsy's clinging embrace. Lily shook her head behind Betsy's back, and Skye wondered fearfully just what she was about to be told.

'Right after the telegram came I got a letter from some medical friend o' Justin's, Skye,' Betsy gabbled, 'and 'tis worse than I feared. How my poor boy will cope, I don't know. 'Tis a blessing his father's not alive to see this sad day—'

'Come and sit down, Betsy, and tell me exactly what's happened,' Skye said carefully. 'Show me this letter.'

Her heart lurched painfully as soon as she scanned the words, couched in a formal, unsentimental manner of which Justin would have approved, being a medical man himself, but which completely demoralised Betsy.

Dear God, Skye thought in horror, as she read the clinical words. Justin had not only been blinded, but it seemed as though half his face had been blown away... For a moment, she felt her innards turn to water at the thought, and then guiltily willed the ghastly images away.

'He says Justin don't even want to come home to us,' Betsy moaned, her face scarlet, and her eyes flooding with tears. 'He says Justin has to deal with his blindness in his own way and he don't want nobody's pity, nor nobody seeing 'im until they've rebuilt his face. His *lovely face*, Skye,' she almost screeched. 'Just as if we'd be giving 'im pity, anyway. 'Tis love he wants, love and comfort, and that's what he'd get from his own fam'ly!'

Skye met Lily's glance, and knew they were both thinking the same thing. No matter what she said, they knew that if Justin came home, he would be simply smothered with all the love and pity that Betsy could give him. He'd be as helpless as a puppet, completely dependent on her, and she would slowly love him to death. He would be killed by devotion – if he didn't take his grandfather Walter's way out and kill himself. But how could you say such a thing to a grieving mother who wanted him back in the womb?

Skye was still hugging Betsy close and wondering when the keening would end when Sebby came bursting into the room.

'Adam told me when I got to the pottery, and I came back at once. How bad is it?' he said abruptly.

Lily took the letter from the table and handed it to him.

'It seems it all happened a few weeks ago, but Justin refused to let any of us know until he was back in England, had got the full medical opinion and had decided his own future,' she told him. 'This is from a close friend and colleague.'

Sebby said nothing for a few minutes, and then he nodded.

'I'll go to London and see him,' he said.

'Oh, we could do that, couldn't we?' Betsy said at once, sudden hope in her voice. 'We could take him things—'

'No, Mother, I'd said *I'd* go and see him. The last thing he wants right now is for folk to descend on him when he's in a vulnerable state. He's not a peep show.'

'I'm not *folk*. I'm his mother.'

He put his arm around her bulky figure. He rarely made a great show of family affection, but no one could miss his awkward concern for her.

'Ma, listen to me,' he said gently, reverting to his old childhood name for her. 'I know something of what Justin's going through now, because I've been through it too. I know that feeling of not wanting to see anybody, or having anybody see me. My wounds have healed and I've little more to show for it than a limp. Justin's wounds will take far longer, and you have to accept that he's never going to see again.'

'You're cruel to say so,' Betsy cried out.

'I'm being honest, Ma. Justin's blind, and his senses will be heightened because of it. He won't be able to see, but he'll sense the pity that people feel for him, and he won't be able to bear it. Not yet. Maybe not for a long time. And that's why we have to stay away until he's ready.'

'Except for you,' she said accusingly.

'I'm his brother,' Seb said simply. 'He'll know I understand.'

Seeing the indecision on Betsy's florid face, Skye spoke swiftly. 'Seb's right, Betsy. No matter how much we want to help, we have to let the young ones fight their own battles. You must know that from the boys you've had living here. Some want to talk it all out, and others want to shut themselves away until they're ready to face the world again.'

After what seemed an age, Betsy nodded.

'But my Justin's never going to face the world again, is he?' She swallowed deeply, then spoke more resolutely. 'You go to him with my blessing then, Sebby, and tell him when he's ready to come home, we'll be here, just like always.'

–

'It was a very traumatic afternoon,' Skye reported to the family over supper that evening. 'I felt desperately sorry for Betsy. She's done so much for the boys in her care, yet when it came to her own, she felt completely rejected.'

'I can imagine,' Nick said. 'It's a bit like God throwing back all your good works in your face.'

'Oh Nick, I wouldn't say that exactly!'

'You might if it was Olly,' he said reasonably.

'Is Justin going to be blind for ever, Mrs Pen?' Butch said nervously. Hoping they wouldn't notice, he had experimented on the thought by closing his eyes, feeling across the table for the salt cellar, and knocking it flying.

'You little idiot,' Celia snapped, home for the weekend and jittery with nerves at this latest happening in their family. 'Of course he's going to be blind for ever. It's not like a cough or a cold that you get over next week. What do you suppose he'll do, Mom? He's too young to sit around in a Twilight Home twiddling his thumbs. He'd go mad in a week.'

'I don't know,' Skye said in distress. 'I simply don't know. We'll find out more when Seb's been to London and spoken with him and his doctors.'

'At least he seems to have a good friend in this fellow who wrote to Betsy,' Nick said. 'A medical man, is he?'

'I suppose so,' said Skye. 'He seemed to know all about Justin's condition, anyway.'

—

Seb Tremayne took the first available train to London and found his way to the military hospital on the outskirts where his brother was being treated for his wounds. He had enough experience of hospitals to know the kind of smells that would assault his nostrils the minute he walked through those doors. The sickly, nauseatingly sweet smell of gangrene and the stifling scent of starched uniforms, carbolic and polished linoleum floors, all mingling with other smells too indescribable to define, well masked by the overpowering stink of disinfectant.

It was enough to turn the strongest stomach, as was the sound of the poor wretches who would be doing just that, heaving their guts out into the nearest receptacle – providing there was one near enough. Seb prayed that Justin wouldn't be one of them.

He thought he had forgotten that time when he too had been brought in to a field hospital to be patched up and sent back as gun fodder. He considered he'd got off lightly when they didn't think him fit enough. But there was bitterness as well as guilty relief in the fact, and before they sent him back to Blighty, he'd still had to go through the ordeal of sharing a ward with men who were never going to get through another night or another day. He had been unable to avoid listening to their screams and agonies as they struggled for one last precious breath.

He had waited inevitably for the heaviest silence a man ever knew. It wasn't the peaceful ending of the very old, dying after a lifetime of fulfilment. It was the jagged silence of a life cut short, long before its time, and it was a silence like no other.

Here and now, returning to one of the hospitals where such nightmares happened, day after day after day, Seb knew he would never forget it. It was a rite of passage and only those who had endured it would ever really know what it was like.

'Can I help you, sir?' said an orderly.

Seb felt momentarily irritated by the officious voice of the young man in the stained white coat that proclaimed his pride in his work. In civvies now, Seb knew he had no status here. He wasn't one of the honourably wounded, or the 'nearly-deads' as he and his equally macabre fellow patients had called those in the beds nearest the door... he was just a visitor. However, he quickly regretted his assessment of this young man, seeing the weary way he pushed his hair back from his forehead. They were all stretched to the limit these days.

'I've come to see my brother. He's a patient here. MO Justin Tremayne,' he added with professional efficiency.

The orderly's eyes grew more respectful. 'I think there's someone with him right now, but I'll tell him you're here.'

'I can wait if he's receiving treatment—'

'Oh no, it's a friend who comes to sit with him for the best part of every day. I'll show you to his ward.'

'Is this friend a Captain Giles Peterson?' Seb said casually, not knowing why his heart should be thudding a little faster. Good friends were more precious than gold, but some friends were more precious than others.

He had no idea why he should suddenly be having these thoughts, and these feelings. Justin was his brother, and he thought he knew him as well as he knew himself…

'He's in here, Mr Tremayne,' the orderly said, pointing to a side ward. 'Just go on in.'

'Is it usual for a man with his injuries to be placed in a side ward?' Seb persisted.

'He was very badly burned, and delirious enough to warrant it. We have to consider the other patients, you know,' the orderly added delicately.

'You mean he was raving. It's all right, I've been invalided out myself, so I know the form.'

The orderly gave a slight smile. 'Then I don't need to explain. Besides, Captain Peterson made a generous donation to the hospital for equipment that's badly needed. The least we can do is to give his friend as much comfort as we can.'

You're too young and too naïve to see what's right under your nose, thought Seb. *And I pray to God that you are, and that maybe I'm wrong.*

As the orderly hurried away to attend to his duties, Seb pushed open the door of the side ward and paused.

The man in the bed was lying perfectly flat, with varying pieces of equipment attached to him. Because of the heavy bandages covering most of his face and the pads over his eyes, he was completely unrecognisable.

In that fraction of a moment, Seb felt the gorge rise in his throat, remembering how he and Justin had romped with their cousins as children, up, up on the moors, breathing in the crystal clear air, sliding down the sky-tips that were part of their heritage, and dreaming of the days beyond childhood when all dreams were possible. And now there was this wreck of a man, still young, for whom all dreams had ended...

His attention was caught by the middle-aged man sitting beside the bed. As yet, he hadn't turned around to see who had entered the ward. He was too busy leaning forward toward the patient, speaking softly, his strong hand holding the lifeless one, the thumb gently caressing Justin's, the murmured words of comfort as deep and intimate as if from a lover. And at once, Seb knew.

He cleared his throat, and the man turned around. He was handsome, full of military bearing, his face etched with pain until he adjusted his expression on seeing a stranger.

'I'm sorry,' he said in an educated voice. 'I'll wait outside if you need to examine him—'

'I'm not a doctor,' Seb said in a strangled voice.

The figure on the bed moved its head the merest fraction.

'Seb, is that you? I knew you'd come.'

Seb moved forward, and saw how Justin's hand slid away from his companion's clasp.

'Of course I came, if only to report home how you are and prevent Ma from tearing up here with armfuls of home-made produce, convinced that they're not feeding you properly.'

He had to be jocular and talk quickly, because if he didn't, he knew he would simply fall apart. He was a man, and everyone knew that men didn't cry... except in wartime. Except when someone they dearly loved was reduced to this...

He felt the touch of Captain Peterson's hand on his shoulder, and just managed to resist recoiling from it.

'I'll speak to you later, if I may, Mr Tremayne,' he said quietly. 'You'll want to spend time alone with your brother.'

'Thank you.'

He left them alone, and Seb realised he was completely out of his depth, not knowing how to begin an impossible conversation. It was one thing to be faced with the most terrible injuries he could have envisaged for his brother. It was something else entirely to be confronted with this new situation that was as shocking as it was unexpected.

To his amazement he heard Justin give a small laugh. At least, he presumed that the thin sound that came through the bandages was intended to be a laugh.

'Poor Sebby. You had no idea, did you?'

'Well, I didn't expect to see you quite so swathed in bandages,' he blustered.

'That's not what I mean, and you know it. But don't worry. We're outwardly respectable citizens, despite the fact that I shall come out of these bandages looking like a gargoyle, I dare say. But Giles will take good care of me. He's got one of those places in wildest Yorkshire they call stately piles. Ironic, isn't it? All that money and no heir to leave it to. Well, he couldn't have, could he?'

'Are you sure you should be talking so much?' Seb said, when he couldn't think of anything else to say.

'I'm supposed to talk, no matter how painful it is. It exercises the facial muscles and stops them seizing up. So what do you think of my friend?'

Seb winced. 'Oh, don't ask that of me—'

'Good God, bruth, I never realised you were so narrow-minded and insular. And you in the Forces too. Didn't you ever see *friends* together?'

Yes; saw them disgraced and hounded out of the army, and shunned them as much as possible...

When he didn't reply, Justin went on, his voice still muffled behind the bandages, but with an edge to it now.

'Let me tell you something, Sebby. There would be no future for me now without Giles. I thank God for him every day. For his wanting my companionship in the good days, and still wanting it now. When the doctors and surgeons have finally done with me, we shall move to Yorkshire. He's retired from the army now, and he's promised to look after me as long as I live. Wouldn't you say that's the best kind of friend there is for a wretch like me?'

Seb couldn't doubt the sincerity in his voice, and he sensed Justin's need for his approval too. It was against his own nature to approve of the kind of lifestyle these two shared, but it was their lives.

'I say that anyone whose friend thinks that much of them is fortunate indeed,' he said at last. 'But Justin – you are discreet, aren't you?'

'I've been discreet for years,' Justin said simply. 'But I'm still your brother. Aren't I?'

'And always will be,' said Seb.

Chapter Thirteen

'So did you meet this stuffy Captain Peterson who wrote to me?' Betsy wanted to know, when she had exhausted every ounce of information she could get out of Seb on his return to Cornwall, and been reassured that Justin was in the best possible hands. 'What did you think of him? What was he like?'

Seb paused. *What was he like?*

How could he possibly repeat the emotional conversation he had had with Justin's companion, without admitting to this homely countrywoman that there were more kinds of love in this world than he had cared to believe, and that only the completely bigoted – or those who were as truly blind as his own brother – would condemn it?

In his heart Seb still condemned it too, but his love for his brother overcame his revulsion. Even so, such a revelation would break his mother's heart, and since it was against the law for two men to indulge in the kind of relationship that would disgrace a family, it was a secret Seb had vowed to reveal to no one outside the three people who now knew it.

'Well, go on, what was he like?' Betsy persisted.

'He's intelligent and well-spoken, and being a medical man himself he's taken a great interest in Justin's future. He's a wealthy man, retired from the army now, and he's offered to move Justin to his private clinic in Yorkshire to study his case,' he invented quickly.

Betsy sniffed. 'Treating him like one o' they specimens, is he? I don't think Justin will take kindly to that.'

'I think Justin will be thankful to be so well looked after, Ma. Strangers can sometimes be the best people to have around you in times of trauma. Your boys here know that, so you should understand a little of how Justin feels. I truly think it's the best thing for him, at least until he regains his self-confidence.'

'And then he'll come home to us?'

'Well, that's for him to decide,' Seb said vaguely. 'But Captain Peterson's promised to send me regular reports until Justin feels well enough to try writing to us himself.'

Betsy looked at him as if he was stupid. 'And how's he going to do that with no eyes to see? How will he be able to read his own words, or even keep the lines straight on the paper?' she said, bursting into uncontrollable tears at the thought of all that frustration and wasted education. Justin was always so proud of his achievements, and so was she.

Seb put his arm around her. 'He'll be taught Braille, Ma. Captain Peterson – Giles – will see to it all in his clinic. Justin was always quick to learn, he'll discover how to read with his fingers, and when he wants to write to us he'll dictate the words he wants to say. Just don't expect things to happen quickly. They have to patch up his face first, and it'll be a long time before he's done with hospitals.'

Now that he had had that long conversation with Giles Peterson he had to admire the man for standing by Justin. It wasn't a lifestyle Seb understood, and it wasn't something he cared to think about too much. But he couldn't doubt the genuine feelings the two men had for one another, and once away from prying and curious eyes in the wilds of Yorkshire, he knew his brother would be safe and cared for.

But with an urgent need to prove his own masculinity to himself, Seb had spent his last night in London in the company of an enthusiastic and large-breasted prostitute. And in the best barrack-room vernacular, he had given her a bloody good seeing-to.

—

By the middle of May, everyone knew what was about to happen. There was an undercurrent of excitement in the very air, as if the promised invasion of France was going to mean the imminent end of all hostilities.

'It won't, of course. It will just mean more killing,' Celia Pengelly said to her companions as they paused for elevenses in the field above Penzance where they stooked corn sheaves in the hot morning sunshine.

'You always think you know everything, don't you, Pengelly?' said the one they called East End Gertie, fixing her with a scowl and a flip of her brassy hair.

'That's because she does,' her friend Lizzie said. 'She prob'ly knew the date it was going to happen before she left that posh job of hers with the Ministry.'

'It wasn't with the Ministry,' Celia snapped. 'How many more times? It was just an office job—'

'Oh yeah?' Gertie sneered. 'And since when did the likes of us gels get office jobs? I worked in a button factory before I came down here, and sometimes I wish I'd never bleedin' left it. Just look at the state of my fingernails.'

But Celia wasn't looking at anything except the man making his way over the fields towards them. A man she recognised at once. She got to her feet, feeling as though they were made of lead and as if she was moving in slow motion, dropped her hunk of bread and cheese and began running towards him. She couldn't think why he was here, but in all this time, apart from the tenuous and general information Moonie had been able to give her, this man had been her one link with Stefan, and if he had further news…

He swung her around in his arms, and it flitted through her head that he had grown tall and stout since his years in Ireland. He was no longer merely the young brother of her stepfather, or the gangly youthful champion of the infant Wenna, but a stolid man in his thirties, she realised. A husband and a father.

'Ethan, what are you doing here? There's nothing wrong, is there?' she gasped, when she could catch her breath.

For of *course* he wouldn't have news of Stefan. The realisation was acute, and her momentary surge of hope vanished as quickly as it came. How could anybody have news of a man incarcerated by his own kind, so far away from the reality that was wartime Britain?

'There is, actually,' he said, his voice scratchy now. 'It's Ryan. We've brought him over to England to see if the doctors here can help him. He has a weak chest, Celia, and each winter it gets worse. The doctors in Ireland fear that he might not even grow into adolescence.'

'Dear Lord! Karina must be demented,' she said, shocked.

'She is. So much so that I had to get out of the house where she's weeping and wailing all over your mother right now. I can't take much more of it, which is why I came to see what you were doing these days. It's funny to see you working as a farm girl,' he added without a trace of humour.

Celia glanced around, to see that her companions had already begun work again. She knew she couldn't let her mind dwell on the awfulness of Ethan's family problems for too long. The farmer was a stickler for keeping the girls working.

'It won't be so funny if I don't get back to work,' she said quickly. 'Come and talk to me while I get on with it.'

'I'll come and help—'

'No, you won't.'

'Yes, I will. I need to be doing something, and there's not a farmer alive that won't welcome another pair of hands.'

'And you didn't seek me out for any other reason?'

She had to say it, as casually as possible, knowing how selfish she was being, for his child's health was far and away reason enough to be here at all.

'What other reason?' he said blankly, and then it dawned on him. 'God, no, Celia, there's been no news of that kind. We've had no POWs in the vicinity for months now.'

She nodded, her eyes smarting. There were so few people she could speak to about Stefan. Nor did she even dare mention his name. He was one of the enemy, and her fellow Land Girls, looking at her curiously now, would have spat on her had they known the identity of the man whose ring she again wore on a chain around her neck.

'Who's your feller, Pengelly?' Gertie jeered at once. 'Is this the one you're always dreaming about when you look up at them stars at night?'

'This is my cousin,' she said stonily. 'He's over from Ireland with his wife and their sick child, and he's offered to help us with the stooking.'

'We won't say no to that then, will we, Gertie?' Lizzie said sweetly, smiling at Ethan. Married or not, he still wore trousers and that made him fair game as far as she was concerned.

They might as well not bother, thought Celia. It was obvious to her that Ethan only had Ryan on his mind, and she doubted that even Wenna would stir his heart any more.

As if her thoughts transmitted themselves to him, he forced himself to ask about her sister.

'Been in Italy, a proper little Vera Lynn by all accounts, singing to the troops,' Celia told him. 'But she's back in England now, much to Mother's relief. Olly's God knows where, of course, flying his kites, as he calls them, and I daresay you've heard what happened to Justin.'

Ethan nodded. 'Poor devil. It puts everything into perspective, doesn't it?'

Celia squeezed his hand. 'It doesn't make your concern for Ryan any less important, if that's what you're thinking. What kind of father would you be if you didn't care so much?'

'What kind of husband am I being, to be enjoying myself out here in the fields with three lovely girls, when my wife's crying her heart out back at New World?' he muttered.

Before Celia knew what was happening, he had flung down his fork and was striding back the way he had come.

'Well, he's a johnny-come-lately and no mistake,' Lizzie said, having heard his last words. 'Calls us lovely girls one minute, and then runs out on us.'

Celia glared at her. 'Sometimes, Lizzie, I don't think you have the brains of a flea. If you can't tell when a man's suffering, then it's no wonder you've never caught one.'

'Well, pardon me for breathing, ma'am,' she snapped, reminding Celia suddenly of her time in New Jersey when everyone was ma'am and sir, and people were full of an exaggerated politeness that was almost of another time. In that instant she felt a brief longing to be there again, away from it all, in the sweet-scented apple orchards belonging to the Stone household.

But as she heard the Cornish farmer's angry shout to them to get on with their work and stop dawdling, she knew she couldn't do that. Even if she tried, nothing would ever be the same again. You couldn't ever retreat to a safer world. All anyone could do was to go on.

–

Outwardly, Ryan Pengelly looked like a robust little six-year-old with a healthy tan on his skin, thought Skye. It was only when he began to cough at night, and the wheezing could be heard through the bedroom walls, that it was evident that he wasn't a well child.

Ethan and Karina were making a fair living on their Irish farm, but if Ryan was to have specialist treatment, it was clear they couldn't afford it.

They hadn't come to Cornwall looking for hand-outs, merely the expertise of the British doctors, and they were adamant on that point. But Nick and Skye had other ideas.

'You're our family, and our family deserves the best,' Nick declared. 'We'll send him to a private clinic and see what they can do for him.'

'You must believe that this is not why we came,' Karina protested in her soft Irish voice, tears welling in her eyes at the gesture of kindness.

'You came where you belong,' Skye told her. 'Where else should you be at a time of trouble but with people who love you? We all want to see Ryan able to run and play like other little boys. He's of an age to play with Lily's two now.' She paused. 'You'll go to see them, of course?'

Karina flushed. 'I doubt that Lily's boys will want to bother with Ryan. They must be thirteen now, and won't want to be seen hanging around with a small boy who can't run about very much. Besides, I'm not sure that Lily will want to see me. I've been very tardy about keeping in touch.'

'I'm sure Lily will be as pleased to see you as we are,' Skye said firmly. 'I'll invite them over for Sunday tea. We might even get Celia to come. I know she's glad to get away from the girls she works with whenever she can.'

Ethan laughed. 'Having met them, I don't blame her for that – and you won't stop Skye getting the family together on the slightest excuse, Karina.'

'It's a family thing,' Nick agreed, tongue in cheek. 'A Tremayne thing, or whatever they call it.'

The teasing broke the tension that had surrounded them all like a cloud, and by the following Sunday the house was full of people again. Superficially, anyone could be forgiven for thinking they didn't have a care in the world. Or that there was a war on at all.

Only someone with a crystal ball, who was able to look beneath the surface, would see that nearly every one of them felt a measure of anxiety and grief.

Betsy wouldn't even come to New World, preferring to stay with 'her boys'. Seb reckoned she was being extra diligent on their behalf as a kind of penance. She felt she mustn't desert them just because her own boy was going through such torment.

'It's irrational, of course, but she has to work things through in her own way,' he went on.

'We all do,' Celia said.

'No news then?' he asked without explanation.

'How could there be?' she said in a brittle voice.

He slung an easy arm around her shoulders, and she could still marvel that where there had once been so much anger and conflict between them, there was now the closest friendship.

'I reckon you'll just have to settle for marrying me then,' he said casually.

'And pigs might fly,' she retorted, and then gave an unexpected giggle. 'Did you ever know that we used to call you a prize pig, Seb? Mom and Lily did too. Isn't that awful? But you really were the most insufferable child.'

Butch Butcher wandered near, thankful to hear laughter when most of the grown-ups seemed to be so miserable lately.

'What's an insuff – whatever you said, Celia?'

'Something you're not, kiddo,' she said, putting her arm around him with rough affection and realising to her surprise that he was truly one of the family now. Just like an adopted brother, in fact, and she found herself hoping her parents would finally get around to taking him on permanently.

He wriggled free in embarrassment, his face as red as his hair, and went to find Lily's boys. Celia turned to Seb.

'I'm beginning to think I'm getting soft in my old age,' she said. 'Maybe I'll turn into one of those ancient, toothless spinsters, mumbling into my cocoa every night about the good old days. What do you think?'

But she didn't want an answer, because it suddenly sounded too frighteningly like the legions of elderly spinsters from the First World War. Those who had resolutely never married because their sweethearts had never come back from the Front, but who carried their images in their hearts for the rest of their lives.

'Not you, sweetheart,' Seb lazily. 'You'll *have* to marry me before then.'

'Hey, you're not serious, are you?' she said in alarm. 'Not you and me, Seb—'

'Good God, no,' he drawled. 'Just giving you the option if all else fails, that's all.'

–

Nick fixed an appointment for Ryan to see a top specialist in Bristol, who would then admit him to his private clinic for observation and treatment if the condition warranted it.

He also arranged for Ethan and Karina to stay at lodgings nearby, and insisted on having all the bills sent to him. He wouldn't hear of anything different.

He and Skye accompanied the little family to Bristol and stayed for one night.

'We want to visit some old friends,' Nick told them by way of easing their consciences at all the expense. 'My ex-partner and his wife have an antique shop in Bristol and it will be good to see them again.'

It would also be good to spend the night in the hotel where, long ago, he and Skye had journeyed to Bristol to inspect the retirement home where old Albert Tremayne was to spend the rest of his days. They had gone there as Albert's married niece and lawyer, and come back as lovers.

'Do you remember?' Skye said softly, as they stood at the window of the hotel that night, gazing down at the silvery ribbon of water in the Avon Gorge far below Clifton Downs.

She felt Nick's arms fold possessively around her, and she leaned back against him.

'As if it was yesterday. I don't know how we had kept apart for so long.'

'I do,' she said quietly. 'It was because I was married to Philip, and we knew it was wrong to give in to our desire.'

'But we made a vow not to repeat it as long as Philip lived, and we kept to it, so I don't think God will punish us for that, darling.'

She twisted round in his arms. 'And now I'm married to you and nothing that happens between us is wrong,' she said, her heart beginning to beat faster at the look in his eyes.

It was a dark, passionate look that she knew meant only one thing, and she exalted again in the knowledge that he could still desire her so much and that their feelings for one another had never changed.

'Then I think it's time we confirmed those vows we made all those years ago,' he said more urgently, in a way that thrilled her heart and told her the time for talking was over.

—

They didn't stay in Bristol for more than their one planned night. Next morning, the visit to Nick's ex-partner was a brief but joyous one, full of nostalgic talk of the past and hopes for the future. The city and its docks had had its own horrendous taste of the Blitz and many parts were devastated, even razed to the ground, but the Bristolian spirit had been strong, and would survive, the way it always had.

Skye was filled with a strange kind of euphoria as they caught the train at Temple Meads station and headed home to Cornwall. It had been a journey on account of Ryan's health, but for her, it had also been a renewal of vows, and a reminder that love never dies.

Somehow it had united the past with the present, and all the past impressions, of Bristol and of Cornwall, with her mother Primmy, and Primmy's beloved brother Albert. All that love, through all the generations, seemed to fuse in her own mind into the certainty that Ryan would get well. That the specialist who was treating him would work miracles.

She said as much to Nick as the train rattled westwards, and he smiled at her indulgently.

'Well, let's hope so. Or do I hear Granny Morwen dictating positive thoughts in your head again?'

Her smile was triumphant. 'Well, you said it, not me! So who's using his Cornish intuition now, honey?'

Whatever it was, in two weeks' time they heard that Ryan's condition could be treated with a small operation, and that he would then undertake a long course of medication that in time, it was hoped, would completely cure him.

He would need to stay in the clinic for several weeks, and the specialist advised a further month in a specialised children's clinic in the country, where the parents could stay with him before they went home to Ireland.

'It will cost a fortune, Skye, and we're going to take out a loan to pay for it,' Ethan finished, at the end of a lengthy and exuberant telephone call.

'You'll do no such thing, Ethan! Nick and I won't hear of it. No matter how much it costs, we shall ask Mr Warner to continue to send the bills to us, do you understand? We'll be deeply upset if you refuse to let us do this.'

'How can we refuse without seeming totally ungrateful?' Ethan said huskily. 'You're the dearest people we know, and I'll call you again when I'm not so damned emotional.'

Skye put down the phone. She had no idea how much an operation of this nature would cost, but it didn't matter. All that mattered was seeing that small boy well again.

She turned around to see Butch hovering behind her.

'I've got some pocket money saved up, Mrs Pen,' he said, hot with embarrassment. 'If you want it, I'll give it yer.'

'Oh Butch, honey, that won't be necessary, but you're an angel to even think of it,' she said, hugging him.

'I thought all the fam'ly might be helping, see?'

At once, she knew what he was getting at. It was his way of being included as one of the family, and not just a 'vaccy', as Olly had once called them so scathingly, in what seemed like a lifetime ago. At that moment, Skye knew how important this was to him.

'If we need to call on the family for help, I promise I'll remember your offer, Butch,' she said, and was rewarded by a beatific smile on his plain face.

–

World events overtook domestic ones with dramatic swiftness in early June, when the news broke that the Allies had liberated Rome. It began a wave of patriotic hysteria that at last, the Jerries were on the run.

On June sixth came the announcement from General Eisenhower's HQ that the invasion of Europe had begun. Naval forces, supported by air forces, began landing huge numbers of Allied forces on the northern coasts of France. The actual landing place was not mentioned at first, and the solemn voice of wireless announcer John Snagge made it seem an almost modest achievement. The understated British, Skye thought, with wry and affectionate amusement.

And yet the invasion was so vast in its conception and operation, that it was only when the full facts emerged of the biggest land, sea and air operation of all time, that the plans began to seem so awesome.

Skye went at once to the newspaper offices in Truro, unable to sit at home or do anything else, and quite sure that David Kingsley would have the latest information coming through all day. The more his sources revealed, the more incredible it became that it could have been achieved without the enemy getting prior knowledge of exactly where and when it would all take place.

'It must have been a terrifying sight, to see thousands of parachutes descending on French soil,' Skye said. 'And all those ships discharging the soldiers and tanks at the various landing points must have put the fear of the Almighty into the German troops waiting to repel them.'

'Yes, but we shouldn't underestimate them,' David said. 'They won't have turned tail and retreated, Skye, and the casualty figures are going to be immense on both sides. It's going to be nothing short of carnage.'

She looked at him sharply. 'You don't approve of this operation, do you, David?'

'I don't approve of men killing one another.'

'Not even for the best of reasons, to make the world a safer place to live in?'

'Didn't they say that about the last one, and about every bloody war that's ever been fought?'

'My God, for a newspaperman, you sounded almost human at that moment,' she said flippantly.

'It's not unheard of,' he said, and at the frown on his good-looking face she realised they were practically at loggerheads over a cause.

But she also knew well enough that if a newspaperman revealed everything in print that he knew, the public would be shocked to the bone at the cruelty that existed in the world. Danger didn't only exist these days in hand to hand fighting. Modern warfare had more sophisticated weapons of death and was fought on land, on sea and in the air.

'I wonder if Olly was involved in it,' she said.

Part of her hoped desperately that he was not, while the other part knew that he would have just as desperately wanted to be there, his aircraft zooming through the skies and bombing railways and power plants, or dropping parachutes with men and supplies to support the great and wonderful invasion that was to liberate France and the world...

Suddenly she felt as sick and dizzy as if she too was up there in skies that were darkened with man-made machines filled with death-delivering horror; that she was somehow unable to breathe in the cloying stench of smoke and burning oil in the claustrophobic confines of the aeroplane carrying her son to his destiny—

'Put your head between your knees, Skye,' she heard David order her as if from a long way away.

She obeyed without thinking, willing away the surge of bile that climbed upwards from her stomach and threatened to disgrace her.

'Olly,' she whimpered, without even knowing that she spoke his name.

'What about Olly?' David said, his head close to hers, his hand still pushing hers down to her knees.

But by now the vision had faded, if vision it actually was. Or had it all been no more than an illusion brought about by her natural fears for her son? She had no way of knowing, but right now the last thing she wanted to feel was that it was some kind of premonition. At that moment, she completely rejected any thought of second sight. She didn't want it, and didn't have it... *wouldn't* have it...

'Here, drink this,' David went on, thrusting a glass of water into her hand. 'Sorry it's not brandy, but I can fetch you a drop of that if you feel the need.'

'No thanks. Water's fine,' she muttered, not wanting her senses dimmed in any way. 'I'm sorry, David. I get bad moments at times, worrying about Olly. But they say no news is good news, don't they?'

Instead of reassuring her as she expected, his voice became more clipped. 'And we both know that's one of the most stupid clichés ever invented.'

'What have you heard?' she said at once.

He shrugged. 'Nothing to alarm you. Only that the air force is as much involved in this invasion as anything else. But anyone with any sense knew that it was going to be. This war is very much a battle of the air, darling, even more than the last one was. Anyway, have you heard from Olly lately?' he added casually. Too casually.

She shook her head. 'No. But that's nothing new. He's always too busy to write. For all his one-time longing to be a reporter, he has very poor corresponding skills when it comes to his own family.'

Illogically, she was angry with David for making her feel even more anxious than before. For bringing her foolish fears out into the open instead of keeping them buried deep in her heart, even from Nick.

But, providing she heard from Olly soon, she decided it would be her new talisman for bringing him safely through to the end of the war.

The thought made her equally angry with herself, for putting such faith in pagan values.

'I think I need some fresh air, David,' she said, her chest suddenly tight. 'I'll go and see Lily while I'm in town, and I'll speak to you again soon.'

But Lily couldn't help, and nor did Skye know what help she wanted or needed. She only knew that she was filled with an inner dread that all was not well, and that Olly was the pivot of that dread.

'You need a tonic, darling,' Lily advised her. 'I must say I'm glad the Irish lot have got over their trouble and that Ryan's convalescing now. It seemed to me that no sooner did half the evacuees leave New World than the others moved in, and you always did take other people's troubles too much to heart, Skye. You should give more thought to yourself instead of other people.'

'They used to say that about Granny Morwen too,' Skye said, 'but if that's the way you're born, there's not much you can do about it. Anyway, most of our evacuees left a long time ago now. There's only Butch, and I hope he'll stay for good.'

'You're really fond of that little tyke, aren't you?'

'Why shouldn't I be? He's a honey,' Skye said.

–

The mood of the whole country was lifted by the fact that D-Day, as it became known, had been a success. But there was a price to pay. Early news reports made little of the terrible toll of killed and wounded in the battles of the first few weeks, but eventually the true figures were reported.

In any case, logical reasoning made anyone question how such a heavy bombardment could meet the expected fierce resistance without heavy casualties on both sides – though for families who had lost loved ones, logical reasoning didn't come into it, of course. Those like the Pengellys, who hadn't had to face receiving a dreaded yellow telegram, could still hold on to hope for their sons and daughters.

'At least we can be thankful that Wenna's safely back in England now,' Skye said, but she spoke almost guiltily, still horrified that a family in Truro had heard that their two sons had both been killed in the first wave of Normandy landings.

They had heard nothing of Olly, but by now she was more than ready to hold on to the tired old cliché that no news was good news, however futile. It was by far preferable to thinking the worst.

The wireless news bulletins assured the public that the war was turning in the Allies' favour at last, and that was the important thing. Breaching the Normandy beaches was the first step in liberating France. The recurring theme on everyone's lips now was that the war would soon be over...

And then came a new horror.

–

The telephone rang at Killigrew House late one evening in the middle of June. Seb picked it up quickly, knowing that telephone calls at a late hour held terror for his mother these days. He was thankful he'd answered it when he recognised the cultured voice of Captain Giles Peterson.

'Have you heard the news, Sebastian?' he said formally. 'The Germans have launched their secret weapon, and the city's in a state of panic, though the very south of England's seen the worst of it so far. They're calling it the doodlebug or the buzz-bomb – you take your pick. Whatever it's called, it's causing hellish damage.'

'Is this the V-1 bomb?' Seb said sharply. 'We've all heard about it, even down here in the sticks.' They weren't all country hicks in Cornwall.

'Of course,' Giles said. 'I didn't mean to imply anything else. But I wanted to let you know that Justin's well enough to be moved, and I'm getting him out of London tomorrow morning before the flak really begins here. I have a friend in Derby who runs a private clinic, and he'll continue his treatment there until we can go home to Yorkshire. I wanted to keep you informed, so that your mother wouldn't worry for his safety. The moment we're settled, I'll contact you again.'

'I appreciate your letting me know,' Seb said, unable to doubt the other's sincerity and genuine concern. 'It would have worried my mother to death to learn about these

V-1s flying about, knowing Justin was still in a London hospital.'

'Well, we'll soon be well out of range of the devilish weapons. Do you know much about them?'

Seb realised he wanted to keep him talking. Make contact. Establish a rapport. The way people did with their lover's family. He made himself remember that Justin was dependent on this man, and forced his own feelings of distaste aside.

'I know they're high-speed craft and carry nearly a ton of explosive,' Seb said, dredging up all he had learned.

'And they're already calling the area over Kent and Sussex 'bomb alley',' Giles went on grimly. 'People are being warned to take cover as soon as they hear the peculiar engine-note stop, because within fifteen seconds it will explode.'

Seb cut in. 'Isn't the theory behind it that as long as you can still hear it coming, you can feel safe?'

'Yes. But who can calculate where they'll explode? And with no pilot, what's to stop them being sent over in daylight as well as during the night? First reports are that southern England has been as shaken by the bombardment as if it's suffered an earthquake. Hell on earth is a more apt description.'

He spoke with crisp military precision, but it couldn't hide the anger in his voice.

'Then the sooner you get Justin out of the capital, the better,' Seb heard himself say. He swallowed his pride, and added, 'Thank God he's got you to care for him.'

'Those few words will mean more to both of us than I can say, Sebastian. I'll relay them to Justin if I may.'

When the call ended Seb went into the living room where his mother and her convalescent boys were crowding around the wireless set, listening intently to the latest bulletin.

Thank God Giles Peterson had already put his mind at rest about getting Justin out of the capital, he thought now, seeing the fear in his mother's face as the announcer relayed much of what Seb had just heard.

'Before you start fretting unduly, Ma, that was Captain Peterson on the phone. Justin's being moved to a clinic in Derby tomorrow for further treatment, so he'll be well out of reach of these doodlebugs.'

'Then let's thank the Lord that somebody's looking after him,' Betsy said, almost weeping with relief.

'Amen to that,' muttered Seb.

Chapter Fourteen

Despite the Allies' penetration farther and farther into Europe, hopes for peace seemed constantly thwarted as the German bombardment of London and the south-east became intensified during July, and frantic evacuation began all over again.

The doodlebugs were getting a stranglehold on the capital, and no matter how some of the newspapers tried to shield the public from the worst of it, the public demanded to know the truth. It was becoming clear that no amount of anti-aircraft gunfire seemed able to stop them.

There was no warning as to when the machines would stop their deadly approach, and once the noise of the engine ceased, you might as well say your prayers, according to many eyewitness reports in the newspaper.

It made depressing and horrifying reading, but Skye's attention was caught by another small headline.

'Can you credit this?' she exclaimed. 'The government has revealed plans for building between three and four million new houses in the first ten years after the war with proper kitchens and plenty of hot water. That must be a real comfort to people who are homeless now! What kind of tactless idiots sit on their backsides in Whitehall?'

'They mean well,' Nick said. 'They're planning for the future, and they have to look ahead, just as we all do. This war isn't going to last for ever, and people will want decent homes to come back to. Jerry probably did us a favour in destroying some of the old slums.'

Skye stared at him in disbelief and her voice grew passionate with anger. 'My God, sometimes I wonder if you have any compassion in you at all, Nick! How can you say such a thing? They may have been slums, but they were homes. People married and had babies there. They grew old together and they died there. There's more to a home than a draughty old kitchen and no running water. There's a family's hopes and dreams—'

'All right, don't take on so, Skye. All I'm saying is that if people are better housed after the war, they'll have a higher standard of living than they ever had before. You only have to compare the old clayworkers' cottages on the moors with the smart little town houses in Truro to know the difference. You wouldn't disagree with that, would you?'

'No. It was just the way you said it, that's all.'

He laughed shortly. 'Oh well, not everyone can have your gift with words, sweetheart, especially not a stuffy old lawyer like me. I see facts where you see rainbows.'

'Well, that's not so bad!' she said. 'Everyone knows there's a pot of gold at the end of a rainbow.'

'There's no answer to that kind of crazy logic.'

But she declared that her prophecy about gold being at the end of a rainbow was proved right when Olly sent word that he was coming home on leave, and had "oodles" to tell them.

'*Oodles?*' Nick said, as picky as ever. 'Where the devil do they get these expressions from?'

'It's called youthful enthusiasm, honey,' Skye said, too relieved and overwhelmed by the fact that all was well with their son to care about his censure.

–

Oliver Pengelly had broadened considerably during the last few years, not only in stature but also in maturity. He was twenty-one years old now, and the important birthday had come and gone. It hadn't mattered a hoot to him that the only celebration had been in the mess-room with his mates where he was bumped and cheered and almost drowned in cheap booze.

He had seen and experienced far more in his years in the Royal Air Force than some men knew in a lifetime, and while some of it was good, much of it was more horrific than he would ever tell his parents.

Once he had got over the usual excitement of being home on his short leave, and they had all got used to his presence, it was only to Seb Tremayne, his closest confidant now, that he revealed the gut-wrenching terror that could make a man 'brown-ass' his trousers in mid-flight and be too traumatised even to notice.

On the last day of his leave, they strode over the moors as they used to do when they were children, finding a good vantage point to view the domain of the clayworks and surroundings that were still essentially theirs. Still Killigrew country. Still Tremayne and Pengelly country.

The endless moors and the Cornish sense of mystery and magic were still so peaceful and unchanging that for a while it was easy to forget that war was raging elsewhere. That men were dying and burning, and screaming in agony…

'I sometimes wonder if Justin's so lucky after all,' Olly said abruptly, when they had exhausted all other topics of conversation. 'Sometimes I think he'd be better off dead. Nothing personal, of course.'

'*Christ*, Olly, what kind of a remark is that? It's a hundred times better to be alive than dead.'

'Not when you're only half alive, sport. Not when the images of hell are so indelibly stored up in your head and your heart that you can still hear and smell your companions burning even if you don't have eyes to see it happening. Those memories will never die, no matter how much you wish to God that they would,' he ended savagely.

'You're speaking personally, of course,' Seb said at once. 'This isn't only about Justin, is it?'

Olly shrugged. They sat cross-legged on the short stubbly moorland turf now, with the placid sight of the sea rippling like silver in the distance, and the only sound the sighing of the breeze through the bracken.

As it was Sunday, White Rivers Pottery was closed for the day, and the clayworks were still now, where they used to be constantly alive with the sounds of men and women hollering cheerfully to one another above the hum of machinery.

'I had a good mate in my squadron,' Olly said. 'We shared the same dreams and ambitions for the future, and thought about going into commercial flying after the war. Going into it together, I mean. We could have made a go of it too, except that Hitler's goons put a stop to all that.'

'What happened?' Seb said quietly, when Olly's voice tailed away and he continued staring into space, as if his mind was a million miles away.

'What do you think?' he said, suddenly harsh. 'Nothing exceptional. Nothing that wasn't happening to dozens of other damn good eggs who thought they could conquer the world. We've all got a bloody nerve thinking we can reverse the Almighty's plan and soar like eagles. We should leave it to the bloody birds to fly, and keep our feet on the ground like nature intended.'

Seb snapped back at him, 'People get killed with their feet on the ground, Oliver. People get blown up and blinded. People get bombed in their own homes. You aren't defying God's laws by flying aircraft, if that's what this little bit of self-hatred is all about. You're doing a hell of a good job in helping to win this war, and you should stop feeling so bloody sorry for yourself and remember it.'

Olly turned and glared at him, and after a moment he managed a hint of a smile.

'All right, so I'm a bloody hero—'

'Yes, you are, and so is every other man with the nerve to go up in one of those infernal machines and defend his country, so hate yourself if you must, but don't belittle the rest of them, there's a good chap.'

Olly glared at his cousin again. 'Did you ever think of becoming a head doctor?'

'No, I just use my common sense, that's all. In this war, we can't do without people like you and Justin, and your sisters, and the boys convalescing at Killigrew House. The ones who come home in one piece are the lucky ones.'

'You're forgetting somebody, aren't you?'

'I don't think so—'

'*You*, you bugger! Since when did you become so modest? You bought it too, and this soft-soaping is definitely not the Seb I remember. In fact, it's more unnerving than all Hitler's bombs,' he said with a grin. 'So when are we going to go out and find some girls? There *are* some still around who are looking for a good time, I suppose? And the day you tell me you don't know where to find them is the day hell freezes.'

—

'What did you think of Olly this time?' Skye asked Nick when their son had gone back to his base. 'I thought he was very on edge when he arrived, but I was glad to see that he and Seb got so pally.'

'That's because they did what every healthy young man should do, and went chasing girls,' Nick said easily.

'Well, I'm not sure that's a very nice thing to say!'

'How do you want me to say it? It's natural for young men to want the company of girls, and in wartime, it becomes even more urgent to sow your wild oats.'

'*Nick!*'

'For pity's sake, darling, I'm not suggesting he was bedding every girl who caught his eye, but when you're never sure if you're going to see another tomorrow, you want to make the most of your time. And don't start reading anything prophetic into that remark.'

'All the same, I wish you hadn't said it,' Skye said uneasily. 'I've always been anxious about Olly—'

'And about the girls, and everyone else you ever knew. Let's face it, my love, you've turned into a worrier.'

Had she? Skye felt a little shock at his words, knowing it wasn't the way she thought about herself.

She still thought of herself as the bright and breezy young American girl with the quick New Jersey accent who had burst in on her Cornish family for a year, and stayed for a lifetime. But she was no longer a girl, and she was in danger of letting herself slip into maudlin middle age, she thought with a sudden feeling of alarm.

'Well, I'm not going to worry any longer,' she said determinedly. 'The war must be nearing the end, and I'm going to start planning my booklets properly, ready for the hordes of tourists who are going to discover us as soon as it's all over. There's no reason why I shouldn't get them into shape, even if there's not enough paper available to print them!'

'That's my girl,' Nick said.

–

But as if to dash her determination every time it came to the surface, and remind her that the war wasn't over yet, there was a telephone call late one afternoon at the end of July that had her heart thumping.

'We're at the railway station in Truro, Mrs Pen, so can yer send somebody ter fetch us, because there ain't no bleedin' cabs or buses to be had.'

'Who is this?' Skye said sharply, unable to believe what her brain was telling her.

'It's me and my gel. Edna Hollis and Daphne. Our 'ouse got hit by a doodlebug, and my Gary said we should get straight back down to Cornwall where it's safe.'

Skye gasped as the woman's words poured out with about as much emotion as if she was saying she was dropping in for afternoon tea.

'Your house was hit? You mean it was destroyed?' she said, knowing how stupid that sounded.

She heard Edna Hollis's harsh laugh. ''Course it was, lady. Them bombs don't do things by 'alves. It was lucky me and Daphne wasn't in it when we was doodlebugged.'

Skye felt her mouth go dry, and then she heard Daphne's excited voice burst in.

'Come 'n get us, Mrs Pen, and I'll tell yer all about it. The kids next door was burned to a cinder, what was left of 'em, anyway, but we was all right—'

'Stay where you are, Daphne, and I'll be there to fetch you as soon as I can,' Skye broke in, knowing Daphne's graphic turn of phrase, and not wanting to imagine the scene just yet. It would be bad enough later, when they had to hear it over and over again. And if the Hollis mother and child were assuming they would stay indefinitely, no doubt Daphne would soon be telling the whole school what it was like to be doodlebugged.

The idea of having the pair of them installed at New World for any length of time quickly stretched Skye's charitable thoughts to the limit. She also knew that Edna's incessant chatter, coupled with Daphne's, would quickly drive Nick insane. There had to be another way. And by the time she reached the railway station in Truro she had already begun to plan it, providing it was handled delicately enough.

Daphne threw herself into Skye's arms with a sudden burst of tears that took her by surprise.

'The little bugger missed yer,' Edna observed. 'Always on about 'er posh house in the country, she was, even to my Gary, though he kept telling 'er we'd have a big place in America.'

'I missed yer, Mrs Pen,' Daphne sobbed. 'When Gary comes ter visit us I want to show 'im my lovely room.'

Skye felt alarmed. How many more of them were there going to be? While she had a patriotic affinity with the unknown GI Gary, she realised that she didn't want her house filled with strangers. Not any more.

'I know you must have had a terrible time, Mrs Hollis, losing your home like that—'

'Oh, it weren't much,' Edna said airily. 'Anyway, we'd taken a lot of stuff wiv us while we were staying wiv Gary for the weekend. That's how come we was so lucky, not bein' there. We was glad to see the back of the old dump, and there's no excuse now for not getting spliced as soon as poss.'

They were in the car now and on the way back to New World, and since Mrs Hollis seemed remarkably resilient, Skye decided there was no time like the present to say what she had to say. While she still had the courage.

'It must have been a shock, though, and you may not be feeling it properly yet, so you're very welcome to stay with us for a while until you're properly recovered.'

'We wanter stay wiv you for ever, Mrs Pen,' Daphne wailed. 'At least until Gary takes us to America! All the kids that went back ter London are being sent away again now.'

'I know, Daphne,' Skye said, 'and I was very sorry to hear that. But if you and your Mom are going to be in Cornwall for some time, wouldn't it be nice to have a little place of your own where Gary could come and visit you?'

Edna Hollis snorted. 'We couldn't afford no rent, so who'd be daft enough to give us a place of our own, missis?'

'I would,' Skye said calmly. 'It's only a cottage, but it would be yours for as long as you needed it – and you needn't bother to pay me rent as long as you keep it clean. In fact, you'd be doing me a favour by looking after it.'

When there was no reply, she glanced at the woman sitting beside her. To her amazement Edna Hollis's throat was working painfully. But it only took a moment for her voice to return.

'Blimey, missis, this is such a turn-up you fair took me breath away. Nobody ever gave me nothin' before, see, and now me and Daphne are going to have a house of our own—'

'It'll be just for the duration,' Skye said hastily.

'Oh, o' course! Once the war's over, we'll be off to America, anyway.'

'Where's this 'ouse, Mrs Pen?' Daphne said, scowling in the back seat. 'I fought we was coming ter live wiv you.'

'So you will, for a while. The cottage will need to be got ready for you, but I know you'll like it. It's up on the moors by the clayworks and the pottery—'

Daphne howled right in her ear. 'I ain't goin' ter live all up there! I want me own bedroom at New World.'

Her reward was a clip round the ear from her mother.

'Don't be so bleedin' ungrateful, Daphne,' Edna snapped.

'You ain't seen where it is! How can I go ter school from up there! I won't see Tilly nor my friends ever again!'

Skye thought there would be a good few parents who would be relieved to know that, but she spoke swiftly.

'Daphne, you're nearly eleven years old now, and most children change schools about that time. There's a very nice school at Roche, which is much nearer than Truro, and you'll make all kinds of new friends there. Besides,' she added, 'it probably won't be for very long. As your mother said, once the war is over you'll be getting ready to go to America. You'll be able to tell your new friends all about that.'

She could feel Daphne breathing heavily down her neck. But by now, Skye knew she'd be wrestling with indignity at not staying at New World indefinitely after all, and the thought of bragging about her mother's GI to her new school friends. In the end, pride won.

'I s'pose we oughter have a look at this cottage then. Just ter see what we think, mind,' she said grudgingly.

–

Nick came home from his chambers to have his ears blasted with the gory details of how Daphne and her mother had found out about the doodlebug that had destroyed their house and the row of houses alongside them. By then Butch was as white as a ghost and Daphne was ghoulishly elaborating about the bodies that could only be identified by bits of shoes and other objects.

'Thank God they're not going to be a fixture here,' Nick said, once he and Skye were alone. 'You're a blessed genius to have thought of an empty clayworker's cottage, Skye.'

'I know,' she said modestly. 'And tomorrow I'm taking them up there to show them around. The place will need cleaning and airing, and a bit of paint, but Butch said he'll be happy to help with that. The poor lamb's just thankful that Daphne won't be around here for too long.'

'And you don't think the Hollis woman will think it's a poor place after the promise of an American paradise?'

'Honey, I think Mrs Hollis is ready to grab anything she can get as long as it's free,' Skye said smartly.

But they couldn't get rid of them for a month. The cottage needed considerable repair work, and the roof leaked. Although it was summertime now, no one knew how long the Hollis pair would have to stay there.

However, any unease they might have had about it being beneath Edna's expectations was put to rest as soon as Skye saw her casting her eyes over the hefty clayworkers round about. Some of them were more than ready to lend a hand to their flashy new neighbour, and Skye found herself hoping that Edna's GI Gary was going to be man enough to cope with her.

All the same, it was an uneasy month, and Skye involved herself in securing a place at the Roche school for Daphne. The girl still wanted to see her old friends, though, and cycled all the way into Truro especially to tell Tilly Green about the night the doodlebug had fallen on their house. Nobody else could boast of such a thing, nor had any idea of what it was like, so Daphne had the world at her feet in the telling. By the time she had finished, the bomb had grown to gigantic proportions and killed everyone for miles around.

It was a huge relief to everyone when she and her mother were finally able to move into the clayworker's cottage on the moors, and Daphne could torment the life out of her new schoolfriends at Roche with her outrageous stories. Life at New World could revert to its harmonious level again.

–

Rumours that Hitler had been assassinated, or was about to be, were in full flood during the next few months, more in hope than fact. Plots to be rid of him abounded, even by his own officers, and it was reported in the press that in the so-called People's Court a number of them were cruelly executed for their part in such betrayal of the Führer.

'It's surely a measure of how things are going in our favour,' Skye said, scanning every newspaper. 'Hitler must see that there's no hope for him to win this war if his own officers are plotting to kill him. Paris and much of Europe is under the control of the Allies at last, and now that the Russians have cut off much of the Germans' oil supplies in Romania, the country must be in a state of panic. How much longer can they hold out?'

'I don't know,' Nick said. 'But there's one thing I'm sure about. They'll have their Maker to answer to when the full story of these concentration camps emerge.'

Skye glanced at him. Nick was a good man, but not a religious one, and when he resorted to mentioning God in any form, she always knew his thoughts were serious.

'David showed you some of the horror stories he's not prepared to print, didn't he?' she said quietly.

'He did, and in my opinion he should damn well print every one of them. People should know what kind of evil bastards these men are,' Nick said savagely.

Skye shuddered. The thought that anyone of theirs should ever be imprisoned in such terrible circumstances – as the Jewish friends and relatives of sweet Georgie Rosenbloom, all of who had never been seen or heard of again, had been— was too stomach-turning to think about. And yet, not to think about them was to deny that they ever existed. Georgie had killed himself because the pain of it was too much for him to bear, and such atrocities should never be forgotten.

'In the order of things, we've been lucky, haven't we, Nick?' she said slowly. 'We didn't think so when we heard about poor Justin, but he's safe in Yorkshire now with the friend who's caring for him. We didn't think so when Fanny was killed in an air raid, or when Seb was wounded and Celia had her breakdown. But our three have survived, and we have to be thankful for that. I thank God every day for it.'

'It's not over yet though, and until a peace treaty is signed, it would be foolish to be too complacent, darling.'

'I'm not going to be a pessimist, either,' she said stubbornly. 'It's not my style.'

–

By November it had become common knowledge that the Nazis were retreating all over Europe. The more disillusioned German soldiers were voluntarily surrendering in the liberated French and Belgian cities, and as if to underline Skye's hopes for the future, Celia arrived home like a whirlwind.

'I've had a letter from Moonie,' she announced, her blue eyes blazing with excitement. 'The old darling hadn't given up on me all this time, Mom, and he's got some information about Stefan at last!'

'And from the way you came bursting in here it's obviously good news…'

'The best. At least, it's the best anyone could hope for at this time. It seems that some of the captors holding political prisoners hostage have begun to panic over reprisals at the end of the war, and are letting them go.'

'Is Stefan a political prisoner?'

'More like a moral one, I'd say, for simply refusing to hand over his home to the Gestapo until he had no choice. But it amounts to the same thing.'

'So where does Moonie say he is now?'

Celia's elation faded a little. 'He doesn't know. He doesn't even know if Stefan is involved. It's just general information, but I have to keep my hopes alive that Stefan has been freed, Mom, and that somehow he'll be able to contact me soon. I *have* to believe that, don't I?'

Her eyes shone for a different reason now. They brimmed with the tears she refused to shed, and Skye's heart ached for her. The information was all so hazy, no more than a thread of hope, but she knew how desperate Celia was to cling to it. She could see it by the way she twisted the pearl and garnet ring on her finger.

In all this time, Celia had never lost faith that she would find her lover again, and Skye wasn't about to dash her hopes.

'We all have to believe it, darling,' she said softly. 'I'm sure your Captain Moon wouldn't have raised your hopes unnecessarily. He must think there's a good chance that Stefan will be freed, and he'll be in touch as soon as he possibly can. But you know how difficult that may be, so you'll just have to be patient a while longer, honey.'

'I can be patient for ever as long as I know Stefan's coming back to me.'

At her mother's doubtful look she gave a rueful laugh, because both of them knew it would take more than all the tea in China to give her patience.

The telephone rang as they were speaking, and Celia pressed her shaking hands together as Skye picked up the receiver, certain that fate had sent her here on this very day, and that she was about to hear Stefan's voice at last.

'It's Wenna,' Skye said, turning away from the sick disappointment in Celia's eyes, and holding the instrument away from her ear for a second as her younger daughter's voice came over the wire.

'Darling, that's wonderful, and Celia's had good news too. Stefan hasn't contacted her yet, but we have great hopes that he may be safe,' she added, more for Celia's benefit than Wenna's. 'You'll come down to see us as soon as you can get some leave, won't you? And try to bring Harry home for Christmas.'

She hung up, still smiling. This was turning out to be a very special day, she thought. First Celia, and now Wenna. And then she realised that Celia still didn't know what the call was all about, and she turned around to tell her.

But Celia was more intent on watching a boy on a bicycle toiling up the hill towards New World, and only half heard what her mother was saying.

'Harry Mack has proposed to Wenna and she's said yes! I'm very happy for her, though what difference it will make to her musical ambitions once the war is over, I have no idea. I doubt if either of them have considered that yet, anyway.'

Her voice trailed away as she realised that her daughter wasn't really listening. 'Celia, what is it?'

She caught sight of the boy on the bicycle then, and her heart seemed to leap in her chest. It wasn't Butch Butcher, cycling home from the pottery. It was a boy on a red bicycle, the kind that the boys from the Post Office rode. With her mind still so recently full of Stefan von Gruber, all Skye could think about was that after all Celia's hopes she was about to hear bad news.

Unless, of course, it was *good* news. Telegrams didn't always have to bring bad news, did they? she thought, with desperate optimism.

'Oh Mom—' Celia began.

'Keep calm, darling. It may be the news you're waiting for. You stay here and I'll go and see.'

It was a long while afterwards that she remembered the look on Celia's face when she went to answer the door and took the telegram out of the boy's hand. A look of premonition regarding something that Skye herself hadn't had the faintest inkling about. Her own sixth sense had completely failed her, she realised as she quickly tore open the envelope and stared at the words in sick horror.

It was nothing to do with Stefan. It was a far more poignant message for Skye. 'We regret to inform you… your son… Oliver Pengelly… missing in action…'

–

Wenna managed to get compassionate leave and was home within twenty-four hours, her own news completely overshadowed, her face full of stark misery. Celia was still at New World, having telephoned the farmer to say there was no way she could return to her duties, because she was needed at home. His scathing reply was to tell her not to return at all except to collect her belongings.

'To blazes with him,' Celia snapped. 'There are more important things than turning over his damn turnip fields. I'll resign and go back on the trams for the duration.'

'Can you do that?' Wenna said, glad to talk of anything but the thing that was uppermost in all their minds.

'God knows. And he's not telling. But I haven't even congratulated you on your engagement yet.'

'Oh Celia, I can't even think about that now. It seems so awful that Mom and I were talking so happily, and seconds later this happened. It seems—'

'Now just stop it. If you were about to say it's a kind of tit-for-tat thing because you were so happy, forget it. We've all gone through that kind of nonsense, and that's all it is – just nonsense. I could have said the same thing because I'd just heard that Stefan might be safe – and that's all conjecture, anyway. But I refuse to think there has to be a counterpoint for everything good that happens. It's too ridiculous.'

All the same, she mentally crossed her fingers as she spoke, because it was all so fearfully possible. All the clever-clever professors said as much, and who was she to dispute their learnings? She did, though, and she was damn well going to stick to it, for all their sakes.

'Look, the house is too bloody full of people this afternoon, with all the family rallying round Mom and Dad as ever, and I'm badly in need of some fresh air. It's the one thing I miss about the farming lark, I guess. Let's go up to the pottery. I want to make a phone call, and I can do it easier away from the house. I don't want Mom to hear it. Will you come with me?'

'Gladly,' Wenna said promptly. 'I never thought I'd say it, but the house is stifling me too. In the circumstances I haven't said anything to Mom yet about my future plans, but when Harry and I are married, we're going to live in Canada. His folks have a ranch there, and they breed horses.'

'It sounds wonderful. And Stefan and I will be managing our own hotel in Gstaad,' Celia went on determinedly, 'so we'll all be scattering again, won't we?'

But she avoided Wenna's eyes, knowing they were really thinking of Olly, and wondering if he'd be coming home at all.

'By the way, the infant Butch intends to stay here for ever,' Celia said suddenly. 'Did you know?'

'Thank God for Butch,' Wenna said, and they both knew what she meant. 'Anyway, what's this important phone call you're going to make that you couldn't make at home?'

'You'll see.'

Adam Pengelly was about to close the pottery for the day, and his face became anxious when he saw his two nieces approach. He was clearly afraid to ask if there was any more news of Olly, but Celia forestalled the question.

'We've heard nothing else, Adam, but I want to use the telephone here. Is that all right? Only it upsets Mom to hear me talking too much about it at home,' she said glibly.

'Of course it's all right, my dear. Just click the door shut when you've finished and it'll lock itself... Me and Felicity intended calling at New World this evening. What do you think? Does your mother want company?'

Celia managed a smile. 'When we left, Seb and his mother and all the Kingsley clan were there, and Butch was handing out lemonade and keeping Lily's kids amused. It does Mom good to be surrounded by folk, Adam, so go whenever you like.'

Nice as he was, he was an old fusspot, and she wished he would go away now, so that she could put the call through to the special number she kept locked in her memory. Once there was no one at the pottery but herself and Wenna, she picked up the phone and asked for the number she wanted.

After what seemed like an age she heard the efficient, well-remembered tones come over the wire.

'Hello Moonie,' she said huskily.

'Celia! By all that's holy, it's a joy to hear your voice. How are you, my dear girl? But I hardly need to ask, do I? I take it this call is on account of the letter I sent you, and I wish I'd been able to tell you more—'

'Moonie, it's not because of your letter, although of course I was overjoyed to get it, and I wanted to thank you for not giving up on me.'

'As if I would,' he said heartily. 'But if it's not about your fiancé, then what is it? I must say, you're not quite as bubbling as I expected you to be, so tell old Captain Moonlight what's wrong.'

The sudden kindness in his voice almost finished her, but she held on tightly to the telephone cord and stated the facts as calmly as she could.

'My brother's missing in action, Moonie. We've just heard the news, but I don't need to tell you how frustrating the bare facts can be. There's no real information. Nothing to say if his plane crashed or if he was wounded, or – or worse—'

'Take it easy, my dear,' he said, as her voice began to shake. 'Just tell me what you want me to do.'

She looked at the phone stupidly. What could he do? What crazy idea was in her head when she first thought of him? He wasn't God, able to do what nobody else could do – find her brother among a million other casualties of war…

Wenna took the phone out of her hand and spoke rapidly.

'Captain Moon, this is Celia's sister. Would you mind holding on for a moment while she recovers herself, please?'

'Of course. Tell her to take all the time she needs.'

Celia caught the sound of his booming voice, and bit her lip. "Take all the time she needs"… as if he wasn't one of the busiest men on earth, with a very important job, and no time to spend on a stupid female falling apart with grief…

She took back the phone from Wenna. Like an automaton she gave him Olly's name and service number, and without a qualm she went on with her request.

'I'm asking you to pull rank, Moonie. I know it's not your field, and Olly's only one young man among so many, but if anyone can get inside information, it's you. I know it's a heck of a lot to ask, and I shouldn't be doing it all—'

'I'll do whatever I can, Celia, and of course you had to ask me. I wouldn't have expected anything else. In fact, life has never been the same here since you left. I miss your quick wit and your quirky ways—'

'They're not so quirky now,' she mumbled, her eyes smarting at the unexpected compliment that was clearly meant to cheer her up.

'But they will be again, I promise you. I'll be in touch, my dear.'

She recognised the change in his voice, and guessed that his priorities had changed. She could almost sense the sudden rush of adrenalin and activity as some new decoding message came in – and she missed that feeling. She was no longer in the thick of it, and despite Moonie's many contacts, she knew it was a very long shot to see if he could find any news of Olly. All she could do was wait and try not to give way to the sudden depression that hit her.

It didn't even occur to her until much later that she hadn't even asked if there was any more news of Stefan. But of course there wouldn't have been, or he would have told her.

Chapter Fifteen

The news that Oliver Pengelly was missing spread around the district with the speed of a forest fire. At Skye's request, David Kingsley reported it only briefly in the *Informer*, confirming that the family was still waiting for definite news, and had every hope that their son was still alive.

No one really believed it, of course. The clayworkers were as awkward and inarticulate as Butch with their sympathy, but nonetheless sincere; the townspeople sent cards or stilted letters; and Daphne Hollis arrived at New World with a bunch of wild moorland flowers to make Mrs Pen feel better.

'It's a sweet gesture, but it makes me feel as if everyone has got him dead and buried already,' Skye said, weeping in Nick's arms.

She wavered between being completely out of control and deathly calm, and could do nothing to stop the moods. She refused to take the doctor's mind-dulling pills, preferring to keep her senses alert to whatever fate had in store for them.

She knew that the pills might have helped alleviate the nightmares, when she saw Oliver in the grip of some terrible death, burning or drowning, his body ripped apart or blown to pieces. She couldn't stop the nightmares, and nor would she try to blot them out artificially.

She wanted to feel the pain, and even welcomed it in a macabre way, because in doing so, she believed she was sharing whatever Olly was experiencing. It was wrong, and she knew it. It was virtually trying to take on God's role.

No human being could share another's pain, but the agony she had experienced when he was born had been hers alone, and if in some grisly manner she was now sharing the agony of his dying, she jealously guarded that too as hers alone. But the guilt of knowing exactly what she was trying to do made her constantly scratchy with Nick.

'I'm really worried about you, Skye,' he told her now, as she shook in his arms. 'You're not sleeping properly. You must let the doctor give you something—'

'*No!* Not until I know Olly's safe,' she snapped.

'But what good is it doing to suffer like this?'

'Would you not have me suffer for my son? Are you so damn self-sufficient that you can detach yourself from it all?'

'That's not fair,' he said, not even raising his voice. 'I love him too, Skye, and if you don't know that by now, then I wonder what we've been doing together all these years.'

Hearing the tightness in his voice, she was stricken with remorse at his quiet dignity, and she leaned into him again, feeling his strength, but unable to take comfort from it.

'I'm sorry,' she mumbled.

'You don't need to say it. And any day now we may get word that Olly's safe, and our worst fears will be over.'

She moved slightly away from him and looked up into his handsome face, seeing how his dark eyes were clouded and the lines around his mouth were accentuated with the tension he held so rigidly inside. Seeing how old and drawn her once young and virile lover looked now, she knew how selfish she was in not crediting him with suffering too.

'But you don't really believe he'll come home safely, do you?' she said, her mouth trembling. 'The truth now, Nick.'

After a moment he slowly bowed his head.

'If it's the truth you want, then I believe we've already said goodbye to our son, Skye,' he said.

As if the trauma of saying it out loud was suddenly too much to bear, seconds later his face twisted. He clung to her and wept silently in her arms, and she was at once the comforter and the comforted, and thought all the more of him for breaking down and releasing his feelings.

–

Celia and Wenna returned from what had become their ritual daily walk to get out of the house to find their parents still locked in a close embrace. With one accord they moved silently outside again.

'I can't stand much more of this,' Celia declared. 'I simply don't know what to do for the best. We're not helping, Wenna. They don't want us. We're constant reminders that something's wrong. Until some definite news comes through, they have to get on with their lives, and so do we.'

'I know you're right, but what do you suggest? Are you going back to Penzance after all?'

'I suppose so,' Celia said. 'I daresay they'll have me, much as I hated it, and at least I can get home quickly from there if ever – whenever—' She swallowed hard, and went on more harshly. 'I'd dearly love to ask if Moonie could take me back, but I doubt if the proper channels would welcome back a crazy woman.'

'You're not crazy. You're the sanest woman I know. But *I* begin to wonder how much compassionate leave is reasonable for someone whose brother is missing in action. If everyone did the same thing, there'd be no service personnel left.'

They looked at one another. They had been home for two weeks now, but there had been no more real inform-ation. Moonie hadn't been able to come up with anything more definite than the latest official word of 'missing in action'.

Beyond that, he had stretched the bounds of security and told Celia there had been a spate of missing aircraft that was being hushed up for morale purposes. Among them, several Bomber Command aircraft had been shot down during diversion tactics over Norway. It was suspected at source that Olly's had been one of them, but there was no mention of survivors in the reports, and until there was positive news of the air crews, nothing would be released.

'He could have parachuted out of the plane, Celia, and been picked up anywhere and taken to safety,' was the best Moonie could say. 'If I hear any more, I'll contact you.'

'Thank you,' she said woodenly. 'There's no news of Stefan, I take it?'

'I'm sorry, no.'

But why would there be? Moonie didn't even know him, and he was just a civilian, too old for the early conscription into the army, but not too old to be condemned for refusing to support his compatriots.

Though, in Celia's opinion, anyone who defied the Gestapo regime was a hero.

She hadn't repeated everything to her parents, only the positive thought that Olly might have parachuted into the countryside somewhere. Even if he had been taken prisoner, he would still be alive – but with the recent revelations about the horror camps, no one dared to make any more comments about such a possibility.

'I really think I should go back to my unit tomorrow,' Wenna told her sister now. 'I know Mom will understand.'

'Can you still manage to entertain the troops, with all this hanging over us?'

'I have to. It's not their fault, Celia. They need encouragement to carry on, and maybe in doing it for them, I'm doing it for Olly too.'

'You're a good kid,' Celia said huskily. 'Not such a kid any more, either. No wonder Harry Mack fell for you.'

'We've all grown up, haven't we? And a lot quicker than we would have done if we hadn't gone to war.'

'So I guess I'll do my duty and continue eating humble pie in the turnip fields. How's that for growing up?'

But their cautious laughter held more than a hint of desperation, before they linked arms and went back into the house to tell their parents what they had decided.

–

Long before a mellow Cornish November had slid into December, the newspapers announced that the Home Guard was officially to stand down, and the country gave a cautious rejoicing that surely such things couldn't be sanctioned unless Jerry was truly on the run.

For several months now, towns and cities away from the coast had been allowed to turn on moderate street lighting again, and children who had only ever seen their towns in darkness once night fell were enchanted by the sight.

'Good for them,' Skye said to Nick. 'But we're still denied the best news of all. And if you tell me once more that no news is good news, I shall scream. Until I hear for sure that Olly is safe, I'll be unable to rejoice over anything—'

'Why don't you think positively, the way you always used to, and turn your words around?' he retorted. 'Until you hear for sure that Olly's not coming home, there's always hope.'

After a small pause, she spoke sadly. 'We've changed, haven't we? I used to be the optimist, and you the pessimist.'

'Well, despite what I once said, one of us has to believe that he'll return,' he almost snapped. 'If you must know, I'm beginning to resent the sight of your gloomy face, Skye. It's not the most welcome thing to come home to.'

'Is that why you've been staying out more often lately?'

'Perhaps,' he replied, turning away, and she felt a huge surge of fear in her heart.

There could be another reason, of course. He was still a very handsome man, and he came into contact with all kinds of women in his work. Vulnerable women, needing advice and support. Who was to say that he wouldn't be as susceptible as the next man, when the alternative was coming home to a woman who seemed to have lost interest in life?

She caught sight of her reflection in the overmantel mirror, and was shocked at what she saw. Her beautiful black hair, the family trademark, was more than speckled with grey now, and she hadn't bothered about it properly in weeks. Her once lustrous blue eyes were dulled with anxiety and her private, silent weeping.

She was the one now, she thought furiously, who had her son already dead and buried before they even knew his fate. She owed him the force of her optimism.

'If only we could hear *something*,' she muttered. 'I begin to think there's a conspiracy of silence at the War Office about these missing planes. Either that, or there were so many of them that they daren't let the public know the extent of our losses. They've begun reporting some of them, I know, but how can Olly's plane be missing for so long with no word at all? No wreckage, or sightings, or bodies…'

She said the words deliberately, confronting them out loud, and as she did so, she felt a weird kind of strength seep back into her. Perhaps it was a conspiracy. Perhaps he'd been on some secret mission that couldn't be revealed as yet.

However crazy it sounded, she knew from Celia's guarded conversations about her previous decoding work that such things happened.

Nick held her close. 'Darling, I know he'll be safe. I have a feeling in my bones about it. Despite what I may have thought before, I think we'd have heard about it by now.'

He wasn't sure, any more than any of them were, but he wasn't going to dampen her sudden look of determination to think positively. He wasn't going to admit that he too had frequent nightmares about the chance of his son becoming fish-bait in the North Sea, or blown to pieces in a horrific air crash. He wouldn't let himself think of any of it, because he knew that to blot it out was the only way to keep sane.

But the news announcement in mid-December that Glenn Miller's plane had disappeared over a routine trip to France, and that all passengers and crew were feared dead, was almost enough to crush Skye's sprits again. They could find news of a celebrity plane all right, she thought bitterly, but they couldn't trace an ordinary airman's.

Then, when she had all but given up hope again, came a trickle of information.

A letter arrived from the Air Ministry. She was too afraid to open it until Nick came home that evening, even though Butch had offered to read it for her. But it wasn't his place, and she sent him out of the room before she gave the letter to Nick. Whatever Olly's parents had to face, they must do it together.

'Why didn't you call me?' Nick said. 'I would have come home earlier.'

'I knew you were in court today,' she said, her voice jerky with anxiety. 'I didn't want to disturb you.'

God, how feeble that sounded. How dreadful, too, when she knew instinctively that there had to be news of her son's life – or death – contained in that slim envelope.

'I'm so afraid, Nick,' she went on tremulously.

Her hands were clenched together, the palms damp with sweat. She didn't miss the fact that Nick's face was as white as her own, even as he ripped open the envelope and scanned the page.

'It's all right,' he said rapidly, but his voice was strained. 'At least, it's all right as far as the worst of our fears is concerned. Nothing is confirmed yet – but the news is at least hopeful.'

Skye almost snatched the letter out of his hands. 'What kind of information is that?' she said angrily. 'Are they tormenting us with half-truths?'

She read the formal words quickly. Plane wreckage had been picked up in one of the icy Norwegian fjords, and it was confirmed as one of Oliver Pengelly's squadron. A man had been found wandering in the woods, somehow keeping alive in a half-wild state in the harsh Norwegian winter. Between the lines the Pengellys deduced the terrible state of the man, but he had finally been able to babble out some service information and was now in hospital and identified as a British airman.

The letter went on in similar stilted manner to tell them that although it had been established that the man was not their son, it was hoped that once the airman had fully recovered his senses, more information would be forthcoming, and then the Pengellys would be contacted again.

'And that's all they can tell us?' Skye said, choked.

'At least we know one of them got out safely—'

'You mean *alive*, don't you?' she went on bitterly. 'But presumably his mind had gone and all identification was missing. So if he's the only one they've found so far, how much hope you do really hold out for Olly? You told me recently you thought we'd already said goodbye to him, remember? I can't forget that.'

'I wish to God I'd never said anything at all.'

'So do I.'

She couldn't rid herself of the imagery of the plane wreckage in one of those impenetrably deep Norwegian fjords. The fact that one man had got out alive did nothing to ease her torment. In her imagination she could see the pilot still strapped in his seat, even now, deep in his underwater tomb. And Olly… her sweet baby… his young body ripped apart with the impact of the plane hitting the icy water.

The very thought of drowning – of the sensation of mouth and eyes and lungs filling up with water until they almost burst; of choking and gasping desperately for air, and knowing that there was no escape whatsoever – was filling her with a growing sense of claustrophobia. As if she was the one knowing the terror of sinking into an eternal darkness…

'Skye, put your head between your knees,' she heard Nick order her as if from a distance.

Next minute, a glass was thrust between her cold lips. She opened them and swallowed the bitter-tasting brandy automatically, choking as she did so.

'I'm all right,' she gasped. 'Just for a moment I couldn't breathe, but I'm all right now. I need some air.'

'Let's go outside—'

She touched his arm. 'I need to be alone, Nick. I need space to think by myself. Please understand, honey.'

And although he let her go, she knew he wouldn't really understand. Why would he? He was a lawyer, who solved everything by logical means and by poring over legal tomes, not by the airy-fairy urge to be up on the moors in the place where her ancestors had lived and breathed and died.

The thought was in her head without conscious effort. In a strange and inexplicable way, the moors had always been her family's sanctuary, maybe even more so for the women than the men. It was where they always went in time of trouble or fear. It was where Morwen Tremayne and Celia Penry had circled the old Larnie Stone to discover the images of their future sweethearts, nearly a hundred years ago.

It was where Morwen's brother, Sam, had died in the collapse of Ben Killigrew's rail tracks, on a clayworkers' outing to the sea. And that was the death that had resulted in Morwen and Ben taking in three orphaned children to their hearts and their home; Skye's own mother, Primmy, and Walter and Albert.

Morwen had been born in one of the little cottages overlooking Killigrew Clay, which was the pivot of all their hopes and dreams. It was where the heart of the family belonged, and it was where Skye knew she had to be while she concentrated her mind on praying for the safety of her son. She knew how badly she needed the spirit and passion of those ancestors around her now.

She toiled up the wintry slopes, scorning the use of a car or a bicycle, needing to feel in contact with the earth, and not caring if she was behaving like a madwoman, as crazy as the old witchwoman in the hovel on top of the moors.

Sunlight was thin and watery on this December day, but it still glinted on the soaring sky-tips as it had always done, unchanging and eternal. The clayworks were silent now, with work done for the day, and no endless shifts of men and women and children scurrying about as they had done in days gone by.

The milky green pool where Celia Penry had drowned herself through the shame of being raped was still and deep, hiding its secrets. That other Celia was someone Skye had never known, but whose memory was forever perpetuated in the name of her own daughter. All for Morwen's sake. All for the grandmother she had loved so much…

Without warning, Skye felt a huge bitterness surge in her heart. Hardly aware of her own actions, she picked up a stone and hurled it into the clay pool, watching the ripples spread across its surface and spoil its evil serenity.

Without warning, she was shouting hoarsely into the silence.

'Damn you, Granny Morwen! *Damn* you, and Great-Grandma Bess and Great-Grandad Hal, and Mom and Dad, and every Tremayne and Killigrew who ever lived. I want no part of you. I don't want to be beholden to your past. This is *my* life, and mine alone. I wish I had never come here to be entangled with you all. I was a fool to think this was where I belonged.'

The rippling patterns of the pool grew wider and wider as she threw stone after stone into it, trying to exorcise every memory of those earlier ghosts. The ground was glossed with dew in the late afternoon, but she noticed none of it as her feet slid and slipped.

She was filled with a weird sense of exhilaration, of freedom and excitement, as if the oppression and weight of all those family ties was being abandoned for ever. It didn't feel like a betrayal, more a sense of becoming herself at last, instead of being just a continuation of all that had gone before. And she gloried in the feeling.

She laughed out loud, revelling in the sound, since it seemed so long since she had laughed, or danced or sung. Her feet gave a little skip of pure joy, and the next moment she went sprawling and rolling on the damp earth, her arms spread out to save herself, but still laughing, as if fully aware of how ridiculous she must appear, a middle-aged woman behaving like a wild thing.

But with the sound of her hysterical laughter came a slower and fuller awareness of where she was, and who she was. She was aware of the madness and futility of her actions in denying her past, and above all in denying those loving ancestors who had helped to shape the woman she was today.

'Oh God, forgive me, Granny Morwen,' she heard herself mumble, as her head dropped to the ground and she tasted the dankness of the earth on her lips and felt its coolness on her cheeks. Sobs welled in her throat, where moments before there had been laughter. She knew she had been truly in the grip of madness, for to deny her heritage was to deny her own Celia and Wenna – and Olly too.

She heard a scuffle of feet, and as she sensed the shadow above her, her eyes closed in shame. If this was that grizzled old witchwoman, about to shriek abominations at her, then she would know she had truly let the devil into her heart...

'Have you hurt yerself, Mrs Pen?' she heard Daphne Hollis's scared young voice say. 'Should I go and fetch me Ma or somebody?'

Skye jerked up her head, knowing how stupid she must look, a grown woman lying face down on the moors with her arms spreadeagled as if in supplication, and her face covered in clay dirt. She rubbed at her cheeks and sat up carefully, breathing deeply for a few seconds before she spoke shakily.

'I'm not hurt, Daphne. I slipped and got winded for a minute, that's all.'

'Yer'd better come to the cottage and let me Ma clean yer up then,' the girl said practically. 'If yer don't mind me sayin' so, yer look a real sight, Mrs Pen, like one o' them clayworking gels in the old newspaper pictures.'

'Do I, Daphne?' Skye said huskily. The thought sped into her mind that out of the mouths of babes and vaccies could often come more common sense than ever came from an educated woman's brain.

'Come on then,' Daphne went on. 'We was just going to 'ave our tea, and me Ma will be wond'ring what's happened to me. We've got summat to tell yer, anyway.'

She couldn't hide the excitement in her voice as she put out her arm to help Skye to her feet.

'Have you? What's that?'

Oh honey, tell me anything to help me rid myself of the madness of the last ten minutes, Skye thought.

'We're gettin' hitched,' Daphne announced in triumph. 'Gary wrote to me Ma to say he's bein' sent back to America on account of his war wound. So we're gettin' hitched before Christmas and goin' wiv 'im. What do yer think of that!'

'I'm astonished!' was all Skye could think of to say.

She hadn't known that Gary had a war wound, either, but it was clear that Daphne was totally swept away by the glamour of going to America. And what a coup to tell her school friends about, was her next thought. Above all things, Daphne needed to feel important and this was clearly the pinnacle of her dreams.

'I'm really happy for you and your Mom, honey,' she went on, giving the girl a quick hug.

Daphne squirmed away. 'Yeah, well, as long as I don't have ter start talking funny, like you do,' she giggled.

Skye began to laugh. 'Daphne, you can talk any way you like, and you'll always do me a power of good.'

'Will I?' Daphne said suspiciously. 'It's not what me Ma says then. She says I'm a proper caution.'

'You're that too,' Skye told her solemnly.

–

'Where the hell have you been, Skye?' Nick said angrily when she finally returned to New World, having had her ears stormed by how wonderful life in America was going to be for the Hollises once they were mutually hitched to Gary. 'I was about to send out search parties for you. And what in God's name has happened to your clothes?'

'Oh, don't fuss, Nick. I fell over, that's all, but Mrs Hollis let me have a wash and brush-up at the cottage.'

'You've been up on the moors? Skye, it's practically dark now! Anything could have happened to you.'

'Where else would I go when I needed to think?' she snapped. 'And how could anything bad happen to me with Granny Morwen looking after me?'

She bit her lip. She should be past all that weird stuff at her age, and she knew Nick didn't like that kind of talk, anyway. Besides, she couldn't forget the guilty fact that she had totally rejected it herself just a short time ago. She lowered her eyes, feeling a swift shock that she could have done so, and then she felt her husband's arms fold around her.

'I should have remembered,' he said softly. 'She would never let any harm come to you.'

She caught her breath at his unexpected understanding and acceptance before raising her face for his kiss, and in that moment she had never loved him more.

–

The Hollises were gone before Christmas. Americans moved with admirable swiftness, Skye told Butch when he came home from White Rivers and reported that the cottage was empty. Daphne had already called to say goodbye, and it might have been a far more emotional one, but for her obvious excitement at going on a ship to the other side of the world.

Just for a moment, Skye had felt a huge tug at her heart, imagining Daphne's feelings at her first sight of the New York skyline, and the green Statue of Liberty rising out of the ocean like a fantasy figure, welcoming all who saw her.

Then she grinned wryly. Knowing Daphne, she would probably not even notice Lady Liberty, except to make some rude comment.

'Are we having Christmas this year, Mrs Pen?' she heard Butch say cautiously. At his uneasy look, Skye felt a rush of affection for him.

'Why, what a thing to say, Butch. Of course we're having Christmas. Why on earth wouldn't we?'

His blush met his carroty hairline. 'Well, because of – of Olly, and we've all been so sad lately – I thought perhaps we should all be quiet—'

'Well, we're not going to be quiet at Christmas-time. Goodness me, what would New World be like without celebrating Christmas? We can't let it pass as if it's just another day, can we?'

But she swallowed hard as she spoke, and she didn't let him see how bright her eyes were, or what an effort it was to constantly remind herself that life went on, even if hearts were breaking.

In the end, it was the best idea of all to fill the house with people. Celia was home, and so was Wenna with Harry Mack. All the relatives came as usual, and Skye kept a determined smile on her face as they all drank a toast to Olly, saying stoutly that this time next year he would be drinking a toast to all the stay-at-homes instead.

'And long before this time next year, God willing, we'll all be living in a free world again,' Nick added.

'I can't remember what anything was like before the war,' Butch said, frowning.

'Good Lord, I don't suppose you can, kiddo,' Celia said, glad to change the subject before her mother's smile slipped. 'Well, when it's all over we'll have bananas by the bucket-load, and so much chocolate it will make you sick. You'll get so fat you'll be waddling up to White Rivers every day—'

'Stop it, Celia,' Seb laughed. 'Leave the boy alone. He's doing a grand job at the pottery, and I won't have you teasing my star pupil.'

'He's your only one, isn't he?' she grinned back at him, and ducked as he made a mock swipe at her.

Watching them, and listening to their nonsense, Skye thought what a handsome pair they made. If Celia wasn't still so madly in love with Stefan von Gruber – a hopeless liaison in her opinion – she was sure she and Seb could have made a go of it. It wasn't unheard of for cousins to marry – her own parents bore witness to that – but fate had evidently decided that Celia was a one-man girl.

She had thought that about herself once, when she and Philip Norwood had only had eyes for one another, but fate – and Nick Pengelly – had proved that love could come for a second time, and be just as spectacular.

'What are you smiling at?' she heard Nick say beside her.

'I was just thinking how much I love you, and how good it is to have all our family around us,' she said steadily. 'And even those who aren't here now are still with us in spirit, aren't they, Nick?'

'Always,' he said.

–

The remote Norwegian farmhouse was warm and cosy, the wood fires in every room burning fiercely to defy the bitter cold from the snow outside. The girl with the long silvery hair leaned over the bed of the young man with the ugly jagged cuts on his cheeks and chest.

The wounds were healing satisfactorily now, but they were still too tender for him to bear any bedding touching them. The girl's heart ached for the once-fine sight of the young man's body, criss-crossed with such hideous scars now.

They would fade in time, and few would know the raw vividness she and her brother had seen when they had brought him here a month ago, nearer dead than alive. He had been lucky to be found just days before the first bad snows of the winter had set in. A few days more, and he would surely have perished. Some were born lucky, and Birgitta had known instinctively that he was one of them. She knew about such things… she was acknowledged as a healer and she could sense the need for survival in this man.

The patient stirred in his sleep now, and Birgitta wondered if this would be the day, at last, when he would recover full consciousness. Until that day came, they had no idea who he was. His garbled shrieks and mutterings gave no clue as to his nationality or identity, and all remnants of identifiable uniform and dog-tags had been ripped away from him long before they had found him.

But the hand holding hers was becoming increasingly strong, and she prayed that he would soon awake. It was foolish to fall in love with someone whose gaze was so vague as yet. But his eyes were as startlingly blue as her own, and they made her heart race each time they looked at her.

Birgitta came from fierce Viking stock, and fervently believed in the old legend that said that the man whose life she saved forever belonged to her.

She felt her brother's hand touch her shoulder, and she waited a moment before looking up at him. Her long straight hair fell over her face, and she hoped swiftly that it hid the passion in her eyes for her unknown warrior.

'Come away now, Birgitta,' Rolf said gently. 'You know we can't let this go on much longer. We don't know if he's British or Polish, or even German, but people will be looking for him, and we have to notify someone soon.'

'Why must we?' she said fiercely. 'We've tended to his wounds, and he's healing well. He should be allowed to recover in his own time.'

'But there will be others who are missing him. He may have a wife and family—'

'*No*,' she said. 'I would know if it were so. I would feel it. Besides, I'm sure he's not German.'

Rolf spoke more sharply. 'Birgitta, you can't rely on your instincts in this case. It's time to inform the partisans that the man is here, and let them decide what to do next.'

As if in answer to his words, the man in the bed stirred, and his incoherent mumbling began as usual. But as Birgitta leaned closer, she heard that some of his words were better formulated than usual, and she frowned.

'Olly?' she said, looking up at her brother. 'What does this mean? What is Olly?'

The man's grip on her hand tightened, and she saw that his eyes were a fraction clearer than before.

'Olly,' he whispered painfully and slowly, as if finding it hard to move his dry lips over the simplest of words.

'Olly – Oliver—' he managed, and then his clasp slackened again and he slumped into sleep once more.

'Oliver,' Birgitta repeated after a startled moment. 'I know that name, Rolf, and so do you. It is the name of the boy in the famous British story who asked for more gruel. This is an educated man to speak such a name.'

She looked at Rolf again. 'He's told us something else too, I think. Whoever he is, he's British. Thank God.'

'Then we know where to start. I'll alert the partisans right away, and they will inform the British authorities.'

'Must you?' Birgitta said, all her feelings in her eyes, and desperately wanting to keep him to herself for just a little while longer.

At least until the moment when he opened his eyes properly and realised that she was a vibrant young girl on the brink of womanhood, and not merely a pair of healing and caring hands that had tended his most intimate requirements in these past weeks.

'I must, my love,' Rolf said quietly. 'And you know it. He doesn't belong here.'

Chapter Sixteen

There had been a time, long ago, when all that Stefan von Gruber had dreamed about was becoming a respected vintner like his father. Of following in the family footsteps, and carrying on the tradition of growing the grapes on the vast von Gruber Estates that produced such fine German wines.

As a small boy, still enchanted with his heritage, he had known the magic of seeing how the rows upon rows of the bare winter sticks of the vines gradually came into shining green leaf. There was even more magic in the way the tiny clusters of dry pips developed into the luscious purple globes of the grapes, their sensual aroma enveloping the crystal clear air of the vineyards.

During the boredom of being interned, he used his imagination fully to exercise his mind, recalling the halcyon days of childhood. He could still imagine the lovely, squishy feel of the grapes in his hands, staining his clothes and his fingers purple, and could well remember knowing he was in for a scolding from his mother, and indulgent laughter from his father.

In the last few years, such memories had sustained him in a way he would never have believed. When the Gestapo had so viciously commandeered his home and imprisoned him along with other political prisoners for refusing to co-operate, he had thought himself one of the forgotten men.

Their guards hardly knew what to do with them, since the prisoners were all intelligent and influential men in their own right. They weren't even criminals in the general sense, and they were given as much leeway within their confines as it was possible to have, without allowing them their liberty. The guards were canny men, and while keeping them strictly at arm's length, had become as sociable with their prisoners as dignity and hierarchy allowed.

In the dying months of 1944, they, like everyone else, knew that the end of the war was in sight. Hitler would inevitably be overthrown, and they would want to be known to have been lenient. And when another new year had come and gone, and the Allies were burgeoning their way through Europe, many of the captors simply panicked and fled, leaving the prisoners to discover that their doors were no longer being locked at night.

There was nothing to prevent them from leaving their isolated strongholds and going their separate ways. But for many, the enforced camaraderie of the past years did not spill over into this new freedom, and they knew it was not going to be easy to resume life in a country that was so vastly different now from the way it had been five years before.

–

After his parents' deaths, it had been Stefan's plan to begin a new life in Switzerland with his adored Celia, and he offered up a silent prayer of thanks to whatever God was looking after him that he had thought to deposit the bulk of his fortune in a Swiss bank before the worst happened.

But he had no idea where Celia was now, and she might even think he was dead. As a businessman he had known a great many influential people, but he had become wary of everyone now, and there was no way of knowing whom he could trust.

When he left his prison in the chill of a February morning, he was dressed far more soberly than of old. He needed to merge into the outside world, and try to find out exactly where he was.

But he was also disorientated and temporarily destitute, and he knew he must contact someone who could help him. From newspapers and road signs, he realised he had been held in a remote area some distance west of Berlin.

Then he remembered his old boss, Herr Vogl, with whom Celia's parents had done such good business in the years before the war. He prayed that the Vogls would still be sympathetic towards their old business friends.

Herr Vogl had been a fair and honest man, and Stefan hoped that he might advance his old employee some money so that he could make his way to Switzerland.

It hurt his pride to have to ask such a thing, but he would do anything for the chance of contacting Celia again. So, fighting off the panic attacks that had become all too frequent since his unexpected liberation, he gathered his thoughts and made his plans, and tried to feel slightly more human again.

–

The Vogls were preparing for supper when the doorbell rang, and Herr Vogl answered it with some annoyance. No one trusted late callers these days, although by now everyone knew it was only a matter of time before the Nazi regime was crushed. Then, perhaps, the world could return to normality again after all the suffering and madness of war.

'Yes? Who is it?' he said, opening the door a fraction.

'A friend, Herr Vogl,' Stefan said at once. 'A one-time friend and business acquaintance. Stefan von Gruber.'

Vogl opened the door a little wider and stared at the shabby attire and the spare frame of the man he remembered as once having such a fine physique.

'*Mein Gott*, man, what has happened to you? Come inside and warm yourself by the fire. Have you been ill?'

Stefan gave a bitter laugh as he was ushered into the drawing room. 'Not ill, exactly. But deprived of my liberty all this time due to my convictions—'

Too late, he remembered that long ago the son of this house, the young and earnest Franz Vogl, had become one of Hitler's Brown-shirts.

Stefan wished desperately that he could have taken his words back, but he had walked for miles to get here, and he was near to collapse with fatigue. He simply couldn't think sensibly any longer. But he recognised that these strait-laced people might well view him as a traitor to the Fatherland... He swayed a little, and felt the older man grip his arm.

'Sit down, von Gruber, and take a nip of brandy.'

He obeyed, because he had become used to taking orders. He had not been badly treated during internment, but all liberty and sense of self-respect had been taken away from him and his fellow prisoners. They ate when they were told, slept when they were told, took exercise when they were told.

Once he had recovered a little, he knew this man and his wife would want answers as to why he was here. He steadied himself enough to know he must go carefully.

In the formal German manner of politeness before explanation, he enquired about the Vogl family.

'Our son is dead,' Herr Vogl said abruptly. 'He was killed doing his duty for the Fatherland. My wife and I feel it best to state these things at once, to save embarrassment.'

God, he was a cold fish, thought Stefan. Frau Vogl too sat as rigidly as if a son wasn't part of a loving family, just a commodity to be mentioned in passing. But it was their nature, he thought, with a vague recollection of how Celia had amused him with anecdotes of the Vogls' long-ago Christmas visit to Cornwall, and told him how stiff and starchy they had been in that free and easy household. Clearly, nothing had changed.

'My sincere condolences on your loss,' he said gravely.

Herr Vogl's shoulders sagged for a brief moment. 'We are all casualties of war in one way or another, my friend. The world has changed for the worse, and I fear that the old order is no more, and never will be again.'

His words gave Stefan a glimmer of an opening.

'But once it's all over, we will have to resume normal living again, or it will have been for nothing. Forgive me, sir, but even old enemies must strive to regain something of what's past, wouldn't you agree?'

He saw the flash of anger in Herr Vogl's eyes, and for a moment he thought he had gone too far. Then he saw Frau Vogl put a restraining hand on her husband's arm.

'I suspect that you are thinking of the Pengelly girl, Herr von Gruber,' she said quietly. 'I believe you and she had an affection for one another at one time.'

'For *all* time, Frau Vogl,' Stefan said, ignoring all thought of caution now. 'We loved each other deeply, and were to be married. I pray that someday it will still be possible.'

He took a long draught of the stinging brandy and felt his head spin. It had been a mistake to drink on an empty stomach, and so far he had been offered no food.

The condemned man drank a shot of brandy, he found himself thinking... *and then he was shot.*

'Please forgive me for bothering you like this,' he said, getting clumsily to his feet. 'I shouldn't have come here.'

'Sit down, man. As a former colleague, you are welcome,' Herr Vogl said harshly. 'We were about to eat, and I'm sure my wife can stretch our meagre fare to three. The pantry is not so plentiful as it once was, but we survive. Then we will talk, and if it is your wish, we will be happy to offer you the hospitality of our home until you decide what you are going to do.'

'You are very kind, and I accept gladly,' Stefan said, his heart too full to say more at this unexpected gesture.

–

Now that France had been liberated, Wenna's ENSA concert party was entertaining troops in Paris and other French cities. Everyone said the war would be over soon, and Celia knew how buoyant her sister was these days, eagerly waiting for the day when it all ended, and she and Harry Mack could be married.

Celia was happy for her, and she tried not to let her own sadness show in the regular letters she wrote to her sister. But at the start of the new year she had good news to tell her, since their cousin Seb was now seeing a girl from Roche, and was seriously courting at last. She was happy for both of them, but it did seem to emphasise her own lack of news, and she felt increasingly lonely.

She never lost faith that one day she and Stefan would be together again, and she ached for the day when he would take her in his arms and vow that nothing had changed between them, nor ever could.

But she was wise enough to know that it would never be quite the way it had been before. Not at first, anyway. So much had come between them, and however much they desired it and longed for it, there would be an inevitable awkwardness at being reunited.

In her darkest moments, she wondered if they would both have changed irrevocably. No one could ever know how deep the changes were until the moment of truth when they were together again. Celia shivered, torturing herself with doubts, but facing facts logically, the way she had always done.

–

Even as Celia was writing her letter to Wenna, a wedding was taking place in a small country church somewhere south of Paris.

The ceremony was conducted in French and English, and there was no formal attire among the chief participants or the wedding guests. There was a mixture of army and air force uniforms, and a large sprinkling of local people who had turned out to witness a far happier occasion than had been seen in their bullet-riddled town in recent years.

'Do you, Harry Johnson Mack, take Wenna Pengelly to be your wedded wife? Will you love her and honour her, and keep you only unto her, so long as you both shall live?'

The man looked deeply into his bride's vivid blue eyes.

'I will,' he said quietly.

The priest turned to the beautiful woman in the trim khaki uniform, mourning, as only a Frenchman could, that with such gloriously dramatic colouring she couldn't be wearing virginal white. But the obvious love between the two was the only thing that mattered, and he cleared his throat once more.

'Do you, Wenna Pengelly, take Harry Johnson Mack to be your wedded husband? Will you love, honour and obey him, and keep you only unto him, so long as you both shall live?'

'I will,' murmured Wenna, her voice catching at the solemn beauty of the moment as the priest motioned to Harry to slide the gold ring on to her wedding finger.

'I now pronounce you man and wife,' said the priest. He looked around at the congregation and spoke sternly. 'Whom God has joined together let no man put asunder.'

'Just let anyone try,' Harry murmured so that only Wenna could hear, as he pulled her into his arms and pressed his mouth to hers in their first married kiss.

And then all solemnity was over, and their friends and supporters surrounded them, and kisses and tears flowed in equal measure, together with good luck flowers from the local well-wishers. They had little to give, but everyone loved a wedding, and this marriage of strangers in their midst seemed the best way of all to herald the start of the new year.

'Have we done the right thing, do you think?' Harry whispered mischievously in her ear when they were finally leading the procession down the street to the cafe in the square where they were to hold a small reception.

'No. We're totally mad,' Wenna said, smiling, touched beyond words as local children threw flowers in their path.

'What will your folks think when we tell them?'

She smiled again, sure of herself, and sure of his love.

'They'll love it. How could my mother do otherwise, when she and my father did the very same thing?'

She wasn't sure about Nick – though she knew her mother could always placate him – but from the moment Harry had told her he couldn't bear to wait until the war was over to make her his wife, she had known they would do this.

There had been an undoubted sense of charm and continuity in her mind, knowing that her mother had married her father in the very same way during the First World War – secretly, telling no one but their wartime colleagues, and for no other reason but the need to be together.

Skye and Philip hadn't even told their closest family their secret for some time, but Wenna and Harry intended writing home with their news at once.

But first there was the small reception of food and drink, generously hoarded and donated by their colleagues, and catered by the romantic French cafe owners. There was much laughter and teasing innuendo before it was over, and they winced at the clanking sound of the old tin cans that were tied to the back of the small car they had borrowed.

But finally, as twilight merged into the soft darkness of evening, they were alone to enjoy their brief weekend leave at a small hotel in the country. It wasn't the honeymoon of the rich and famous, but for two people so very much in love, it was more idyllic than anything that money could buy.

'Do you know how often I've dreamed of this moment?' Harry murmured, as he slid the silky straps of her slip from her shoulders, and bent his head to kiss the soft smooth skin of each one.

'Tell me,' she said huskily, her senses tingling anew with every touch of his hands and mouth. She was happy to prolong the moment, knowing that this sweet banter was no more than a prelude to the pleasure they would take in one another, on this night and for the rest of their lives.

'Every day since the day I met you,' he said, his lips moving downwards to kiss the wild pulsing at her throat. 'And every night since then, I've ached to hold you in my arms and make you mine, and to know that no one else could have you.'

'No one else ever could – or ever will.'

She felt his hands moving over her slender shape, finding the curves and hollows through the slip. With a growing fire in her body that matched his own, she longed for him to know every part of her, properly and without restriction or inhibition.

'Harry, I want—' she began tremulously, hesitating for no more than an instant. 'I don't think I can bear to wait a moment longer.'

'Nor I, my sweet darling,' he said, pushing the silky garment down the length of her body until it fell in a shimmering heap on the carpet. 'And I thank God I don't have to apologise for my hunger for you.'

With one movement he swept her up in his arms and lay her on the bed. Moments later he had filled her with himself, and she gloried in the erotic fever of his lovemaking. If there was one coherent thought left in her mind as they soared towards an exquisite completeness, it was to thank God that they had found one another, out of all the world.

–

Normal communication between Europe and Britain was slowly being restored, and the letter that arrived at New World a few weeks later had an unmistakably French stamp on it.

"I've truly been meaning to write to you sooner than this, Mom," Wenna had written. "But after my recent leave we were immediately sent to give a series of concerts to the British and Allied troops in Normandy, and you wouldn't believe how hectic and disorganised everything is there. Still, the reception we got was simply wonderful. Life will never be the same for me after all this adulation."

Skye smiled indulgently, knowing how unbelievably modest her girl still was, despite the lovely voice that must have cheered thousands of servicemen by now. As many as the much-fêted Vera Lynn, Skye thought loyally... She read on, and sat bolt upright.

> *As a matter of fact, nothing will ever be the same for me again after my last leave, Mom. It was no more than a weekend, but it was the most blissful weekend of my life, because I spent it with Harry in the sweetest little hotel in the country. And before you're completely shocked, I have something very special to tell you.*
>
> *Harry and I were married on our last leave. We simply couldn't wait any longer, and I pray that you'll understand, because it was the same for you and Daddy, wasn't it? I know you'll feel a bit cheated out of giving me a big wedding but it*

wasn't what we wanted, or needed. All we needed
was each other, so please be happy for us.

Skye was reading the words for the umpteenth time when Nick came home and found her there, sitting motionless, her mind a million miles away.

Remembering a time when she too had wanted nothing but to be in her beloved's arms, desperate to know the feeling of belonging while everyone around them threatened to blast all the world into oblivion. A threat that was even greater so in this war.

She and Philip had been so in love, exactly as Wenna and Harry were in love…

'What's wrong?' Nick said, alarmed at her silence. 'It's not bad news, is it, darling?'

She smiled at him, the second great love of her life. In many ways the best love of all, because he was her last and most enduring love. She stretched out her hand and he came to sit beside her. She leaned against him.

'No, it's not bad news. For once, it's happy news,' she said. 'But I think you had better read it for yourself while I pour us both a celebratory glass of sherry.'

'Good Lord, it must be good news for you to take a drink in the middle of the afternoon,' he said with a grin, but she could see the relief in his face. There had been enough bad news to contend with over the years, and it was time they all turned the corner.

The next moment her euphoric mood shattered and her hand shook over the sherry decanter as he uttered a savage oath.

'The unspeakable bastard! This was presumably a shotgun wedding—' he said explosively.

'*Nick*, how could you think such a thing! I thought you had more trust in our daughter.'

'I trust *her* all right, but not this conniving bastard. What kind of a hole-and-corner wedding could it have been, anyway, doing it on the quiet and telling nobody until it was all over?'

'*My* kind,' Skye said, her voice stiff with anger. 'The very same kind that Philip and I had in wartime. But I suppose no one could expect a *lawyer* to understand the needs of two people very much in love and far from home, who couldn't bear to be apart one moment longer, and were always aware that every day might be their last.'

The silence in the room was electric. Then Nick had covered the distance between them and was holding her unyielding body tightly in his arms.

'My God, Skye, forgive me. I didn't think—'

'You never do. You can be as objective as ice when it comes to your clients, but not where your family is concerned. Don't you find that strange?'

Her voice still shook with rage and she couldn't relax in his arms. He had spoiled the most beautiful moment of these dark days, and she couldn't forgive him for that.

'Don't you know why?' he said in a strangled voice at last. 'Don't you know it's because I love you all so much, and it tears me apart to know what's happening to all of us? I can't bear to see how Celia still lives in hope for her German fellow – and not knowing if Olly's dead or alive – and now losing Wenna in this way—'

'You idiot,' Skye said, all her stiffness melting away in an instant. 'We haven't lost her. She'll always be ours, and she'll want us to be happy for her now. If she's half as happy as we've been, she'll do all right – wouldn't you say?'

Her eyes dared him to say otherwise, despite their sometimes volatile relationship. Through it all, the love had survived, and always would. All of this was no more than one irregular heartbeat in the steadfastness of their lives together. She truly believed that. She lifted her face for his kiss, and he crushed her mouth with his own.

'I may be a successful lawyer, but my wife is much cleverer than I could ever be,' he mumbled against her mouth.

'That's because I'm a Tremayne at heart,' she told him, just in case he thought she was still harbouring secret yearnings for Philip Norwood after all this time.

'So are you going to write straight back to Wenna?'

'Of course. We both will, and we'll promise them a New World party to end all parties when we're all together again,' she said determinedly.

–

Celia was openly envious.

'The lucky little devil,' she said to her companions in their draughty billet when she heard the news. 'My sister's just got married in France to her Canadian Group Captain.'

'There'll be a right shaking of the old bedsprings going on in the old barracks by now then,' giggled East End Gertie, making a rude gesture. 'Unless she did it just to get her ticket back to Blighty, of course.'

'What do you mean?' Lizzie said, as dim as ever.

'I mean, pea-brain, that married women can have babies – or didn't anyone ever tell you about the birds and bees?'

'Don't be stupid, Gertie. I doubt that my sister would even think about having a family yet,' Celia said.

'And you'd know all about how to prevent it, of course, clever-clogs,' Gertie sneered.

Celia looked at her in exasperation. 'When are you going to stop this stupid inverted snobbery, Gertie? We're all in the same boat—'

'Don't you mean the same dung-heap?' the other girl grinned, and then shrugged. 'Oh well, I dare say you're not so bad, Pengelly – for a country girl, that is. So when are you going to tell us a bit more about this man of yours that you keep so secret? You're next in the wedding stakes, I suppose.'

Celia's nerves jangled, and she gave a forced laugh. 'I'm waiting until after the war before I tie the knot.'

Lizzie spoke up slyly, taking Gertie's lead. 'I don't reckon he exists. I reckon you just made him up!'

'Maybe I did,' Celia said, turning her head away to hide her stinging eyes. 'But you'll never know, will you?'

A sudden knock on their billet door saved her from answering any more probing questions. The farmer's son was calling her name imperiously.

'There's a telephone call for you, Pengelly, and Father says you're to be quick because he wants to use it himself.'

'The old fart probably wants to call his lady friend,' Gertie jeered. 'You take as long as you like, Pengelly.'

Celia was glad to escape. They were coarse and irritating, though they had all got used to one another by now, and rubbed along fairly well. In a perverse kind of way she would miss them when they all disbanded.

Like a hole in the head, she amended grimly, hearing their raucous laughter. It followed her across the farmyard to the house, where she thankfully closed the door and picked up the phone in the passageway.

It was Moonie.

'Celia, I've got some news,' she heard him say, and her heart leapt.

'Stefan?' she breathed.

The silence at the other end was minimal, but even so, she knew instantly that the news wasn't going to be about Stefan. She smothered her disappointment with a huge effort.

'I believe we've located your brother,' Moonie went on, and paused while she gasped audibly into the receiver.

'Is he safe? Is he well?' she spluttered.

She quickly grabbed the nearest stool and sat down heavily on it before she fell down with shock. She couldn't help the agonised thought, coming so soon after Wenna's news, that maybe the Pengellys had used up all their luck now.

'Before I say any more, Celia,' Moonie said, 'let me assure you that he's safe.'

She gripped the phone, feeling as though her stomach was turning somersaults with relief.

'Thank God. Where is he? Was he wounded? What happened to him?' she babbled out all at once, her usual coolness gone in an instant.

'Take it slowly, my dear. I've been in contact with some Norwegian partisans, and it seems he was shot down over Norway, as we've long suspected. Unfortunately the man your family had already heard about has since died, and was unable to tell us any more. But I understand that your brother was pretty badly cut about, Celia, so be prepared.'

'Just as long as he's safe,' she whispered.

He went on unemotionally. 'He was picked up and cared for by some farmers. The woman looked after him very well, by all accounts.'

'A woman?' she repeated stupidly.

'It was a brother and sister who farm in a small way, I'm told. Strictly between you and me, Celia, I gather Olly has begged for her to accompany him to England, where he'll be taken to a military hospital for some time. I don't know if it will be sanctioned for her to go with him.'

'Is she a nurse or something?' Celia said.

'Some sort of a healer, they say. Lucky, wasn't he?'

Bloody lucky, thought Celia. But that was Olly. Always falling on his feet. Always the darling of the gods. Smelling of roses when everyone else was in the proverbial dung-heap... Without warning she burst into uncontrollable tears, because she loved him, and she thanked God he was safe, even if it meant she had used up all her own luck in the process.

So the woman was a healer, was she? Some sort of a crank... but how could she think that, and she a Cornishwoman! Her throat was tight with tears.

'I'm sorry, Moonie. I'm finding it hard to take it all in. Just give me a minute, will you?'

'Take as long as you like.'

'I can't do that. The farmer here wants to use the phone. Can I call you back in a little while?'

'Of course. I'll be here all evening, and I still need to say more to you.'

She hung up and went back to the billet, not wanting to face anyone right now. She couldn't quite believe it was actually true that Olly would be coming home. While she knew she should feel like singing, she prayed for her mother's sake that it wasn't all a cruel hoax... but it couldn't be, if Moonie had got the information from the partisans on their elaborate short-wave wireless system. She trusted him totally.

Still, she tried to think rationally. It had been a long time, and as yet she didn't know what Olly's injuries were. Moonie's voice had been cautious, and she knew they couldn't expect to see the same happy-go-lucky Olly who had gone away.

Everyone knew that war changed people. Nobody ever came out unscathed. Her mother would know that. So would everyone of her generation; they had seen it all before.

She felt more rational by the time she managed to speak to Moonie again, ignoring the instruction from the farmer not to make it too long or the cost would be docked from her wages.

It soon became clear that Olly wouldn't have survived without these Norwegian farmers who had found him, though Moonie had no more information about them.

'They're angels, that's who they were. Guardian angels,' Celia said.

'Apparently so. Look, Celia, I've got a few days' leave, and I've got clearance to give your family the news myself. I can be at your home tomorrow afternoon. Can you be there?'

'You make it all sound terribly ominous,' Celia said, her first elation slipping into anxiety now.

'I don't mean to, but it's quite complicated, and I'd prefer to explain it in person, and I'd like to see you again, of course. But for the moment, I advise you to keep the news to yourself. So go and tell your boss that you need some leave, and I'll see you at New World tomorrow afternoon.'

She hung up the phone with shaking hands, her mind in a whirl. She wondered uneasily just how serious Olly's injuries were, and how much he wasn't telling her. But then the most important point of all flooded her senses. Olly was alive. For the moment, her joy eclipsed everything else, even the searing knowledge that there was still no news of Stefan. She had been so sure she would have heard something by now...

She was still catching her breath when the farmer came out of the parlour and asked curtly if she had finished her business. He was a boorish man who had no truck with women farm workers, and she hated him.

'I have to go home on family business tomorrow,' she said coldly. 'I'll let you know when I'll be back.'

'Don't bother, miss,' he snapped. 'You've been a thorn in my flesh ever since you arrived, and I'll be more than glad to inform the authorities that you're no longer needed here.'

'Thank you, sir,' she said sarcastically. 'That will save me the nuisance of doing it myself.'

–

Celia didn't want to go home to New World too early. She would be too afraid of blurting out everything before Moonie arrived, and it was clear that however traumatic the news they had to hear was, he wanted her and her parents to be together when they heard it. She was getting increasingly nervous. Olly was alive, but that was all she knew. It didn't bode well.

Tomorrow was Saturday and Nick would be at home. Presumably Moonie had worked that out for himself. She tried not to imagine terrible injuries, and concentrated instead on packing her things and telling the other Land Girls she was going home for good, and that she intended having a long lie-in before she left in the morning.

'Bimey, gel, what's old sour-face going to say about that?' Gertie exclaimed.

'I'm damn sure he'll be giving three cheers to see the back of me,' Celia retorted.

'Well, *we* won't,' Lizzie said. 'We'll miss you, Celia.'

'Go on. You won't have time to miss me! You'll have twice as much work to do without me around,' she said, touched by the words, and throwing a pillow at the girl to soften the unexpected emotion she felt.

It must be because of everything that had happened so suddenly, she thought. Wenna's news, and now Olly's…

But where did that leave her? Out of nowhere a small voice inside her said that two out of three wasn't bad. There was probably a law of averages that said there always had to be one who didn't get everything she wanted—

Her spinning thoughts were halted as a pillow was hurled back at her, and suddenly the feathers were flying, and the three of them were laughing and spluttering and coughing, and the tears went unnoticed.

–

Later, she couldn't have said how she spent the whole of the next day until she got back to New World in the mid-afternoon. She remembered parts. She stayed in bed until it was unreasonable for her to stay any longer, and besides, she was far too jittery to be idle.

She bought a midday snack in a local cafe, idled along the seafront at Penzance, watching the boats jostling in the harbour, and then took the bus as near to New World as possible, before walking the last mile home.

By then, her suitcase felt as if it weighed a ton, and her mother's eyes widened at the unexpected sight of her. Although it was a chilly early March now, Celia's face was as red with exertion and worry as if had been midsummer.

'For pity's sake, honey, come inside. Are you ill or is this an unscheduled leave? You should have let us know you were coming, and Daddy would have come to fetch you—'

'Please don't fuss, Mom. I'm home to stay, that's all. Me and Farmer Giles have parted for good, and that's all I'm prepared to say right now!'

It served two purposes, and Skye knew better than to ask too many questions when her daughter was in one of her scratchy moods. She would explain things in her own time, and right now she looked as if she needed to rest and recover.

In fact, Celia was feeling increasingly guilty at having to keep the news from her mother that Skye would so dearly love to hear. She should never have agreed to keeping it from her until Moonie arrived.

'Is Daddy here?' she asked swiftly now.

He had to be here when Moonie came. She felt the panic rising. It was important that they were all together to face whatever Moonie had to tell them...

'He's in his study. Is something wrong, Celia?'

She shook her head, and then they both looked up as they heard the sound of a car door slam. A taxi had pulled up and Captain Moon was alighting from it.

Skye frowned, not knowing who the visitor was, but Celia ran outside at once, and took both his hands in hers. Her heart pounded, and she looked at him searchingly, but he kissed her cheek and spoke reassuringly.

'It's all right, my dear. I promise you everything will be all right. Let's go inside and talk to your parents.'

Chapter Seventeen

'And he's actually here in England?' Skye gasped, when Moonie had related everything he knew – much more than he had already told Celia.

'My latest information is that he's in a sanatorium south of Bristol that specialises in his injuries,' Moonie said carefully. 'I must warn you, Mrs Pengelly, that it may be some time before he's allowed home. When he is, of course, I doubt that he'll see active service again.'

'I should damn well hope not,' Nick said angrily. 'The boy enlisted under age, and he's seen enough active service for any man.'

'But that's what he is, Nick. A man,' Skye said with huge pride and dignity. 'And I'm terribly proud of him.'

'We all are, Mom,' Celia put in. She turned to Moonie. 'But what about these Norwegian people? Did the farming woman come with him after all?'

'Apparently. I gather your brother refused to be moved without her.'

Celia spoke uneasily. 'Well, I thank God he's safe, of course, but I hope this doesn't mean he's become dependent on some crank healing woman.'

'Can we visit him?' Skye asked swiftly, wanting to prevent Nick from saying anything scathing, and knowing she and Celia would both be remembering the old witch-woman on the moors at that moment. There was a cranky old healing woman if ever there was one, she thought feelingly.

'I have the address of the sanatorium,' Moonie said. 'There are no restrictions on visitors.'

There was an awkward silence for a few minutes. Moonie had said all he had come to say, and he sensed that these folk would be burning to get away to visit their son as soon as possible. Besides, it wasn't for him to urge caution, to advise them not to bombard the boy with emotions and tears.

Seeing his face, Celia spoke swiftly. 'You'll stay with us for a while, won't you, Moonie? I'd like to show you my little piece of the world.'

'Just overnight, if that's all right with your parents. I have some visiting of my own to do in the area.'

'Of course you must stay, Captain Moon,' said Skye, but she was already mentally packing a small suitcase with which to travel to the Somerset sanatorium.

She simply couldn't think about entertaining. This was Celia's friend and colleague, and it was up to Celia to make him welcome. All Skye could think about was that Oliver was safe, and as soon as his wounds had healed, he would be coming home. God had been good to them, and for the first time in ages, she felt a great urge to be inside a church and thank Him properly. She had said many prayers in her lifetime, in many places, and she knew that they all counted. But this time, no other place but God's house would do.

'Do you mind if I spend some time alone?' she said to Nick, once Celia and Moonie had left them, and the tears of relief had dried. 'I know it's not your feeling, Nick, but I need to go to church to give thanks for Olly's survival.'

'I need that too – if you don't mind,' he said quietly.

She put her arms around him and felt him shake. Then she lifted her face for his kiss, and they went out of the house together, their arms entwined.

–

Olly was recovering more quickly that the doctors and nurses had believed likely when they first saw the extent of his still suppurating wounds. Without the initial application of Birgitta's herbal remedies, he would almost certainly have died, and even so, it had taken all the doctors' skills to deal with the wounds – just as it had taken all Olly's mental energy to insist that Birgitta came to England with him.

By now, he knew he could never thank her enough for all she had done for him. He knew he owed his life to her, and that he could never love anyone as much as he loved her. He knew all the guff about a patient falling for his nurse, but this was different. This was the love of his life.

She was sitting by his bedside, her silvery hair falling over her face, when he realised there were people entering the ward who weren't wearing the obligatory medical uniforms. He sighed, not wanting visitors. Not wanting anyone but the beautiful Norwegian girl he adored. And then, as if in a dream, he heard his mother's voice.

'Olly. Oh, Olly, darling—'

He turned his head carefully, aware of the sting of the stretched, tender skin on his cheeks where the scars were still vivid enough to reveal the extent of his injuries.

'Mom? They didn't tell me you were coming—'

He had been strong for so long, but now his face crumpled and the unmanly tears trickled over his scars making them smart still more as he saw his parents and sister.

To Skye, he was no longer a hero, but simply her boy, her baby, and she rushed forward and held him in her arms.

'Hey, hold on, Mom. It hurts,' he said weakly, though the hurt didn't really matter. In any case, it was a very little hurt compared with the searing pain he had endured.

'I'm sorry, darling,' Skye said in a choking voice. 'It's just so wonderful to see you—'

'You too. But don't drown me in tears. I've had enough water to last a lifetime...'

They were crowding him, words pouring out of them all now in their relief at finding him coherent, and apparently still capable of teasing, despite everything. He loved them all, but he had been too long in an isolated Norwegian farmhouse to be able to cope with too much attention too soon.

His lady was standing quietly by now and saying nothing. He reached out his hand and drew her into the circle.

'This is Birgitta, Mom and Dad,' he croaked. 'She rescued me and brought me back to life. She's my angel, and I hope you'll all love her as much as I do.'

Celia saw the girl lower her eyes, and knew at once that nobody on earth could love her as much as her brother did. She hoped fleetingly that it wasn't a case of a young man falling for his nurse, but her sixth sense told her it was far more than that. Lucky Olly, as ever, she thought next – but without rancour, because if anyone deserved to find love, he did.

He would have to remain in the sanatorium for another few weeks, but then he could go home, providing he continued to have nursing care. And since he insisted that the only nursing care he would accept was that of Birgitta and his family doctor, the staff knew better than to argue with this strong-willed young man, and let him have his way.

–

'It's wonderful that Olly will be coming home,' Lily said to Celia, when the glad news had spread throughout the family. 'Do you think he and this Norwegian girl—'

'Oh yes,' Celia said with a smile. 'There's absolutely no doubt about it. You only have to see them together.'

'So it seems as if Wenna has got her man, and Olly has virtually come back from the dead. What of you, my love?' Lily said next. 'What's your news?'

Celia turned away, not wanting her cousin to see the raw despair in her eyes. More than ever she was certain that the famed Tremayne luck had all been used up, and there was none left for her. She was the one who had lost out in the game of chance, the one that fate forgot. She swallowed the lump in her throat and tried not to sound bitter.

'What news could I have?' she said.

'Well, David says many German towns have fallen to the Allies now, and the terrible concentration camps have been liberated – not that I'm implying that your Stefan would have been incarcerated in one of those, of course,' she added quickly. 'But it's all over bar the shouting, as they say – isn't it? Oh Celia, I'm sorry—'

She was aghast as she saw the girl's face, as white as their own china clay. Celia had always been so strong, so flippant and brittle, taking everything life threw at her in her capable stride. Except this.

'Oh, take no notice of me, Lily. I'm all right, really. I just get these moments, that's all,' Celia said with a huge effort to gain control of her emotions. 'Sometimes I have this image of myself in years to come, like one of those poor elderly spinster women from the last lot, full of useless memories and little else.'

'Don't be ridiculous,' Lily said briskly. 'You're made of sterner stuff than that. You'll find a new love some day—' At Celia's aggrieved look, she knew at once it was the wrong thing to say.

'Have you written him off as well then? That's the difference between me and everybody else, Lily. I haven't, and I never will. I'd rather grow old without him, than ever think I could love someone else.'

–

The news that Hitler was dead came at the end of April, at the same time that Berlin finally fell to the Allies. German towns and cities everywhere were flying white flags now, and Allied soldiers were organising the movement of refugees.

Oliver had returned home to New World with Birgitta by his side, and it was tacitly assumed that she was going to stay in Cornwall for the foreseeable future. Olly still didn't want to see anyone but the family. They all accepted that he needed time to adjust, and were prepared to give it to him.

Wenna's concert party had already been disbanded, and she too had arrived home, awaiting her husband's discharge papers to come through at the earliest opportunity. Then they would make known their plans to depart for Canada.

Learning of Hitler's death sent the whole country into rapture, even though it was morally wrong to feel happy at the death of a man. But this had been such an evil man that no one could be anything but relieved at reading the huge black headlines in the *Informer* and every other newspaper telling of Hitler's suicide, with his mistress dead beside him.

The war wasn't officially over yet, but tentative celebrations were already being arranged in many households. New World had always been the scene of great parties, and the Pengellys anticipated a gathering of the whole clan when the peace treaty was finally signed, as it surely must be soon.

Whether in sorrow or in happiness, families needed to be together at such times, and when Birgitta asked shyly if her brother Rolf could be invited to join them, Olly added his voice to the request, and perked up so much at the suggestion that Skye and Nick agreed gladly, knowing how huge a part these two had played in their son's recovery. It was arranged that Rolf would arrive in Cornwall at the earliest opportunity.

During the first week of May, it seemed as if David Kingsley telephoned New World almost hourly as the news came through that everyone had been waiting for.

'The Germans are surrendering everywhere,' Skye exclaimed. 'Italy, Holland and Denmark – and now Norway.'

Birgitta's eyes blurred with tears at the news.

'I am too full to speak, Mrs Pengelly. It is hard for me to express the feelings in my heart at knowing that my country is free again.'

'Will you want to return, Birgitta?' Skye said, knowing it would break Olly's heart if she did.

She shook her head. 'Not until Olly is tired of me.'

'Can pigs fly?' he said, laughing at her puzzled look and taking plenty of time to explain the Englishness of the joke.

–

Their happiness was almost too much for Celia to bear. She begrudged them nothing, but for her there was only a deep void in her heart as the news broke that the peace treaty had finally been signed and it was all over. Six years of war had ended in a small schoolhouse in Rheims where the Allied Supreme Commander, General Eisenhower, had his HQ.

'There are still the Japanese to contend with, of course,' Nick said, cautious as ever, but nothing could dim the joy of knowing that victory celebrations could begin, bonfires could be lit all over the country, and the organised and disorganised street parties could finally take place.

Rations that had been hoarded for weeks could be brought out and displayed on tables groaning with food, while flags flew and balloons soared skywards all over the country. In every city and town the lights were turned on again, and searchlights lit the sky in jubilation instead of fear.

'I'd love to be in London right now,' Wenna said wryly. 'The people will be out in force to see the royal family come out on the balcony of Buckingham Palace – and Prime Minister Churchill too, I dare say. There won't be an inch of space among the cheering crowds in Piccadilly.'

'Do you miss it, honey?' Skye asked her. 'And Fanny?'

Wenna took a deep breath. 'In some ways I miss her more now than when she died. It's knowing that all this will be going on, I suppose, and that she'd be there in the thick of it. She did so love a knees-up, Mom.'

They hugged one another, both remembering the brash, vivacious woman who could cuss like a trooper and had the proverbial heart of gold.

'And what of that life, honey?' Skye persisted. 'Will Harry be agreeable to you going back on the stage?'

Wenna took a deep breath. 'I won't be, Mom. There won't be much call for singers in the wilds of Canada… I didn't mean to blurt it out like that.'

'You didn't have to. I guess I always knew.'

'And you don't mind?' Wenna said cautiously.

'We all have to go where our hearts are, Wenna, and yours is with your husband. Of course I shall miss you, but you'll go with my blessing.'

–

The world was celebrating the peace, and so was Berlin. The bombing and destruction had all but obliterated many fine buildings, centuries old, and reduced much of that beautiful city to rubble. Those whose homes had survived, whether hovel or mansion, could count themselves among the lucky ones. There were thousands who could not.

Frau Vogl learned of her country's final surrender with unaccustomed tears in her eyes. She was not given to showing emotion, but now that it was all over she could remember her son, and wonder what it had all been for. It was a feeling that was echoed by her husband, even though it was unsaid. Herr Vogl was a man who would remain loyal to the Fatherland, and she respected him for that, despite her maternal sadness at the loss and waste of a young life.

But there was another young man in the household who had needed all their care and attention in the time he had been with them. Not that Stefan von Gruber was such a young man, except when compared with themselves. But when he had succumbed to the vicious attack of pneumonia shortly after his arrival in their home, his life had hung on a thread for many weeks.

The Vogls had discussed the matter thoroughly, and finally decided not to even try to inform the Cornish family that he was safe and well until they knew for sure which way the illness would go.

Now he was well and strong again, and it was time for him to leave them. It would be a wrench, for he had become almost as close as a son to them, but he had chosen his path in life, and it was his to follow.

Stefan himself was well aware that he owed his life to the Vogls and their family doctor. His delirium had been so intense that he had hardly known whether the hammering in his head and the flashes of light that burned his eyes came from inside his head, or from the British bombardment of the city.

When he had slowly started to recover, he was filled with a weird kind of superstition that was worthy of his Cornish sweetheart. Through the darkened window of his bedroom he had watched the searchlights criss-cross the sky and picked out the British planes dropping their death-laden bombs. He had tried not to imagine one of those bombs hitting this house and obliterating them all while he lay helpless.

He had watched the skies like a hunter searching for its prey, his mind tormented and muddled as he sought to find one bright star, while hardly knowing why he did so. Fighting to remember some words from long ago that reminded him that as long as that star still shone, something very precious would survive in this hell.

Now he knew what it was. Now, his mind was lucid and clear, and he knew that if God, or fate, or luck, was on his side, Celia would still be waiting for him. But, still with that feverish near-Cornish superstition, he had decided not to contact her until he returned to their special place.

He had money now. The Vogls had generously seen to that, and his self-confidence had returned. His mind was alert in a way it hadn't been for months, and he knew exactly what he had to do, and where he had to be before he saw Celia again.

As the train took him over the border into Switzerland with a sense of freedom so new it was almost painful, the sight of the mountains ahead gave him a feeling of almost sexual ecstasy. He vowed that once he and Celia were reunited, nothing in this world was ever going to separate them again.

–

Harry Mack arrived at New World a few weeks later, to the delight of his bride. He treated Olly like a hero, until Olly told him in embarrassment that he'd far rather he didn't. Rolf had arrived from Norway, but stayed only a short while, saying he would return for his sister's wedding before Wenna and Harry departed for Canada in the late summer.

'It's far too soon for Olly and Birgitta to marry, of course,' Celia said to Lily, her closest confidante now. 'But how can you destroy their happiness by telling him to wait a while? They wouldn't take any notice, anyway.'

'Would you?' Lily asked. 'The three of you have always gone your own way and got whatever you wanted.'

'I hardly think that applies to me.'

'You haven't given up hope, have you?'

Celia shook her head slowly. 'Of course not, but it's sometimes hard to hold on to a dream. I keep torturing myself with the thought that surely Stefan would have got in touch with me by now if he was still – still able to.'

She didn't dare say "if he was still alive", because it was tempting fate to put such thoughts into words.

'David says that Germany's in a terrible state,' Lily told her, quickly changing the subject. 'It's practically in ruins, and people are still emerging from shelters, not even aware that the war's been over for a few weeks. Perhaps—'

'Don't even say it,' Celia said sharply. 'Stefan's not the sort of man to hide in a shelter for weeks on end without knowing what's happening.'

But what sort of man *was* he, she thought, if he was still alive and hadn't bothered to contact her? Was his love so shallow after all? She couldn't believe it, but neither could she dismiss it. People changed. And there was always the possibility that he had met someone else.

She had always steadfastly refused to think about such a prospect, and she pushed it out of her mind now. Instead, she reflected on Lily's sensible comments that they must all look to the future now, or it would all have been for nothing.

Olly and Birgitta would marry and live happily after, presumably at New World. Wenna and Harry would go to Canada and raise horses or whatever they did out there. Her mother would begin in earnest on her china clay history booklets and her plans for the open-air museum that would attract hundreds and thousands of visitors to Cornwall in the bright new tomorrow that was now today. And Butch Butcher would be their surrogate son.

And she – where did that leave her? Celia Pengelly, who had once been the brightest and most self-confident of all of them, who had thought she had the world at her feet…

She caught her breath on a sob as she neared New World, and then slowed the car to a stop at the side of the road, scattering dust and gravel everywhere.

'What the devil do you think you're doing?' she yelled at the carrot-headed vision that had suddenly loomed up in front of her on the road, dancing about in a frenzy and waving its arms hysterically. She ignored the fact that her thoughts had been too taken up with misery to see him, or anyone.

'Have you lost your senses, Butch?' she yelled again when he seemed too stupefied to speak for a moment. She leapt out of the car and shook him by the lapels. 'I nearly ran into you, you idiot.'

'There's been a phone call for you, Celia,' he screeched, his face as red as his hair. 'He's going to try again in an hour or two – though he says he's having a terrible time getting through – and you're to wait indoors for him.'

Her eyes blazed with sudden hope, and if he could have done so, Butch would have backed away at their brilliance. But she still held on to him so tightly he was almost choking.

'He? Did you say *he*? Who was it? Tell me at once!'

Common sense should be telling her not to get over-excited, but common sense was the farthest thing from her mind now. Of course, it might be Moonie… or Ethan in Ireland… or someone giving her the news she dreaded…

'Mrs Pen says it's your feller—' Butch croaked.

He howled with rage as she let go of him so quickly that he had to stagger crazily to keep his balance. Celia hardly noticed. She almost fell back into the car and screeched it into gear. She couldn't wait for Butch to get inside, and left him there, hollering after her. She heard none of it.

All she could hear in her head were the magical words: "Mrs Pen says it's your feller"...

'Stefan,' she almost sobbed. 'Oh, please God, let it be really you.'

Once home, she slammed the car door behind her and rushed into the house, shouting for her mother.

'Hey, sis, where's the fire?' said Olly with a grin, coming out of the drawing room with his arm slung loosely around Birgitta's waist.

'There was a phone call,' Celia stuttered.

'Was there?' he said, unconcerned. 'I wouldn't know. We've just come in from a stroll, which is all I'm allowed.'

She turned away from him, resisting the childish urge to stamp her feet in frustration. 'Where's Mom, Olly?'

'I'm here, Celia,' she heard her mother say quietly.

She whirled around, clutching at Skye's arms, all the hope in the world mirrored in her eyes. Almost too afraid to ask, and yet needing so desperately to know...

'There was a phone call for me,' she said hoarsely. 'Butch told me.'

Her mouth trembled and her legs began to give way. She felt so dizzy that she swayed and would have fallen if her mother's arms hadn't held her so tightly.

'Hold on, my darling. It's everything you hoped for. It was Stefan, and he's going to try again later, just as soon as he can, but the telephone system between here and Europe is so appallingly overloaded now, of course—'

Celia heard no more. She slid to the floor, and a few minutes later found herself lying on the sofa, with people fussing around her. Someone put a glass to her lips, and she pushed it away. She didn't need it. She just needed answers.

'Tell me I wasn't dreaming,' she whispered. 'After all these years of hoping and praying – tell me it was really Stefan, Mom, and that it wasn't all some cruel hoax.'

'It was no hoax, honey. It was definitely his voice.'

Celia hid her face in her hands, not wanting any of them to see the raw emotion on her face that she knew she couldn't hide. Such acute joy was almost agonising, and she didn't want to share this moment – the moment when she thanked God deeply for sending her lover back to her – with anyone.

Then reality came rushing back. She still didn't know if he was well, or where he was. All she knew was that he had telephoned. Someone else had heard his voice first, and she was beset with the most ridiculous feeling of jealousy because of it. She was desperate to hear his voice for herself, to be reassured that he still loved her and wanted her. That every night, when she had searched the heavens for their star, he had looked for it too, or thought of it, and planned for the day when they would see it together once more.

'There's no telling when he'll manage to get through on the telephone next,' Skye said, more firmly now. 'So we must carry on normally, Celia. Dinner will be at the usual time, and with so many of us in the house, you could do worse than to keep busy and help Cook with the preparations.'

'I don't think so, Mom, unless you want me to chop my fingers along with the cabbages,' she said shakily. 'I couldn't concentrate on anything at all right now, and I need to be alone with my thoughts. Please understand.'

She fled upstairs to her bedroom before anyone could argue. In a little while, God willing, she would hear Stefan's voice again, and she would know instantly if everything was still the same.

But dinner came and went, and the day softened into twilight and then darkness, and still the telephone hadn't rung. Celia toyed with the meal, eating no more than morsels of food, in an agony of suspense.

At last the shrill sound of the instrument shattered the quiet of the evening.

Her heart pounded as she rushed to answer it. She made herself take deep breaths and held on to the receiver as tightly as if it was a lifeline. And then she heard his voice.

'Celia, at last, my *liebling. Mein Gott*, the waiting has been so long. I began to think I would never hear your voice again.'

'Is it really you, Stefan? Please tell me I'm not dreaming,' she stuttered, knowing how inane she must sound, and not caring. 'I can hardly believe it's true. I've imagined this moment for so long—'

There was a mechanical delay at each end before either of them could hear the other's reply, and Celia held her breath as she waited for him to speak again.

'No one could have imagined it more than I, my sweet darling. I can picture you now, standing in the hallway of that lovely house. Take a moment to look out of the window, my Celia, and tell me what you see.'

She looked to where the long French windows reached the floor. Outside, the night had deepened to a soft velvet blue, and shining high above was a shimmering silver star, brighter than all the rest. The breath caught in her throat.

'I see a star...'

In the small enforced silence, she tried to collect her senses, but it was almost impossible, knowing their thoughts were still so in tune, despite the distance between them.

'So now we know it isn't all a dream, and that our lives together can begin at last,' he said gently.

'But where are you? Are you still in Germany? In Berlin? What's happened to you all this time? I heard you had been interned, Stefan, and about your lovely estate.'

She had so often wondered how much he mourned for all that had happened to his old home in the intervening years.

'It's no longer mine, Celia, and I'm no longer in Germany, although I remained in Berlin for a long while in the care of the Vogls.'

She gasped, and would have asked more, but he went on speaking gravely.

'Their son is dead, my love, serving his country, but the Vogls took great care of me when I became seriously ill. If it had not been so, I would have contacted you much sooner. But when everything seemed to be over, I decided to wait just a little while longer until I could offer you what we always dreamed about.'

He paused, but before she could say any more, his voice became a touch more tentative than before. She could hear the strain in it, as if he too wondered if the time spent apart had changed them irrevocably.

'So how soon can you come to Gstaad, *liebling*?'

'You're in Gstaad?' she repeated stupidly, hardly able to take in all that he was saying.

'In a certain hotel that in due course, I hope, will have my name over the entrance, Celia. *Our* name.'

She swallowed. Everything was happening so fast that she couldn't think straight. But one thing was certain. She hadn't waited all this time to be put off by the little matter of finding transport. The old mercurial Celia asserted herself.

'I'll come as soon as I can get a flight, Stefan. I'll telephone the hotel to let you know the time of my arrival.'

'I'll be waiting,' he said. 'And there's something I haven't told you yet. I love you with all my heart.'

'I love you too,' she choked. 'So very much.'

–

It was a little while before she felt able to join her family in the drawing room and speak sensibly.

'Was it your feller then?' Butch said daringly.

'Come on, Celia, tell us what's been happening to him, and put us out of our misery,' Olly said, with a hint of impatience in his voice. All the attention had been his until now, and Celia guessed that with the selfishness of the invalid, he wanted to get this new drama over and done with. She didn't blame him. It was the war...

Wenna looked more anxious, knowing how very important this was to her sister. She and Olly both had their own futures assured now with loves of their own, but for Celia there had been so much uncertainty. And none of them would readily forget, she thought uneasily, that Stefan was German, and that these two ex-airmen had been doing their best to bomb his country out of existence.

But none of that was going to stop Celia's resolve, and it was to her mother that she looked for reassurance.

'Tell us your fiancé's news, darling,' Skye said softly, bringing him into the family circle with one simple word, and daring anyone to dispute it.

'He's in Gstaad, Mom. He's been very ill, but the Vogls have been looking after him. Can you believe that? And he says that Franz Vogl was killed, so they had their casualties too.'

She didn't mean to make it sound as if that compensated for the fact that Stefan was a German, but if they took it that way, so be it. Her voice was jerky as she went on.

'I have to get in touch with Moonie as quickly as possible. I need to go to Gstaad to be with him, Mom, and I'm sure Moonie will be able to organise a flight for me. I have to go. You know that, don't you? All of you?'

Her eyes pleaded with them to understand. She needed the approval of her family. They were important to her, but Stefan was her love, her everything, no matter what else he was. If they couldn't see that, then she would be estranged from them for ever, because she could never give him up.

'Cor. I reckon your feller must be somebody special,' Butch said in a hushed voice.

'He is,' Skye told him, and then turned to her daughter. 'You go and contact Captain Moon right away, darling.'

Nick added his piece. 'And when it's settled, we'll drink a toast to the good times ahead of us all, to wash away old hurts, and to welcome a long and lasting peace.'

'Amen to that,' said Skye. To Celia's enormous relief, nobody questioned it.

And it was Olly who moved across to her and kissed her, his tender cheek bearing witness to the fact that if he could forgive an old enemy, so could anyone.

'I love you all,' she said in a choked voice, before she rushed out of the room again to telephone Moonie.

–

A week later, she stepped out of the rickety train that had sawed its way into Gstaad, and breathed in the sweet summer air of the mountains and the flower-strewn meadows. She had contacted the hotel to say what time she was arriving, but nothing was reliable these days, and the train was inevitably very late, causing even more frustration in Celia's heart.

Just then she saw him, standing by the gate, as dear and handsome as ever, if older. Oh yes, he looked older. But so did she, thought Celia. No one had come out of this war unscathed, however peripheral a part they had played in it.

And then all thinking was over, as they ran towards each other and were caught in one another's arms. His kiss was sweet on her lips, the same as ever, and yet never so fresh or so cherished as in those first emotional moments.

'I've missed you so much, Stefan,' she sobbed against his shoulder. 'I've longed for you so much, and I never gave up hope for a single moment—'

'No more did I, my darling,' he said unsteadily. 'How could I, with our star never failing to appear? But we mustn't stand here entertaining the local folk. Let's go home.'

A porter picked up her luggage as they walked outside the station still hugging one another, and Stefan drove them to the picturesque hotel in the soft shadow of the mountains that she remembered so well.

The hotel where they had met and had afternoon tea together, when the darkly handsome German had interviewed the beautiful blue-eyed Cornish girl for an employment post, during what seemed like a lifetime ago. They had both known then that it was destined to be far more than a business meeting.

Now she learned that the hotel was actually going to belong to them, and there was a sweet sense of inevitability about it that was as Cornish as her name. They explored every bit of it, renewing themselves through memory, and talking long into the afternoon about all that had happened since their enforced parting. Learning about one other all over again, taking it slowly, and exulting in knowing that nothing had changed. Their love was still as bright and new as ever.

Celia turned to him with shimmering eyes, holding his hands tightly as they reached Stefan's bedroom.

'I asked for your luggage to be brought in here,' Stefan said carefully. 'Or was I presuming too much, too soon? You must tell me if it's so, my love, and I'll understand.'

She put her fingers to his lips, smiling into his eyes, and she was at once the old assertive Celia he adored, who had always known exactly what she wanted.

'Will you? Well, I would not! Do you think I've waited all this time, and longed for you with all my heart, for us to worry about petty conventions? Whose hotel is this, anyway?'

'Yours and mine very soon, sweetheart,' Stefan said, with the laugh that she remembered that could warm her heart.

Then the look in his eyes deepened into something far more intimate and sensual as he lifted her in his arms and walked purposefully towards the huge four-poster bed.

'I think it's more than time I showed you just how much I've missed you,' he went on, his voice deepening with desire. 'Or is that too presumptuous a suggestion so early in the evening?'

'Of course not,' she whispered, her senses soaring to meet his. 'Now that we're together, we have no more need to watch for the stars to come out, my love.'

'Except that when they do, I shall want to make love to you all over again,' he told her, as he began to unfasten her blouse, teasing every bit of newly exposed flesh with small, erotic kisses. 'Tonight and every night, for the rest of our lives, until I'm far too old and weak to do so.'

'May that day be never,' Celia said softly, as her feverish undressing matched his now.

Their mutual need overcame any thought of strangeness after being so long apart, and her arms reached out to draw him down to her. And then all the waiting was over as Stefan covered her and filled her with himself, and she surrendered to the exquisite fulfilment of belonging.

For them, tomorrow had already begun.